REMNANT FACTION

BOOK 5

PEACEKEEPERS
OF SOL

REMNANT FACTION

GLYNN STEWART

This edition published in 2022 by:

Faolan's Pen Publishing Inc.

22 King St. S, Suite 300

Waterloo, Ontario

N2J 1N8 Canada

ISBN-13: 978-1-989674-28-4 (print)

A record of this book is available from Library and Archives Canada.

Printed in the United States of America

1 2 3 4 5 6 7 8 9 10

First edition

First printing: September 2022

Illustration by Sam Leung

Faolan's Pen Publishing logo is a trademark of Faolan's Pen Publishing Inc.

Read more books from Glynn Stewart at faolanspen.com

1

A STAR SYSTEM is a vast expanse of mostly nothingness, but it is never truly *empty*. A star on its own was a massive presence, and most at least had debris fields even when they didn't have planets.

Sometimes, though, the absence of technological civilization was enough to qualify as "empty" for the immediate purpose—usually when there was *supposed* to be something there.

"I was expecting at least a picket ship," Commodore Henry Wong observed as he reviewed the sensor data on the Ra-78 System. They were only a single short skip from their final destination, already eleven days into their mission.

The tall Chinese-American United Planets Space Force officer was one of three people on the small flag deck on his destroyer flagship. *Paladin* was alone today, her gravity engines allowing her to leave her friends behind, but Henry was in command of the *mission*—and that meant being with the single ship leading the way.

"Our information on Rashova and what the Rashovans have been up to is limited," his flag captain replied. Lieutenant Colonel Okafor Ihejirika had been with Henry for a while now, first as his tactical officer on Henry's last starship and now as his flag captain on *Paladin*.

"But what the E-Two have reported says there should be a picket here."

The large African officer shook his head on his video link to Henry. The Eerdish-Enteni Alliance—christened "the E-Two" among the UPSF for ease of discussion—were newly reforged friends of the United Planets Alliance.

Henry was there as much for the E-Two's protection as the UPA's, his mission to make contact with the Rashova System a step toward a wider alliance. They'd been warned, in the Eerdish home system, that the old war was returning.

The Kenmiri Empire had once ruled ten thousand stars before they'd been driven into retreat and a slow genocide by, among others, Henry Wong. Now a faction of their Warrior Caste was threatening the Ra Sector—the stars closest to the UPA—and Henry had been tasked to find allies to stand against them.

Key among those allies would be the former Kenmiri colonies on the inward frontier of the sector, worlds once occupied by the Kenmiri themselves and now abandoned by them. They had more advanced industries and tech bases than the former slave worlds—and there had been tens of millions of slaves on the colonies, too, to use those industries.

But if the leaders of the Rashova System, once the capital of the Ra *Province* of the Kenmiri Empire, had recalled their pickets…

A chill ran down Henry's spine as he considered the possibilities.

"That could be a very real problem," he said quietly. "Tell Lieutenant Charmchi she is authorized to use *Paladin*'s full acceleration. Get us to Rashova, Captain."

"What about the Flotilla, ser?"

"Send a drone. They're to advance to Ra-Seventy-Eight and wait for further orders. We don't want to threaten the Rashovans."

And if the situation was as bad as he feared…the handful of allies he had tailing *Paladin* weren't going to make a difference.

PALADIN WAS EFFECTIVELY unique in UPSF service at that moment. She'd been built with two sisters, *Cataphract*—the name ship of the class—and *Maharatha*, but *Cataphract* had been sent back to UPA space with crippling damage and *Maharatha* had been destroyed.

Henry had taken his three-ship squadron in pursuit of the Drifters after they'd betrayed a peace summit, and the price had been high. His success in that mission had allowed them to learn of the threat from the revanchist Warrior faction, which led directly to his flagship hurtling toward the Rashova System at an acceleration very few ships in the galaxy could match.

Paladin was equipped with the first starship-scale gravitational maneuvering system the United Planets Space Force had ever built, allowing her to accelerate at two kilometers per second squared without any apparent thrust to the crew aboard her.

Compared to the standard half-KPS^2 of the UPSF's pre-GMS fleet, she was unbelievably fast. But even as Ihejirika's ship blazed across the star system toward their destination, Henry couldn't shake the feeling that things had already gone wrong.

"Permission to enter the flag deck," a sharply feminine voice asked.

He turned to see the sharp-edged platinum-blonde Russian woman standing at the entrance to his working space and smiled. Even in his current concerns, the sight of Sylvia Todorovich warmed his heart. "Granted, Ambassador."

"We'll go check in with CIC, ser," Commander Georgina Eowyn said instantly, the operations officer rising from her seat and leveling a pointed look at the other officer in the room. "See if anything else has fallen out of the sensor data."

That *probably* wasn't needed, and Henry wouldn't have asked for it —but it was going to be five more hours before they hit the skip line, and he couldn't justifiably leave the flag deck until then.

If his staff were going to volunteer to leave him and his girlfriend to talk in private, he wasn't going to argue.

His staff were out the door almost before he could object, anyway, leaving him alone with the woman who spoke for the United Planets Alliance there, almost fifty days' flight from the closest UPA star system.

"I will take that as a pointed hint," Sylvia told him, stepping into his personal space and leaning down to give him a fierce kiss.

"Unnecessary on their part but not unwelcome," Henry agreed. Both of them were well aware of the need for public propriety in their relationship. While Henry was no longer the senior UPSF military officer in the Ra Sector—there was an entire UPSF battle fleet at the Eerdish System now, watching over the captive Drifter Convoy—he remained the second-in-command of the Peacekeeper Initiative, the ongoing effort to reestablish contact with everyone in the sector and stabilize the political and economic situation.

And Sylvia Todorovich was, without question, *the* senior civilian official of the UPA in the Sector. In many ways, Henry was certain she was significantly more important than he was. *Paladin*'s role today, after all, was basically to be her taxi.

"I heard that Ra-Seventy-Eight came up empty," she told him, taking a seat in the flag deck's single observer seat. "Which wasn't what we expected, right?"

"The Eerdish said their diplomatic mission to Rashova met with a picket squadron here, and the limited trade had similar encounters." Henry waved a map of the stars around them into existence on the main screen.

Paladin lacked holographic emitters in her combat stations. They were too fragile to be relied upon on in battle, so screens and links to personnel's internal networks served the purpose for sharing and reviewing information.

They were eleven days from the Eerdish System and any kind of support. That *support*, though, was Twelfth Fleet, anchored on three UPSF fleet carriers, plus the E-Two fleet, plus the UPA's allies in the La-Tar Cluster and, hopefully, the Kozun Hierarchy.

Henry was certain the allied fleet was sufficient to take on anything the Kenmiri had in play, but it was always a guessing game. The main reason he hadn't brought more ships with him to Rashova, though, was that Twelfth Fleet still had an important task in E-Two space—namely, ending the war between the E-Two and the Kozun.

The Ra Sector needed to face the returning Kenmiri as one. War between two of the UPA's allies had gone from *inconvenient* to *unaccept-*

able, and Admiral Cody Rex had been planning on making that point to the Hierarchy with a carrier group or two.

Henry also preferred not to arrive in hopefully friendly star systems with an entire unannounced battle fleet.

"We are one skip from Rashova," he told Sylvia. "It's a short skip, only five hours. I'm honestly surprised the Rashovans haven't built up an out-system infrastructure here, if only for raw resources.

"Not everyone has another star system only five hours' travel away."

The skip drive—formally the Icosaspace Traversal System—gave a ship a twenty-dimensional velocity that could bypass regular three-dimensional space. Under normal circumstances, though, that was a curiosity that didn't provide a great deal of extra pseudo-velocity.

Along the carefully calculated lines drawn between high-mass stars, however, it allowed a ship to catch the flow of the gravity wells and "skip" along the line like a rock traveling along a river's current. Distance and the mass of the stars on either end drove the travel time between systems.

"Rashova is surprisingly disorganized, from what the Eerdish told us," Sylvia told him. "They're operating with a series of basically trade guilds running segments of their society and economy, with limited system-wide cohesion. They might not be organized enough to arrange colonial efforts."

"That's fair, but they *were* organized enough to have defensive pickets in the surrounding systems. And those pickets are missing."

Henry glared at the screen. The Rashovans, disorganized as they might be, had managed to keep a lot of secrets from the limited traffic they'd allowed into their system. He believed that they had access to capital ships of the former Empire, but he didn't *know*.

The only thing he really knew was that there had been a pair of former Kenmiri escorts in the system when the Eerdish Sovereign of Sovereigns had sent a diplomatic and trade mission to Rashova eight months earlier, and later merchant ships had reported the same picket.

And that picket was now missing.

"You're nervous, love."

"I'm more than nervous, Sylvia," he admitted. "I can't think of many reasons for the Rashovans to have recalled their pickets—and the most likely reason is very straightforward.

"If they saw the Kenmiri coming, they would have recalled every ship they had to defend their system."

They were a long way from home and in systems the United Planets Alliance hadn't had people in since the end of the war. Ra-78 had been the seventy-first system visited by the UPSF in the sector, but the UPA government had limited interest in operating in the former Kenmiri Empire now that the threat to the UPA was gone.

Except that now a faction of Kenmiri was doing...*something*. And Rashova was only a few skips and a handful of days' travel from the border of the Osiris Province, the closest territory still claimed by the Kenmiri Remnant.

"You think the Warriors are already here," Sylvia murmured.

"Or at least on their way. The whole affair with the Drifters was supposed to keep us distracted and divided, and in the end, it only cost them two dreadnoughts and a few escorts." He shook his head. "There was no point in a distraction like that if they weren't close to moving; we knew that. But it appears it may already be later than we dared to fear."

2

PALADIN SKIPPED INTO A NIGHTMARE.

Even toward the end of the war, as the Vesheron alliance of rebels and outsiders had built up their resources compared to the Kenmiri Empire, the Kenmiri had maintained a near-monopoly on their heavy capital ships. El-Vesheron powers, the outsiders like the UPA, had fielded their own capital ships, but the Vesheron rebels inside the Empire had relied on stolen Kenmiri ships.

Less than twenty dreadnoughts had ever fallen into Vesheron hands. The rebels had learned to match mass with numbers, meeting individual dreadnoughts with swarms of refitted freighters and stolen escorts, backed where possible by El-Vesheron capital ships like Terran battlecruisers.

Even with the gravity shields that allowed them to shrug aside the Kenmiri warships' heavy plasma cannon, the UPSF had hesitated to engage dreadnoughts more than one at a time. Henry had commanded a battlecruiser through the last few years of the war, providing fire support for Vesheron operations across the entire Kenmiri Empire, and he had seen full dreadnought formations only a handful of times—and had *run* from them more often than not.

Watching thirty-six dreadnoughts, six full Kenmiri battle

squadrons, advance across the Rashova System sent chills down his spine. Ten dreadnoughts were accelerating out from Rashov, the system's inhabited planet to meet them, with swarms of escorts and gunships around both forces.

Henry wasn't sure he'd *ever* seen forty-six dreadnoughts in one system before.

"I'm sure no one needs the confirmation, but the ten dreadnoughts accelerating out from Rashov are local ships," Ihejirika's tactical officer, Lieutenant Commander Medb Bach, said drily. "All are six-megaton designs mounting six heavy plasma cannon."

"And the Warriors?"

Bach glanced at the pickup Henry was watching the bridge through.

"Eighteen superdreadnoughts, massing sixteen million tons apiece, with an estimated fifteen cannon apiece," she reported. "Eighteen regular dreadnoughts of several variations, average mass eight million tons and an estimated total of a hundred and thirty-five cannon.

"Escorts and gunships are hard to distinguish from each other at this range, and we don't have a solid count on the lighter warships."

"Understood." Henry met his flag captain's gaze through the video feed.

"Your orders, Commodore?"

"We came here to make allies, not watch them die. Set a rendezvous course with the Rashovan fleet and keep our sensors running at full power."

Paladin was the newest and most advanced warship the UPSF had in commission. Her sensors put the suites available to anyone during the war to shame, which meant that they were about to get a *lot* of useful data.

If anyone lived long enough to use it.

"We won't arrive in time to affect the battle, ser," Ihejirika warned. "Assuming the Kenmiri are heading for zero-zero with Rashov orbit, they'll interpenetrate the defenders in just over an hour and reach orbit in four hours."

The Remnant fleet wasn't even pushing particularly hard. They were accelerating at point-eight KPS^2, less than their inertial compensators could handle, let alone what their engines could put out. The Rashovans were at the full KPS^2 that was the maximum stolen Kenmiri compensators could handle.

The locals would intercept the fleet as far away from the planet as possible, but Henry had to agree with Ihejirika's unspoken assumption: the Rashovan fleet wouldn't survive clashing with the attackers.

"Set course for Rashov orbit," Henry ordered with a sigh. "Get sensor probes headed toward the expected intercept zone. Let's get as much data on these bastards as possible."

Whatever happened in Rashova, the UPSF knew they were going to have to fight this fleet. The more they knew, the better.

IN THE RASHOVANS' place, Henry probably would have paid more attention to the unknown destroyer appearing in their star system on the verge of a massive battle. On the other hand, he supposed, *Paladin* was transmitting her identity on a channel shared by all the former Vesheron rebels.

The Rashovans should have a pretty good idea of who Henry and his people were and had clearly decided either that *Paladin* wasn't a threat or was something they could deal with later.

As the minutes ticked toward the two dreadnought fleets engaging, Henry found himself poring over the sensor data, looking for any answer he'd missed. A weakness of the superdreadnoughts leading the Kenmiri advance. A secret weapon on the Rashovans' part.

Anything that would change the hard arithmetic of thirty-six dreadnoughts versus ten.

"Missile launch detected. Rashovans are launching… Kenmiri are launching."

One of the results of the rebellion being heavily based on stolen Kenmiri ships and the new successor states being based on Kenmiri industrial systems was that basically *everyone* was using the same missiles and launchers.

Electromagnetic launch systems provided a thousand kilometers per second of additional velocity, and fusion engines provided ten

KPS^2 of acceleration for five minutes. There were enough variances between different manufacturers and styles to allow the identification of a missile's source, but the performance envelope was almost universal.

The closing velocities and accelerations extended the missile range to over five times that of the heavy plasma cannon that were the dreadnoughts' main shipkillers, three and a half million kilometers, and the space between the two fleets filled with tiny icons.

Henry's people still didn't have a solid number on the escorts and gunships in either fleet. Counting *missiles* from halfway across the star system was impossible. Even the Rashovans were launching enough that the icons more resembled a tidal wave on the displays and datafeeds than individual weapons.

The first salvos struck home before the two fleets reached plasma-cannon range, in catastrophic tsunamis of nuclear fire. Shaped-charge fusion warheads turned missiles into plasma shotguns at point-blank range, hundreds of megatons of short-lived firestorms lashing at dreadnought armor.

But this was the threat environment the Kenmiri had built their dreadnoughts *for*. Only one Rashovan dreadnought disappeared from the screens before the two fleets reached cannon range.

There was no way to follow what happened after that. Hundreds of heavy plasma cannon, each capable of obliterating most lighter warships, hammered at each other for ten seconds. Twenty. Thirty.

It took just over eighty seconds from the moment the two fleets entered plasma-cannon range until they interpenetrated, the Kenmiri Warriors continuing to decelerate toward Rashov…and the scattered survivors of the Rashovan fleet began aggressive evasive maneuvers, trying to avoid destruction.

"Warriors lost three dreadnoughts," Bach reported. "Unclear how many escorts. None of the Rashovan dreadnoughts survived, but I've got about thirty escorts or gunships on screens."

"Poor bastards," Ihejirika muttered.

"They've got courage; you can't deny that." Henry was watching the escorts' vectors. They'd increased their acceleration and added side vectors, spiraling away from the vector they'd fought the Warriors on —but their vectors were also all turning back toward Rashov.

They hadn't given up on their planet yet.

Henry, on the other hand…had to make a call.

"Captain, Ambassador," he addressed Ihejirika and Sylvia. "Your assessment of whether it's worth making contact with Rashova at this point?"

"Militarily, it's already over," Ihejirika observed softly. "There are a few orbital platforms, and those escorts are trying to swing back around, but escorts can't fight equal numbers of dreadnoughts."

"That's focusing entirely on the spaceborne assets," Sylvia replied. "I'm not as fluent in the tactical displays as you two, but I'm not seeing any landing ships in the Kenmiri formation. The battle for the system might be over, but the battle for the planet has yet to begin—and we made a lot of allies who were occupied by the Kenmiri before."

"Agreed." Henry was running the vectors in his head. They could divert away from Rashov easily enough, but they had enough velocity in-system to make just turning around impractical. They were going to see what happened to Rashov, no matter what.

"Let's adjust our course," he told Ihejirika. "Keep us at least five light-seconds from Rashov, but let's try to open a channel to the government and get the Ambassador talking."

"It never hurts to forge links, even if they have to go dark in short order," Sylvia agreed. "I'll see what I can do."

"And we'll see what data we can pick up. The more we know about that fleet and those superdreadnoughts, the better off we all are."

The superdreadnoughts in the Warrior fleet were new, built after the end of the war and vastly larger than any ship the Kenmiri had possessed before the Fall. Henry had destroyed two of them rescuing Drifter Convoy Blue Stripe Green Stripe Orange Stripe from their control, but *that* had been by ambush and surprise.

He didn't know as much about the big warships as he'd like. No one did.

3

AFTER ALMOST TWO years of working together, being together as romantic partners for over six months and walking into hell together repeatedly, Sylvia and Henry Wong had a solid sense of the limits of each other's sphere and a strong professional partnership.

Sylvia knew exactly which members of *Paladin*'s crew she could impose on to help her and which ones were too busy operating the ship in a combat environment. Lieutenant Commander Mehitabel Jackson, for example, was the destroyer's communications officer. Right now, she was managing the connections with the sensor drones that the UPSF ship had sent into the teeth of the Kenmiri formation.

Commander Chan Rong, on the other hand, was *Henry's* communications officer. Their main role was to maintain links between *Paladin* and other ships under the Commodore's command. With no subordinate or allied ships in the system, Commander Chan wasn't *unoccupied*, but they had availability to help the Ambassador.

"We're pinging the capital city and the orbital platforms to establish a link," they informed Sylvia. "We're still a full light-minute out, so time lag is going to be an issue."

"I'm used to it, Commander," Sylvia told them. The screen in her office had full access to the tactical reports and sensors set up for the

Commodore, but she wasn't as fully trained and able to read them as the destroyer's military crew.

She definitely *could* read the distance to Rashov, though. And she understood enough about the vector diagrams to know that *Paladin* was beginning a long curve that would take her right back to the skip line she'd arrived through.

The United Planets Alliance liked to pretend they didn't abandon their friends and allies, but Sylvia Todorovich had been one of their representatives working inside the Kenmiri Empire. She'd armed and encouraged multiple revolutions that she'd *known* the rest of the Vesheron wouldn't be able to support as quickly as the new rebels were hoping.

As best as she could, she'd never *lied* to any of the assorted alien races she'd convinced to rise up against the Kenmiri, but she'd definitely let them draw their own conclusions. This wasn't the first time she'd fled a star system aboard a UPSF destroyer, leaving the theoretical allies behind her to the mercy of the Kenmiri.

But that was the job sometimes, and she raised a sharply groomed eyebrow at the link to Chan as the timer ticked down.

"Any response, Commander?"

"Not ye— Wait." The heavyset Chinese officer held up a finger as they listened to something on their internal network. "I have a link. Someone is sending an active channel under Vesheron encryption protocols. I'm isolating it for security and can link you in—" They paused, finishing a task Sylvia couldn't even see. "—on your order."

"Connect me."

Sylvia didn't even need to check what her surroundings looked like. *Paladin* had more space than most destroyers—she needed less fuel for the same range, as Sylvia understood it—which had allowed them to squeeze in a small Presence Mission Section to provide working space for a diplomatic detachment.

That meant she had a permanent office, with the flag of the UPA—a blue banner with a curved V of eight gold stars—to her right and the flag of the UPSF—the same V on a stylized rocket—to her left. *Paladin*'s silver helmet commissioning seal was positioned directly behind her.

She'd had to improvise an impressive office enough times in her career to appreciate having the space aboard *Paladin*. She might be hundreds of light-years and weeks of travel from Sol and the UPA Security Council, but here and now, Sylvia Todorovich spoke for the United Planets Alliance.

The screen in front of her shifted as Chan linked the channel to her systems, the plot of the system vanishing to be replaced by the command center of a Kenmiri prefabricated defense platform. There were at least two dozen people working in the background, but the video feed was centered on a Tak woman.

The stranger wore an unfamiliar black uniform that faded oddly into the Tak's gray skin and head tentacles, but she was definitely in command. She was also, at the moment the channel was established, looking aside at something else.

There would be a two-minute round trip for every message back and forth between Sylvia and the stranger, so Sylvia leaned in to her own pickup and spoke rather than waiting.

Thanks to the scale of the Kenmiri Empire and its shadow across the Vesheron and the successor states taking shape, she didn't need to worry about language. She spoke the Kenmiri trade language, Kem, fluently—and could reasonably expect that any senior civil or military official of Rashova did the same.

"Rashovan representative, I am Ambassador Sylvia Todorovich of the United Planets Alliance. I was on my way to warn you about a rogue faction of Kenmiri Warriors threatening the Ra Sector, but it appears that we are far too late.

"Unfortunately, I do not believe my ship has the capacity to turn the tide of this battle. We are prepared to establish contact protocols with whatever emergency continuance plans you have and arrangements for further aid going forward, but..."

She spread her hands helplessly and leaned back to wait.

Tak were one of the Ashall species, the Seeded Races. Other than having small waving tendrils instead of hair and skin tones that were odd to human eyes, they could easily have been mistaken for human. No one was entirely sure *why* some seventy percent of the races in the Kenmiri Empire and the surrounding space could pass for each other at a distance.

First war and now the chaos of the Empire's Fall had been far more important since humanity had discovered that oddity of the universe.

She could see the moment, about two minutes after she'd connected, when the Rashovan officer saw the channel link up. The stranger waited through Sylvia's introduction, then leveled a grim gaze on the camera.

"Ambassador, I am Guild Admiral Chat," the woman said softly. "Until a few minutes ago, I was the *second*-in-command of Rashov's defenses, but my commander died aboard our dreadnoughts.

"Responsibility for the safety of the Rashova System is now mine, but the Kenmiri have not yet transmitted any demands or terms for our surrender. I have no choice but to accept whatever terms they impose, which also leaves me with no choice but urge you to flee the Rashova System as quickly as you can.

"I can neither guarantee the safety of your vessel, Ambassador, nor guarantee that I will not be required to use Rashovan security forces to hunt you down."

"Guild Admiral!" one of the other officers on the channel shouted. "The enemy are splitting their force."

Sylvia brought the tactical feed up in her internal network, giving mental orders to her implants to overlay the feed above her display. She saw what the officer above Rashova was seeing in a few seconds of examination.

The Kenmiri fleet had split into three clear detachments. One, led by a solid phalanx of at least twelve superdreadnoughts, was continuing their approach to Rashov. Another, mostly consisting of escorts and gunships, was clearly maneuvering after the surviving Rashovan ships.

The last, anchored by two more superdreadnoughts and demonstrating the increased acceleration of the Kenmiri's new ships, was now very definitively heading to intercept *Paladin*. Sylvia wasn't sure of the exact balance of power—UPA ships had a near-monopoly on the gravity shields they used for protection and could fight well above their weight—but she *knew* that the destroyer couldn't fight two superdreadnoughts.

Even if Henry had already done it once.

"Ambassador, you *must* leave," Chat told Sylvia. "I and many of my people were Vesheron once, and we owe you the warning for that. For now, I will do what I must to save my people."

The channel cut off and Sylvia swallowed a curse. Their mission in the Rashova System was now a clear failure, which left them with *problems*.

A mental command reopened the channel to the flag deck as her tactical feed reappeared on the main display.

"Henry, the locals are surrendering as soon as the Kenmiri let them," she told him crisply. "Slavery before death, I suppose."

"They're making assumptions I wouldn't in their place. That pursuit wing heading after their escorts isn't calling for surrenders."

"And the ships coming for us?"

Henry's image in her mental feed shrugged. "We're already running," he admitted. "Ihejirika is adjusting course to cut it even more sharply, and we're increasing acceleration to maximum.

"We'll be clear in time."

"They're going to follow us," Ihejirika warned. "That could get messy."

"I'm counting on it," Henry told them both. "The E-Two *want* to test their fighters against dreadnoughts in a more-controlled environment. They don't want to have the first strike by their shielded starfighters against dreadnoughts to be in a full fleet action."

Paladin had brought friends with her, at least as far as Ra-78. Among those friends was the Enteni carrier *Fronds of Will*. Sylvia wasn't sure how to match the new E-Two carriers and their fighters against Kenmiri ships, but she *did* know that a UPSF carrier wouldn't blink at sending their strike group against two regular dreadnoughts.

"And the Rashovans?" she asked.

Henry shook his head.

"I hate it, but surrendering is the right call for them. We can pull together our allies and make contact with the other two ex-Kenmiri colonies before the Warriors reach Anderon.

"We'll be back, Sylvia, and they know it."

Anderon and Kori were the other two systems in the Ra Sector that had served as homes to the Kenmiri themselves. All three had last seen

UPSF warships during Golden Lancelot, the genocidal operation that had ended the war by wiping out the Kenmiri's Kenmorad reproductive caste.

Without the Kenmorad, no new Kenmiri could be born. It was possible that the Kenmiri Artisans would find a technological solution before old age claimed them all, but Kenmiri society was built on the labor—physical and intellectual—of non-Kenmiri slaves and Kenmiri Drones.

That was why the Kenmiri had abandoned the outer provinces of their Empire, leaving six thousand stars to their own devices while the Empire focused on eight provinces and a *mere* four thousand stars.

"We will be back," Sylvia repeated. "We broke the Kenmiri once. We can do it again. The part that worries me, though…"

The screen in front of her marked the rapidly dispersing Kenmiri task forces, but it didn't magically produce the answers she was looking for.

"They haven't communicated with the Rashovans at all," she told Henry and Ihejirika. "They're *trying* to surrender, but the only people answering their hails in this system are *us*."

"Weapons fire is a form of communication," Ihejirika said drily. "They've definitely exchanged that."

"Kenmiri Warriors are pompous jackasses who know most of their opponents understand Kem," the Commodore said slowly. Henry Wong had served through the entirety of the seventeen-year war against the Kenmiri Empire.

His take on them meant more to Sylvia than most peoples', and not *just* because he was Henry Wong.

"They *will* taunt, belittle and condescend until they are actually losing," Henry continued. "Something is wrong. These Warriors… they're angry. Angry like the Kenmiri never were before Golden Lancelot.

"And that means I'm not sure I know what they're going to do."

The channel was silent for several seconds, and then she heard Ihejirika swear softly as the tactical feed updated with new icons.

Whatever formal report was on the bridge wasn't relayed to Sylvia —her link with Ihejirika and Henry was almost entirely mental, a link between their internal networks—but she was also getting the tactical feed.

"Why are they launching?" Sylvia asked. "They can't hit at this range, can they?"

She knew that the range for missiles wasn't always the standard seven hundred and fifty-thousand kilometers that the missiles could achieve from rest, but the Kenmiri fleet was still over twenty-five light-seconds from the planet, over ten times that range.

"Range on a missile is an arbitrary thing," Henry explained, his voice strangely distant and clinical. "We generally calculate it based on how far the missile can travel under power, since even orbital defense platforms engage in some level of evasive maneuvering.

"But the missile *keeps going* after that. Forever, really. We have to include failsafes on our missiles to keep them from continuing for all eternity."

Sylvia had been vaguely aware of that—mostly in the context of the need to make sure those failsafes had *no* external access once fired. But she wasn't sure of the point. If the orbital platforms could still evade…

"What are they shooting at if they can't hit the orbital platforms?"

"The planet."

Suddenly, she understood why Henry had gone so clinical. Like the vast majority of the officers in Golden Lancelot, he hadn't been *told* that his strike on a Kenmorad creche was part of an Empire-wide campaign of genocide.

And his had landed last. Hundreds of ships and thousands of officers and spacers had participated in the campaign to destroy the future of the Kenmiri, but it was his ship that had killed the last Kenmorad.

His ship that had truly doomed the Kenmiri to a slow death. And if the Kenmiri were firing missiles at a *planet*…

"How bad?" she whispered.

"We're estimating a full salvo launched from the entire fleet. Hard to get exact numbers, but at least fifteen hundred missiles," Ihejirika told her. He wasn't quite as clinical as Henry…but he didn't have the shields Sylvia's boyfriend had built against guilt and PTSD.

There was fear and anger in Ihejirika's voice.

"The Rashovans will try to stop them. But each of those missiles is likely carrying a five-hundred-megaton fusion warhead. And they'll just…keep firing."

There was a long and chill silence on the channel Sylvia shared with the two military officers. She glanced at the tactical display and checked the numbers through her internal network. Five minutes of flight time on the part of the Kenmiri missiles. Another five minutes with their terminal velocity before they reached the planet.

"I'll be on the flag deck in three minutes," she told them.

4

HENRY MADE no pretense of trying to convince Sylvia not to join him on the flag deck. There was an observer seat in the small space for just that reason, and it wasn't like they were going to actually fight a battle today.

The Kenmiri missiles were reaching the end of their powered flight as she took that seat, and the flag deck was entirely silent as the bridge and CIC updated the estimates.

"The Rashovans are tracking the missiles and are maneuvering the defense platforms to shield the planet," Commander Eowyn said after a few moments, glancing back at both Henry and the Ambassador with a heavy look to her eyes.

"It might help," she suggested.

"We have a second launch from the Kenmiri fleet," Lieutenant Commander Bach reported. An entire wall of the flag deck was now given over to a link to the bridge, allowing the bridge crew to report directly to Henry.

In a battle, that was a distraction he wouldn't inflict on them. Today, *watching* a battle that was already lost, he needed the updated information.

"They estimated that the defense platforms would take down too many missiles for whatever they're planning," Henry said grimly, bloody memories running through his mind. He'd never participated in mass bombardments of planets, but he'd fired enough missiles at ground targets to know the math.

The Kenmiri missiles were going to be coming in at a measurable percentage of lightspeed. The thermonuclear warheads were almost redundant.

"Rashovan escorts have pushed their acceleration to one-point-five KPS-squared," Eowyn told him. "That...won't work for long."

"No. Some of their engines will overload and do the Kenmiri's work for them. Some will burn their engines out and never fly again... but after today, it won't matter, so they'll do it anyway."

He drew strength from Sylvia's silent presence, but he knew how little they could do.

There were no more reports for a few minutes. Every eye on *Paladin* that could watch the sensor feeds was doing just that, watching as death descended on the planet they'd come here to save.

Guild Admiral Chat did more than Henry expected—more than anyone had any right to ask of her—but no mortal power could have stopped that tsunami of fire with the tools she had.

None of the defense platforms survived. Not a single missile had been targeted on them, but they intentionally put their shields and hulls between their planet and its doom. It wasn't enough and it cost them their lives.

Hundreds of missiles dove into Rashov's atmosphere and detonated. None of the first salvo even reached the ground, exploding high enough to spread radiation and violence through most of the atmosphere.

Henry *heard* Eowyn's sharp exclamation of fear.

"Commander, report," he snapped.

"Computer runs an automatic spectrographic analysis of most sensor data, ser," she whispered. "We have analysis of the..."

She swallowed.

"We have analysis of the additives presents in the explosions," Eowyn said. Her voice was firmer now, but still very quiet. "Strontium.

Cobalt. Gold. Others, too, but those are the key three. All would be activated into radioactive isotopes by the fusion bombs.

"Half-lives are in the decades, and they're…scattered across the entire planet."

Henry knew what that meant. Especially if another salvo of over a thousand missiles, similarly salted with radioactive isotopes, struck home. The Kenmiri weren't content to wipe a planet out and kill an entire population.

They were *destroying* Rashov. No one would ever be able to live on the planet now. The biosphere might survive the nuclear Armageddon being unleashed on it. It might even survive the winter that would follow from the water and ground strikes filling the atmosphere with debris.

But nothing but bacteria would survive all of that *and* decades upon decades of radiation.

"How many people?" he finally asked.

"Rashov's Empire-era population was one-point-nine billion Kenmiri supported by approximately three billion slaves," Sylvia said, her voice gentle.

Three billion.

Three *billion*.

"We should have been faster."

"We didn't think the Kenmiri would be here this quickly, Henry. We needed to build alliances, prepare for a war. Just warning the Rashovans wouldn't have been enough."

Sylvia squeezed his forearm. It was a gesture neither of them would normally make in the eyesight of others, but he knew his people would understand.

"Captain Ihejirika," he said calmly, turning to meet the Lieutenant Colonel's gaze—the UPSF had removed the rank of Captain from the organization tables, limiting it to being the title of a starship commander to avoid confusion.

"Your orders, ser?" his subordinate asked.

"Bring us about and stand by all beams and missile launchers," Henry ordered. "We cannot let this stand."

In the back of his mind, he knew that wasn't an order *Paladin*'s

Captain should have welcomed. But the big African officer visibly straightened when Henry gave it and nodded firmly.

"Bring us about," Ihejirika repeated loudly. "Draw me targets on those superdreadnoughts!"

It would take them at least half an hour to close with the dreadnoughts, and they'd end up passing each other at speed. But *Paladin* would have ten minutes to hammer the crap out of the Kenmiri ships, assuming her gravity shield withstood their return fire.

Henry gave it fifty-fifty chances at best, but he *knew* that his people couldn't stand by and watch a world die and do *nothing*.

Icons and numbers flickered through his network feed and across the screens around him as *Paladin* flipped in space to once again accelerate away from her skip-line exit.

"Henry, you can evade them completely," Sylvia whispered. "You're risking the ship."

"We can't do *nothing*," he hissed back. He turned to Chan.

"Commander Chan, prep six drones with all of our information and send them ahead of us through the skip line," he ordered. "Three to the Forward Flotilla, three back to Twelfth Fleet."

He wished he'd brought the rest of the Forward Flotilla, his command of UPSF and allied ships, to the Rashova System. They'd have been later, since none of the Flotilla could match *Paladin*'s acceleration, but it seemed that wouldn't have made any difference anyway.

He could *feel* the anger in his crew, a rekindling of the deep, burning hate that had driven the UPSF in pursuit of the aliens that had attacked their worlds even after the Empire had been driven from UPA space.

Hate was no true shield against the crimes Henry had committed. He knew that *he* couldn't hate enough for that—and he feared, in some ways, the officers who *could*.

But standing within sight of an artificial apocalypse, that hate would drive his people into a conflict the Kenmiri would regret.

"Henry, I'm not going to tell you you're wrong," Sylvia murmured, very clearly controlling her voice so no one else could hear her. "This is your area and we've always held that balance. But please...tell me. What do you expect to *achieve* today? Is it worth losing *Paladin*?"

That question cut through his anger like a hot knife, and he swallowed his immediate answer.

"We *cannot* let the death of a world stand," he finally whispered back. "Three billion lives. I cannot ask our crew to have watched that and do *nothing*."

Henry's own anger burned hot, hotter than it had since Golden Lancelot.

Sylvia was silent, watching the flag deck's main display for several seconds. Vector cones had appeared on the display, and Henry joined her in studying them.

He realized he was calculating the point of no return, the moment at which their charge toward the Warriors became irreversible. Part of him recognized the danger.

"What happens if *Paladin* is destroyed?" Sylvia finally said. "We die. What purpose is served?"

"We have to send a message."

"And *that* doesn't?"

The Ambassador's pointing finger indicated the icons of the remaining Rashovan fleet as they hurled themselves into the teeth of the dreadnoughts sent to finish them off. It was a pointless strike, Henry knew that—the *Rashovans* had known it—and thirty escorts died in exchange for at most five.

"We can survive," Henry said grimly, but for the first time, uncertainty undermined his will.

He glanced at his staff officers. Eowyn and Chan were focused on their tasks, either unable to hear the quiet conversation or determinedly ignoring it. *Paladin* didn't have a squadron with her today, but that only meant they were supporting Ihejirika's people.

"Maybe," his lover murmured. "I won't tell you you're wrong," she repeated. "But again…what do we gain by dying for the honor of the flag?"

He convulsively clenched his fist, staring at the display and automatically recalculating that point of no return. *Paladin* was still over almost an hour from missile range of the detachment heading for her, but there were only five minutes left that he could turn her around in. After that, the existing velocity would bring the single UPSF destroyer into range of two superdreadnoughts, each sixteen times *Paladin*'s mass.

"The Rashovans told us to run. To carry word and gather allies and come back to rescue them," Sylvia told him. "The only difference is that now we have to *avenge* them...but we can't do that if we're dead, either."

She wasn't going to overrule him; Henry knew that. She didn't have the authority, but in his heart of hearts he knew that if she *told* him to run, he would. Her position as the senior ambassador and civilian authority in the Ra Sector put her in an odd position versus the military chain of command, even *before* he factored in his trust in her judgment.

Or their relationship. If he sacrificed *Paladin* today, he'd not only die himself but get *Sylvia* killed. And Okafor Ihejirika, and Georgina Eowyn, and Chan Rong, and...and...and...

His people were angry. Were willing to fight and die for that anger. But it was *his* responsibility, as the flag officer and commander, to set aside his emotions and make the *right decision*.

"They killed three billion people," he whispered. "And we couldn't do *anything*."

"We can avenge them. But not today."

"No," he conceded. "Not today."

He nodded and gave her a sad facsimile of a smile before turning back to his link to the bridge.

"Captain, new orders," he told Ihejirika. He sighed heavily as the Lieutenant Colonel met his gaze. "We... We cannot risk this ship for the honor of the flag. Not when our sensor data may make the difference in a future battle—and not when we have reinforcements so close.

"Break off the attack run and set a course back to the skip line at full thrust."

"Ser, we—"

"That isn't discretionary, Captain Ihejirika," Henry said sharply. "We cannot let our emotions—our anger—lure us into a mistake that costs the lives of the people under our command.

"We *will* avenge Rashov. You have my word. But a single destroyer against a battle fleet won't achieve that."

"Yes, ser."

New numbers flickered across Henry's tactical feed as the destroyer flipped in space again, twisting her artificial gravity well to point toward the skip line back to Ra-78.

He took a few seconds to confirm that the Kenmiri Warriors wouldn't bring them into range, then leaned back in his seat and muted the signal to the bridge.

"Thank you, Sylvia," he murmured. "I *hate* this. But you are right."

"Don't think for one moment that I don't want to see those bastards burn," she told him fiercely. "But we'll make them burn with Twelfth Fleet and a thousand allies…not a suicide charge by one destroyer."

5

WHILE THE PROCESS of entering a skip line, as well as the secondary impulses used to maintain transit along the line, was an indescribably uncomfortable experience, *finishing* a skip was relatively calm. There was a sensation of falling in dimensions other than the usual three, and then reality settled back in around Henry.

"Skip complete," Lieutenant Fulvia Charmchi, *Paladin*'s navigator, reported. "Course set for the rendezvous point with the Flotilla."

"Thank you, Lieutenant," Henry told her. He turned his attention to his staff.

"Chan, do we have any contact from the Flotilla yet?"

"Not yet, ser."

"Forward our course and sensor data as soon as Ihejirika's people have located them," Henry ordered. "Those dreadnoughts are closer behind us than I like, and I'll feel a lot more comfortable once we've made contact with everyone else."

By any reasonable standard, the Allied Forward Flotilla was too large to be the command of a single Commodore. Henry's *official* command, Destroyer Squadron Twenty-Seven, currently consisted of just *Paladin*. His secondary role as second-in-command of the Peacekeeper Initiative was the source of his authority over the other UPSF destroyers in the Flotilla.

The Enteni carrier group and the La-Tar escort wing that made it an *Allied* flotilla were both commanded by officers who were at least Henry Wong's equal in rank. But since Twelfth Fleet was arguably the most powerful combat formation in the Ra Sector and none of the successor states had any illusion about how they stacked up against the industry and military of the United Planets Alliance overall, he'd been effectively *elected* as the leader of the Flotilla.

"We've confirmed the Flotilla is at the rendezvous point," Commander Eowyn advised. "Collating and classifying beacons now, but I agree with CIC's assessment that no one *else* is likely to have eighteen ships out in the middle of nowhere."

"What's our ETA to the rendezvous?"

"That depends on whether the Flotilla comes to meet us or not. If they hold their current position, we'll zero-zero with them in an hour and forty minutes. If they come out to meet us and we pass them, we'll intercept in just under an hour, but we'll pass each other at over ten thousand kilometers a second."

"We'll coordinate to rendezvous somewhere in the middle," Henry said calmly. "Once we have a communication link, we can make better plans. How long until our 'friends' catch up?"

"Ninety minutes, give or take."

That gave Henry and his subordinates and allies *time*. And given that the Flotilla had another five UPSF destroyers, an Enteni carrier and two Enteni destroyers, and seven Kenmiri-style escorts from both the E-Two and La-Tar navies…the Kenmiri might live to regret giving Henry that time.

If nothing else, they should be able to get the logistics freighters out of the way. The UPSF ships could go a *long* time without resupply—or resupply themselves, if push came to shove—but neither the Kenmiri-style ships nor the new Enteni ships had been built for the same conflict environment.

UPSF destroyers had needed to scout across the entire Kenmiri Empire with minimal or no logistics support. The Kenmiri had expected to have logistics facilities *everywhere*—and the Enteni hadn't expected to need to send their new ships very far at all.

There were plenty of reasons why a Kenmiri escort carried twice as many weapons as a UPSF destroyer despite being *half* the size.

THE KENMIRI HADN'T MADE it through the skip line yet by the time *Paladin* decelerated into formation with the rest of the Forward Flotilla, but Henry could still *feel* the palpable relief of the destroyer's crew.

They'd been willing to follow him on a suicide charge to avenge Rashov, but he doubted there was anyone aboard *Paladin* who wasn't delighted to be surrounded by over a dozen other warships.

"Tactical network linked and updated," Chan reported. "Telemetry updates on the feed."

"No particular surprises," Eowyn continued, smoothly taking over from the communications officer. "All ships have replenished fuel from the logistics vessels. *Bringer of Cloths* reports she is down to seventy percent capacity and could use some quality time with a gas giant."

"I'm not certain that Captain Vara would phrase it that way."

Captain Vara was a Beren officer from the Atto System. Since the gentleman wasn't *human*, Henry doubted he would even understand the double entendre.

"No, that one is on Lieutenant Colonel Byrne," the coms officer confirmed.

Lieutenant Colonel Decimus Byrne was the senior of Henry's five destroyer captains, one of the first officers to volunteer for the Peacekeeper Initiative when it had formed. His ship, *Paramount*, was one of the most modern destroyers in the UPSF...or had been, until the *Cataphract*-class ships had arrived and rendered every non-GMS warship obsolete.

"Any concerns that you see?" Henry asked Eowyn as he ran through the data feeds himself. He had more information on the five Peacekeeper Initiative destroyers than on the dozen allied ships, but nothing leapt out at him on any of them.

"Nothing, ser. All ships report green and ready for combat."

"Ser, Defender Falling Rain is requesting a full update on the pursuit force," Chan told him.

"Forward them our scan data," Henry replied. "Then set up an all-captains virtual conference."

Defender Falling Rain was both the captain of the carrier *Fronds of Will* and the commander of the overall Enteni-Eerdish Alliance carrier group of the Forward Flotilla.

The Enteni officer was of equal rank to Henry, but they'd been a freighter captain during the war, not even the commander of a rebel Vesheron ship. They recognized that Henry had far more experience at war and command than they did, and had readily conceded command to the human officer.

Anyone who doubted that the carnivorous plant-like alien was Henry's second-in-command, though, was going to have a rude shock.

"ETA for our Kenmiri friends?" he asked, looking back at the main display again. The Flotilla was now at zero velocity relative to the skip line, twelve million kilometers from where *Paladin* had emerged.

The Kenmiri wouldn't necessarily emerge at the same point on the line. The skip line was just that: a *line*, and a ship could fall back into realspace anywhere along it.

"Five minutes," Eowyn said grimly. "How long to weapons range... Well, that depends on what everyone does."

"That's what that conference is for. Chan?"

"I've got most of them online," they reported. "Ready to link you in on your command."

✦V✦

THANKS to the internal network hardware woven through Henry's skull, switching to a private virtual conference didn't even require him to move. His implants were entirely capable of inducing muscle ataxia and dropping him into a full virtual-reality space.

His nonhuman officers, whose societies were built on Kenmiri technology, had *significantly* less trust in their computers and implant technology than the UPA did. Internal networks and neural implants were ubiquitous in human space and utterly unheard-of in the successor states of the Empire.

Still, all of them were linked in via systems that allowed Henry to see them. They made for a riotous collection of color, ranging from Falling Rain's mauve-tinted dark green skin to the nearly transparently pale skin and orange eyes of Captain Vara.

"Captains, thank you," Henry greeted them in Kem. "We are short on time, so I will lay out what we know as swiftly as I can."

He swallowed hard as he faced his next words.

"The Rashova System has been…exterminated. The rogue faction of Kenmiri that we were hoping to recruit the Rashovans to fight got there first. We arrived in the middle of the battle, and *Paladin* was far too little to turn the tide of the fight.

"The Kenmiri bombarded Rashov itself with heavy-metal-laced fusion warheads, both devastating the planetary population and salting the surface with radioactive isotopes to render the planet uninhabitable for decades."

Three of the captains of the Forward Flotilla were Enteni, utterly alien beings that resembled mobile Venus flytraps with stalked eyes concealed inside their mouths. Henry had spent enough time with them to begin to be able to read the body language of eyestalk and tentacle, but he wasn't confident in it yet.

The other nine nonhuman captains were Ashall. Two of them could pass for human on even close inspection, though the rest either had skin tones well outside human norms or visible tertiary characteristics like horns or Vara's orange, slit-pupiled eyes.

While the Ashall were diverse in both appearance and culture, they all had sufficiently similar facial musculature to create shared patterns of emotional reaction. Culture would decide how someone interpreted a smile, but every Ashall Henry had ever met tensed muscles in their temples when stressed.

Those were the microexpressions that Henry and many other UPSF officers had learned to read from extended interaction with nonhumans—a skill that led to some *entertaining* conversations in casinos, in his experience.

Right now, it allowed him to feel the horror that his officers felt at what had been done in Rashova.

"As of our last sensor data, the Rashovan fleet has been completely obliterated," Henry continued. "The Kenmiri took at least some of the orbital infrastructure and shipyards intact, so I expect to see them repair and refit in place before moving on.

"The immediate concern, however, is that the Kenmiri identified *Paladin*. They may not have recognized her as a *Cataphract* destroyer, but they certainly recognized us as a UPSF warship."

"That is-was not difficult," Falling Rain pointed out. "Your gravity shields are-were quite distinctive and still unique."

"Indeed. I believe they realized *Paladin* was no capital ship, but they still detached two of their new superdreadnoughts and what looked like twenty-two escorts and gunships to pursue us."

Henry smiled grimly.

"I am flattered, if a tad concerned, by their level of overkill. But if our rogues are willing to send a detachment after us, I am perfectly willing to engage them in detail. Between our shields and our starfighters, I believe we have a clear and distinct advantage over a task group of two dreadnoughts and escorts."

What he wasn't going to admit to his officers was that he was *less* certain of their advantage over a task group of two *super*dreadnoughts. The new Kenmiri capital ships were still unknowns in many ways.

"If they kept up their pursuit, I expect them to arrive any minute now. Barring serious objections, I intend for us to engage them in the Ra-Seventy-Eight System."

Ra-78 was a UPA designation, marking the seventy-eighth system the UPSF had surveyed in the Ra Sector. Since they didn't know any local name for the star and the Kenmiri designation was equally bland, the allies had grown used to the UPA names.

Henry's main focus as he waited for objections was on Falling Rain. The Enteni Defender not only commanded the largest contingent of non-UPSF ships, but their carrier was also key to any chance of actually engaging the Kenmiri successfully.

"Any chance to injure-maim the rogue fleet can-should not be allowed to escape," Falling Rain replied. Unlike the Ashall members of the meeting, their voice was translated into Kem by a computer on their ship. It was fluent enough, except that the Enteni had an odd sense of time and a partial imperative tense that didn't exist in Kem.

Or English, for that matter, which Henry was able to translate Kem into without a thought.

No one else said a word to counter Henry and Falling Rain, and the UPSF Commodore nodded once with a grim smile.

"The destruction of this detachment is a small repayment for the deaths in Rashova, but it is what we can inflict on them today," he told his people. "We will divide the Flotilla into two segments separated by fifty thousand kilometers."

That was close enough to allow the second line to engage in the missile duel and *far* enough to allow the front line to shield the second.

"The forward line will consist of the UPSF ships and the Enteni and Eerdish escorts and destroyers. The rear line will consist of *Fronds of Will*, the logistics ships and the La-Tar escorts."

He would prefer to send the logistics ships entirely away, except that they were limited to the same acceleration as his older UPSF destroyers. At half a KPS^2, the transports weren't going to escape Kenmiri warships.

His destroyers could at least send their crews to acceleration tanks to withstand the subjective gravity of higher thrusts. The tanker and the replenishment ship couldn't.

"I am not certain that my crews will be content to lurk in the rear," Squadron Leader Tol Azan said grimly. The La-Tar officer had drawn askance looks from the E-Two officers in their early meetings because he was Kozun, with the clearly visible armored head-plates of that race. While the E-Two were at war with the Kozun homeworld, Tol Azan's family had been removed from the Kozun homeworld over a hundred years before.

Many of the slave worlds in the Ra Sector had at least one group of Kozun "tributes" dumped on them. That was how the Kenmiri had populated their slave worlds, after all—the race homeworlds had kept limited self-governance in exchange for giving up millions of their people to their overlords as slaves.

"The problem, Squadron Leader, is that your ships lack shields of any kind," Henry said bluntly. "My ships have gravity shields. Defender Falling Rain's ships have energy screens. Your ships have neither."

The La-Tar escorts were decently armored and had decent antimissile defenses—but so were the E-Two escorts, and those ships had shields.

The Kenmiri had not, prior to the Fall, miniaturized their energy screen technology sufficiently to fit it on anything much smaller than a dreadnought. The Kozun Hierarchy, born from the Kozun homeworld, had managed to build energy-screened cruisers, but the majority of the Ra Sector's successor states were operating with either Kenmiri-built escorts or new-built copies of the same.

Scientists on the Enteni homeworld had solved the miniaturization problem, allowing the E-Two to mount energy screens on everything down to their starfighters.

Tol Azan and his people might not *like* it, but the four La-Tar escorts in the Forward Flotilla were the squishiest units Henry had except for the lightly defended freighters.

"I want your ships close enough to provide missile-fire support," Henry told Azan, "but I am unwilling to risk exposing your people to Kenmiri fire when we have gravity- and energy-shielded ships that can take that fire without damage."

He met the Kozun's gaze levelly.

"I understand that is never easy to be asked to hide behind others," he conceded. "But there is no sense to risking your ships unnecessarily."

"And I must-will need your ships to stand guard over *Fronds of Will*," Falling Rain told the La-Tar officer. "If I send my escorts forward to join the shield wall, I will need others to provide missile defense.

"We can-will not afford to lose *Fronds of Will*'s ability to rearm the starfighters."

Tol Azan's expression told Henry that he wasn't entirely reconciled, but he made an accepting gesture and leaned back in his seat.

"If that is accepted…?" Henry waited a moment more, then turned to Falling Rain. "We will want to open with the fighter strike. The

Kenmiri have never met your Shieldwings and will expect them to be the usual unshielded starfighters of the Vesheron."

What the UPSF indelicately called "TIEs," unshielded starfighters were a tool of desperation, used to put vast numbers of missiles on target in exchange for *knowing* you were going to lose too many of them.

The UPSF had gravity-shielded starfighters, but Henry had none of them with him today. The Enteni starfighters—"Shieldwing" was the UPSF's reporting name for the new spacecraft, though the E-Two contingent of the Forward Flotilla had adopted the Kem translation themselves—were the first shielded fighters he'd seen that *weren't* Terran. They'd hopefully be as much of a surprise for the rogue Warriors as they'd originally been for his people.

"That can-will allow us to send them in closer," Falling Rain said, their tentacles lacing together firmly. "The destroyers and shielded escorts can-will come in behind them. We must-will teach the Kenmiri to fear the Ra Sector."

"We'll want to get your fighters into space immediately," Henry told them. "Are they ready?"

"They are-will-be."

"Ser." Eowyn's interjection wasn't heard by anyone else, feeding directly to his internal network. "We have disturbance along the skip line. Looks like the Kenmiri mirrored your skip almost exactly— they're about three minutes late, but they're here."

Henry could see that the rest of the officers were getting similar updates from their own officers.

"So it begins, officers," he told them. "Let's be about it."

6

THERE WERE STILL times Henry missed command of a single starship. There was an immediacy to being captain that no squadron command could match—and he'd have given at least his right arm, if not his dominant left, to have either of his old battlecruisers with the Forward Flotilla.

But watching eighteen starships maneuver to his orders still triggered an atavistic shiver of awe.

The six UPSF destroyers led the way. *Paladin* was the newest, but Henry also had three of the modern *Significance*-class ships and two of the older *Tyrannosaur*-class vessels. Even the *Tyrannosaur*s were likely more survivable than any non-UPSF ship in the Flotilla, though their gravity shields were weaker than the *Significance*s.

The two E-Two destroyers were simpler ships than their UPSF counterparts in many ways. Triangular prisms almost two hundred meters long, they lacked the missile-launcher-equipped "wings" and were more lightly protected.

In exchange, they were more heavily armed and faster than the Terran ships. Their size and energy screens put them ahead of the Kenmiri-style escorts that made up the rest of the Flotilla, even the ones the E-Two had refitted with energy screens of their own.

Eleven ships with gravity shields and energy screens formed Henry's forward line, spread out into a rough square to allow mutual support against missiles.

Behind them, the four La-Tar escorts positioned themselves in a protective formation around *Fronds of Will* and the two logistics ships. They held off on their acceleration for a few moments, allowing the shield wall to open up the distance between the two segments.

And as the whole formation took shape, *Fronds of Will*'s energy signature flared repeatedly on Henry's feeds. The Enteni and their Eerdish allies were still feeling their way into carrier warfare, and their ships couldn't clear their decks as quickly as a UPSF fleet carrier—but they still put ninety starfighters into space in as many seconds.

The Remnant fleet was still forty light-seconds away. They had *time* to sort out their formations—Henry could see that the Kenmiri were doing the same thing, even as they began to accelerate toward his ships.

"Ser. Are we going to talk to them?"

Henry arched an eyebrow at his flag captain. Ihejirika's image was running through his internal network, a small virtual window to the left of his vision no matter where he looked. The big man shrugged at the wordless question.

"We *could*," Ihejirika pointed out. "The Ambassador has a silver tongue, after all. She's talked us out of a few messes over the last few years."

"These people killed three billion civilians," Henry said. Just *saying* that sent a spike of anger through him that took conscious self-control to keep out of his voice. "We might be *able* to talk them into some sort of truce here today...but even putting aside Protocol Twenty-Seven, Captain Ihejirika, why would we *want* to?"

Peacekeeper Initiative Protocol Twenty-Seven required Initiative ships to engage any Kenmiri warship found in the Ra Sector. It was a recognition that the war with the Empire had never officially *ended*. The Kenmiri had abandoned half their Empire without a word, let alone a peace treaty.

"We don't." The flag captain smiled grimly. "We really, really don't. But it's my job to poke at the things you haven't said, ser."

"That it is, Captain," Henry conceded. "But no. I think every sentient in the Forward Flotilla is united on this: today will be a small down payment on the sins of these Warriors, but it is a payment they are *going* to make."

AFTER FLITTING around the galaxy using *Paladin*'s full two-KPS^2 acceleration, moving at half a KPS^2 with the rest of the Flotilla felt like swimming through molasses. The warships *could* go faster, but it would require putting the crew of the five older UPSF destroyers in gel-filled acceleration tanks.

Henry did *not* miss needing acceleration tanks to get up to full power and wasn't sure they needed the loss of crew efficiency that came with that step. Plus, the two logistics ships *didn't* have that capability.

He wasn't going to leave the freighters unprotected. They might be all but certain that they'd located the entire Kenmiri force, but they also knew that the Kenmiri had penetrated the Ra Sector with a small fleet of stealth ships.

It wouldn't take a warship to destroy the two logistics vessels. A boxed one-shot missile launcher would be more than enough if he left them undefended.

"Shieldwings have commenced their run," Eowyn reported. "Thirty-five minutes to missile range."

For the fighters, at least. Just over an hour for the main body of the Flotilla to range on the enemy. The fighters would burn through their envelope of the Kenmiri fleet at about three percent of lightspeed, holding their missiles until the last sane moment before salvoing everything they had at the two superdreadnoughts.

Ninety starfighters would put over three hundred and fifty missiles on their targets. With the extra velocity from the starfighters' approach, the missiles would come in *fast*. The volume and speed of the strike were what made fighters so dangerous, even the unshielded TIEs the Vesheron had built—and lost—in vast numbers during the war.

Ten minutes after the fighter strike, Henry's first line would launch their own missiles and follow up with heavy lasers as they drew closer. The Kenmiri would do everything in their power to close the range, their plasma cannon the key to the battle if they could bring them to range—though that same range would bring the Flotilla's lasers into play.

Henry knew most of what both sides were going to do over the next hour. His people would follow up the fighter strike with more missiles and try to keep out of cannon range. The Kenmiri's superior acceleration would eventually bring the Flotilla into cannon range, and the Flotilla would engage with their lasers.

The question was how much would be *left* of the Warriors at that point. The fighter strike *should* badly damage both dreadnoughts, clearing the way for the Flotilla's missiles.

Unless the superdreadnoughts were even tougher than Henry expected, this fight wasn't going to go the Kenmiri's way. Of course, unless the superdreadnoughts were *less* tough than he expected, this fight was going to hurt.

Time and skill would tell…and Henry Wong had confidence in everyone around him.

V

WAR HAD a reputation of being ninety-nine percent boredom and one percent absolute terror. Space battles, in Henry's experience, often took that same ratio into the actual combat action. Thirty minutes passed in a professional false calm, even as tension ratcheted up across *Paladin*'s flag deck and bridge.

"All ships reporting in," Chan told Henry. "All weapons and defenses have passed systems checks. We're green."

That was the third time they'd run a systems check across the Forward Flotilla in the last three hours, but Henry *knew* everyone was being twitchy. The checks distracted people, focused their attention on the task at hand.

"That's weird."

Henry turned a sharp look on Commander Eowyn.

"Those are dangerous words, Commander," he said slowly. "What have you got?"

"It *looks* like the superdreadnoughts are launching missiles," she told him. "I've got a pretty decent handle on their launchers' energy signature, and they're cycling like they're launching.

"But I'm only seeing blips that *might* be thrust signatures. No missiles—and even the Shieldwings are well outside missile range of the superdreadnoughts."

"*Weird* and *that's funny* are words that can get a lot of people killed in a battle. Link up telemetry with the rest of the Flotilla," Henry ordered. "Nail down just what the bastards are doing, Commander."

Now he remembered that the Remnant Warriors had been prepared to send two of their superdreadnoughts against Twelfth Fleet. Part of that had been the size of the new warships and the expectation of surprise...but part of it, according to the Drifters the Kenmiri had forced to bait their trap, had been the belief that they could neutralize Twelfth Fleet's starfighters.

And Twelfth Fleet had three fleet carriers and six battlecruisers, with a total of almost four hundred starfighters. Not ninety.

"Integrating telemetry from our ships into a VLA," Eowyn said grimly, her hands flying across her console and the air above it, tapping commands only she could see.

Henry could only wait, watching the Shieldwings blaze closer to the earliest point they could effectively launch their missiles at the Kenmiri.

"I've got ten times as many ghosts now but *nothing useful.*"

Eowyn turned the last two words into a curse, and Henry pulled her data into his own network feeds. Sparks of intermittent data flared across the sensors, picked up by multiple ships but too vague to be resolved into anything useful. They *might* be missiles fired on lower power than usual but decreasing power didn't increase delta-V or range. Anything that could threaten the fighters they should be able to detect.

"Fighter missile range is in two minutes," he checked aloud. "Is whatever it is going to reach them before then?"

The silence that answered him took too long…long enough that he knew the answer even before Commander Eowyn said anything.

"Assuming the current pattern continues, the contacts will interpenetrate the Shieldwing formation fourteen seconds before they enter missile range."

Henry had been a starfighter pilot before he'd been a starship captain. He still wore pilot's wings on his chest—and his were painted red, to mark that he'd survived the brutal first campaign against the Kenmiri, where less than thirty of the pilots deployed had lived to come home.

He knew the feeling of charging into the dark against an unknown enemy with an unknown weapon. Without knowing what the Kenmiri had deployed, there was *nothing* he could do.

The only option was to order the pilots to launch their missiles before the ghosts intercepted them—but that would result in the missiles arriving at the superdreadnoughts with no time left on their engines.

And without running engines, the missiles would be easily dodged. If they launched early, the pilots would give up over ninety percent of their weapons' effectiveness.

He didn't have enough time. Everything he was seeing was fifteen seconds old, and everything he could send his pilots would take fifteen seconds to arrive. It was already too late.

"Intercept in eleven seconds," Eowyn murmured. "We'll see in thirty."

"Inform the captains," Henry ordered Chan grimly. "And Defender Falling Rain. Whatever is coming…I'm afraid it's going to be ugly."

"Their shields should protect them," his operations officer replied, but even *she* didn't sound like she believed herself.

Henry would have given a lot for Eowyn to be correct, but as the energy signatures started spiking across his feeds, he knew that wasn't the case.

He'd expected a wave of missiles, somehow concealed and potentially with extended ranges. What they got was something else entirely. Seconds before the still-unidentified ghosts interpenetrated the fighter strike, their stealth finally failed—as the weapon finally came online.

The ghosts they'd been tracking *were* missiles, he thought—but as they reached the fighters, they broke apart into drones a tenth of the size of a standard warhead at most. Visible even at over fifteen light-seconds, arcs of electrically charged plasma linked the drones together in high-energy webs.

Webs that were drawn toward the approaching starfighters like moths to a flame. As soon as any arc or drone impacted a Shieldwing's shields, the rest wrapped around from the sides. Shields designed to withstand a blast from a plasma conversion warhead or a laser pulse failed in the face of inexorable pressure and sustained energy.

The webs only lasted for a few seconds before their power cells failed...but then a second wave of plasma webs lit up behind them, crashing down on the surviving fighters before their pilots could adapt to the sudden change in the threat environment.

There was a chill silence on all of Henry's communications channels as the last icons flickered out.

"Report," he ordered. He knew his voice was flat and cold. It was the only way he could function when things went *this* wrong.

"No survivors, ser," Eowyn whispered. "They took out every one of the fighters."

And that changed *everything*.

7

"ALL SHIPS, THIS IS COMMODORE WONG," Henry announced, trusting Chan to expand the link to the captains. "We have misestimated our enemy. Adjust course ninety degrees to the ecliptic and maneuver to evade the enemy."

Maneuver cones flickered across his screen and he swallowed his anger and grief, focusing on the task at hand.

"We can't break off, ser," Eowyn warned. "Our velocity is toward the Rashova skip line. If we attempt to retreat, they'll overhaul us long before we make it out."

She paused.

"*Paladin* might make it, ser. The rest of the Flotilla will be run down and destroyed."

"They'd bleed for it, but I won't order people to die to cover our retreat," Henry replied. "We need another option. Get me the full map of the system."

His view expanded, the maneuver cones pushing out farther with his view. The overlap told him everything he needed to know about the truth of Eowyn's statement. Only *Paladin* had the acceleration to lose the enemy fleet inside the Ra-78 System, and even she would need to play cat and mouse at high speed to make it back toward Ra-77, the first system of the route back to Eerdish.

"There," he said aloud, highlighting the answer. "Eowyn, check my calculations on the route to the Ra-One-Fifty-Two skip line."

That course wasn't outside the maneuver cone of the Kenmiri fleet, but they'd only be in missile range before they skipped.

"I make it one hundred fifty-two minutes before transit, assuming we transit without slowing."

Hitting a skip line at speed was neither wise nor safe—but it was safer than getting into a cannon-range engagement with a superdreadnought division.

"How long is the Flotilla in range of their missiles?" he asked.

"At least twenty minutes," she warned. "I don't know if the logistics ships can take that...but they're the ones holding us to point-five KPS-squared."

"And the ones we can't afford to lose if we have a chance in hell of getting through."

Ra-152 didn't lead anywhere useful other than *away*. It would buy them time to get away from the Kenmiri, but it was also going to be a long way around. They'd need every drop of fuel on *Bringer of Cloths*—and probably every missile and spare part on *Rightful Chieftain*!

"Chan, get me Captain Vara and Captain Caijus," Henry ordered. "Eowyn, tell the UPSF squadron to get to the acceleration tanks. Whatever happens, we're going to need every scrap of acceleration we can get."

He left passing the orders to the Commander as the two Ashall captains appeared in front of him. The two were a study in contrasts. Vara was orange-eyed and nearly translucently pale, as alien-looking as any of the Ashall races. Caijus, on the other hand, could have passed for a cousin from Okafor Ihejirika's home of Nigeria. He was a large and broad-shouldered dark-skinned man, without even the green tinge many Eerdish had to separate him from a Black human man.

"I need to know how fast you can push your ships," Henry told the two Ashall without preamble, his Kem as fast as the somewhat stilted language allowed.

"*Bringer of Cloths* can likely get up to point-eight KPS-squared,"

Vara said instantly. The translation between Kem and Terran numbers was automatic for Henry now. That number, though, surprised him.

"*How?*" he asked bluntly.

"We expected the problem and rigged up some crude acceleration couches," the pale captain told him. "Neither engines nor crew can handle the same thrust as your UPSF warships, but we can make more thrust than designed."

Caijus looked impassive, but Henry could spot the microexpressions of his stress.

"We cannot accelerate that fast," he admitted. "I do not have any acceleration couches or pods—except possibly in our cargo holds. Even if we did, I do not believe *Rightful Chieftain*'s engines can sustain the power.

"At point-six KPS-squared, we are subject to five subjective gravities. Our engines can sustain that and my crew can endure that."

"It will have to do," Henry told them. "Make whatever preparations you need. You will not have long."

"Understood."

He dropped the channel and turned back to Eowyn.

"Assume the whole Flotilla maintains point-six KPS-squared. What does that cut the time in missile range to?"

"Sixteen minutes," she said instantly. "I'm…"

"The freighters can't survive sixteen minutes in range of two superdreadnoughts," Henry finished for her. "The Warriors are vicious enough to target them first—even if they *don't* think we're likely to escape and need the logistics support."

He studied the maneuver cones again. His ships were now building a significant side vector, opening up the closest approach they'd make to the Kenmiri ships.

But as soon as the Kenmiri adjusted course to intercept them, that gap would start closing.

"Get the orders out," he told his staff. "The Flotilla will make a straight run for the Ra-One-Fifty-Two skip line at point-six KPS-squared."

"On it."

Before Henry could even give further orders, his link to Ihejirika chimed.

"Ser…I can run the same math as everyone else," his flag captain told him. "Ra-One-Fifty-Two doesn't lead anywhere but into Osiris. Kenmiri space."

"Right now, it only matters that it isn't going to get us burned down by those superdreadnoughts," Henry admitted softly. "And we need to buy the time for the rest of the Flotilla to make that journey safely."

Ihejirika exhaled heavily, then nodded.

"We have full sensor data on their new toy and they know it," he observed. "Courier-drone salvo?"

"I was going to use *Paladin* as bait, but that works even better," Henry replied. "Chan, I want every ship to do a full data download to their courier drones and fire a spread to Eerdish."

The courier drones were tiny skip-capable ships, their engines bearing more than a slight resemblance to the shield-skipping penetrator warheads in the UPSF ships' magazines. But the UPA had used them before it had discovered subspace communications.

And when they'd learned that their subspace communications had been in a frequency zone artificially stabilized by the Kenmiri, they'd gone right back to them. Not least because the Kenmiri had *shut down* whatever had been doing said stabilizing, cutting off FTL communications across the galaxy.

"The Kenmiri may not recognize the drones, ser," Ihejirika pointed out. "We probably want to use *Paladin* as bait regardless."

"That's not going to go well for your ship, Captain, but she's the only one that can do it," Henry said. "Are you ready?"

"*Paladin*'s crew has walked into hell with you before, Commodore. We'll play matador for you if you need us to."

Henry had to consult his internal network to find out just what a matador *was*—and grimaced as the description processed.

"The difference is that the Kenmiri are even *more* dangerous than a bull," he pointed out. "And unlike the bull, they deserve whatever we can do to them."

New icons sprinkled the tactical feed as the courier drones

launched, screaming back toward the Ra-77 skip line at five KPS^2. The Kenmiri had enough of a velocity advantage that they'd be able to bring the drones into missile range—but only if they stayed on a pursuit course.

The logical move on the Kenmiri's part was…

"There they go," Henry observed. "Ten escorts just split off to pursue the drones. Remainder are with the superdreadnoughts, arcing out to intercept us."

"Time for bait?" Ihejirika asked.

"Bait, yes, but first…" The Commodore studied the Kenmiri ships on the displays for a few long seconds, then forced a grim smile.

"First, I'm going to punch the bastards in the nose. Chan, get me Kenmiri open-channel com protocols."

THE UNITED PLANETS ALLIANCE'S Operation Golden Lancelot had been cold-blooded genocide, enabled by a thorough understanding of their opponents' culture and biology combined with an absolutely ruthless division of information and need to know.

Not a single officer aboard any ship on the offensives had known Lancelot's full objectives. The analysts and planners who had set it into motion had kept the full scope of the horror the UPSF had embraced to themselves until after it was over.

Then, though, the UPA had fully briefed the other El-Vesheron powers and the major Vesheron rebels on what had been done and what had happened. Only key personnel in key formations had known anything before it happened, but *afterward*, it had become common knowledge that Colonel Henry Wong and the battlecruiser *Panther* had fired the final shots and killed the last Kenmorad evacuation transport.

Henry Wong *hated* the nickname "Destroyer"—but as Sylvia Todorovich had once told him, he'd paid for it, so he may as well use it.

Now he leveled his coldest gaze on the camera pickup, knowing that Chan was carefully limiting what was recorded and sent to the Kenmiri fleet.

"Kenmiri Warriors, you know who I am," he told them, the sharp syllables of Kem accentuating his words. "I am the Destroyer, the man whose hand *ended* your race. It seems that your desperation has led you to dishonor your ancient traditions and rain fire on a living world."

Ancient tradition called on the Kenmiri to *protect* the Ashall and the worlds that could support life. That didn't seem to be enough to stop them turning inhabitable worlds into the pollution-ridden hellholes of Kenmiri industrial slave worlds, but for all the Kenmiri's *many* crimes, carpet-bombing planets was a new one.

"I would tell you to look inside yourselves for the true answer to your crimes, but to have done what was done...you are no longer Warriors. I do not know what you have become, but you have forsworn the most ancient oaths of the Kenmiri.

"Turn back now, or I will once again become the avatar of your destruction."

He cut off the recording with a hand gesture, then shook his head.

"Think that will do anything, ser?" Eowyn asked.

"I'll tell you in about five minutes. Captain Ihejirika? Execute Matador."

Up to that moment, *Paladin* had been maneuvering with the rest of the Forward Flotilla and heading for the Ra-152 skip line. Now she flipped in space and began accelerating on a new vector at full power.

Like the course the Flotilla was on, the Kenmiri would bring *Paladin* into range. But since *Paladin* could out-accelerate the Remnant fleet, doing so would require them to break off from pursuing the rest of the Flotilla.

"Superdreadnoughts are changing course," Eowyn reported. "I think you might have hit a sore spot, ser."

"Good." New maneuver cones were updating on his screens, and Henry studied them mirthlessly.

He imagined that the Kenmiri had considered sending just one superdreadnought after *Paladin*—or even just the escorts. That was why he'd punched them in the nose, after all.

The *escorts* couldn't take on the rest of the Forward Flotilla. Henry would even take bets on five UPSF destroyers versus *one* superdreadnought, leaving the escorts to the allies.

In the more traditional battle they were facing today, *Paladin* wasn't going to beat a superdreadnought one-on-one. But if the Kenmiri sent one after her, they wouldn't have enough ships to really threaten the Flotilla.

So, they were bringing the *entire* fleet after him.

"I'm guessing there's no way we're going to get through to Ra-Seventy-Seven to carry news home, is there?" he asked Eowyn.

"Not a chance, ser. I'm not sure we'll be able to avoid their fire at all —but the only way we're getting out of this system is into Ra-One-Fifty-Two on the tails of the rest of the Flotilla."

"Help Charmchi plot the course," he ordered. "We'll want to cut it as tightly as possible—if it's a choice between the Flotilla getting hit or *Paladin*..."

"We take the hit," she finished for him. "We're on it."

8

SPACE WAS MOSTLY empty and very large. That gave Ihejirika and Charmchi a lot of space to play with, even as their existing three-thousand-odd kilometers per second of velocity relative to the Remnant fleet limited their options.

Still, *Paladin* had a lot more acceleration to work with than the Kenmiri fleet, and Henry was content with the final maneuver pattern his people worked out. The math was clear: *Paladin* could have broken clear of the Kenmiri fleet so long as she wasn't trying to get back to Ra-77.

The problem was that if the vectors said they'd escape without entering missile range, the superdreadnoughts had no reason to pursue the GMS destroyer instead of the rest of the Forward Flotilla. The Warriors appeared to *really* want Henry's blood—and the deployment of half of their escorts to deal with the drones also proved they wanted to keep any data on their antifighter plasma webs away from Twelfth Fleet for now.

But given the choice between *no* chance of stopping Henry getting away with that data and destroying an entire formation of allied ships, they'd go after the Flotilla.

They'd picked a course that, hopefully, looked like they were heading back to Ra-77 and willing to risk a fight with the Kenmiri to make the run for the skip line.

"Escorts have ranged on the drones," Eowyn reported quietly. "I'm detecting a full two-hundred-missile salvo. If there are any gunships, they're still with the superdreadnoughts."

Gunships traded half of the missile launchers and all of the lasers of an escort to carry a single heavy plasma cannon of the same style as the dreadnoughts'. At long range, they were less effective—but outside of luck or overwhelming numbers, missiles didn't decide capital-ship actions.

Today, the Kenmiri had overwhelming numbers *and* the Forward Flotilla's only capital ship was *Fronds of Will*—and with the carrier's fighter wing gone, the Flotilla had no business in a capital ship action.

If they brought any of the now-divided Flotilla into plasma-cannon range, it was going to be very ugly.

"Second salvo from the escorts. Third."

Henry exhaled a surprised breath. His six UPSF destroyers had each launched five courier drones. Their allies had a more limited supply—neither the La-Tar Cluster nor the E-Two Alliance were manufacturing their own skip drones yet—and had only added another ten between them.

They'd sent forty robotic spacecraft across Ra-78 to carry a message home. The Kenmiri had just launched fifteen missiles at each of those drones.

"We need to improve the defenses of our drones," he observed mildly.

"Our drones *have* no defenses," Eowyn said. "They have an evasive maneuvering program and five KPS-squared of acceleration. That's it."

"That would be my point. As we are seeing, if the Kenmiri are prepared to spend the missiles, they can cut off the interstellar coms of any engaged force using drones."

The drones had been sufficiently new in most of their engagements in the Ra Sector that no one had yet treated them as a target. The Warriors had clearly been paying attention to their intelligence reports.

That was part of the reason why Henry had written Protocol Twenty-Seven into the Initiative's core rules. He hadn't anticipated that the Kenmiri would develop and roll out an entirely new generation of stealth and communications technologies to enable their scouting efforts in their former territory, but he *had* wanted to blind any attempt at aggression on their part.

"All drone signatures lost," Eowyn concluded. "Twelfth Fleet really isn't going to know what happened here, ser. Or in Rashova."

"I know." Henry shook his head. "There was a plan for this, at least. Right now, we need to get the Flotilla out of this system intact."

"Twenty-three minutes on this vector until the Remnant task force can no longer bring the rest of the Flotilla into missile range before they make the Ra-One-Fifty-Two skip line."

He nodded and glanced at Ihejirika's image. "When do we divert, Captain?"

"In forty-two minutes, we break for the skip line ourselves," his flag captain replied. "We'll hit the line four hours and thirteen minutes from now, roughly two hours after the rest of the Flotilla.

"It's a twelve-hour skip…but I have to remind you, ser, there isn't much in One-Fifty-Two."

"That's a future-us problem," Henry said. "Our current problem is how long are we going to be in missile range of the Kenmiri?"

"We will enter missile range in approximately ninety-six minutes and remain in range for seven and a half minutes. Any orders, ser?"

"None, Captain. You know how to fight your ship."

Ihejirika nodded. "I suggest you strap in, ser," he warned. "We will be using all of our systems in defensive mode, but we are badly outgunned. The likelihood of us making it through this without being hit is middling at best."

"Better *Paladin* is damaged than the entire Flotilla is lost," Henry murmured. "And *Paladin* is the toughest ship in the Flotilla."

Destroyer or not, her gravity maneuvering system had replaced fusion rockets and massive fuel tanks with powerful gravity projectors. The same system that provided her acceleration *also* provided her primary defense.

The gravity shield worked by creating a shear zone, where gravity went from nothing to thousands of gees, then right back to micro-gravity over the course of about twenty centimeters. The shear gravity of *Paladin*'s shield was easily on par with Henry's last command, *Raven* —a modern *battlecruiser*.

Paladin was no more heavily armored than her *Significance*-class sisters and probably comparable to the E-Two destroyers, but her gravity shield was the most powerful in the Flotilla.

If Henry had to pick one of his ships to get shot at, it was *Paladin*.

Except, of course, for the fact that the senior civilian—who also happened to be his girlfriend—was aboard her. *That* was definitely a mark against the plan…but it was still the best plan.

"VAMPIRE."

Henry had heard that code-word announcement in just about every tone of voice possible. The announcement of "hostile missile launch," depending on circumstances, could be utterly expected to the point of being as boring as anything in combat or a complete horrific surprise or just about anything in between.

Lieutenant Commander Medb Bach's announcement this time was of the cool and collected professional variety. Not bored, not terrified. Calm and ready for what was coming.

Henry was in much the same state of mind as Commander Bach, but he had sympathy for anyone who *wasn't*. With two superdreadnoughts and ten escorts bearing down on *Paladin*, the number of missiles in space was mind-boggling.

"Looks like their escort force was structured on the standard four-to-one ratio," Eowyn announced. "All four gunships are with the dreadnoughts."

That reduced the number of missiles coming their way to a *mere* three hundred. In the first salvo.

"Deploying our missiles in defense mode," Ihejirika intoned. "I have missile control. Bach, you have the standard defense array. I'll clean, you sweep."

The "plasma shotgun" of a standard conversion warhead made for an effective but expensive counter-missile weapon. The icons for

Paladin's twelve launchers flashed on Henry's feeds as they went to rapid fire, spitting out missiles every fifteen seconds.

They couldn't sustain that fire for long, but the only munitions *Paladin*'s engineers couldn't replace given time and a gas giant with nickel-iron in its rings were the skip-drive penetrator warheads—and those were useless for antimissile fire.

The Kenmiri fire was steadier, a salvo every forty seconds. They could match *Paladin*'s spew of missiles, but even dreadnoughts struggled to manage hundreds of missiles at maximum range.

"Eowyn, have we scanned for disruptor and penetrator missiles?" Henry asked. The skip-drive penetrator missiles had only been seen in UPSF hands so far, and the resonance-based disruptor warheads had been developed by the Drifters—but Henry wasn't willing to assume that the most powerful race in the galaxy *hadn't* duplicated them.

"All scans suggest standard warheads so far," Eowyn reported. "We're watching as they come in. We'll know more after the intercepts."

The first of those intercepts was at two minutes, *Paladin*'s missiles detonating in shaped blasts of plasma that vaporized or disabled multiple missiles apiece. Four more intercepts tore into the first salvo before the antimissile lasers engaged.

They'd spent sixty missiles—ten percent of *Paladin*'s magazines—and Henry could already tell that the missiles were going to get through the laser defenses. That was inevitable. He was throwing a destroyer against multiple capital ships, after all.

"Prepare for impact!"

Explosions rippled through space around *Paladin*'s shield, and Henry watched them with a careful eye. There were no unusual tricks or surprises in the salvo, just sheer numbers as the warheads duplicated the fire of dozens of plasma cannon.

"No blowthrough, no blowthrough," Bach chanted, her voice still cool and calm. "Second salvo incoming. Brace!"

There was nothing for Henry to say. For seven minutes, all they'd be able to do was writhe in the storm as the Kenmiri's fire hammered down on them.

"We're at reserve levels for missiles," Ihejirika told Henry quietly. "Permission to continue counter-missile engagement?"

That meant they were down to ten missiles per launcher, twenty percent of the magazines. While Ihejirika *had* the authority to fire those missiles, it was considered a bad idea without solid logistics support.

It also meant that they'd *already* started warhead-swapping on missiles. Only sixty percent of the magazines were loaded with conversion warheads by default. Since Henry had seen neither penetrator missiles nor unshaped warheads in the defensive salvos, they'd been swapped before firing.

"Do it," Henry ordered. "Might be the only thing that gets us through this."

And there were more missiles on *Rightful Chieftain*, even if they didn't get time to fabricate more. The Flotilla also had enough spare parts aboard to replenish their full magazines, plus the reserve on *Chieftain*, at least four times over, given the raw materials.

Given enough time, they could even fabricate those parts, too. There was no reason to hold back when those missiles could make the difference between survival and destruction.

"Blowthrough!"

Henry felt *Paladin* shiver around him in the moment Bach's report sounded on the bridge. Hundreds of explosions had battered the gravity shield, but it had served as well as any battlecruiser's defenses.

Now, for the first time in the fight, a bolt of plasma wasn't warped enough to miss. It washed over *Paladin* in a tidal wave of heat that sent warning lights flashing across the screens.

"Coronal hit," Bach reported after a moment. "External sensors and heat radiators have been badly damaged, but the hull is intact."

"Engineering is extending the secondary radiators, but that will take time," Ihejirika warned. "They have to cool the reactors. Defense lasers on capacitors only!"

Unlike most older designs, the *Cataphract*-class ships had enough reactors aboard to run all of their systems at full power. That came with the price of having very little extra heat-radiation capacity at full power—but they also carried the same capacitor systems that allowed older ships to operate while rotating what was being powered.

That would let the defensive lasers operate for sixty seconds without power—but Henry could map the maneuver cones.

They were still going to be under fire for another *ninety* seconds—and another blowthrough clipped the starboard wing as he did the math. The destroyer spun in space, only inertial compensators keeping the crews' stomachs where they belonged as Charmchi got her back on course.

"We've got this," Ihejirika muttered.

Henry didn't think anyone had been supposed to hear that. His private link to his flag captain was more sensitive than most of their internal coms.

He wasn't sure he agreed with Ihejirika, but he didn't correct the man's self-assurance. There were still four salvos of missiles inbound on *Paladin*, and they'd have to take the last two without lasers or defensive missiles.

Paladin's magazines were dry, and her last missiles detonated amidst the Kenmiri salvos as Henry watched. The enemy couldn't add *more* missiles now, at least—the geometry had moved them out of range well before their last missiles had reached the targets.

"For what we are about to receive, may the lord make us truly thankful."

Henry jerked up to look over at Eowyn. The farcical prayer wasn't something he'd heard often before, but he got her intent.

She met his gaze and shrugged as he shook his head reprovingly.

Another wave of fire swept over the ship before he could say anything. Like the first hit, the plasma blast had been disrupted enough to cause a "coronal hit"—whatever central mass packet remained missed *Paladin*, but the expanding ball of plasma around it washed over her hull and disrupted her external systems.

Henry grimaced as he realized that they'd lost the set of secondary heat radiators that the destroyer's engineering team had been busy deploying. That was a problem. A *real* problem.

UPSF ships looked vaguely feathery to the untrained eye due to the use of vast numbers of easily replaced vaned heat radiators. Secondary sets were concealed behind protective panels for exactly this situation, but they could only have so many of those.

The squadron-status report he had on the ship said she'd lost over sixty percent of her radiators, and that was *after* eighty percent of the secondaries had been unveiled. They weren't getting the defensive lasers back anytime soon!

"Capacitors dry," Bach reported. "Missiles gone. Two more salvos incoming, and we're taking them on the shield."

"And that's why it's a damn good thing it's *us* and not anybody else," Ihejirika replied. "*Paladin*s to the front of the line!"

Cliché as the declaration might have been, Henry *saw* the bridge crew stiffen in their seats as Ihejirika spoke. It might not make a difference, but who knew?

The moral was to the physical as three was to one. And when fire washed unstoppably over *Paladin*, the only thing her crew had left was faith.

Faith in whatever divinity they believed in.

And faith in the gravity shield that had brought so many UPSF ships home when any other ship would have died.

"Blowthrough! Multiple blowthroughs!"

Bach's calm finally broke as that wave of plasma breached their shield, multiple jets of superheated gas blazing through the inviolate bubble *Paladin* lived in. Charmchi twisted the ship around, trying to keep them intact.

It wasn't enough. It could never be enough, and Henry winced as the ship lurched underneath him.

Red icons flashed across *Paladin*'s entire starboard wing. The hit was bad. He couldn't tell *how* bad, but six missile launchers were now offline—and he wouldn't be surprised if they were just *gone*.

"Clear, we're clear," Ihejirika snapped. "That was the last salvo, people. We are *clear*!"

Unspoken was the chill knowledge, shared by everyone with access to the overall damage schematic reports, that thirty-two officers and spacers had battle stations in the starboard wing.

9

SYLVIA HAD LOST track of the number of skips she'd made over the years. She could probably look it up if she needed to—she certainly knew which systems she'd visited and how often, after all—but the number was definitely in the hundreds. Probably over a thousand.

Despite that, she found the sensation involved indescribable. The moment of skipping or of "secondary impulse generation" involved giving a three-dimension object a *twenty*-dimensional vector and the human brain and body had no concept of how to handle that.

She processed it differently every time. This time, her brain had been sufficiently confused that she perceived the moment of *skip* as a taste. Like the more "normal" sensation of falling in seven directions at once, it was an excruciating, indescribable thing.

And *unlike* the sensation of falling or being punched or twisting or any of the other interpretations of the twenty-dimensional impulse, the taste decided to stick around for several seconds after the pulse was complete.

That left Sylvia, who took pride in being cool and collected in almost all circumstances, gagging and scrabbling at the controls of her office drink machine to get it to produce hot chocolate when Henry Wong stepped into the room without knocking.

"Ah. Apologies," he greeted her as she finally hit the right button and the machine started whirring.

"Have you ever *tasted* a skip?" Sylvia demanded, turning on her boyfriend—who was one of the few people she was certain had endured *more* FTL journeys than he had.

"Once, in my first year of service," Henry replied instantly. "It is…a *memorable* version of the experience."

Sylvia gagged against the mere *memory* of the taste and grabbed the hot chocolate the drink cabinet produced. The smell hit her like a ton of bricks, far sweeter and richer than her usual taste in hot chocolate, let alone her preferred hot drinks, and she only managed to swallow a single mouthful before she realized it was too much for her.

It was, at least, a *pleasant* overwhelm.

"Sorry, Henry," she told her lover. "I'm assuming you didn't come here to watch me fight with skip nausea."

"Sylvia, I have met seven people in my life who claim to have got used to skips," he pointed out with a smile. "And one of *them* lost her stomach when we hit a skip at this kind of velocity. I just felt like I was falling up, sideways and inward."

"'Just,'" Sylvia echoed, then sighed. "Icosaspatial travel. Not the best way to travel faster than light."

"Just the only way," her boyfriend agreed. He took a seat across her desk from her, eyeing the flags and ship commissioning seal behind her.

"I do need you, as you figured," he continued. "Professionally, that is," he noted after she arched an eyebrow.

Sylvia laid aside the cloying hot chocolate and told the machine to give her a proper black tea. "I assumed, but poking at your double entendres will never grow old, Henry."

He shook his head repressively at her, a gesture she suspected he'd long practiced on his subordinates.

"So, what political mess are we finding this time?" she asked.

"If it was only one mess and only political, I'd feel a lot better," he admitted. His network requested access to her office systems, and she allowed it with a thought.

The holoprojectors in her desk flickered to life, showing a three-dimensional map of the region.

"First off, the political mess of the Forward Flotilla itself," Henry said. "The La-Tar Cluster detachment and the E-Two detachment were temporary, intended more to show mutual support when we met the Rashovans than to actually fight together.

"We worked together well in Ra-Seventy-Eight, but that was *before* we got every single one of Falling Rain's fighter pilots killed."

Sylvia knew, better than most, that Henry identified strongly with the fighter pilots under his command. The losses aboard *Paladin* would hit him the hardest, but even alien fighter pilots would sting.

She also knew that Henry was underestimating the deep well of respect their allies had for him specifically.

"If it was another UPSF Commodore in command of the Forward Flotilla, I might be worried," she admitted. "If we'd sent Commodore Barrie, for example."

That was a palpable hit and she watched Henry sigh. Commodore Peter Barrie, captain of the fleet carrier *Scorpius*, had about two years as Commodore on Henry—but was *also* his ex-husband.

A marriage, like so many others, sacrificed on the altar of the war. Sylvia was, so far as she knew, only the fourth or *maybe* fifth person Henry had ever been attracted to—but given that the list included at least one alien, she was well aware that her boyfriend's interest wasn't restricted by anything so minor as *gender*.

"Peter would be more senior, better able to argue that he should be in command over Defender Falling Rain," Henry pointed out.

"But I guarantee you that Falling Rain would be less likely to concede command without that argument. Whereas they *volunteered* for you to command the Flotilla over them. No one could have seen what happened in Seventy-Eight coming. Falling Rain and their people won't blame you for it."

"Perhaps, but the suddenly longer *term* of the Flotilla is a concern we need to watch," he said. "I trust your judgment assessing if we're in trouble. I just want you to keep an eye and a thought on that area."

"Always," she promised. "But…what do you mean, *longer term*?"

He gestured to the map.

"Ra-One-Fifty-Two has skip lines to four star systems," he observed. "Ra-Seventy-Eight, obviously. Rashova—inconveniently, if the Kenmiri call for backup, though that's a long skip. Ra-One-Fifty-Three, which is the absolute opposite direction of anywhere we want to be.

"And here."

He highlighted the fourth system and Sylvia saw his point.

"Osiris-Sixteen," she said aloud.

"Remnant space."

And *that* opened a can of worms the size of a fleet carrier.

"If we jump through One-Fifty-Three," she said slowly, "where does that get us?"

"Fifteen-and-a-half-hour skip to Ra-One-Fifty-Three. Not entirely sure how long it would take us to make the skip line, but from there… twenty-two days to La-Tar. Eighteen by drone, I think.

"Thirty days, at least, to make Eerdish. Probably twenty-five for our drones to get there and update Twelfth Fleet."

"There's a catch to that, isn't there?" Sylvia asked.

"Yeah. We're supposed to have sent a drone back already, which would have arrived in ten days. Which means that in *fourteen* days, Admiral Rex activates his backup plan and takes the main fleet to Anderon.

"They're fifteen days out from Anderon at Eerdish," he noted. "So, in thirty days, when we'd be arriving at Eerdish, Rex will be in Anderon.

"And remember that it's only sixteen days from Rashova to Anderon. If the Kenmiri deploy immediately, Anderon is…doomed. We can't communicate with our allies or Twelfth Fleet in time to get anyone there before the Kenmiri."

"But they won't go immediately, will they?" Sylvia wasn't a military or logistics expert, she'd freely admit that, but she knew that very few organizations could immediately turn around and launch a new offensive within days, let alone hours, of a battle like they'd seen in Rashova.

"Most likely not. Most likely they will use the shipyards they carefully left intact in Rashova to repair and rearm their fleet before they move on Anderon. Fortunately, given that Kori is roughly thirty-three days from Rashova, we can presume they're moving on Anderon."

Kori, Rashova, and Anderon were the three Kenmiri colonies. With Rashova burned and Kori far away, Anderon made sense to her. And based off what they'd seen at Rashova, Sylvia also understood why Henry and the other officers had all been so convinced that the Kenmiri would definitely move on their own former colonies first.

The homeworlds had orbital industries that could be refitted to build warships. The industrial slave worlds already had yards designed to churn out freighters and escorts in mass batches. Some of the industrial worlds even had gunship yards.

But the former Kenmiri colonies were the only places with true capital-ship yards, capable of melting and spinning up asteroids to manufacture dreadnoughts. In the Ra Sector so far, the only sources of new capital ships were the yards in those three systems.

Well, and one yard in the Kozun home system—but every one of the Kozun's cruisers was gone now, the last of them wrecked by the Drifters when they'd betrayed the peace talks.

If the Kenmiri took out the three former colonies, the UPSF would be the only people able to send capital ships to the Ra Sector's defense.

Unfortunately for the Remnant, they'd convinced the Drifters to betray the Kozun-La-Tar peace talks, and Admiral Cody Rex's Twelfth Fleet had been sent into the Ra Sector on a punitive expedition—and that meant there were six battlecruisers and three fleet carriers from the regular UPSF to challenge the rogue Warrior fleet—plus the Initiative's sole operational battlecruiser.

"So long as they pause to refit, Admiral Rex should beat them to Anderon, right?" Sylvia asked. "That gives them a chance."

"Yes." Something in Henry's voice told her she was missing something, and he was still staring directly at the link to Osiris-16.

"Henry, I think I need to remind you that I am no soldier. I don't always see what you see."

"The Warriors misestimated, I think, the level of our response to the attack on the peace conference," he said slowly. "I think they were only expecting two carrier groups at most. Two *Crichton*s, four battlecruisers. But..."

Sylvia let him think in silence.

"They thought two superdreadnoughts could handle that."

"And they have a lot more than two superdreadnoughts now," Sylvia conceded.

"We saw their new antifighter missiles in action. I'm glad that the system is size-limited by their missile chassis—because if they upsize it, it will be a serious threat to gravity-shielded *warships*."

Sylvia had been a wartime diplomat, as intimately part of the war effort in her way as Henry had been in his. She had seen a dozen space battles even before she'd ended up working with the Peacekeeper Initiative and being on the front lines of the attempt to stabilize the Ra Sector.

She understood how bad the Kenmiri's having an effective anti-gravity-shield weapon could be. The UPA's outsized role in the Vesheron, their ability to dominate the Ra Sector with only a handful of ships, their ability to fight the Kenmiri on an even footing *at all*…all of those came back to the fact that a UPSF warship was among the most survivable starships in existence.

"But they can't?" she asked.

"I honestly don't know. I know that in their current form, the missiles are only a bit more dangerous to, say, *Paladin* than a standard conversion warhead. But their current form is bad enough. They *obliterated* our fighters in Ra-Seventy-Eight, Sylvia.

"*Fronds of Will*'s fighter group should have been an easy match for at least one superdreadnought. The damage they inflicted on two *should* have turned the tide of the battle in our favor.

"Instead, we lost every single fighter before they could even launch their missiles, and were forced to run for our *fucking* lives."

He inhaled sharply, pulling a shield of calm around himself that Sylvia didn't often see him do in private. She could still read the tension in his microexpressions and from the fact that she knew Henry Wong like few others did now.

"Henry, you couldn't have predicted that," she told him. "We did everything right after that and we got every ship out."

"We lost thirty-two of *Paladin*'s crew," he said flatly. "Plus ninety of the Enteni's pilots. That's a lot of letters home for getting everyone out.

"And a part of me that is very logical, and makes me very angry some days, is more concerned about the fact that we lost four of *Paladin*'s missile launchers—and we were *lucky* to only lose four!"

There were times to maintain professionalism in private, and there were times when Sylvia Todorovich's lover was wrestling with his demons. She rose and walked around the desk to put her hands on Henry's shoulders, willing some strength into the man as she looked at the map with him.

"But we're still alive," she murmured. "We don't know what will happen in Ra-One-Fifty-Two, but it sounds to me like if we can evade the Kenmiri there, we're home free back to La-Tar."

"In theory," Henry agreed. "Except that if we go that way, even our drones won't make it to Twelfth Fleet before they will engage the Warriors. The E-Two are putting up three more carriers of their own—they're only keeping one at each of their homeworlds, after *Fronds of Will* is with us!

"So, six carriers collide with that fleet. Admiral Rex is a carrier commander, a good one. The E-Two officers don't have experience with proper shielded fighters, but they've run exercises and they have some solid operational concepts.

"With over six hundred gravity- and energy-shielded starfighters, those ships form the main offensive weapon of the allied fleet."

He leaned back into her hands, staring straight ahead. "And unless we do something rash, they won't know anything about the plasma webs. They'll know what I knew before Ra-Seventy-Eight: that the Kenmiri *believe* they have an effective antifighter weapon."

"And not what that weapon is," Sylvia finished. "How big a difference does that make, Henry?"

"Drastic. Without *knowing* that they're using a low-profile flight mode on missiles carrying a weapon that is *devastating* to shielded small craft...their fighters will suffer the same fate ours did.

"Twelfth Fleet and whatever Anderon has for defenses won't be able to run the way we did. There are millions of people on Anderon that have to be protected."

"One and a half billion, according to the information we had before we lost coms," she told him. "Anderon's defenders won't run."

"Admiral Rex and I have different points of view on a lot of things," Henry said slowly. "But I think he'd jump the same way in that situation as I would."

"He'll fight."

"To the death. And against a Kenmiri return to the Ra Sector? Every ally he can bring to the field will do the same. But if the Kenmiri wipe out their fighters…they *will* be fighting to the death."

Sylvia was aboard *Paladin* because they had needed their best negotiator to talk to the former Kenmiri colonies. Even the Kozun Hierarchy, a mostly friendly former enemy at this point, could be trusted to fight the *Kenmiri*.

But forging new alliances with people that the UPA hadn't talked to since the Kenmiri shut down the subspace network—people who had fought the Kozun, in Kori's case, and might see the UPA as allies of their enemies—had required their best.

She couldn't negotiate with the laws of physics and skip lines. She wasn't a navigator. Whatever the answer was to this, *she* didn't see it.

But…

"So, what is the answer, Henry? I assume it's something you want me to help sell the rest of the Forward Flotilla on?"

"Osiris Sector." He gestured at the link to Osiris-16. "We transit through nine Osiris systems, two of them inhabited, and then enter Ra-Two-Oh-Five, which has a skip line to Anderon."

"Assuming we can make it through Kenmiri space without having to fight a war," Sylvia murmured. "But we'd get there…?"

"Twelve hours to Ra-One-Fifty-Two. Assume it takes us thirty-six hours to rendezvous with the Flotilla, evade the Remnant and get to the Osiris-Sixteen skip line. About twenty, twenty-one days after that to make it to Anderon."

Twenty-three days. Sylvia knew that space travel times were always a bit variable, but that told her what she needed to know.

"Ten days after the Kenmiri *could* make it there," she murmured.

"If those Warriors move that quickly, there is nothing we can do to stop them attacking Anderon," Henry admitted. "If they're that prepared, that determined, we may not even be able to save Kori. We may even need to wait for reinforcements from back home."

"And there isn't as much back home as we'd like."

Sylvia had fought hard to keep the Peacekeeper Initiative's budget separate from the main UPSF budget, but the Initiative's budget paid for *maintenance*, not construction. They'd sliced two battlecruisers and twelve destroyers from the UPSF—but currently, one battlecruiser and one destroyer were laid up for major repairs, and two destroyers were gone and not yet replaced.

The main UPSF fleets, on the other hand, were being rapidly drawn down to ease the UPA's overall budget. Every pre-*Crichton* carrier had been decommissioned, along with every battlecruiser older than the *Panthers* and *Corvids*.

They'd lost a quarter of the UPSF's active ships in Golden Lancelot —and over the three-plus years since the war, they'd lost just as many ships to the scrapyard. The entire UPSF was down to only twelve carrier groups.

Sylvia suspected that footage of Rashov burning would help change that. Her distaste for waving a bloody shirt had never overcome its effectiveness in her own mind.

"So, we have to hope they're pausing in Rashova," she noted. "And then get the Flotilla to Anderon first."

"But, as you said, we have a route out of Ra-One-Fifty-Two that should get everyone home safely."

Sylvia smiled at her lover as she squeezed his shoulders.

"My Henry," she murmured. "You underestimate how far the officers of the Forward Flotilla—human, Ashall and Enteni alike—would go because *you* asked them to. More than that, the ships of the Forward Flotilla were sent knowing they were going to fight the Warriors.

"You hit them high, I'll hit them low, but I don't think any is going to blink at violating Kenmiri space to save a world of over a billion innocents."

10

Twelve hours of inviolate peace had allowed Henry to get some sleep, even while planning for being pursued and for how to get to Anderon. Now it was time to get to work again.

Ra-152 wasn't much of a star system in many ways, but it was definitely *impressive*. A mid-sized blue giant, six hundred times the mass of Sol, it served as a skip line nexus next to Rashova and an intersection between the Ra and Osiris Sectors.

The single uninhabited planet was inconveniently located to any of the four skip lines. The Kenmiri had maintained an observation-and-refueling post in the system, maintained from the Rashova System, but that had been destroyed during the war and never replaced.

Like Ra-78, Henry's intelligence said that the Rashovans should have had a picket in the system. This time, though, he *knew* where that picket had gone—the Rashovans had recalled all of their ships for the desperate and doomed battle for their home system.

"Have we located the rest of the Flotilla?" Henry asked, glancing over at Eowyn.

"The star is really messing with the scanners. We're talking a million times Sol's luminosity. Computers are adjusting, but we're not used to dealing with this kind of radiation density."

"That's not a bad thing for the next stage," he said. "But I'd very much like to find the Flotilla before our insectoid friends arrive."

"Ser, we're picking up a beacon at two light-seconds," Chan reported. "Looks like it was watching for our identity beacon and activated when it detected us. UPSF encryption protocol."

"Someone was being clever. Good."

"It's a navigation course from Captain Byrne on *Paramount*. I'm transferring it to the bridge and activating the beacon's self-destruct. Falling Rain set the Flotilla course for the planetoid, apparently."

"Could be worse." The Defender at least hadn't taken the Forward Flotilla and run for home.

Henry hadn't really expected Falling Rain to do anything of the sort, but he suspected it would have been harder to talk people into his plan if they'd already been on the way home.

"We're swinging around to follow them," Eowyn reported. "With the course, we've picked them out."

"That gives me some ideas," Henry murmured. "While Captain Ihejirika's people get us to our friends, Commander Eowyn, I want your team to run an analysis.

"If the Flotilla cuts their engines in three hours, when we're expecting the Kenmiri to arrive, will they still be able to see us?"

THERE WERE enough components to Henry's request that it took Eowyn's team almost twenty minutes to get him an answer, by which point they'd nailed down the location of the rest of the Flotilla—forty-plus light-seconds away.

"Right now, even without the beacon telling us the Flotilla's course, we'd have picked them out well enough for pursuit in about ten minutes," Eowyn warned him. "*Paladin*'s sensors are better than anything we know the Kenmiri to have, but not *that* much—and we can't be sure they haven't upgraded their sensors along with everything else."

"Assume they have at least the same sensor fit as *Paladin*," Henry told her.

"Already did."

She waved a projection of the courses onto the main display.

"Falling Rain brought the Flotilla back down to half a KPS-squared once they were here in One-Fifty-Two," she reported. "They are continuing that acceleration and won't make turnover for almost twenty-four hours if they maintain the course toward the planetoid.

"*We* are accelerating at two KPS-squared and will enter the formation with matching velocity in approximately two hours, three and a half light-minutes from the skip line.

"We can assume that the Kenmiri will match our vector well enough to emerge at roughly the same point as we did—they did it coming from Rashova; they can do it again.

"Unless they found some new reserve of acceleration, they hit the skip line three hours after we did. Physics works the same for them as us, so they'll *emerge* in two hours and forty minutes.

"At that point, we and the Flotilla will be five light-minutes away from the skip line. If we cut our acceleration ten minutes before we anticipate their arrival, we will be a long damn way away, with the lowest energy signatures we can manage, and that star is pumping out a *lot* of heat and light."

"So, we've laid out why I'm asking the question," Henry said. "But not an answer."

"Long answer short? They'll detect us *eventually*. This is deep space, the open void. There's nothing to hide behind and we don't have whatever fancy heat-sinking stealth technology the rogue Remnant have been using to scout the Ra Sector.

"But we'll be a long way away in a system that helps distort their sensor feeds. Going cold will help, but we're looking at six hours. Maybe twelve at the outside. That opens the maneuver cones up and might give us enough distance to make it to a skip line."

"But even if we're running hot, they'll take an hour to see us?" Henry asked.

"Seventy-five minutes, plus or minus ten percent," she said instantly. "*Paladin* could run at point-five on the GMS and have the six-hour timeline—we don't release a lot of heat at that level—but the rest of the Flotilla are..."

"Big ships with big engines," Henry concluded. "All right. That gives us something to play with, but it depends on where we're going, doesn't it?"

He traced two mental lines across the map. If they went cold, they'd gain six hours—but those six hours would take them *farther* from the Osiris-16 skip line. Unless the Kenmiri did something unusual in their search, they'd be better positioned to intercept the Flotilla after those six hours than they would be when they arrived.

Which *did* make the decision, he supposed. It was just a question of whether he could sell his allies on it.

11

BY THE TIME *Paladin* had caught up sufficiently to have a live conference, Henry was vividly aware how short on time they were starting to run. They had barely forty minutes left before they were expecting the Kenmiri, and were still twelve hours from the skip line to Osiris-16.

The sooner they diverted, the more likely they were to evade the Kenmiri and escape without being pursued.

For now, nineteen starship captains and Ambassador Todorovich joined Henry Wong around a virtual conference table. The centerpiece of that virtual table was a holographic tactical plot showing the Ra-152 System and the Forward Flotilla's current position.

"We are-were delighted to have you with us again-now," Falling Rain told Henry in their computer-generated Kem. "We understood the plan, but there is-was significant risk to *Paladin*."

"I cannot pretend we did not get hurt," Ihejirika said grimly. *Paladin*'s Captain didn't look like he'd slept since the battle. "Our magazines are empty, and we lost four missile launchers and a number of our people."

"We all mourn your dead," Tol Azan said softly. "The Kenmiri's shadow once again blots out lives. They will pay."

"If they want a war, we will bloody give them one."

Henry leveled a repressive look at Lieutenant Colonel Bart Denison, CO of *Ankylosaurus*. The two *Tyrannosaur*-class destroyers were the oldest ships in the Peacekeeper Initiative, let alone the Forward Flotilla, and Denison was his newest and most junior Lieutenant Colonel.

"That is the plan," he conceded. "But how we do that is going to depend on where we go from here."

"We fall back on Ra-One-Fifty-Three and then to the La-Tar Cluster," Byrne suggested. "We can make contact with the Salar Cluster on our way if we need support, though we lack information on how many ships the Hierarchy will have available there."

"We would-can prefer to avoid interacting with Kozun formations until-unless the diplomatic situation between the Hierarchy and the Alliance is-was resolved."

"Falling Rain is correct," Henry said. "Bringing Enteni and Eerdish warships into Hierarchy space is…unwise. We *could* avoid Salar's worlds easily enough, which would result in only encountering patrols or civilian shipping."

None of the Salar Cluster—a collection of four industrial slave worlds fed by a single agricultural slave world, the standard organizational unit of the Kenmiri Empire—inhabited systems were on the route to La-Tar, after all.

"But."

Henry let the word hang in the conference, drawing it out to make sure he had everyone's attention.

"Regardless of where we go from here, Twelfth Fleet and our allies will execute on the fallback plan that I organized with Admiral Rex and his people," he told them. "They will proceed to the Anderon System.

"They will arrive in the Anderon System in about twenty-eight days. No drones of ours sent along the La-Tar Cluster route will reach Twelfth Fleet prior to that. Since we have no idea what the rogue Warriors' plan is, I believe we must assume that they will either be in Anderon when Twelfth Fleet arrives or attack shortly afterward."

He scanned the virtual room, meeting the gazes of his officers.

"We all saw the plasma-web antifighter system these rogues deployed," he noted. "Two superdreadnoughts equipped with that weapon massacred our fighter pilots. *Eighteen* superdreadnoughts, with such a weapon, will almost certainly inflict equal catastrophe on Twelfth Fleet's pilots if they are unwarned."

"You already said we have no way to warn them," Tol Azan pointed out. "We cannot bear guilt for not achieving the impossible."

"Except it is not impossible," Henry replied. "There is a route through the Osiris Sector that would get us to Anderon roughly six days before Twelfth Fleet. We cannot safely send *drones* along that route, for obvious reasons, but we *can* take the Forward Flotilla into Kenmiri space and transit the systems between here and Anderon."

Everyone was looking at the map now and Henry smiled grimly.

"The fastest route is neither easy nor simple," he admitted. "We pass through the Brell System, home to an industrial slave world still in the hands of the Kenmiri, and then through Traste, a Kenmiri colony which had two billion Kenmiri and three billion slaves before the Fall."

While the short-lived Drones made up eighty percent of the Kenmiri population—and the law of averages said about forty percent of them had died in the four years since Golden Lancelot—the Empire had also moved entire planetary populations into the core sectors from the outer provinces.

Traste probably had *more* Kenmiri now, even with their Drone population dying of old age.

"It seems unwise to run from the enemy into the hands of the enemy," Captain Byrne said slowly.

"The political situation with the Kenmiri is far more complicated than we tend to assume," Sylvia interjected, the Ambassador glancing at Henry more to warn him that she would handle this than for anything resembling *permission*.

"One of the things we are keeping confidential is the source of our intelligence on the faction of Warriors that has attacked the Ra Sector," she continued. "Since it is relevant to this, however, I feel that you now need to know.

"This information cannot be shared with your crews—not even your command staff. Even in the successor states, learning the source of our intelligence could lead to harm and misery for innocents. I must have your word."

There was no hesitation on the part of any of the officers in the room. The UPSF officers were bound by their own disciplinary codes; Henry wasn't concerned about *their* ability or willingness to keep secrets.

But the Ashall and Enteni officers were leaning forward, committing their words and sacred honors to keep something secret from their subordinates.

Though *not*, Henry had noted in Sylvia's phrasing, their *superiors*. The La-Tar Cluster and the E-Two Alliance's leaders already knew who had warned them about the Remnant's rogue Warrior faction.

"During the ceremonies around signing the peace treaty with Drifter Convoy Blue Stripe Green Stripe Orange Stripe, Commodore Wong and I were brought to a private meeting with a caste of Drifters we had not encountered before," Sylvia told them. "That caste, now effectively dissolved, were known as Interfaces—and their role was to stand between the Drifter Convoys and the Kenmiri Empire.

"And to fulfill that role...they *were* Kenmiri."

Henry leaned back in his chair, watching his lover lead his officers down the path she needed them to understand.

"We did not discover the genocidal faction among the Remnant on our own," Sylvia told them. "A Kenmiri Artisan, authorized by the Council of Artisans that has taken control of most of the Remnant, gave us that warning."

That brought the entire meeting to silence, waiting on Sylvia's next words.

"The Kenmiri are no longer unified," she finally said. "But more importantly, what unity they *have* under the Council of Artisans is defied by the Warriors ravaging our systems. The Council has decided that they cannot deal with this rogue faction themselves, but they did not object to an agent of theirs warning us.

"These Warriors *are* rogue," she concluded. "Whatever support structure they have is limited, and I suspect the resources and ships they command are effectively *stolen* from the rest of the Remnant.

"I believe—I have *reason* to believe—that the majority of the

Remnant may be engaging in surveillance operations in our space but have no interest in a renewed war. They want to focus on survival, on cracking the codes in their genetics that the Kenmorad hid from them.

"There is sufficient evidence to believe that we will be able to safely pass through Kenmiri systems so long as *we* do not engage in active aggression against them."

"Let us be very certain of one thing," Henry told them all. "The leaders of the Remnant *do not care* if the worlds they have abandoned live or die. The very structure of the slave-world clusters was designed to doom them without Kenmiri shipping, and they walked away from *hundreds* of those clusters.

"As the Ambassador says, I do not expect them to fight us if we transit their systems. But there is no treaty between us. No peace. And they will do *nothing* to restrain these rogues.

"Rashova is gone. Her innocent billions massacred. Left unchecked, these rogue Warriors will slaughter everyone they can find. So, we will stop them. And while I hope and believe that the Kenmiri Remnant will not bar us from traversing their space, I am entirely willing to destroy them if they try."

He met Sylvia's gaze and smiled.

"We will sneak by where we can. We will negotiate passage, if they offer. But we will fight where we must. We *must* get to Anderon before the rogue Warriors. The sensor data we carry may make the difference between victory and defeat when the main fleets clash.

"I have the authority only to order the UPSF ships into this transit," he conceded, glancing at Falling Rain's wavering eyestalks. "I believe we are more likely to succeed in the passage if we have enough force to make the Kenmiri hesitate—and the *Remnant* will not know that *Fronds of Will* has empty hangars."

"You will need *Bringer of Cloths* either way," Captain Vara pointed out, stroking his head tendrils thoughtfully. "And to rearm *Paladin* from *Rightful Chieftain.*"

"The UPSF ships have sufficient fuel to make a seven-system transit without a tanker," Henry said. "But it would make our lives easier with one, yes."

"I do not believe I could go home, look my Arbiter in the eyes and tell Casto Ran that we left *Henry Wong* to make a journey through Kenmiri space to save the day without us," Tol Azan pointed out. "The La-Tar Cluster owes you and yours a debt of blood and honor that no duty, no gold, no favor could ever repay.

"My ships will fly with you."

Henry tried not to look *too* directly at Falling Rain. He *suspected* that the two Eerdish ships in the E-Two squadron could detach themselves from the Enteni Defender's command if they wanted, but the main decision was Falling Rain's.

"As Captain Vara notes, it would-will be difficult to return home without his tanker," Falling Rain observed. "But I can-will not hide my decisions behind obfuscations.

"I watched a world die. I can-will not permit that to occur once more. My people's departure from their world, our alliance with the Eerdish and the Makata Cluster—even our alliance with the UPA. These are-were born to preserve the lives and freedoms bought at a high price."

Their entire body shivered in a way that sent a spike of atavistic concern down Henry's spine.

"We can-will not stand aside while others fight for the lives of the innocent. We join-joined the Forward Flotilla to fight alongside our allies. We can-will not run now."

"Thank you," Henry said softly. "It means a lot that you are prepared to fly with us. From here into the belly of the beast, my friends.

"But the next step is to lose our Warrior friends."

12

Eowyn's report was later than expected. Henry had expected the Kenmiri to arrive almost an hour earlier—which meant the concern was whether the enemy had delayed their skip entry or if the Forward Flotilla had failed to detect them.

"Estimated time of arrival in Ra-One-Fifty-Two?" he asked.

"Current data is light-delayed by approximately six minutes; it appears they emerged from the skip line two minutes prior to that," she reported swiftly. "Hostiles have been in-system for eight minutes."

Henry nodded thoughtfully, considering the tactical plot. New maneuver cones were appearing on it, but they didn't tell him anything he wasn't able to estimate at first glance.

The Forward Flotilla was eleven hours from the Osiris-16 skip line, still shedding their velocity out-system. The Kenmiri's delay had cut the window for interception in half, but there was still a chance where they could bring the Flotilla into range.

Their current course, however…

"I make their course for the Ra-One-Fifty-Three skip line," he murmured.

"CIC just finished their analysis and confirms," Eowyn reported.

"Kenmiri are at full acceleration of one KPS-squared toward the Ra-One-Fifty-Three skip line. ETA at the skip, nine hours."

The analysis team in *Paladin*'s combat information center were the minds behind the maneuver cones on Henry's display. Much of that was automated, based on the known performance envelope of the Kenmiri ships, but some of it was an estimate of the enemy's intent.

It would be five minutes before the Flotilla would know if the Warriors turned toward them. Anticipating that was as much art and guesswork as science—and as much or more Henry's job than CIC's.

"You made a guess," he murmured to himself. "Not a bad one, either. But you guessed wrong."

The irony was that if he was running for Ra-153, the delay in the Kenmiri's arrival would have made all the difference. They wouldn't even have brought the Forward Flotilla into missile range before the allied ships skipped away.

Of course, they *would* have brought them into range in Ra-153 if they continued the pursuit. The Kenmiri ships had higher acceleration than the two logistics ships. The question, of course, was whether the Kenmiri fleet had enough fuel aboard to overhaul the Flotilla.

That was still going to be the question with the course into Osiris. Just the fact that the Kenmiri had to get *back* to their logistics while the Flotilla had *Bringer of Cloths* made a stern chase a winning chase for Henry.

"Every minute they burn toward Ra-One-Fifty-Three cuts two minutes off the interception window," Eowyn reported.

"What do we estimate their fuel reserves at?" Henry asked. "They probably refueled before entering the Rashova System."

"CIC assumes the same," she confirmed. "Standard Kenmiri fuel allotments would allow them to cross six systems in total, roughly. A three-skip operating radius."

One skip to Rashova from wherever they'd refueled. A second to Ra-78 and a third to Ra-152. The Kenmiri's logistics train would be in Rashova now, which opened up the Kenmiri's range a *bit* more—especially since Ra-152 also linked to Rashova.

The Kenmiri could pursue into one more system but not past that. Not without a resupply.

Henry's ships, on the other hand, included Kenmiri-design ships and E-Two ships with a similar endurance. But he *also* had *Bringer of Cloths*, with enough fuel to resupply every ship in the Flotilla twice.

He could outlast the Kenmiri pursuit, even if he couldn't fight them.

"Thirty minutes," he said aloud. "They likely won't risk pursuing us into Osiris, not if they are unlikely to catch us."

"What happens if they turn in those thirty minutes, ser?" Chan asked.

"That's why we're rearming from *Rightful Chieftain* while under power. It's *not* the safest option, but it's better than going into battle down eight launchers because we don't have missiles for them!"

That was enough to reassure his limited staff, and Henry interlaced his fingers as he watched his enemy charge headlong in the wrong direction.

"So, the answer rests entirely on whether or not you upgraded your sensors, doesn't it?" he whispered to his unknown opponent.

Henry *wanted* to assume they hadn't. The Kenmiri had rolled out at least two entirely new types of ships—the vast superdreadnoughts and the tiny stealthed scout raiders—plus an entirely new weapon system, the stealth system for the scout raiders, and an entirely new generation of subspace communicators.

He would have loved to assume that represented the full research-and-development capabilities of the Remnant over the last three and a half years—especially given that the main focus of the Remnant's scientists had to be on trying to find a way to reproduce!

Unfortunately, he suspected that physicists and weapons engineers weren't very useful to reproductive biologists, which meant that the vast R&D apparatus of the Empire remained. It was entirely reasonable that the Kenmiri had also updated their sensor technology since the end of the war.

His flag deck was silent. Even Henry had to resist the urge to hold his breath. No sound any human could make would affect how detectable they were, but they were hiding and the brain interpreted that as requiring quiet.

Their only actual chance of hiding, though, came from the fact that

Ra-152's massive star was bright enough to overwhelm a lot of normal sensor equipment. It wasn't like they *weren't* blazing massive fusion engines to hurl the Flotilla across the system.

Patience was the only answer and he waited, watching seconds tick into minutes as the overlap zone of the maneuver cones shrank. He was confident in the Flotilla's ability to absorb *some* long-range missile fire from the Kenmiri task force, but the logistics ships would always be in danger.

A soft chime rang through the flag deck, and he started, looking over at Eowyn to see what was going on.

"That's it, ser," she reported. "They've crossed the line where they can no longer reverse course in time to intercept us before we skip out."

Henry exhaled a long breath. It would be another ten hours before the Flotilla actually made the jump toward Osiris-16, but that was the moment of truth. If the Kenmiri couldn't catch them in Ra-152, the first hurdle had been overcome.

He even had to wonder, after all, if the rogue Warriors *could* pursue him into Remnant space.

✦✦✦

"WHAT THE *HELL* took them so long?"

Henry had to chuckle at just how *offended* Ihejirika sounded when the Kenmiri Warriors finally turned. It had apparently taken seventy-six minutes after they'd entered the system for the rogues to finally realize that the allies were sailing in the opposite direction.

"Unless their sensors or computers have *degraded* since the war, they should have seen us at least thirty minutes ago," Eowyn noted. "Though…"

"Your thoughts, Commander?" Henry asked after her silence lasted about ten seconds.

"Their vector is now toward Rashova, ser," she reported. "They're giving up on chasing us as a waste of time, I suppose."

"Which, I think, gives us our answer as to what took so long," he pointed out. "Though my suspicion of the answer raises a few dozen *other* questions."

"Ser?" His flag captain looked…*lost* wasn't the right word, but Ihejirika definitely wasn't following Henry's train of thought.

"Their sensors haven't degraded. We can take that as gospel, I think," Henry said. "So, the only reason they wouldn't have picked us up for this long was if either the sensors and their analysis hardware were all pointed in the wrong direction for a minimum of thirty-five or forty minutes.

"Now, they *can* do omnidirectional scans and computer analysis, but they clearly *didn't*." He waved a hand. "That said, potentially they realized what had happened sometime after interception became impossible and continued on their existing course until they decided whether or not to pursue, but that feels uncharacteristic for Warriors.

"What *is* characteristic for Kenmiri Warriors, especially ones that haven't been burned by it in the past, is a degree of tunnel vision that the UPSF wouldn't tolerate in a *cadet*, let alone a senior officer."

That was probably more cultural than biological, Henry figured, but the "go for the kill" mentality of the Warriors—combined with their arrogance, condescension and other bad habits—had made for some interesting psych-based tactics during the war.

"The counter to that is often the fact that the *sensor* departments, especially, usually contain significant numbers of Drones and Artisans."

Henry let that hang in the air as he watched his enemies give up on pursuing him.

"If they fell into the trap of tunnel vision and pursued the course they *expected* us to take until it was absolutely clear we weren't heading for Ra-One-Fifty-Three, they detected us about when I would have expected—about five minutes *faster* than they would have with their wartime sensor fit."

"But they *know* that's a weakness, don't they?" Ihejirika asked.

"Indeed. Which suggests a few possibilities," Henry noted. "The most obvious is that whoever is in command over there has never fought the UPSF. We burned that tunnel vision out of the officers who faced us repeatedly. The ones who couldn't learn, died.

"But even with a more inexperienced flag officer, experienced juniors might have run their own scans—and an experienced Artisan or Warrior scanner section chief would have done so too, on their own initiative."

"So, they have no experienced personnel?" Eowyn suggested.

"More than that," Henry murmured. "Not just no experienced personnel, but they're missing key non-Warrior personnel. Even *Drones* don't have that tunnel vision. But if they're using Warriors to do jobs that are normally handled by Artisans and Drones…"

"They could have the most experienced crews in the Remnant and still fuck up in pretty basic ways if they've never handled the sensor rooms on their own before," Ihejirika said.

"Exactly. Our rogue faction here may be more universally Warriors than I thought."

From what their Drifter contact had told them, Henry had known that the faction was led and organized by Warriors, senior officers who refused to quietly sit down and wait to die. He could see very easily how the Warriors' usual list of cultural views would lead into the "If we're going to die, *everybody* is going to die" response the rogues were following.

But if they *only* had Warriors, that was a key and useful thing to know. Only about fifty percent of the crew of a Kenmiri warship was usually from the Warrior Caste. Ten percent would be Artisans and the rest Drones.

If the Warriors were filling *all* of those jobs, that suggested all kinds of possibilities to Henry.

"It's something to keep in mind," he murmured. "I think I'm going to have to talk to our diplomats. Sylvia knows the mindsets of the Kenmiri castes even better than I do."

Henry, after all, had really only ever learned the mindset and culture of the Warrior caste—because *that* had made fighting and killing the red bugs a *lot* easier.

13

SYLVIA WOKE up to Henry whimpering in his sleep. It wasn't the first time his nightmares had woken her up while they'd slept together—and the reverse had happened a few times as well.

Paladin was a small-enough ship that her rooming with the Commodore helped squeeze her staff in. While the *Cataphract*s had enough space for both a squadron commander and a diplomatic mission, neither space was particularly *large*.

So, her staff had divided the official ambassador's quarters into space for four more people. Her usual chief of staff was currently being Admiral Rex's pet diplomat, but Sylvia's team knew their work well.

And no one on either the military or civilian side of the ship had any illusions about the relationship between the Peacekeeper Initiative's second-in-command and the Peacekeeper Initiative's senior ambassador. Sylvia suspected that most of the Initiative had worked out what was going on before *Henry* had.

He twitched again and she reached out to grip his shoulder. Like her, Henry had spent a *lot* of time in hostile space and normally woke up easily. She imagined that being a starship captain had helped solidify that habit as well—but this time, he didn't wake at her touch.

A full-body shiver rocked Sylvia's lover, knocking her hand away from him, and she grimaced.

"Henry?" she asked, gripping his shoulder and shaking him gently. "Love, you need to wake up."

For a few seconds, she thought even that wasn't going to work—then his eyes snapped open. He stared blankly at her, then exhaled raggedly as his entire body relaxed at once.

"Henry?"

"Thank you," he whispered. He was still staring past Sylvia at the ceiling, ignoring her nakedness.

"You're usually easier to wake."

He exhaled again and nodded shakily, levering himself up on the bed and blinking as he finally managed to focus on Sylvia.

"Nightmares decided to play a greatest hits collection," he admitted. "Gallows on La-Tar. Bombs on Rashova. Golden Lancelot... Other times, too."

There were parts of Henry's career even Sylvia didn't know about. Black stretches in his record that no civilian could ever access. She suspected he'd *tell* her about them, if she asked—little, if anything, about the Kenmiri war was classified outside her reach.

For all that the Kozun Hierarchy were allies now, their occupation of La-Tar prior to Henry's liberation of the planet had been *brutal*. Sylvia had seen the gallows being torn down and had her own nightmares of the footage the locals had shown them.

Nothing about what she and Henry did was easy, and nightmares were a price of doing business. So were neurotransmitter regulators in their internal networks and regular therapy sessions. Every physician in the United Planets Space Force was supposed to be a fully qualified psychiatrist as well as a surgeon.

In practice, there was usually a psychiatrist *and* a surgeon on a ship, but enough of the UPSF's doctors handled both to meet the theory.

"You okay?" she finally murmured to him, her hand still on his shoulder.

He covered her hand with his own and smiled sadly.

"I will be. Osiris has memories; that's all. And Rashova..."

Sylvia shivered as her own memories of the bombs falling came rushing back. Despite everything, the destruction of entire worlds was a line neither side had crossed in the war. It almost felt out of character for the Kenmiri Warriors—which she supposed said something about how *broken* the rogues were.

"Osiris is new to me," she told Henry, focusing on the small things. "I spent most of my time in Isis and the sectors around it. Working with and for the Londu."

Her career had started with the expedition sent to convince the Londu—a race outside the Kenmiri Empire, like the UPA—to join the Vesheron in their rebellion and war. She'd been one of the UPA's "Londu experts" and worked in their area of operations after that.

"Osiris was our...hunting ground when I commanded *Bulldog*," Henry said softly. "We were barely able to penetrate that deeply then. We were commerce raiders, trying to pick targets that would hurt the Empire's industry without harming the slaves."

He shook his head, his gaze flicking away from Sylvia again.

"Which was impossible, of course. Even the ships had slaves aboard, and we didn't have the GroundDiv troopers for boarding actions. We tried to validate what the cargo was and not blow up food ships, but I know we got it wrong."

Bulldog had been his first destroyer command, Sylvia remembered. She'd been a *Hunter*-class destroyer, the predecessor to the *Tyrannosaur* class.

And if Sylvia recalled correctly, *Bulldog* had been blown apart under Henry's feet, with half of her crew lost in action and the rest rescued by the Vesheron with barely an hour of air left in the wreckage.

Commerce raiding was an ugly type of war at the best of times. UPSF IntelDiv had improved by leaps and bounds over the course of the war, too, but their data on what Henry and the other raiders had been hunting had started off...nonexistent.

"It was a shitty war and it was supposed to be over," Sylvia told him.

"It was." Henry kept staring into space for a few more seconds. "We did what we thought would help protect the UPA and maybe liberate some slaves. And it all worked, I suppose.

"And now these bastards come back in, murdering and destroying in revenge for what we did. What *I* did."

"You didn't do it on your own. And you were *lied* to."

"You'd think watching them carry out mass murder would change how I feel about genocide," Henry observed. "But all I can think is that this is a predictable, if irrational and violent, response to what *we* did."

"Henry Wong, if you try to blame yourself for this, I will smack you," Sylvia told her lover. "Fluke may have left you firing the last shot, but you didn't plan Golden Lancelot, and the Kenmiri have made their own choices since.

"Lashing out may be *predictable*, but it's still irrational, violent and *their action*."

"I know." He sighed, turning away to study the bare metal wall. "But what's the difference between their attack on the Ra Sector and our own counterattack into this same space sixteen years ago?"

It had taken the UPA three years to drive the Kenmiri invasion forces out of their own stars. Another year to scout and survey and find the Empire. But when they had launched their first offensives into Kenmiri space, they had known *nothing* about the Empire, the slave worlds, the Vesheron…any of the realities of the Kenmiri Empire.

Their attacks had been launched for revenge. The hope to liberate uncountable trillions had come later.

"We did not murder worlds," Sylvia murmured. "We fought a war against the people who attacked us, but we didn't unleash salted nukes on planets that did *nothing* but take the independence they were given."

That was the worst part, she realized. There were worlds that were ruled by Vesheron factions. The Kozun had even managed to liberate their homeworld before the fall of the Empire, though everyone realized that liberation would have been short-lived without Golden Lancelot.

But the worlds led by former Vesheron rebels were the minority. Kozun was *unique* in having expelled the Kenmiri by force. Most, like Rashova, had just found themselves abandoned by their former overlords and left to find a way to survive.

The slave-world clusters had been *designed* to fail in the absence of

Kenmiri shipping—and the retreating Empire had only left behind ships they didn't have crews for. Only the fact that the Kenmiri had waited a year to disable the subspace-communications network had allowed the industrial and agricultural worlds to link up again and survive.

The industrial worlds could build transports, after all. They had just needed to know there was a point in doing so.

But those worlds had not chosen to revolt against the Kenmiri. They'd taken their liberty gladly, but they hadn't taken it by force. And now the rogue Warriors were burning those worlds for…what?

Not dying on command?

"These rogue Warriors are the worst of the Kenmiri, given an excuse and unleashed without checks or controls," Henry finally said. "They need to be stopped. Destroyed, most likely."

He shook his head. "Weirdly, I think even the main Remnant would agree with us there. There was always a degree of…I don't know. Patronization? In the Kenmiri rule over their slaves.

"They liked to pretend that they were *protecting* the other races. The Vesheron who lived under them never believed it, but as an outsider…"

As Henry trailed off, Sylvia was reminded that—*unlike* her—Henry Wong had actually *met* Kenmiri. Her focus had always been on meeting and negotiating with Vesheron factions—but Henry had fought them for seventeen years, taking prisoners and negotiating along the way.

"What?" she asked.

"I really do think there was always a core of truth to it," he admitted. "Twisted and warped and turned into something dark as the void, but there was truly an intent to protect the rest of the galaxy. The problem became that the thing we ended up needing protection from was *them*."

Sylvia sighed and squeezed his shoulder.

"If we're not going to get back to sleep, I think I'm going to take a shower." She smiled at him as he finally appeared to register her level of dress. "Join me?"

14

THE OSIRIS-16 SYSTEM WAS, in and of itself, nothing special. Six rocky worlds, an asteroid belt and a gas giant orbited a small yellow star. There were no energy signatures on Henry's tactical feeds except for the ships of the Forward Flotilla.

And despite that, entering the system was crossing a line that hadn't been passed since Golden Lancelot and the Withdrawal of the Kenmiri. The Fall had changed the universe, and the former Vesheron powers had let the Remnant be—certain, after all, that the Kenmiri had less than a century to live.

Ticking clock or not, though, the Remnant remained the single most powerful entity in the galaxy, one that the UPA was explicitly still at war with—and the Forward Flotilla had just entered their space without permission.

"Paramount, Kepentingan, Betekenis, Vazhnyy, Ankylosaurus, Dilophosaurus," Henry reeled off, pinging the captains of his four *Significance*-class and two *Tyrannosaur*-class destroyers. He smiled slightly when he looked at *Dilophosaurus*. Back when the *Tyrannosaurs* had been brand new, she'd been his replacement for the wrecked *Bulldog*. She was a good ship, even if none of the old crew was aboard her now.

"Formation Delta-One," he ordered. "Security perimeter around the Flotilla."

Delta-One was basically a sphere with the six ships at the cardinal points. Henry's UPSF ships still had plenty of fuel left from their last refill. The rest of the Flotilla was at half or less.

"Captain Vara, move *Bringer of Cloths* into the center of the formation," Henry continued, switching to Kem as he spoke to the La-Tar ship. "Get your hoses ready. We will start with the Eerdish and Enteni destroyers, then the escorts, then *Fronds of Will* and *Paladin,* then the UPSF destroyers."

Bringer of Cloths could refuel four escorts at once, but the destroyers and carrier were enough bigger that only two of them could be filled simultaneously.

"Eowyn, sort out the order. Chan, make sure it is communicated. We'll continue moving toward Osiris-Seventeen while we refuel and resupply."

"One presumes that *Paladin* needs to finish her visit with us," Captain Caijus of *Rightful Chieftain* told Henry on the main channel. "We have been prepping the rest of the missiles for transfer to *Paladin* since we skipped."

"We are already on our way," Ihejirika said as Henry nodded. "I feel rather naked with half-empty magazines."

The UPSF destroyers were missile ships in a way that the larger battlecruisers weren't. Their lasers gave them a punch at shorter ranges, but it was nothing compared to the spinal gravity driver of Henry's last command.

Missiles were long-ranged but unreliable in the face of both shields and antimissile defenses. There was a reason that the main shipkiller of the Kenmiri Empire was the plasma cannon—and the main shipkiller of the UPSF was either the starfighter or the gravity driver.

It wasn't even that the UPSF *couldn't* build plasma cannon at this point. Henry had even seen a prototype cruiser packing four heavy plasma cannon under a gravity shield go through trials once. The conclusion had been that the need for multiple gunports in the gravity shield and the loss of the possibility of variable munitions had more than offset the gain in brute firepower.

Henry figured he knew what the eventual result of that would be, but if anyone in TechDiv had the logical three-million-ton next-gen battlecruiser with both weapons systems in more than schematics, they hadn't told *him*.

THE LOGISTICS SCRUM took almost fourteen hours in the end. Fourteen hours where Henry couldn't quite bring himself to leave the flag deck. There were conversations he needed to have and paperwork he needed to do, but none of them felt quite as urgent as mother-henning his Flotilla through its most vulnerable moments.

They were reasonably certain the pursuit from Rashova was over, but that was no guarantee that no one *else* was going to show up in Osiris-16. This was Kenmiri space, and while the Flotilla was en route to Osiris-17, there were two other skip lines from the system.

One led to Osiris-15 and another led to a system the UPSF had never visited. The Kem label was a string of characters that anglicized as I8LH&DD9.

Neither was inhabited, but that didn't mean there wasn't traffic through them. Osiris-16 was uninhabited too, and at one point the system had held a patrol base and a fueling depot.

What Henry hadn't told Sylvia was that he had not only been to Osiris before, he'd been to *Osiris-16* before. He had the fourth planet up on his screens as the Flotilla crept across the light-minutes between the two skip lines, looking for the scars from his last visit.

"Looking for something in particular, ser?" Ihejirika asked.

Henry looked up in surprise. He hadn't realized the destroyer's captain had been watching sensor access.

"Captain?"

"You've been staring at Sixteen-D for fifteen minutes now, Commodore," his flag captain pointed out. "So, either you saw something the rest of us didn't, or you're looking for something."

Henry chuckled.

"*Teta*," he conceded. The Kem word meant "struck" and served much the same purpose in formal combat contests for the Kenmiri Warrior caste as *touché* did in Terran fencing.

"So, what are you looking for?"

"I was XO aboard the battlecruiser *Romulus* when she came through here," Henry told his subordinate. "There was a fueling and logistics depot for the Kenmiri here."

"'Was' being the operative word?"

"Yeah. We were hunting dreadnoughts, and blowing up the fuel station seemed like a good way to lure some out." Henry shivered at the memory of the *end* of that particular mission—the first time he'd commanded a battlecruiser, after a blowthrough had obliterated *Romulus*'s bridge and left him conning the ship from the CIC.

The point of the mission had been to test the *Hercules*-class battlecruisers against dreadnoughts. They hadn't been *quite* a match for a dreadnought one-on-one, it had turned out, and only a lucky shot by one of her destroyer escorts had saved the cruiser.

Like the *Hunter*-class ships, the *Hercules* battlecruisers had been decommissioned at a pace that said a great deal about the capabilities versus their enemies—and a pace that Henry couldn't quite bring himself to disagree with.

"Unfond memories?"

"Not as bad as some others," Henry admitted. "I was looking for the crash site where the depot station fell. I was expecting there to be more left, since it doesn't look like they rebuilt their infrastructure here."

"I can get the tactical department to take a look," Ihejirika offered.

"That's unnecessary," Henry said with a shake of his head. "I want *them* watching the skip lines for unexpected visitors. Sixteen is quiet so far, but we're the first UPSF ships to enter the Remnant since at least the Great Gathering."

Disastrous as the attempt to bring together the Vesheron powers for a grand conference had proven in the end, it also marked the end of the subspace-communications network and any attempt by the United Planets Alliance to exert power outside the closest sector.

The irony to the UPA's efforts to keep the *Vesheron* from knowing where the UPA's stars were was that the *Kenmiri* knew perfectly well where at least a third of the UPA was. The Red Wing Campaign had been a Kenmiri invasion of Terran space, after all.

"Do we even know which systems the Remnant is hosting fleets in?" Ihejirika asked. "The IntelDiv briefings I get are pretty…sparse."

"Then you're probably getting the same ones I am. There are a few things I'm not going to mention, but they don't give us enough data to make it worth keeping classified."

Henry didn't officially know about the five IntelDiv listening outposts that had been positioned through the Ra Sector—but Initiative ships had deployed the prefabricated facilities and the personnel to crew them. So, he knew more than he'd been told.

But since the listening posts were mostly limited to lightspeed data and had to use drones to report in, their data was *very* stale by the time it made it into briefing packets.

"We know where the inhabited worlds are," Henry continued. "But we have no live data on them. Our intelligence assets inside the core sectors…" He shook his head. Sylvia probably knew more about that than he did, but his understanding was that most of those had been Vesheron, and what *had* been direct UPA assets had been lost when the subspace network went down.

"We have no way to talk to them, if nothing else," Ihejirika noted, following Henry's silent thoughts.

"Exactly. We have some encryption protocols and code phrases to try to make contact with agents in Kenmiri space, but…" Henry spread his hands. "We haven't talked to any of them in at least two years. If they're still alive and still willing to talk to us, they may not even have the hardware to hear us calling anymore—and are almost certainly not checking it regularly!"

The Kenmiri had built a new variety of subspace communicator, but they were much more advanced than anyone else in that area. The revelation that the subspace "frequency" everyone had been using had been entirely artificial was a harsh proof of that.

"Well, should we be looking for war scars on any other planets we pass by?" Ihejirika asked after a moment's thought.

"In the end, we're just passing through. We don't want trouble and I'd rather not remind the Kenmiri of their reasons to hate us. We need to get to Anderon. Everything else is secondary right now."

"That's what I figured. Skip in nine hours."

15

THE FORWARD FLOTILLA was three star systems deep in Kenmiri space before they saw any sign of life. The skip into Osiris-18 was almost *more* nerve-wracking because Osiris-16 and Osiris-17 had been empty, though.

"Emergence...now."

The universe flickered back into existence around *Paladin*. The rest of the Forward Flotilla were in perfect formation with them, *Fronds of Will* and the two logistics ships in the well-protected center.

"Contact!" Bach snapped. "Multiple contacts. Closest range is... fourteen light-minutes."

"Get them on the plot," Ihejirika ordered.

Henry let *Paladin*'s Captain give the orders to his crew while he and his people looked at the information taking shape on their new location.

Two gas giants marked clean circular orbits that kept two asteroid belts and five rocky planets in place around the red giant star. Henry's destination was a twelve-and-a-half-hour skip line to the slave world of Brell. A third skip line, closer to the star than both the emergence and exit points of the Forward Flotilla, linked the system to a slave industrial world called Pok. Brell and Pok were part of the same cluster, linked to the agricultural slave world of Ki-Tar.

Fortunately for the Forward Flotilla, the link between Brell and Pok through Osiris-18 was historically mostly unused—and the current layout of the contacts suggested that was still the case.

The main focus of the energy signatures Henry was seeing was the dual-planet system ten light-hours from the star only a few hours' flight from the Pok skip line but almost two full days' travel from the Brell skip line.

The distance from both the Pok line and what looked like a mining base around the dual planets meant that all but one set of contacts were light-hours away—which meant it would be hours before they knew the Flotilla was there and there was no chance of them intercepting them.

That one set of contacts, though…

"Eowyn, let's nail down the details on Bogey One," Henry said softly. "Everyone else is far enough away that they're no threat, but fourteen light-minutes is close enough to worry."

The twenty-five-and-a-half-hour transit time they'd calculated for Osiris-18 called for them to decelerate into the skip line and jump at a low velocity. Anything else was too dangerous—even with the risk to Anderon, the odds were against them every time they took a skip at high speed.

They *had* to get through. Risking the lives of everyone in his Flotilla *and* everyone on Anderon and Twelfth Fleet wasn't worth the hours they'd carve off. Especially when Henry was reasonably sure he had the time to take it safely.

"Distance is two hundred and fifty million kilometers," Eowyn told him as they resolved the contacts further. "CIC makes their course from Pok to Osiris-Seventeen. We will be well clear unless they change their course."

"Which depends on who they are and what they're doing," Henry murmured as the contact began to resolve into individual ships.

There were twenty-six starships headed in his direction, which was a *lot* more than he'd been counting on. A quarter-billion kilometers of distance was reassuring but not a solid defense.

More details resolved as the combat information center team went through their data and fed it into the warbook. The first dozen ships they identified were freighters, transports making no attempt to conceal their signatures.

The thirteenth ship was a standard Kenmiri escort, and her position was enough confirmation for Henry to know what he was looking at.

"Cargo convoy. I'm guessing four escorts, twenty-two ships," he told Eowyn. "Why headed to Osiris-Seventeen, though?"

"Resupply for the fleet?" his operations officer asked. "Though Seventeen and Sixteen do have other skip lines. From Seventeen I think they can get to the Niov homeworld in a few days."

Henry studied the convoy grimly. The Niov were one of the Ashall races native to the Osiris Sector, and if the convoy was headed toward *them*, he didn't want to get involved. But…

"If it's resupply for the fleet, we could almost justify going after them," he murmured. "We could take four escorts."

So long as the Flotilla went toward Brell and the convoy headed toward Osiris-17, they wouldn't even pass within extreme missile range of each other. But the Flotilla hadn't built up any velocity yet, and the convoy's velocity was *toward* them.

"Maintain current course," Henry ordered slowly. "But Chan?"

"Ser?" the coms officer replied.

"Get Falling Rain, Tol Azan, Ihejirika and the Ambassador on a conference call."

WITH THOSE FIVE in a virtual conference, Henry had the commanders of both of his allied contingents on hand—with Ihejirika standing in for his UPSF subordinates and Sylvia there to provide her diplomatic and civilian perspective.

"We have an opportunity in front of us," he told them all. "But it comes with a lot of questions."

"The convoy," Tol Azan said instantly. The Kozun officer was rubbing his forehead armor plate thoughtfully, almost drawing attention to his lack of hair—unusual even for his race with their armored skulls.

"We do-can not know if the convoy is-was supporting the rogue Warriors," Falling Rain said.

"We *do* know that they are Kenmiri and vulnerable," Ihejirika pointed out, *Paladin*'s Captain eyeing his Commodore aside. "For some of us, that might be enough."

"The question is whether we want to fight *all* of the Kenmiri or just the bastards attacking the Ra Sector," Henry said. "If I *knew* that was a resupply convoy going to the Warrior fleet, we would already be on our way to attack it.

"But if there is any way to distinguish between the Kenmiri who are minding their own business and the Kenmiri who have signed on for a campaign of xenocide against us, we have not recognized it yet."

"I do not believe that we want to create *more* enemies," Sylvia warned. "At this point, we have every reason to believe that the Warrior fleet represents a rogue faction of the Remnant, one with limited logistical support from the main Kenmiri population."

"And if we attack this convoy, we do-must risk bringing the entire Remnant to war."

"The Kenmiri are both hated and feared by all of our personnel," Tol Azan warned. "I do not believe you Terrans will ever fully understand how massively their rule weighs upon our souls. If we order our people to attack Kenmiri in Remnant space, they will obey.

"But they will fear the consequences and it will eat at them. *I* fear the consequences."

Henry nodded, glancing around them all.

Ihejirika was impassive as usual, but Henry could read his flag captain. He wanted to attack the Kenmiri—regardless of whether *these* Kenmiri were the ones who'd attacked Rashova.

Henry could sympathize, but he also had to realize that it wouldn't be the UPA who would bear the consequences if they enraged the entire Remnant.

"I believe we can-will avoid all close contact with the Kenmiri," Falling Rain suggested. "These are not our stars. Our mission is-was to reach Anderon. Why will-should we start a fight we can-do not need?"

"That really is it, is it not?" Henry asked. "I did not want to let the convoy pass without considering it, but Falling Rain raises the real problem: any fight we start risks losing ships and people that we will need at Anderon."

"If they were trying to pursue us, there would be no question," Sylvia said. "But the fate of Anderon and our allied fleets rests on this Flotilla getting to Anderon, doesn't it?"

"It does," Henry agreed firmly. "And I think that sets our strategy for the entire journey, people. For the same reason we are taking the skip lines slowly instead of at speed, we cannot engage enemies who we do not need to fight.

"If the Kenmiri will let us pass…then I say we pass."

"I must-will agree."

"I *want* to fight the red monsters," Tol Azan replied, then he shook his head sharply. "But you are correct. There is no purpose to risking our ships here when we will need them in the Ra Sector to hold the line."

Henry arched an eyebrow at his flag captain after a few seconds of silence.

Ihejirika chuckled in response. "This is no democracy," he pointed out. "Our people will follow where you lead, Commodore. We will chase Kenmiri across the galaxy if you ask it, and we will pass through their systems peacefully if you ask that."

"Every system we pass without a fight is a hope for a future with, at least, *less* war," Sylvia told them all. "The Kenmiri may be fading, but there are four thousand stars in the core sectors and over three hundred inhabited worlds.

"If we can prove to the Kenmiri that we are not out for blood, then perhaps we can talk to them—and if we can talk to them, we may be able to lay groundwork for a peaceful transfer of the worlds they still control."

She shrugged.

"That is a slim hope, and I expect to either fight them or wait for them to die out…but it costs us very little right now to make the gesture."

Henry wasn't entirely sure that *not shooting* at the Kenmiri when the Forward Flotilla was violating their space was that large of a "gesture," but she was right. It cost them nothing right now to avoid fights they didn't need.

So long as the Kenmiri played along, at least.

16

BY THE TIME they were halfway through Osiris-18, there was a clear pattern to the Kenmiri activity in the system. Neither Henry nor his staff had managed to make *sense* of the pattern, but it was definitely a nonthreatening one.

The Kenmiri convoy continued on its way toward the Osiris-17 skip line, almost completely ignoring the Forward Flotilla. The ships concentrated around the dual-planet system were staying close to home. They had to know that the Flotilla was *present*—*Paladin* was the only ship *not* firing a plume of superheated gas into space behind them, after all—but they weren't reacting to them at all.

The oddities left Henry in his office, leaning back in his chair with a steaming coffee as he tried to make sense of it all. There was definitely a mining operation around 18-D's pair of planets, but he would have expected to see traffic between 18-D and Pok if nothing else.

Instead, there were about thirty freighters that he assumed were skip-capable and a few dozen smaller mining ships clustered in orbit of the double planets, under the careful watch of six escorts and a gunship.

"You're not scared of *us*," he murmured. "You were already clustered up when we arrived. So, what am I missing?"

Shaking his head, he gestured a feed of the convoy into the air. Osiris-18 was busy for an uninhabited system, with almost sixty FTL ships present even before the Forward Flotilla had arrived. The clear division between the convoy and the mining base, though…

"Wait." He zoomed in on the convoy and highlighted the escorts.

His admittance chime sounded before he finished his thought, and he blinked away the virtual screen and looked up. "Enter."

Lieutenant Colonel Ihejirika stepped through the door, looking exhausted.

"Ser."

"Grab a coffee and a seat," Henry ordered *Paladin*'s Captain. "What do you need?"

"About twelve hours' more sleep than I expect to get," Ihejirika replied. "May I…speak somewhat freely, ser? I need advice."

"Okafor." Henry's use of his flag captain's first name got the younger man to look up and meet his gaze as Ihejirika poured the indicated coffee.

"You were my tactical officer before you were my flag captain," he continued once he was sure he had Ihejirika's full attention. "If *Raven* hadn't been crippled and needed to go in for a full refit, you would be Iyotake's XO aboard her."

Tatanka Iyotake—now *Colonel* Tatanka Iyotake—had been Henry's executive officer on *Raven*. He'd served as the battlecruiser's passage commander back to UPA space and had been slated to take command of a different battlecruiser there.

Henry's promotion to Commodore had already been in the cards when the Drifters had wrecked *Raven*. The *plan* had been for Iyotake to take over the battlecruiser while Henry moved to being the Peace-keeper Initiative's forward commander.

It would have been a nightmare for Iyotake and Ihejirika if Henry had flown his flag from *Raven* after that, and he'd been *planning* to move aboard one of the *Cataphract*s just to clear the way for the new command crew to find their feet.

"As it is, you don't have Colonel Iyotake to lean on. You command one of our newest warships, one of the most powerful ships of her size in existence, and she is your first starship command.

"If you didn't need advice from time to time, I'd be shocked. So, yes, Okafor, you have my permission to speak freely."

The Black man took a heavy seat across from Henry and took a huge swallow of coffee that was almost certainly still too hot.

"This ship and crew have been running since I took command, ser," Ihejirika finally said. "It was good for us for a while, but now it's starting to wear. This crew prides themselves on being the elite—we have the only *Cataphract* left in service, after all!

"But even *I* am starting to feel the drain of constant active operations. And in Kenmiri space, it feels like I can barely step away from the bridge."

"You and me both, Captain," Henry conceded. "Would it make you feel better if I admit that I'm sitting in my office with a tactical feed because it's the *only* way I can drag myself off the flag deck?"

Ihejirika chuckled grimly. "Yes, actually. It's good to know I'm not alone."

"You're a conscientious officer in a highly demanding new role, and you are, whether you realize it or not, creeping close to the edge of burnout," Henry warned gently. "I *suggest*, though I will not order it, that you sit down with Dr. Uehara and assess your schedule.

"The Captain always has to be on call. But you do not always have to be on *duty*. You need, in fact, to take some time to do your paperwork, sleep…read a damn book, if that's how you relax.

"As senior officers, we have to be available twenty-four-seven. But that puts even more weight on us to find ways to relax *while* still being available.

"This *is* me telling you to do as I say, not as I do," Henry acknowledged with a thin smile. "But it is a skill that we all must master to one degree or another. For the moment…"

He studied Ihejirika and sighed.

"You need to take a downshift and sleep, Captain."

"Fair. I'm just beating my head against what's going on in this system," Ihejirika admitted.

"Me too." Henry considered his subordinate for a long few moments, then activated the holoprojectors in his office. That allowed him to hang the same tactical feed he'd been studying when the captain arrived in the air between them.

"Everyone at the planet seems to be hunkered down like they're expecting an attack, while the freighter convoy is ignoring *everyone*," Henry observed. "I'll admit that I *like* them ignoring us, it makes our lives a lot easier, but I still feel like I'm missing something."

"I feel like I've seen the pattern around D before," Ihejirika said. "Like…in the aftermath of Vesheron attacks?"

"Yeah." Henry looked at the planet's defenders again. It was very much a "sheepdog and flock" formation. Any ship that would have been outside the dual-planet system was *in* it right now, clearly under the envelope of the defensive squadron and whatever forts were in place.

"And the convoy is much the same." He brought up the convoy, studying the formation of the Kenmiri ships. "Those escorts are in tight; no one is getting near those ships with anything."

"That fits," Ihejirika agreed. "So…it sounds to *me* like someone local is causing the Remnant issues. Maybe not all of the Vesheron in the core sectors gave up?"

"It's possible. Maybe even likely." Henry surveyed the display again and shook his head. "If any of them *are* still fighting the Kenmiri, they have to view what happened to the Vesheron after the Fall as the greatest betrayal in all history."

The various rebel factions had let the Kenmiri draw back into the core sectors without a fight—even as vast numbers of civilian Kenmiri were transported in relatively vulnerable convoys. The Great Gathering had, among other things, been meant to decide if the Vesheron and the outer sectors were going to continue the war to try to free the core.

Except the Great Gathering had disintegrated into violence, and the loss of the subspace network had destroyed all interstellar communication. The Vesheron had died that day. Anyone continuing the fight in the Remnant had lost their support and their allies.

"Have we scanned for subspace communications?" Henry asked as the thought of the Fall reminded him. "We should have the communicators on all of the destroyers set up for direction-finding."

There was an ongoing debate on whether the UPSF should include subspace communicators on new ships or even remove them from existing ships, but so far, all of his ships still had the system. And while UPSF technology couldn't duplicate or intercept what the Kenmiri were doing to send messages now, they *could* detect it.

"It's a relatively passive process; we have it ongoing," Ihejirika confirmed. "There haven't been any subspace transmissions while we've been in Osiris-Eighteen."

"Now, *that* is fascinating," Henry murmured. "You'd think someone would be warning Brell that we're coming, wouldn't you?"

"Unless no one here has the new subspace communicators. If they're limiting them to key military ships and infrastructure…"

"And the surveillance outposts in the outer sectors." Henry nodded thoughtfully. "That suggests that they may be more limited in their manufacturing capability for the new communicators than we thought."

His own estimates and assumptions to the Peacekeeper Initiative's commanding officer, Admiral Sonia Hamilton, and the main UPSF had presumed that the Kenmiri Remnant had reequipped at least all of their warships with the new communicators.

But if there were no communicators across an entire star system with a dozen warships in it, plus forts, plus civilian mining infrastructure, that suggested that the new system was more restricted than he'd dared hope.

"We might actually surprise Brell, then?"

"Maybe. Or there may be a scout ship close to the skip line that already slipped through without us detecting it," Henry said. "Either way, there is no one within twelve hours' flight of us right now, Captain. So, I really do suggest you go get some sleep."

"Should I check in with the Ambassador on what *you* should be doing?" his flag captain suggested archly.

"No," Henry conceded with a laugh. "The pot is calling the kettle black, so I will *also* go rest."

It wasn't like there weren't at least four different mechanisms for waking the captain and Commodore up if something went wrong, after all!

17

OSIRIS-18 WAS an uninhabited system with a mining outpost and only a handful of ships. Brell, on the other hand, was a star system anchored on an industrial slave world. Two gas giants divided up seven rocky planets, providing the fuel for the massive fields of factories and foundries that covered the second planet—also named Brell.

Of the entire ten-system route to Anderon, Brell was the first one where Henry was expecting to run into real trouble. Industrial systems like it were where the Kenmiri Empire had built its escorts, gunships, freighters and other vessels. *Dreadnought* construction had been more restricted, but the lighter warships and big civilian ships came from the hundreds of industrial systems.

So did weapons, armor, tanks, agricultural equipment, et cetera, et cetera. Planets like Brell had their original ecosystems obliterated by the pollution of highly efficient but highly destructive Kenmiri factories, run by millions of slaves imported from the homeworlds.

Henry had spent time on over thirty industrial worlds, and only nine of them *hadn't* required a breath mask to go outside. The Kenmiri had the ability to match the industrial facilities from the slave worlds without the pollutants—the worlds they'd colonized for their own people had just as many factories but were beautifully preserved.

They just didn't want to expend the resources. The fact that the industrial worlds were rendered practically uninhabitable without assistance—and *definitely* couldn't grow crops—was a feature, not a bug.

The entire concept behind the slave-world clusters left Henry coldly furious. The Kenmiri had set up groups of five worlds, none of which could survive without each other. Only the slave-race home-worlds and the Kenmiri colonies were able to both feed themselves and maintain their own infrastructure.

That had led to utter chaos in the outer sectors when the Kenmiri had withdrawn. Thanks to the Vesheron and the subspace network, *most* of the clusters had managed to sort things out before the Great Gathering and the death of the communications network.

So far, Henry had not yet encountered any worlds where the links had failed—but he knew they existed and that billions had died because the Kenmiri had simply not *cared* about the costs of their withdrawal.

There was a very clear and direct argument that those deaths were the result of Golden Lancelot and the deaths of the Kenmorad—and hence, one Henry Wong's fault, among others.

That was a rabbit hole his therapists had taught him to keep out of, though, and he managed to dismiss the thought and focus on the slave-world cluster in front of him.

Brell and Pok were part of the Ki-Tar Cluster, and *that* cluster was still operating under Imperial rules. Kenmiri shipping only with escorts and janissary soldiers to keep everyone in line.

"Three minutes to skip exit."

Charmchi's report echoed through the entire ship.

"Every time we enter an unknown system, I wish for magic eyes to see what we're getting into," Eowyn noted. "We know what Brell looked like the last time a UPSF ship was here. *Five years ago.*"

There had never been Kenmorad on the slave worlds. Golden Lancelot hadn't struck Brell, which left the UPSF's data on the system horrendously out of date.

"If they know we're coming, we could be in serious trouble,"

Henry observed. "But that is why Ihejirika brought the ship to battle stations."

Every other ship in the Flotilla would have done the same, but he had no coms with them until they emerged into the Brell System. The only status markers on Henry's internal network feed were for *Paladin* herself.

"Sixty seconds to skip exit."

He glanced at the screen to his left and barely managed not to smile at Sylvia Todorovich. "You ready to talk the Kenmiri down, Ambassador?"

"I never actually negotiated with Kenmiri," she pointed out. "This should be interesting."

IN HIS OWN MIND, Henry had expected to emerge into a fight. They'd picked their emergence point on the skip line to stay away from the usual exit spots, but he'd ordered the Flotilla's ships to expect combat shortly after arrival.

The Kenmiri knew, better than anyone, how to patrol skip lines to make sure they intercepted incoming ships.

"We've got telemetry links with the rest of the Flotilla," Chan reported moments after they fell back into three-dimensional space. "Synchronizing sensor data."

"Formation held through the skip. No contacts nearby," Eowyn added. "We are clear out to one light-minute."

"Huh." Henry updated his feed and checked. Not only was there nothing close to them, but there were also no ships positioned along the skip line to intercept. Either the news of their transit hadn't reached Brell, or the Kenmiri had chosen to let them pass.

"Where *are* the defenders?" he asked.

"Sweeping the system," Eowyn replied. "Contacts above the inner gas giant. Contacts above Brell and the third planet. Looks like gas refineries on Six and mining operations on Three. Some in-system traffic between them, but most of the ships look like they're going into lockdown in planetary orbits."

So, the news of their passing *had* arrived, Henry realized. The Kenmiri commander was choosing to see what the Forward Flotilla did before they did anything, but they were pulling their civilian shipping in under the protective envelope of the planetary forts.

"CIC makes it twenty-four escorts in orbit of Brell itself, supported by an equal number of forts," Eowyn finally said. "Six forts above Three, eighteen above Six. They're in defensive formations, but it will be another five minutes before we see the light of their reactions to us."

"If they were going to fight us, they'd be out here," Henry murmured. "Though I suspect the Kenmiri commander can match twenty-four escorts against eight UPSF destroyers in their head—*I* certainly can."

Even without the rest of the Flotilla, his UPSF ships could handle three-to-one odds against the smaller escorts. The forts were a problem, though, and he could see what the Kenmiri were thinking now.

"Which explains their positioning," he continued, as much for Sylvia's benefit as anything else. "They know they can't take the Flotilla with their mobile force—but add in twenty-four forts with the shields the escorts lack, and it becomes a far-more-even fight.

"So long as in they're in orbit of Brell, the Kenmiri have concentrated as much force as they can in orbit of the one thing really worth protecting in this system. If we want to fight, we have to come in at a disadvantage—but if we're just passing through, they aren't provoking an engagement their warships can't win on their own."

"Scans suggest Brell's population is mostly unchanged," Eowyn said quietly. "Seven hundred and fifty million or so."

And that was the joker in the deck, the part that made Henry want to *take* the risk of leading the Forward Flotilla into an unnecessary action. Three-quarters of a *billion* slaves.

"We have to focus on our mission," Henry finally replied, checking to be sure that his link to Ihejirika and Sylvia was active. He didn't want to have to repeat the point more often than necessary. "We want —*all of us* want—to free those people. But today they are alive and they are not at risk of starvation.

"If we pick a fight over one world, we risk leaving them out on a logistics line that is far too long and unstable to protect or feed them.

And the fight would risk our ability to reach Anderon and Twelfth Fleet."

He knew his control of his features was good enough that most of his crew wouldn't realize how much that thought upset him. Most of his officers and crew were veterans of the war still, but even those veterans had rarely walked still-occupied Kenmiri worlds.

Henry had. He *knew*, intimately, the gray drudgery and totalitarian restrictions he was leaving the people of Brell to. But he also knew that attacking Brell would guarantee a fight in the Traste System—and the next inhabited system on their trip was a Kenmiri colony, which meant he could all but guarantee dreadnoughts.

"I'll send a transmission," Sylvia said into the quiet. "We'll tell them that we're just passing through."

"Nothing else," Henry suggested. He trusted her judgment, but… "They don't need to know about Rashova. If they don't already know, I doubt it will serve any purpose. Especially if they're already letting us pass."

"I'm not so concerned about Brell," the Ambassador told him. "I want to create a pattern that the leaders in Traste will see. If we can pass peacefully through Brell, it may buy us some trust when we enter Traste."

"And Traste is where we are actually in danger," Henry agreed. "Talk them up, Ambassador."

HENRY WATCHED as Chan set up the transmission for Sylvia. The Ambassador took five minutes to relocate to her office, with the banners of the UPA and UPSF and *Paladin*'s commissioning seal. She didn't need to live on the flag deck, after all.

Neither did Henry, now that he knew the Flotilla was well clear of the Kenmiri. His biggest worry now was that one of his successor-state allies would detach from the main body to do something stupid.

"Good to go," Sylvia announced, and Henry turned his attention back to her.

She looked levelly at the camera, and he could *see* every part of her stiffen as her full professional mask came up. Even relaxed around him, she was still sharply built with tight control of her emotions and expressions.

But the professional mask sharpened those edges. Her shoulders straightened further, her position shifted into a near-loom at the camera, and her face went completely flat.

"Kenmiri forces in the Brell System," she began in crisp and fluent Kem. "I am Ambassador Sylvia Todorovich of the United Planets Alliance. While a state of war arguably continues to exist between the United Planets Alliance and the Kenmiri Empire, we are *not* here as an act of aggression against the Kenmiri.

"We are transiting through your space on a mission of our own. We have no intention of attacking or engaging any vessels, military or civilian, and will transit to the Osiris-Twenty-Five System in approximately thirty-five hours."

She held her gaze on the camera in silence for several seconds.

"We will defend ourselves against any aggression with maximum force—and you can assess the survivability of your local fleet against our forces as easily as I can. If you attack us, we will destroy you. If you permit us to pass unchallenged, we will simply pass through.

"The choice is yours."

The recording cut off, and Henry watched Sylvia relax back to her normal "working mask" pose and expression. She arched a silent eyebrow at him, and he didn't bother to conceal a smile.

"Always a pleasure to watch a professional at work," he told her in English. "Think they'll play along?"

"I don't expect to receive a response," she admitted. "But I also don't expect them to pick a fight they can't win."

18

PART OF SYLVIA'S job was to soothe ruffled feathers in their allies. Though the Forward Flotilla's officers had accepted Henry's command authority and would run *most* of their concerns through him, she still wasn't surprised when Tol Azan pinged her for a video call.

The Kozun Squadron Leader looked more refreshed than he had on the last command conference, but his agitation was showing through his admirable self-control.

Sylvia had no idea what quirk of fate or unknown players had created the Ashall and rendered dozens of races passingly similar to each other. Like humans, there was no question that every Ashall species was related to everything else on their homeworlds, too.

But they were similar enough that Sylvia had learned tells shared across all of the Ashall, and Azan was showing them. The Kozun, born and raised on Skex—an industrial world just like Brell—had every reason to be agitated in her mind.

"Squadron Leader, how may I assist you?" she asked in Kem.

"You can tell me what the UPA's plan is for the core sectors," he said bluntly. "I see a billion innocent souls trapped in bondage, and we must simply…fly past. Do nothing."

"Today, yes," Sylvia agreed. "Henry has given the lecture, and you know the strategic situation as well as he does, Squadron Leader. *Today* we fight for the Ra Sector."

"And tomorrow? Do we take the war back to the Kenmiri and free those still enslaved?"

Sylvia sighed. *That* was the question she'd known was coming.

"You were never Vesheron, were you, Leader Azan?" she asked gently.

"No," he admitted. "I was an engine tech on a Kenmiri food transport. A *favored* slave."

Sylvia had seen what the slave-crew quarters on Kenmiri transports looked like. "Favored" was relative. While even the slave worlds had enough flexibility to have definite classes of rich and poor, managers and workers, there was a very clear line of "everyone was a slave."

Even the short-lived Kenmiri Drones were considered more important than the slave races. There generally wasn't much in terms of summary executions and such, but the possibility was always there. The Kenmiri were *always* more important.

"The Fall was a surprise to the Vesheron," she told him. "Nobody expected the Kenmiri to roll over after we took out the Kenmorad. We knew it had to be a body blow to their culture and capability, but a full-on withdrawal from twelve sectors?

"First, we were scrambling to make sure the factory worlds did not starve. And then we had the Gathering and the Kenmiri took out the communications network."

The United Planets Alliance had already been working on their peace dividend by then. They hadn't started standing down ships until after the Gathering, but they'd cut new construction to the bone.

"After the network was down, there *was* no grand Vesheron alliance anymore. The view of every faction shrank down to the tasks in front of them. We made an effort to secure the Ra Sector, but even *that* has taken time."

The UPSF would never have had the hulls to be the primary security in more than a handful of sectors—but they'd also never even tried. Sylvia had fought hard to see the Peacekeeper Initiative created, but it had only ever been aimed at the Ra Sector as an experiment.

If they could stabilize the Ra Sector in a network of alliances and trade treaties that made the UPA's borders secure and their corporations wealthy, it would expand. Until then, though, the UPA was *delighted* to have shaved their military budget by sixty percent.

The member worlds and nations of the United Planets Alliance valued their individual sovereignty, after all, and the fact that only the UPSF was allowed skip-capable warships still stuck in many throats after a century.

"You have not answered my question," Tol Azan pointed out, though his expression told Sylvia he understood her point.

"There is no grand alliance to liberate the core sectors, Leader Azan," she said gently. "The United Planets Alliance lacks the strength to fight the Remnant alone—that is why we have gathered allies even to protect the Ra Sector. We must look to the free worlds to protect *themselves*."

"And expect the slave worlds to *free* themselves? As so few did?"

"It took the massed effort of a hundred rebel factions and seven external powers to break the Kenmiri Empire once, Tol Azan," Sylvia warned him. "Without that grand alliance, all we can do is wait for the Remnant to die out."

Which she suspected had been the original plan for the aftermath of Golden Lancelot. A hundred-year siege, driving the slowly dying Kenmiri inward and inward. Instead, the enemy had…given up.

"So, those people," Tol Azan pointed, presumably at whatever tactical display was in his office, "are just left in the hands of their enslavers? And what happens when the Kenmiri decide that they no longer need their slaves and wipe them out?"

"I do not have the answers you seek, Squadron Leader." She met his gaze levelly. "The war with the Kenmiri Empire is over. These rogue Warriors have started a new conflict, one the United Planets Alliance will see through to the end to honor our commitments here.

"But none of us have the power to free the people who remain in the Kenmiri's hands. I hope that will change, but we must survive the challenge in front of us, Squadron Leader. We must fight for Anderon. Avenge Rashova. Protect the La-Tar Cluster and our allies. We cannot argue about a future when the present is in danger."

"I have to believe, Ambassador, that we can free these people,"

Azan told her. "I have to. Or my people will fall apart. We see our cousins—Ashall and slaves of the Kenmiri, if not directly of our blood —bound in iron, and you ask us to do *nothing*."

"I know." Sylvia let that hang in the air. "*I know*. There is no one in this Flotilla, Squadron Leader, who does not understand what you feel. Who would not break all that remains of the Empire to free her slaves.

"But the Kenmiri chose their weapons well. To rebuild the alliance that defeated the Empire will take decades. In the end, we can hope to forge a new alliance. The survival of the worlds of the outer sectors and their own growth will make that alliance more powerful than the Vesheron ever were—more powerful than the Kenmiri's worst nightmares.

"But it will take *time* to forge that alliance. Time in which the victims of the Kenmiri must endure."

"I was born into a universe in which the Kenmiri would never fall," Tol Azan told her. "I live now in one where they are broken. Perhaps I will die in one where all people are free."

"A dream I think we all share." Sylvia sighed. "I have to believe," she told the Kozun, "that if the call to arms is raised against the Kenmiri again, the United Planets Alliance will answer. I do not think that we will raise that call—but if it is raised by the people of the Empire, old or new, we will answer."

"So, it falls to us to build that alliance?" Azan asked.

"I would say the Ra Sector is well on its way to forming the base of it, but yes," she agreed. "But that battle is for the future. We must save the Ra Sector from the Kenmiri's rogues before we can plan how to deal with the Remnant itself."

"WE'RE CLEAR," Henry told her, stepping into her office and claiming the chair in front of her desk.

"We're still eight hours from the skip line," Sylvia observed. She mentally ordered her coffee maker to start up and make her Commodore a black coffee.

"Yes, but we're now outside any possible maneuver cone of anyone who isn't already in Osiris-Twenty-Five," he replied. "And since we haven't detected any subspace pulses in Brell, it appears they haven't sent any warning on ahead."

"Assuming there was no courier at the skip line and they have no drones," she pointed out.

"Always," he conceded. "There was *definitely* a scout ship of some kind at the skip line in Osiris-Eighteen that warned them we were coming. And they may well have sent one ahead to Twenty-Five, but they can't bring ships *back* from Twenty-Five to ambush us. It's a twenty-one-hour skip each way.

"Without a subspace pulse to send an instant message, they'd need a forty-plus-hour turnaround to bring in an ambush force. So, we're *almost* certainly safe for the rest of the trip through Brell."

Sylvia nodded. A lot of the details of accelerations and vectors and maneuver cones were lost on her. She could read the tactical feed that came to her network, but the details were Henry's expertise, not hers.

"And as expected, they have not replied to our message," she told him. "From what Chan says, they even had most of their internal communications locked down. They *really* don't want to talk to us."

"Would you?" Henry grimaced. "In their place, I'd just be glad we're not picking a fight. Of course, *I* know that *Fronds of Will*'s fighter group would have turned any fight for this system into a joke."

"And we also know that *Fronds of Will* no longer *has* a fighter group," Sylvia said. "Which they don't."

"True, but all they can really tell from a distance is that we have a three-megaton warship in the middle of our formation," he pointed out. "She's smaller than our carriers, but she's bigger than most ships the Kenmiri have seen other than dreadnoughts."

The seven El-Vesheron powers had all brought their own capital ships to the war, but most of those had been in the same four-megaton range as the *Crichton*-class fleet carriers. The Vesheron, on the other hand, had almost universally used Kenmiri warships—mostly escorts and gunships, though some smaller dreadnoughts had fallen into rebel hands and some of the homeworlds had played sufficient games to provide capital ships to factions they supported.

Fronds of Will was smaller than the cruisers the Kozun Hierarchy had built, but they were what she'd been built to fight. None of those cruisers had survived the Hierarchy's conflict with the La-Tar Cluster and the Peacekeeper Initiative, which had been a large piece of the stick Sylvia had authorized her old chief of staff Felix Leitz, now Ambassador to the Eerdish-Enteni Alliance, to use to talk the Hierarchy into standing down.

The Eerdish-Enteni Alliance had *six* ships like *Fronds of Will*, plus an ex-Kenmiri dreadnought. They'd held the carriers and shielded escorts and destroyers back to train, fighting the holding action with the traditional ships.

The Hierarchy had believed they could overrun the Alliance with escorts and gunships. Leitz and Rex were supposed to convince them not to try—with the combined revelation of just how outgunned the Hierarchy *actually* was and the fact that the UPSF carrier fleet was not going to tolerate the war.

Not with the Kenmiri Remnant rogue faction that was pounding on the Ra Sector's borders, anyway.

"So, they have to assume she's on par with one of our battlecruisers except with their style of shields?" Sylvia guessed.

"Yeah. Without *Fronds of Will*'s fighters, I wouldn't want to try to take Brell with the Forward Flotilla," Henry admitted. "But *they* have to figure that *Fronds* is enough to tip the balance in our favor. The commander had to know they couldn't fight us and win."

"So, they let us go and hope that Traste makes a decision before we get there. Which means they have to have sent a ship ahead of us. The local leadership does *not* want to have the conversation that would follow us arriving in a Kenmiri colony system without warning."

"True," Henry conceded with a shrug. "But like I said, no subspace coms. At this point, I have to assume the Brell System doesn't *have* a communicator."

"Or they have one we can't detect?" Sylvia didn't want to assume that the Kenmiri *weren't* communicating, after all—especially when they *knew* that the surveillance outposts had been equipped with FTL communicators.

"I won't pretend to fully understand the physics, but I am told by my communications people that we will always be able to detect that they are communicating. We're a long way from being able to duplicate their carrier wavelengths—either their current temporary systems or the original mass-scale stabilizing structure—but knowing what they are, we can definitely *detect* them."

His admission that he didn't understand the communications systems made Sylvia feel better about her general lack of technological knowledge about the ships she rode around on. She knew, for example, what the skip drive *did* and how that affected the crew—but she had no idea how it *worked*.

"I wouldn't have expected them to cripple themselves this much," she told him. "No one was surprised to find the new communicators in the outpost in the Moti System. The Diplomatic Corps was assuming that they had a smaller version of the original carrier-wave system that covered the core sectors."

"If they did, I'm *told* we'd be able to detect it," Henry repeated. "And there's nothing here. So, our rogue Warriors have subspace coms but the regular day-to-day Kenmiri operations don't."

"Do you have any evidence that the Warriors have them?" she asked slowly. "We *know* the surveillance outposts did, but did we see any use of it at Rashova or in the pursuit?"

He was quiet for a few moments in thought, then got up to grab the coffee that had been waiting for him for several minutes.

"No," he admitted. "I have to assume, from a military perspective, that they have it and have been maintaining constant communications with each other. But on the other hand, our scan data suggests that the plasma web uses radio for its communications. I'm not certain if even the Kenmiri engineered FTL coms small enough to mount in those drones, but I imagine they at least *tried*."

"So, potentially, those surveillance outposts are the only places with the subspace communicators. Who would be able to receive them?"

"I'm not sure. I'll have to check in with Chan and Jackson."

Lieutenant Commander Mehitabel Jackson was *Paladin*'s coms officer—and the other half of the team that had identified the subspace communicators in the first place.

"If the communicators and surveillance stations belong to the main Remnant, then the rogues may have less intelligence than we thought."

"Again, I have to assume they know everything," Henry warned. "They don't necessarily know where the Forward Flotilla is, but they can guess. And I have to assume that they know where Twelfth Fleet is and exactly how strong the allied forces attached to Admiral Rex's ships are."

He chuckled bitterly.

"Even *I* don't know how strong the allied fleet will be," he admitted. "If Leitz successfully talked the Kozun down, Rex could easily be looking at a hundred escorts and gunships between everyone—plus the E-Two destroyers and carriers and Twelfth Fleet itself.

"But you saw the fleet that the rogues have mustered. It's going to be an ugly fight no matter what, and if the Kenmiri wipe out our fighters with the webs..."

"You have to assume the worst possibility," Sylvia agreed. "I need to consider what the possibilities mean. Not least that the Remnant's internal communications are clearly not as solid and reliable as we expected.

"That may create opportunity."

After all, she'd talked a *lot* of people into rising up against the Empire before the Fall—and that had been when the Kenmiri would have reaction forces on their way within hours. And now it would be weeks or *months* before the Kenmiri even realized there was a problem, if they were remotely subtle about it.

19

AFTER PASSING through the Brell System unchallenged, Henry had figured they would either be ambushed immediately in Osiris-25 or pass through peacefully.

He'd figured peaceful passage was more likely, and they'd either guessed right or lucked out. Nothing in the next two star systems raised a challenge, with the handful of warships they saw in either Osiris-25 or Osiris-26 staying well clear of the Forward Flotilla.

They'd been in Osiris-26 for a full day, skirting around the second massive blue star on their route through Kenmiri space. The two blue giants were the key that had made the entire journey possible, as their mass meant that skip lines to and from them were faster and traveled farther than those between smaller stars.

With four hours left to the skip line to Traste, Henry watched his ships once again fueling from *Bringer of Cloths*. They were close enough to Anderon now—a purely relative number, all things considered— that after this, the Flotilla should be able to make the journey on their onboard tanks.

Bringer of Cloths wasn't dry yet, but he was eyeing her tank quantities carefully. A full load of fuel for every ship in the Flotilla was equal to the three-megaton mass of *Fronds of Will*. *Bringer* was the heaviest ship in Henry's little fleet, having started the mission massing just over eight million tons—the vast majority of it highly compressed deuterium and tritium.

"Contact, multiple contacts!"

The report cut through the almost-meditative observation of the fueling station.

"Distance and direction," Henry barked as he turned his attention on Medb Bach. Eowyn was off duty, as they'd been alone in Osiris-26 up till that moment. Everyone had found that suspicious enough that he'd assumed they were being *watched*, but they hadn't seen any ships.

"Twelve ships, range estimate forty-six light-minutes," Bach replied. "They emerged from the Osiris-Sixty-Three skip roughly fifty minutes ago. Warbook makes it an eight-megaton dreadnought plus escorts and a tanker."

That *probably* wasn't enough firepower to challenge the Forward Flotilla—and it was too far away to catch up to them. Henry's fear, one of the options that would doom the Flotilla, was a dreadnought *squadron* emerging from the skip line to Traste.

"What's in that direction?" he asked.

"Osiris-Sixty-Three is a nineteen-hour skip, but there's nothing there," Bach told him. "The most likely origin is the Sovat System, three days along that line. Homeworld of the Sovar, one of the Osiris Sector's Ashall races."

"Dreadnought is Remnant, though, right?"

It was *possible* that the Sovar had liberated their homeworld and were sending a dreadnought out to scout the nearest Kenmiri colony. Henry didn't think that was what was going on—mostly because the force looked like a standard dreadnought-anchored security patrol— but it was *possible*.

"We're still having problems sorting out post-Fall Kenmiri identity beacons," Bach admitted. "They've definitely changed since the war, and we don't know what any of them mean now. It's definitely a *Kenmiri* beacon, though."

From what the Kenmiri Drifter Interface had told Henry and Sylvia, the division between the rogues attacking the Ra Sector and the Council of Artisans was only the most blatant and potentially violent division in the Remnant. The Kenmiri had lost their parents, their leaders, and their *gods* to Golden Lancelot.

Henry suspected that the lack of any likely future was impeding their ability to reorganize a new government.

"Well, they're a long way away from us," he noted. "They would have seen us as soon as they emerged, though. How did they react?"

Whatever faction the dreadnought belonged to, they seemed to be carrying out the kind of security patrol that Henry had seen a hundred times—and the Forward Flotilla was exactly what that kind of patrol was looking for.

"They're assuming a broad formation, spreading their sensors wide for a clearer picture of us," Bach replied crisply. "As of forty-six minutes ago, they were still assessing."

Henry leaned back in his seat and reviewed the long-distance tactical feed. There was no chance of the dreadnought catching up to them in four hours. The dreadnought and her escorts could even evade back down the Osiris-63 skip line and avoid combat if Henry went after them.

His old instincts said to go for the kill. He had the advantage in both numbers and weight of metal. The dreadnought might run, but if she fought, the Forward Flotilla would easily overcome her.

During the war, punching out a solitary dreadnought would have been an unquestionably good thing. Right now, though…he didn't need to fight the Kenmiri. He *needed* to get to Anderon.

"Keep an eye on her, Lieutenant Commander," Henry told Bach. "If I need to worry about her coming up behind us in Traste, I want to know that. But right now…she's no threat to us and we have bigger priorities than her."

"Understood, ser. We'll keep you updated."

AFTER AN HOUR, it was clear that the dreadnought and her escort group were, if nothing else, disinclined to pick a fight with eighteen warships. They weren't vectoring in direct pursuit of the Forward Flotilla, though their course was definitely toward Traste.

"They're practically dawdling," Henry murmured.

"I'm not used to watching a Kenmiri dreadnought group *try* not to be threatening," his flag captain noted. "They'll enter the Traste skip line almost thirty hours after us. They're running at thirty percent of standard thrust."

"They don't want a fight, and they don't want us to feel threatened enough that we'd rather turn and kick them in the chops," Henry agreed. "Like you said, it's uncharacteristic for Warriors."

"A lot of what we've seen recently has been uncharacteristic for Warriors," Ihejirika told him.

The two of them were on a private internal network channel, though Henry was on the flag deck and Ihejirika was on *Paladin*'s bridge. It was the kind of swift and silent communication that had left more than a few of the UPSF's Vesheron allies wondering if the Terrans had a hive mind.

"I prefer the 'caution and concern for their people's lives' side of it to the 'massacring other people' side," Henry said. "I can respect their desire to survive. The ones who have fallen into xenocidal nihilism…"

"Those we're going to blow to hell. And from what you've said, while the Council of Artisans aren't going to *help* us, they are going to sit back and cheer when the Warriors go away."

"I'd worry about the impact we're going to have on the power games being played inside the Remnant," Henry admitted, "except that we *have* to stop these bastards, no matter what."

"The tactical department is working on some counter-tactics to those plasma webs," Ihejirika told him. "I have a few thoughts myself that I've been running through simulations."

"Me too," Henry said. "I can see a few ways our starfighters, at least, can protect themselves against the system. It's nasty, though. Counteracts the one big advantage of our grav-shields."

The web had been utterly overwhelming to the energy screens on the E-Two Shieldwings, but it was *designed* to take down Terran grav-shielded starfighters. The new SF-130 Lancers shared the same gravity drives as *Paladin*, which meant their shields were more powerful than the Kenmiri were expecting.

But the grav-shield depended on sending plasma off in a dozen different directions. The web would bring the arcs in from all directions, vastly increasing the chance that one of those plasma beams would connect.

And starfighters didn't have the mass or volume to spare for armor that could survive that.

"In hindsight, it's a surprise that it took the Kenmiri that long to develop a countermeasure against grav-shielded starfighters," Ihejirika said. "From the first battles of the Red Wing Campaign to Golden Lancelot, the fighters carried a lot of the weight of our war."

"And grav-shields in general carried the rest of it," Henry agreed. "*I* never expected us to maintain our monopoly on them through the entire war. IntelDiv figured we had a decade."

Henry was senior enough that he understood just how ruthless the UPSF had been at protecting their secrets during the war. His orders as a warship captain had been clear: he would do everything possible to evacuate his crew, but if it came to a choice between catching his people in the blast or allowing the Kenmiri to take his ship intact, he was to self-destruct his ship with everyone aboard.

One other El-Vesheron power, the insectoid and *actually* semi-hive-minded Terzan, had gravity shields. They'd been very quiet about their level of gravity tech, which led Henry to believe that the Terzan were probably *ahead* of the UPA on gravity-well projection, the key tech of the gravity shields and drives—as opposed to gravity-well *generation*, which was a well-known tech across the known galaxy.

"We're mostly looking at seeding destroyers through the fighter strike," Ihejirika said. "Everyone poking at it, of course, has their own focuses. The biggest problem is that the best way to make it work would be to have a dozen GMS destroyers in the middle of the fighter swarm."

"And we have one," Henry agreed. He chuckled. "The entire UPSF has *one* right now. The second-wave *Cataphract*s aren't due to commission for another year."

He'd been advised that they had been accelerated some time ago, after the initial success of the Lancer GMS fighters, but he had no idea how much difference that had made.

"I heard a rumor that those were all the *Cataphract*s that were going to be built? I was surprised, though I suppose I have a bias, as the captain of one."

"I have heard slightly solider rumors, I suspect, but nothing definitive." Henry shook his head. "The failure of *Cataphract*'s shield in combat with the Drifters caused some waves back home."

The Drifters had developed their own weapon to breach gravity shields. So far, the resonance warheads hadn't shown up in anyone else's hands, but they turned out to be even *nastier* versus a ship with a gravity maneuvering system and had devastated the name ship of the class.

"That said, I understand that the *Cataphract* class was always seen as an experiment, a test bed for the new technology to lay the groundwork for the mass-refit program—and, potentially, for a wave of true next-generation ships."

"I'll buy they built something better when I see her," Ihejirika told him. "*Paladin* is a damn good ship, ser, even if her crew is in desperate need of R&R."

"We'll get it for them," Henry promised. "After we deal with the Warriors at Anderon.

"We're three hours from entering the skip line to Traste," he continued. "I need to touch base with everyone. If there's any problems, Captain Ihejirika, now is the time to raise them."

"Do we have any idea what's waiting for us in Traste?"

Henry grimaced.

"The last time the UPSF was in the Traste System, we dropped a five-hundred-megaton bunker-buster on the Kenmorad creche," he pointed out. "There *were* six dreadnoughts in the system then, but we wrecked five of them."

And lost three UPSF destroyers and eighteen Vesheron warships in the process.

"They almost certainly built new ships and reinforced. I guess we expect another six dreadnoughts?"

"At least," Henry agreed. "More firepower than we can handle, that's for sure. So, make sure your crew is ready, Okafor. Traste is where the rubber hits the road for this journey."

20

THE TRASTE SYSTEM hovered around Henry's office. The holographic presentation told him much of what he needed to know about the system: even before the Kenmiri had moved one of their colonies in, it had been a busy chunk of space.

Nine planets, three of them gas giants, were split by three asteroid belts: two between the fifth and sixth and one outside the ninth planet. As of that last information he had, three billion people—one-quarter Kenmiri of all stripes—had lived on Traste itself, the third planet. A moon named Allamar, around Traste-IV, was also habitable, inhabited by another half-billion people—unusually, almost three-quarters Kenmiri.

Allamar had been the site of a Kenmorad creche before the UPSF's Golden Lancelot Task Force Seventeen had nuked it to hell. Already chillier than most people would like, Henry's estimates said it was probably suffering a minor nuclear winter.

With Traste itself only a few hours' flight away for a Kenmiri transport, Allamar was almost certainly fine, if less pleasant to live on than usual.

When TF17 had hit the system, the dreadnought squadron had been anchored at a resupply facility in orbit of Traste-IV, enabling them to defend the heavily fortified moon with the Kenmorad. Traste itself had relied on its own fortifications supported by several wings of escorts.

The report from Rear Admiral Caroline Micheli told Henry that basically the entire mobile force in the system had been wiped out by the time TF17 had retreated. The forts above Allamar had been gone as well, but they'd never engaged the forts above Traste.

Even if the subspace network had still been online, Henry wouldn't have been able to ask Micheli her opinion. *He'd* mouthed off at a superior and had a medical team sent to his office before he'd managed to swallow his own gun.

Caroline Micheli hadn't been so lucky. She hadn't even lived long enough to know just how broad Golden Lancelot had been—just nuking *one* planet had been too much for her in the end.

And Henry didn't blame her for one second.

The creche *he'd* nuked had been on an artificial island in the middle of an ocean. The Kenmorad had fled aboard an evacuation ship whose destruction had heralded the end of their race, but he'd still blown the island to hell. There'd been hundreds of thousands of eggs and larvae and juvenile Kenmiri on the island, plus Drone and Artisan caretakers.

Allamar's creche had been in the middle of a city of forty-five million people, half of them non-Kenmiri slaves. The damage assessments TF17 had made before retreating from the system had suggested there were few or no survivors in the city.

"So, do you hate us as much as I would in your place?" he asked the hologram. "You've probably rebuilt the dreadnought yards. Churned out new warships. Found ways to crew them.

"I have to think you've got the guns to take us out, and the geometry is not in our favor."

His skip line into the system was handily distant, five light-minutes from the current position of Traste-IV and ten from Traste-III. The problem was his *exit*. The Forward Flotilla needed the Osiris-66 skip line, which was out in the orbit of Traste-IX.

Eight *billion* kilometers from his entrance point. At the half-KPS^2 that was the best the two logistics ships could manage, it would take thirty-five and a half hours.

And he had to decelerate into the skip line, because if he tried to transit at their peak velocity of ten percent of lightspeed, he'd be leaving bits and pieces of starships across a dozen or so light-years.

And his most direct course took him just over one light-minute from the planet Traste. If the Kenmiri wanted to give him a fight, they were going to have *every* opportunity.

Every detour added more time. Worse, the thirty-two thousand KPS of the peak velocity their current course called for was about as fast as he could really risk taking the ships sublight. Adding more time didn't increase the peak velocity. Evading the planets might make it easier for the Kenmiri to pretend he wasn't around…but it wouldn't make it any harder for them to intercept.

"This one is on you, love," he whispered. "I hope your tongue is as silver as I think it is."

Once they were through Traste, Henry could send com drones on ahead and at least be sure that Twelfth Fleet would get his information when they arrived at Anderon.

But until he was clear of this system, he couldn't safely send drones. They had to get at least one ship through Traste—and if Henry had to fight the star system's defenders, getting even one of his eighteen ships clear would take a miracle.

Or *Paladin* abandoning her allies to use the full power of her gravity drive.

Henry was prepared to hope for a miracle.

21

"CONTACT. CONTACT AT ONE LIGHT-MINUTE! *DREADNOUGHT!*"

Sylvia suspected that at least half of the people aboard *Paladin* had been holding their breath—and *that* almost-shouted announcement from Medb Bach wasn't going to help. The other shoe, it seemed, had finally dropped.

The Ambassador was seated in her office, ready to give the best possible impression of the Forward Flotilla to the local authorities. To keep up with what was going on, she had direct links feeding into her internal network from the bridge and flag deck.

"Verify that!" Ihejirika snapped.

"Formation Delta-One; all ships hold position," Henry ordered—in Kem, so presumably he was on a channel to the entire Flotilla.

"Confirmed," Bach said crisply. "Twenty-six contacts at one light-minute. Two dreadnoughts, unknown ratio of gunships and escorts totaling twenty-four. They are…at zero velocity relative to the system primary."

Sylvia wasn't sure of the importance of that, but she suspected everyone *else* on the network links was. It certainly seemed to give Henry pause, and she fired a wordless question to him.

The formation is standard skip-line patrol, but to intercept an incoming ship or ships requires a base velocity, his text message explained a moment later. *They're in the right place and right formation to be trying to prevent us intruding, but they don't have the right vector.*

They knew we were coming, there's no way they didn't—but this isn't a counterattack.

It's a show of force.

"Hold position," Henry repeated aloud, still speaking in Kem. "Azan, pull your ships back to protect the logistics transports and *Fronds of Will*. Defender Falling Rain, please send your destroyers forward to form a defensive line with mine.

"Formation Delta-Six, everyone."

Sylvia watched as the initial spherical defense formation shifted toward a conical structure with the Enteni carrier at the point—and on the far side from the Kenmiri battle group.

"Ambassador Todorovich," Henry addressed Sylvia aloud—for the benefit of the rest of the Flotilla still, she realized. "If they were accelerating *toward* us, they would be ready to fight. But if they were ready to fight, I can see another six dreadnoughts in the system now.

"Which leads me to think that the Kenmiri are playing games. They have sent a large-enough force to *threaten* us—but a small-enough force and a distant-enough force to suggest that they are looking for an alternative.

"That makes it your area now, I believe."

"So do I," Sylvia confirmed. She nodded to Henry, and he returned the gesture with a slight bow of his head.

This was why the UPA's senior ambassador in the Ra Sector had been aboard *Paladin*. Sylvia wasn't objecting to the bonus of spending the trip with her boyfriend, but she had been with the Forward Flotilla to negotiate with the Rashovans.

And now she was going to negotiate with the Kenmiri. Because every enemy she talked down was a battle they didn't need to fight.

"TRASTE SYSTEM FORCES, I am Ambassador Todorovich aboard the UPSV *Paladin*. We are holding position at the skip line to request unimpeded transit through the Traste System to the Osiris-Sixty-Six System en route back to the Ra Sector and our own territory.

"We have no desire to engage in conflict with the Kenmiri, but we *must* pass. I am prepared to negotiate terms for said passage. In the absence of a return communication, we will proceed to our exit skip line and defend ourselves against any and all aggression by Kenmiri vessels."

A situation that Sylvia *knew* could only result in a danger at best and violence at worst. But it would allow the Kenmiri to ignore them, as they had in Brell.

"How long?" Henry asked softly in her network.

"Theoretically, the dreadnought commander could answer us in two minutes," she said. "But I doubt they've been given the authority. They will need to confirm with the governor, who is either on Traste or Allamar. Either way…"

She shook her head.

"Give them two hours, Henry, then we proceed to the Sixty-Six skip line like they don't exist. If they ignore us, we ignore them."

"Sounds like living with cats."

"Have you ever *had* cats?" she asked. Sylvia had grown up with several in the family home, and most of those cats would *not* tolerate being ignored for long.

"No," her lover admitted. "My father had a ranch in Montana, so we had *animals* but no pets."

"Stereotypes have as many problems with animals as they do people," she told him gently. "And if we'd lived down to our initial assumptions, where would you and I be?"

"Dead."

Sylvia concealed a wince at his bluntness. He wasn't wrong; that was for certain. She would never have guessed that the stiff-necked officer she'd met in Procyon over two years earlier would have become *her* stiff-necked officer.

She figured he felt the same about the sharp-edged and sharp-tongued diplomat he'd met the same day.

"We're past the minimum timeline for direct response from the dreadnoughts," Chan reported. "We won't be able to see if they transmit to the planet unless they're using subspace coms."

"And the new subspace coms, at that, yes?" Sylvia suggested. "Though I imagine you'd have mentioned if there were stabilized carrier waves here."

"We *think* we can detect anything of that sort, yes," the coms officer confirmed. "We are not detecting any stabilized carrier waves, temporary or permanent, but to be frank, we don't fully understand how the Kenmiri are doing it in the first place.

"Which means they may well be able to hide it from us."

"Because *that's* a pleasant thought," Henry said. "We'll wait out your two hours, Ambassador. But that's all the time we can really spare. We *really* don't know how long the rogues are going to take rearming and repairing in Rashova."

"INCOMING TRANSMISSION... Receipt complete. Not a live channel."

Chan's clipped report cut through the molasses-like tension of the wait like a hot knife. Sylvia would never admit it to anyone, not even Henry, but she had a collection of ancient video games stored in her implants for these kinds of waits.

She'd spent a *lot* of time sitting and waiting in her career, and the simplified games originally made for mobile phones were relatively straightforward to play in a virtual window without anyone realizing what she was doing.

"What kind of message do we have, Commander Chan?" Sylvia asked, returning her attention to the task at hand. "Video?"

"Negative. Still processing on a standalone server, but does not appear to be video," the heavyset coms officer replied. "Raw numerical data. CIC is analyzing."

"It's a course," Henry told them. "Tell CIC to run Kenmiri translation protocol thirty-nine-tango-six. Scrub the result for malware, then forward to the main feed."

That took about twenty seconds, and then a green line appeared on the plot of the star system. From what Sylvia understood, it wasn't quite the course that the Flotilla had been planning on taking, but…

"Looks like they want us to stay at least fifty million kilometers from both Traste and Allamar," she said as the officers were still running through it. "But it's otherwise a direct course to Sixty-Six, right?"

"Yes," Henry confirmed. "But there's a secondary vector in here…"

"For their dreadnoughts," Chan told them. "Origin point is correct for the Kenmiri battle group; vector has them paralleling us at one million kilometers."

"With matched velocities, that's outside missile range," Eowyn said quickly. "They'll be shadowing us, but we won't be in range to fire on each other effectively."

"It's instructions, Commodore," Sylvia told Henry. "They're not going to directly communicate with us; they're not going to stoop that low yet.

"But if we follow this course, they'll escort us through the system and, hopefully, no one is going to shoot at us."

"It's a trap." Ihejirika jumped into the conversation, the destroyer's captain looking concerned. "If we follow their course, they could lay mines, they could have a second battle group, they could arrange all *kinds* of trouble."

"They could, yes," Henry agreed. He glanced over at Sylvia. "Your assessment, Ambassador?"

"We asked for terms for peaceful passage," she reminded them all. "They have provided those terms. I trust the Kenmiri as far as I can throw a dreadnought, and I don't work out much.

"But they have done what we asked. An escorted transit through a system with over three billion of their people and a major military-industrial complex *is* them being friendly."

"They have eight dreadnoughts, at least a hundred escorts and gunships, and an unknown number of orbital forts, Captain," the Commodore said calmly. "We are spectacularly outgunned here.

"If they wanted to fight us, they would have assembled a hammer and smashed us to pieces. Warriors are capable of deceit and subtlety, don't get me wrong, but unlike their Artisan cousins, they long ago mastered the KISS principle.

"They're not going to play games when they have the firepower to overwhelm us in a direct fight with few or no losses of their own."

He raised a hand before anyone replied.

"I am not saying that it *isn't* a trap," he admitted. "I am saying that it is unlikely to be a trap and that Ambassador Todorovich is correct. We asked for terms of safe passage. They've given them. If we weren't going to trust their terms, we should never have asked.

"Now, if there is to be any hope of any discussions and peaceful contact between the Ra and Osiris Sectors in the future, we *have* to honor the terms they have given.

"And conveniently, so long as they don't betray us, that gets the entire Flotilla on its way to Anderon without a fight."

"And if they do betray us, ser?" Ihejirika asked.

"'In difficult ground, press on. In encircled ground, devise stratagems. In death ground, fight.'"

Sylvia enjoyed the surprised look the officers all gave her.

"Diplomats, like military officers, must read their Sun Tzu and their Clausewitz," she told them. "If they betray us, we have to fight. But our best chance of getting through this without a fight is to follow instructions.

"Even if I really wish they'd actually talk to me."

She still wasn't surprised that the Kenmiri had gone straight to "peremptory command" as a method of diplomatic communication. Their previous experience with diplomacy was mostly limited to accepting surrenders, after all.

"Chan, package up the course and transmit it to the rest of the Flotilla," Henry ordered. "We do as we've been told. For now.

"But we make the trip with every sensor on full and every weapon charged. Our 'escort' is probably going to do the same. Today is an absolutely essential trust-building exercise—which means neither of us trusts the other one millimeter further than we absolutely have to."

22

HENRY KNEW, from close exposure and examination of a thousand Kenmiri buildings and artifacts, that no Artisan would *ever* make something plain and functional when they could make something baroque. If they couldn't get gold plating on something, they painted it. If they couldn't paint it or plate it, they sculpted it.

On the other hand, an Artisan would *also* rather die than make something that didn't work perfectly. The UPSF had learned the hard way not to underestimate Kenmiri systems just because they had gold-plated grotesques.

For all of that, he'd never been close to an undamaged Kenmiri dreadnought that was still in Kenmiri service. Not without being in active combat with it, at least. He'd been *told* they were high examples of the Artisan art, but every dreadnought he'd really *looked* at had either been captured or crippled.

The two dreadnoughts escorting the Forward Flotilla had settled in a million kilometers away and showed every sign of sticking with them for the entirety of the thirty-eight-hour-with-detour journey across Traste.

Dreadnoughts were forged from conveniently sized asteroids via laser boring and using plasma systems to melt the exterior. Even knowing the level of processing involved, part of Henry's brain still assumed "built from an asteroid" meant "still looked like an asteroid."

That part of his brain was very, *very* wrong.

The two warships were matched sisters, each nine hundred and fifty meters long and a third of that wide at their broadest. The original nickel-iron asteroid had been melted and smoothed to a fine polish before the external systems had been installed, each of the turrets and weapons ports equipped with its own shell of hyper-advanced ceramic armor.

The lines flowed smoothly into each other in a way that drew the eye directly to the fact that the heavy plasma-cannon turrets were each painted in an all-encompassing mural of a Kenmiri Warrior.

Decorative statues, grotesques, encircled the ports for the lasers and missile launchers. They were mostly animals from the ten thousand stars of the Kenmiri Empire. With a thousand habitable worlds' worth of ecosystems to draw on, the Kenmiri hadn't needed to bother with myth to find terrifying-looking creatures for their statues!

But the part that held Henry's attention as he watched their guard dogs shadow them was the vast expanses of armor. Presumably, there were heat-radiation elements built into those iron plains, but they had to have been incorporated into the art.

And *art* was the only word he could possibly use to describe the immense sweeping murals that covered every square meter of the dreadnoughts' hulls that wasn't taken up by turrets, sensor blisters and port hatches. These two ships, at least, were painted with vast landscapes—likely recreated at something around *actual size*—though Henry didn't recognize the planets in question.

They were baroque and overdone and gorgeous—and at ten million tons, they would have been the most powerful warships in the Kenmiri arsenal before the new superdreadnoughts were built.

"I suppose in space, there is no real *need* to paint our ships gray," he told Sylvia on their private channel. "Tradition! The European Union Extrasolar Security Force painted their ships gray, so the United Planets Space Force paints their ships gray!"

"The Novaya Imperiya painted them blue, I think?" Sylvia said with a chuckle. "Don't quote me on that. *Especially* in Epsilon Eridani, we treat the Imperiya as an old shame."

Much how post-WWII Germany had regarded the Nazis, as Henry understood it. The Russian Novaya Imperiya and the United States Colonial Administration had been the two major superpowers in human space, and their clash had triggered the Unity War.

Most accurately, the USCA had turned their battle with the Imperiya into a humanity-wide conflict when they'd seized the Chinese colony at Tau Ceti after the Chinese had refused to provide basing and supply assistance.

There was a reason the United Planets Alliance existed and held a monopoly on FTL warships. The Unity War had mostly stayed out of the Sol System itself, but it had been a near-run thing over eleven years of brutal fighting in the colonies.

"At least we didn't get the USCA paint pattern," Henry told her. "Have you *seen* that?"

"I vaguely recall something about a bird?"

Henry pulled up an image from the historical archive in his network. His great-grandfather had served in the United States Marine Corps when they'd found themselves becoming basically the USCA's private army. Much of Lei Wong's service had been aboard the destroyer *Piranha* and that was the image he shared with Sylvia now.

Piranha was tiny by modern standards, a bullet shape roughly seventy-five meters from bow to stern. Her stern was painted a black-and-silver star pattern, which was fine enough to Henry's eye, but her *prow* was painted with a bright golden eagle against the same black backdrop.

"I think that you won with the plain gray paint job, yes," Sylvia said after examining the image for a moment. "Though who knows? Maybe the Kenmiri would have respected us more if our warships had looked like that."

"I'm not sure that would have been worth it."

The Kenmiri were keeping to the one-million-kilometer line exactly. More exactly than he would have expected, really, given that they weren't *talking* to the Forward Flotilla. He supposed they knew the course that had been given to the Flotilla and were matching that, but it was still impressive ship handling.

Even if the silence was unnerving.

"We'll make our closest approach to Traste at fifty million kilometers in about two hours," he told Sylvia after a few moments' silence. "We don't get that close to Allamar. They appear to be twitchy about letting us near Traste-Four, let alone the moon."

"We *nuked* that moon, Henry," she reminded him. "I'd rather not get close enough for them to be overly reminded of that."

"Fair," he agreed. "We're picking up all the data we can. I'm sure IntelDiv will *salivate* over detailed scans of a Kenmiri Remnant main system."

"Today, I just want to get this fleet and the data we *already* carry through. I've done my part, though. I get to sit on my hands until we reach Anderon now."

Henry chuckled softly. "We hope, at least. Though I suppose if the Kenmiri decided to have an actual conversation before we skipped out, that would be a good thing."

IT WAS an eerie and intimidating day-and-a-half journey across what was technically an enemy system. The two dreadnoughts and their escorts maintained their silent vigil just outside weapons range, matching every acceleration and deceleration as the Forward Flotilla traveled through empty space.

The rest of the star system completely ignored them. In-system transit between the industrial platforms, the asteroid belts, Allamar and Traste carried on as if they weren't there. The only sign that the local civilian population knew the Forward Flotilla *existed* was that none of those ships approached within fifty million kilometers of Henry's command.

"Rendezvous with the skip line in fifteen minutes, ser," Ihejirika told Henry as he reentered the flag deck.

He'd been trying to sleep. Not very successfully—being in a hostile system wasn't conducive to sleeping easily—but he'd been trying.

Now they were into the final stretch. If the Kenmiri were going to pull a surprise out of their bag, it was now or never.

"All ships are at full battle stations and watching the Kenmiri like hawks," Eowyn reported. "I think the E-Two and La-Tar crews are finding this even more nerve-wracking than we are."

"They were Kenmiri slaves once," Henry said. "They never held any Terran systems for long."

Long enough that tens of thousands of humans had been shipped back into the Empire as slaves, but not long enough to impose their administration on any of the UPA's worlds. So far as Henry knew, every one of those victims had been retrieved by the end of the war.

But he knew that the former Kenmiri slaves had a *very* different attitude to the slaving insectoids than he did. The UPA wanted to make peace with the Kenmiri now and wait out their inevitable demographic annihilation.

The liberated people of the successor states were a *lot* angrier.

"Vector change on the dreadnoughts!" Eowyn snapped.

"Get me a lock on where they're going," Henry ordered. "Was this in the courses we were given?"

New energy signatures flared across his display as two-dozen-plus Kenmiri warships went from keeping pace with his ships to accelerating at full power.

"No," Chan replied. "The course they gave us for the dreadnoughts and their escorts ended an hour ago. We have no further information on their intentions."

"Eowyn?"

"They're breaking off," the ops officer reported after a few more seconds. "Opening the distance on a wide vector that looks like it will take them to Traste orbit."

"Sharpen your eyes," Henry ordered. "This *looks* good, but it could also be a trap."

"Permission to use active scanners?" Ihejirika asked.

"Granted. Chan, Eowyn, link up the whole Flotilla and pulse the *hell* out of that void in front of us."

That was impolite at best and hostile at worse, but he'd rather be rude than risk being ambushed—and whatever trust was present between him and the Kenmiri wasn't up to causing him to fly into the dark blind!

New icons and markers flashed across his tactical display in silence for several seconds.

"Sweep complete," Eowyn reported. "We are clear to the skip line. There's nothing in our path."

"Huh." Ihejirika sounded surprised. "They actually gave us safe passage. I...didn't expect that."

"I only gave it fifty-fifty chances myself," Henry admitted. "But we had to take the chance. We couldn't fight the fleet here."

"Ser, we just received a burst transmission from one of the dreadnoughts," Chan reported in a surprised tone. "It's addressed to you by name."

"Me?" Henry asked. "I'm not sure I like the fact that they know *I'm* aboard this ship."

"You *did* rub it in the Warriors' faces, ser," Eowyn reminded him. "Though I think we all assumed they weren't talking to the main Remnant at this point."

"Sanitize it and send it to my network," Henry ordered. "Let's see what they have to say."

A minute later, the file arrived in his internal network. It was a simple video file in the standard Kenmiri data format, and he activated it in a private virtual window.

The video was of what he guessed was the flag-deck equivalent on the dreadnought, an airy space with unnecessary buttresses and a mural of a Kenmorad Queen bestowing gifts on the back wall.

There were a dozen Warriors visible in the transmission, but the details of all but one had been blurred. So had any technology or displays that might have allowed Henry to make an assessment of the ship beyond what the sender wanted.

The only thing clearly visible was the Kenmiri Warrior in the center of the flag deck. They were seated cross-legged on an elevated circular chair, their elongated and carapaced torso looking surprisingly graceful in the odd-looking seat.

While the Kenmiri had much of the overall form of an Earth ant, they also had a very similar skeleton to the Ashall races underneath the surface carapace. The Warriors had *two* layers of carapace, the dull brown underlayer they shared with the Artisans and a thick black outer carapace that protected their vital organs and limbs from attack.

Warrior rank insignia was carved into their chest carapace, a series of ever-more-complicated lines inlaid in bright gold. This one was a Star Legate, the equivalent of Henry's own Commodore rank. The similarity to the Drifter Protector-Legate rank was obvious now that he knew about the links between the Drifters and the Kenmiri.

The Legate focused multifaceted eyes on the camera and crossed sharp-looking arms in front of themselves.

"I am Star Legate Amvash," they said in sharply accentuated Kem. "You are known to me, Commodore Henrywong."

The alien slurred Henry's name together into a single word, a common discourtesy on the part of Kenmiri dealing with other races. It wasn't that Kenmiri weren't capable of recognizing that other cultures used two names. It was that *Kenmorad* were the only people in Kenmiri culture who had two names—and the Kenmiri would never give anyone else that courtesy.

"My leaders have decided that you are to pass, despite your sins and the blood you have shed. We know your mission. My leaders would have us escort you without words, to keep a wall of silence between us.

"But while we have traversed my star system together, I have learned the fate of Rashova."

Amvash closed their eyes for several long seconds. Unlike Ashall, Henry couldn't read Kenmiri body language...but he could guess what that meant.

"I do not know what lies between our peoples in the future," they told him. "The blood of our parents cries out for justice.

"But I do know this. We of the Warriors were forged, born, and molded to stand guard. We were charged by gods and Kenmorad alike to protect the Ashall, not slaughter them.

"Tomorrow you and I may meet in battle, but today you sail to a duty we share and I cannot fulfill. May your blood guide you to victory!"

The message ended, and Henry stared blankly into space for a long time before Sylvia mentally poked him.

"I do believe, Ambassador, that the local Kenmiri commander may just have wished us good luck in finding and kicking the ever-loving shit out of their genocidal cousins," he told her. "I'm forwarding you the video.

"It might be the politest conversation I've ever had with a Kenmiri…and they were the only one talking!"

$$23$$

THE RUN from system to system, skip line to skip line, was beginning to wear on Henry's people. He didn't know how well his allied contingents were taking it—he was primarily interacting with the ship captains and the two detachment commanders—but he had a solid sense of how the UPSF crews were doing.

It showed in the readiness reports his captains were forwarding him. Daily maintenance was needed to keep the destroyers in top fighting condition, even without them getting into battles. Running at speed for days on end wasn't good for the starships, but they couldn't afford to go any slower.

Faster would have been better, but everything beyond half a KPS^2 would put subjective thrust on the crews—and the two logistics ships were fundamentally civilian. They were *Kenmiri*-style civilian, which meant they could match the UPSF destroyers for acceleration, but they didn't have the acceleration tanks that allowed the UPSF ships to push harder.

Henry gave his steward, Arthur Quaid, a thankful nod as the noncom laid a fresh coffee and a breakfast sandwich on his desk. They were almost at their emergence into Osiris-66, and he was *trying* to assess the mood of sixteen warships, only seven of which had to send him detailed reports.

"How is the stewarding team holding up with all of this, Arthur?" he asked Quaid before the man ducked back out of the office.

"Ser?"

"You're the Commodore's steward," Henry pointed out. "That inevitably means you're helping run the mess deck and the rest of the steward team. I don't think anyone on any ship sees more of the crew than the people feeding them."

"True enough, ser." Quaid was still standing, but he looked thoughtful. "Permission to speak freely?"

"Granted. It's not fair to ask that question without permission to speak."

"The crew is tired, ser," the steward told him. "We lost two-thirds of the squadron, took a few days off as we assembled the Flotilla, and then charged right back into the unknown. They understand the mission and its weight, but no one has had real leave since the ship commissioned.

"And this is a new ship."

"Which means we're finding all kinds of teething problems and maintenance is a nightmare," Henry filled in.

"Exactly, ser." Quaid shrugged. "I'm not sure what you want to know, ser. The crew saw a world die and they are *angry*. They're on mission and focused...but rumor has it the Chiefs broke up two fights yesterday."

That was news that wouldn't officially reach the Commodore's ears unless something had gone *very* bad. And yet it was something Henry needed to know. SpaceDiv's personnel were consummate professionals. *Brawling* was extremely out of character.

"Thank you." That confirmed what Henry already suspected. There wasn't much he could *do*, but he needed to know the limitations of the weapon he had to hand.

Quaid nodded and turned to leave, then paused.

"But, ser..."

Henry waited.

"The Kenmiri killed a world in front of this crew," Quaid reiterated.

"I think most of them understand that the bugs aren't one monolith anymore, but it still goes against the grain to play nice with *any* Kenmiri after what we saw in Rashova."

Henry nodded, keeping a calm mask as he took that in.

"Thank you," he repeated.

That was telling for the hope of any long-term peace, he feared. But the United Planets Alliance was still exhausted from the seventeen-year conflict against the Kenmiri. There was no appetite for a forever war to finish them off.

The soldiers wanted to liberate the Kenmiri's slaves, if not necessarily wipe out the Kenmiri themselves. And while Henry knew that the leaders of the UPA were sympathetic to that goal, there was limited political will for another decades-long war hundreds of light-years out of UPA space.

"WE ARE FORTY-FIVE MINUTES FROM EMERGENCE," Eowyn told Henry's staff meeting. "Osiris-Sixty-Six is a red giant star system with a thick asteroid belt and not much else. The line from Traste is inconveniently located related to anything else, and we will have over two days of transit through the system."

"Given the needs met when laying out this course, I'm surprised we haven't had more long-distance system crossings," Ihejirika observed.

Paladin's Captain and his executive officer, Aruna Giannino, were the other half of the meeting. Henry couldn't link to the other ships while in the skip line, but he could, at least, pull his two staff officers and *Paladin*'s senior command crew into a room to make plans.

No one was particularly surprised that Sylvia was also present. Henry would have included the senior diplomat even if they weren't in a relationship—after almost three years of working with each other, he trusted her judgment more than life itself.

"It could have been a lot worse," Henry agreed. "This kind of roundabout course can be a nightmare—and if we'd wanted to avoid

Kenmiri-controlled worlds, we'd have added another six or seven days to the journey.

"We are in the home stretch now," he continued. "Only one more system in the Osiris Sector before we're back in Ra—in space that I expect Anderon's military to patrol unless they've done something weird the last few years."

"Given that they are one of the closest inhabited systems to Kenmiri space, it seems very likely they have developed their military as rapidly and completely as they could," Sylvia said. "And given that Ra-Two-Oh-One is that connection to the Remnant…"

"They would be foolish to leave it unguarded. Though I have to wonder why the rogues hit Rashova instead of Anderon first," Giannino said. *Paladin*'s executive officer was a petite tanned-looking woman from the 70 Ophiuchi A System—simply "Ophiuchi" normally.

"Anderon is closer to an active Kenmiri colony world, but that might actually be why they didn't attack it first," Sylvia suggested. "As we have seen, it appears that while the Remnant isn't going to *stop* their rogues, they certainly don't *approve* of them."

"I think it may be simpler than that, in some ways," Eowyn noted. "The Golden Lancelot reports from Anderon note that our local allies staged an attack on the military shipyards as a distraction to clear the way for the bombardment force.

"Rashova could build dreadnoughts and, given warning, could become a powerful force for protecting the sector against the rogues. Anderon lost the ability to build capital ships and is, in some ways, a lesser threat."

"And Kori was enough newer of a colony that they may have never had dreadnought yards," Henry recalled aloud. "So, they hit the one place they *knew* they'd face capital ships first, expecting to deal with them in isolation."

Which was exactly what had happened. On the other hand…

"Admiral Rex has nine of our capital ships all told," he noted. "Assuming Anderon has any material defenses of her own to stand with us, the Kenmiri aren't going to enjoy their visit to their system.

"But that means we need to get the information about what we know and have seen *to* Admiral Rex. Chan, do we have a data package assembled to send drones to Twelfth Fleet via Anderon? Once we're in Sixty-Six, we will need to begin launching drones on a regular twelve-hour cycle to make sure Rex is updated when we meet him."

There was a long pause.

"I thought Commander Jackson's people were assembling that," Chan finally replied, their voice sheepish.

Henry concealed a moment of frustration and turned to Ihejirika.

"I don't suppose they were?" he asked.

He'd actually assumed that *both* communications departments would be assembling drone downloads as a matter of course. But since no drones had been sent or even planned to be sent for the last week, he supposed it wasn't a surprise that had dropped off the list.

"We have a skeleton of one, I believe," Ihejirika said slowly. "But, no, I don't think we have a full download ready for transmission."

Henry knew that, to Sylvia at least, his desire to roll his eyes was probably obvious. Still, he refrained from any blatantly condemnatory words or gestures.

Praise in public, teach in private was the mantra of good officers for a reason.

"Chan, coordinate with Commander Jackson and get a full telemetry download ready," he ordered. "We'll fire it off to Admiral Rex as soon as you're finished, and then resume a standard cycle.

"We may not get all of the drones through. These aren't systems that we mapped for drone transit, and the Anderon defense forces may well shoot down our drones, not knowing what they are."

He shook his head.

"Sylvia, do we have any protocol we could potentially use to send drones to Anderon? I'd *like* them to at least know we're coming."

"Unfortunately, no," she admitted. "If there are any active Vesheron groups in the system, they weren't there by the Great Gathering. There was minimal contact from any of the three Kenmiri colonies in the Ra Sector before we lost the network."

"That's what I was afraid of," Henry said. "We'll send our messages to Rex, and we will send a drone to Anderon with standard Vesheron com protocols. They may not be able to read them, but it's our best bet short of sending a drone that's transmitting in the open."

And if they did that, everyone in the systems on their route would be able to access the drone and download its contents. That was far from ideal when Henry *knew* that the rogue Warriors were supported by at least some Kenmiri in the Remnant.

They hadn't built a new fleet of superdreadnoughts on their own, after all.

24

HENRY WATCHED the two skip drones blaze away on pillars of fusion fire. At ten times the acceleration the Forward Flotilla could manage, the robotic spacecraft would reach their destination far sooner than Henry's little fleet.

The download package for Admiral Rex had taken time to assemble, but it was at least a standard item. The drone for Anderon was more complicated in many ways. Henry didn't want to hand over his complete sensor data to a *potential* ally, but they'd sent a recorded warning from Sylvia on ahead.

Now it was a question of waiting. Outside of a pair of escorts patrolling the skip line from Traste—who had acted like the Forward Flotilla wasn't even there, though they *had* made sure to never enter missile range—Osiris-66 was empty. There wasn't enough there to really be worth investing in habitats—especially when Traste, the most likely system to do any exploiting, had multiple asteroid belts of its own to exploit.

"Forty-two hours left," Eowyn muttered. "In a system without even anything entertaining to look at."

"A system with *five* skip lines," Henry reminded her. "So, we'll want to keep an eye on those, even if they aren't particularly 'entertaining.'"

"We've got two full ships' tactical teams watching each of the skip lines, ser," she said. "I'm running oversight with my own people and *Paladin*'s tactical team. If any of those skip lines *hiccups*, you'll know."

"We shouldn't see anything coming from Traste," Henry noted, studying the map. "It's Vosha I'd be watching."

Vosha was one of the Kenmiri slave agricultural worlds, the centerpiece of a cluster that their route took them past. They were one short skip from Vosha in Osiris-66—though the skip line was even farther from *Paladin* than the one to Osiris-65—and would be a single skip from Olat, one of the cluster's industrial worlds, when they were in Osiris-65.

At least this time, Henry wasn't going to be in the same *system* as the slave planets and have to consciously walk away from millions of innocents trapped in forced labor.

"Speaking of Vosha," Eowyn said softly, "we have contacts emerging from the skip line. Time delay is about sixty-five minutes."

"I told you this system wouldn't be boring," Henry replied. "What have we got?"

"I've got other ships adding to *Fronds of Will*'s scans to increase resolution, but it looks like about thirty ships moving at point-five KPS-squared. CIC and I are both calling it a civilian transport convoy."

"Running from Vosha to the Osiris-Sixty-Five skip line, I'm guessing?" Henry asked.

"Looks like, ser," she confirmed. "They'll hit the skip line about twelve hours before we do. We won't even be close to them."

"Keep an eye on them anyway. We don't want to make the mistake of *assuming* someone isn't a threat." Henry eyed the data filling in on the feed. "We certainly have enough allies using ships with freighter hulls and freighter engines as warships."

La-Tar wasn't likely to send their refitted freighters outside their own territory, especially now that they *had* enough proper escorts and gunships to send. The crude carriers and arsenal ships that had been the Cluster's interim fleet would probably be decommissioned in short order, Henry suspected, but they'd bought peace of mind at a critical juncture.

And at sixty-five light-minutes, he wouldn't trust *anyone* to be able to tell the difference between those ships and an unarmed freighter.

THE LAST THING Henry did before he went to sleep was check on the location of the Kenmiri ships in the system. The first thing he did when he woke up was the same thing, confirming that the watch squadron at the Traste line was still behind them and that the civilian convoy was still en route to Osiris-65.

Everything was where he expected it to be. The Flotilla still had twenty-four hours in the star system, and the transport convoy, following its own route, would hit the skip line in just under twelve hours.

"You know, you could at least *pretend* I'm more interesting than your network feed," Sylvia teased him, letting the blanket slide aside as she stretched.

"You are significantly more pleasant to look at, yes," he told her, taking a moment to very obviously look her over. "But your breasts are also less likely to get my people killed if I don't look at them immediately."

"Oh, I know." She smiled sleepily at him. "I have a lot fewer active tasks in front of me right now than you. Once we are in Anderon, I will be just as undistractable as you."

"I keep expecting another shoe to drop," he admitted. "Whether it's one of our allies deciding they have different priorities than us or… Well…"

"The Kenmiri."

"The Kenmiri. We've detected a lot less in terms of subspace communications than I was expecting, but they're definitely getting news around anyway. Legate Amvash knew about Rashova.

"Which means that the rogue fleet knows about *us*. It seems that they lack the support in the Remnant to pursue us at full speed, but once we are into Sixty-Five…we are into stars where they could have sent someone ahead of us merely by bypassing Anderon."

"And if they did, you'll handle it," Sylvia told him, reaching out to grip his arm. "We knew the job sucked when we took it."

"We *created* the job. Without us, there wouldn't *be* a Peacekeeper Initiative and we wouldn't be involved in this war."

Henry was *pretty* sure the Ra Sector was better off for the existence of the Initiative. Without them, the La-Tar Cluster would be under Kozun control, the Kozun wouldn't have been reined in, and the Drifters would still be occupied by the Kenmiri.

And the rogue Kenmiri Remnant would *still* be rampaging through the Ra Sector, with no one coordinating any alliance or resistance against them.

"We created the job, but somebody had to do it," Sylvia told him. "We couldn't help wreck the galaxy and then do nothing to deal with the rubble. Not morally, anyway."

Henry covered her hand with his own and squeezed.

"We created the job and we took the job and we knew the job would suck all along," he agreed. "But if the game was easy, they wouldn't need the best. They could have sent anyone."

"But they had to send us." She layered her other hand on top of his and squeezed tightly. "And we are not going to screw this up, Henry. We couldn't save Rashova…but we can damn well save the rest of the Sector!"

"We can," he agreed. "And those Warriors are never going to know what hit them."

HENRY HAD WATCHED MORE Kenmiri convoys than he could easily count. Usually, his watching had come with malicious intent, even if it was only to provide information and intelligence about what was going on.

But the UPSF's first incursions into the Kenmiri Empire had been scouting missions turned commerce raids. It hadn't been until well after humanity had encountered the Vesheron that more complex and long-term objectives had become available.

Which meant that Henry had participated in the destruction of a lot of convoys just like the one now calmly entering the skip line to Osiris-65. It had been his second-least-favorite part of the war, and there were few parts of the nearly two-decade-long conflict he'd call *pleasant memories*.

Now he'd seen two active Kenmiri convoys in the last few days, each full of Artisans and Drones just…doing their jobs. And he'd been able to let them go. It was easier to swallow that than it had been to be in a slave-world system and just leave.

Of course, there were slaves on those transports. Favored slaves, ones trusted with technical training and access to high-tech systems, but slaves nonetheless. The crews of transports like those had been the main source of Vesheron recruitment since long before humanity had become involved in Kenmiri affairs.

"All ships in the convoy have transited," Eowyn reported. "There is nothing on screen. We can barely pick up the guard ships at the Traste line at this point."

They'd traveled two and a half light-hours in roughly thirty-four hours—and there was another half-light-hour left between them and their destination. In reality, the Kenmiri convoy had transited half an hour earlier.

The transports would still be in the skip line when Henry and his people entered it, but if Henry read the maps correctly, they'd not only be out of the skip line in Osiris-65 but also be at the skip line to Olat when the Forward Flotilla emerged.

That transit was shorter than the one to the Ra-201 skip line. With speed-of-light delays, there was a good chance that the convoy would never even see the Forward Flotilla arrive in the next system.

"They were no threat to us, and we had no reason to threaten them," Henry murmured. He chuckled. "Of course, without Defender Falling Rain's starfighters, we would have been hard-pressed to reach them."

"Forty-eight hours until we're out of Kenmiri space," Eowyn observed. "I don't know about you, ser, but I think most of the crews are going to be *very* relieved to enter the skip line out of Osiris-Sixty-Five."

"It'll take some stress off."

Henry wasn't going to admit aloud that he didn't think he'd be able to manage *relief* until the rogue Warrior fleet was debris and prisoners.

25

THE OTHER SHOE that Henry had been dreading since they'd outrun their pursuit in Ra-152 dropped the moment they entered Osiris-65.

"We have contacts in multiple positions across the system, and we have weapons fire," Eowyn reported crisply as the data started flowing in. "Convoy appears to have aborted their run for Olat and split into two segments. They used their base velocity to break free of their attackers but have looped enough to make their courses clear.

"One is headed back to Osiris-Sixty-Six; one is heading to Ra-Two-Oh-One."

"They've got to be desperate if they're heading into the Ra Sector," Henry noted. "We're pretty sure there's Anderon warships in Ra-Two-Oh-One, though I imagine they stick close to the skip line home.

"What's driving the scatter?"

"We've got what looks like a dreadnought battle group with reinforced escorts. There are twelve escorts pursuing the convoy fragment headed for Ra-Two-Oh-One, and ten plus the dreadnought heading our way in pursuit of about half the survivors."

Less than half of the original convoy, Henry realized as he looked at the data. They'd identified thirty-two freighters and five escorts in the convoy before it had skipped from Osiris-66. There were fourteen transports running toward the Forward Flotilla and eleven running for Ra.

Neither group had *any* escorts left, and Henry didn't need to check the scan data for the weapon traces to know what had happened to them. The freighters had managed to spot their attackers before they'd entered range, but their existing velocity and relatively low acceleration had doomed them.

No one would *ever* say Kenmiri Warriors weren't brave. The escorts would have charged, trying to force the enemy to fire on *them* instead of the transports, buying time for the convoy to reverse course and scatter to avoid the enemy.

Seven freighters hadn't made it out of weapons range, but the rest had. But the escorts the attackers had deployed were slowly but surely gaining on both groups—and the dreadnought was ignoring *both* convoy chunks and heading toward the Osiris-66 skip line.

Until Henry and his people had arrived, that would have the dreadnought in position to prevent the convoy escaping back the way they'd arrived and running for Traste's security. The ships were slow enough that they never would have made it, but a dreadnought sitting on the skip line was going to guarantee the capture or destruction of the convoy.

Except now that dreadnought was heading directly toward Henry's Forward Flotilla, with her smaller siblings scattered across the star system chasing Kenmiri transports.

"Command conference, Commander Chan," Henry ordered. "Get me Azan, Rain and Todorovich."

"Defender Falling Rain is already on the call, ser," his coms officer replied. "I'll have Azan and the Ambassador for you in a moment."

"Understood. Linking in."

The virtual conference room exploded into "existence" around Henry—as did a cavernous toothy maw that for a moment was about to close around him. His heart rate spiked—but he managed to access his controls and adjust the scaling glitch before he did or said anything embarrassing.

He hoped.

Enteni were discomfiting at normal size. At *five times* regular size, it was impossible not to find the carnivorous plants utterly terrifying.

"Is-are you unwell, Commodore?" Falling Rain asked. The translated Kem emerging from their vocoder was unable to carry concern, but their words worked well enough.

"Systems glitch," Henry explained, running through a mental exercise to calm his racing heart. "Apologies."

"Unnecessary."

Tol Azan and Sylvia Todorovich appeared around the virtual table before they could say more, and Henry gratefully focused on the task at hand.

He was going to have to talk to Chan about that glitch. The last thing he needed to start critical conferences was feeling that he was Falling Rain's current snack!

"We have a situation," he told them once everyone was online and he'd calmed from his unexpected surprise. A gesture brought a three-dimensional version of the tactical plot he'd been examining.

"We knew we were following a Kenmiri transport convoy in Osiris-Sixty-Five, but by all standard references, they should have been skipping toward the Olat System around the same moment we arrived.

"Instead, they've split into two groups and are attempting to avoid a hostile force that is hunting them down. While a number of ships have been destroyed, I would *guess* at this point the pursuers are attempting to capture them.

"Our most immediate concern, however, is this dreadnought." Henry highlighted it with a thought and checked the datafile that came up.

"She masses eight million tons and is headed our way. We have not determined who she belongs to, but she is big, nasty and going to be in weapons range of us in about seventy-five minutes."

"We can evade her, though," Tol Azan pointed out. "Side vector and then swing around to our target exit line. Without knowing who is attacking the Kenmiri, I do not see why we should become involved."

"I must-will agree," Falling Rain said. "This is-was not our fight. Our crews can-will not fight to protect Kenmiri."

"The only reason that I am considering doing anything is that we all know there are slaves on those transports," Henry pointed out. "Plus, that convoy left an agricultural world and is headed for an industrial world."

He let that sink in—especially to Tol Azan, who'd been born on an industrial world. The Kozun *knew* how critical those food shipments were.

"While the destination world will probably survive the loss of this convoy, it will cause undue suffering. Believe me," Henry said flatly, "*I know.*"

He had vivid memories of visiting industrial worlds during the Kozun blockades of the La-Tar Cluster...*and* after UPSF commerce raiding had cut the food supply in earlier times.

"Without information, it is risky for us to get involved," Sylvia noted. "Certainly, if the dreadnought belongs to some new iteration of the Vesheron, we do not want to protect the convoy.

"On the other hand, if this is some internal conflict of the Kenmiri, rescuing the convoy may buy us goodwill we can use in the future."

Not my monkeys, not my circus, Henry reminded himself. He had dark memories about convoy raiding, and part of him wanted to save *any* civilians, no matter who they were, from attack.

"We will vector away," he decided aloud. "Evade the dreadnought and make our course for the Ra-Two-Oh-One skip line.

"Make sure your communications links are solid and keep your eyes and ears open," he continued. "We want to avoid committing ourselves to anything, but it may yet prove necessary for us to get involved.

"Can we trust your crews to follow that order if it is given?"

"They will-are-be angry," Falling Rain told him instantly. "But you have-will forever earned the trust of my crews. We will strike if you ask it of us."

"My people are tired and angry and hate the Kenmiri more than you can possibly imagine," Tol Azan said slowly. "But the same history that drives that hatred warns me who will suffer from this. My people will leave any Kenmiri to die without question, Commodore Wong, but if you ask it of us, I believe I can convince them to fight."

"The course will be forthcoming from my staff," Henry promised.

"The Kenmiri have not seen us yet, either group. Let us see what happens when they do!"

THE ORDERS FLOWED and Henry's ships began accelerating "sideways"—not quite toward their final destination of the skip line to Ra-201 but definitely *away* from the approaching dreadnought.

The dreadnought was the closest of the five collections of ships in play, just over a light-minute from where the Forward Flotilla had emerged from the skip line, and was continuing its deceleration toward them.

The convoy ships fleeing toward the skip line to Osiris-66 were making the best of a bad position, but they were still a light-minute away themselves and had no chance of reaching the skip line before the dreadnought.

They'd managed, *barely*, to stay out of missile range of the escorts pursuing them, but even that was going to end before they escaped. Their only real hope, Henry knew, was for the attackers to try to capture them.

Then, they might get *some* of the ships through the skip line to safety. Maybe. Most likely, each escort would capture a ship, then the dreadnought would catch or destroy anything that made it past them.

The ships heading for Ra-201 were using enough of their original velocity toward Olat that they had a slightly better chance—but their pursuers also had enough hulls to catch all of them. *Their* best chance was to make it to the skip line and discover that Anderon had a battle group right on the other side.

Henry assumed that the Anderon defenders had ships in the Ra-201 System, but he doubted that they were right at the entrance. There was no part of the convoy that wasn't doomed.

"Well, everyone on this side of the system has seen us now," Eowyn told him. "We're seeing the light from their reaction to us, even."

For the few moments after light completed its round trip between the two groups of ships, nothing changed. The convoy continued the curve backward from their original flight, aiming to come into the skip line at an oblique angle. The dreadnought was still on course to cut them off, and the escorts were still pursuing them.

"Ser, we're receiving a transmission. Wait, no…make that *multiple* transmissions," Chan reported. "One from the dreadnought, one from the convoy."

"Interesting," Henry murmured. "Loop the Ambassador in and play them in sequence, Commander."

"Transmission from the dreadnought is audio-only," the coms officer replied. "It also *did* carry combat malware, but we have sanitized it."

"Well, that does suggest their opinion of us," Henry noted, checking to make sure he had Sylvia in the loop. "Play it for us."

"Terran vessels." The voice spoke with the hyper-accentuated Kem of a Kenmiri Warrior. "This matter is none of your concern. You do not belong in this star system. Any attempt to interfere will be met with your destruction."

"That's clear enough," Sylvia said. "It does tell us that the dreadnought isn't Vesheron or otherwise a rebel vessel, though. Does that impact your plans, Henry?"

"Maybe," he conceded. "Most likely, though, I'm willing to let the Kenmiri kill each other.

"Chan, play us the message from the convoy."

That one was a video, a feed showing one of the extremely standardized bridges of a Kenmiri transport. Like the escort-type warships, Kenmiri freighters were built in their tens of thousands across the industrial worlds of the Empire. The ones that ended up in the hands of Artisans were rapidly decorated and updated, but the *bones* of the standard dozen or so designs were all identical.

The focus of the camera was a Kenmiri Artisan, the human-height antlike worker caste of the Kenmiri. This Artisan had a bright red carapace over their dull underlayer, glittering in the lights of their starship and reflecting the bronze plating around them.

There were two other Artisans on the bridge, but the rest of the crew were the more delicately built Drones, with their iridescent blue-green carapace-like skin. The Drones lacked the heavy outer carapaces of the Warriors and Artisans, though their skin was tougher than the underlayer of the two "elder" castes.

"United Planets Alliance and allied warships," the Artisan said, their Kem smooth and formal. "I must assume that you believe the situation you see before you is irrelevant to you. That the internal warfare of the Kenmiri is a boon to your conflict against Vengeance Fleet.

"You would be wrong. I am Kakat of the Kenmiri Artisans, and the ships that pursue my convoy serve the Vengeance Fleet. They entered this system from the old province of Ra and laid an ambush for the supply convoy headed to Olat.

"Their desire is to use the food, fuel and medical supplies aboard my convoy to resupply and support the Vengeance Fleet itself. We share a mutual enemy. I wish to preserve my convoy and my fellow Kenmiri from capture or destruction. You will wish to prevent the Vengeance Fleet from acquiring new supplies to support their campaign in the old provinces."

Kakat spread their pincers wide in what Henry suspected was as much a gesture of helplessness in Kenmiri as in humans.

"I will beg or grovel or plead as you demand," they said. "Five hundred irreplaceable Kenmiri lives have ended already today. Over a thousand remain in my care and I cannot save them. I cannot save those who will risk starvation if our cargo does not arrive.

"I cannot save anyone from the Vengeance Fleet, here or in the old province. You can. *Help us.*"

The video froze as it ended, and Henry looked at the tiny image of Sylvia in his network displays.

"That changes…a lot," she guessed.

"If we can believe this Kakat," he noted. Part of him didn't want to. If the dreadnought and her escorts were Vengeance Fleet—apparently the Kenmiri name for the rogue Remnant faction attacking the Ra Sector—he had *every* reason to engage them, regardless of whether they were going after civilians.

If they were trying to steal supplies, he had even more reason to attack. Kakat knew all the right levers to pull to get Henry Wong to save them. Enough that it was suspicious—except that it also made *sense*.

More than anything else, Vengeance Fleet would need food and fuel. They could refine fuel from any gas giant, and they could fabricate most spare parts given a nickel-iron asteroid or six, but they couldn't grow food. Recycling only went so far, and Henry had never met a race that liked to think about what recycled ration bars were made of.

Not getting the supplies on the convoy wouldn't stop Vengeance Fleet. It might not even *slow* Vengeance Fleet—but getting those supplies would sharpen the rogue Warriors' edge. Any weakness he could inflict on Vengeance Fleet would be worth it when the clash of titans arrived.

"Ser, we have a problem," Chan suddenly interrupted his thoughts. "The dreadnought transmission was wide-focus; the entire Flotilla picked it up."

"And?" Henry asked. "We all know what we're—"

"The malware, ser," his coms officer snapped. "*We* sanitize every transmission through standalone servers. We identified the malware and neutralized it without any issues. The La-Tar Cluster built their doctrine on *Vesheron* doctrine. And the Vesheron learned not to trust Kenmiri transmissions a *long* time ago, so their process resembles ours. But..."

"The Eerdish and Enteni," Sylvia whispered. "They had few Vesheron to learn from and had to build everything up from scratch."

Scarlet alerts flashed across the icons of Henry's allied ships as he triggered a full update of the main plot. None of the six E-Two warships or the E-Two supply ship likely even had the right kind of air-gapped systems to sanitize hostile transmissions.

And all seven had lost shields. Engines. Sensors.

"That dreadnought isn't decelerating anymore, is she?" Henry asked calmly.

"She's still maintaining her course," Eowyn reported. "But the escorts have abandoned the closer convoy detachment and are coming to back her up at one-point-two KPS-squared.

"They'll reach their missile range of us in approximately sixty-two minutes. If neither of us adjusts course, the dreadnought will *not* range on us at any point, but we can assume she'll adjust course to drop missiles on us at about the same time frame."

"Understood," Henry said. "Do we have a link to Falling Rain?"

"Negative," Chan reported. "*Fronds of Will*'s computer systems are completely down. I would guess the E-Two ships will need to reboot from hourly backups."

Henry swallowed a curse.

"Cut the Flotilla's acceleration," he ordered. "All ships match velocity with the E-Two."

The Kenmiri knew *exactly* how to pin him in place. They might not have counted on their malware taking out half of Henry's force, however temporarily, but they knew he wouldn't abandon any of his allies without a fight.

"What do we do, ser?" Eowyn asked.

The entire situation had changed in a few seconds, partially because of the realization of the true nature of what they were looking at—but mostly because his allies had a lesser level of cybersecurity than his own ships.

"Get me Tol Azan," he ordered.

The Kozun clearly had expected the link, as Chan had him on the channel before Henry finished speaking.

"Squadron Leader," he greeted Azan in Kem. "You saw both transmissions. Our E-Two friends did not have the same experience your Vesheron advisors did with Kenmiri traps. They are temporarily disabled and we do not know how long it will take to get them back online."

The Kenmiri had held their computer technology more closely than anything except Kenmorad biological sciences. That was why none of the Vesheron would ever trust the same level of network implantation as was normal in the UPA—their computer hardware was Kenmiri, and the Artisans had always been able to make it do things the users hadn't expected.

"What do we do, Commodore?" Tol Azan asked. "The situation is more complicated than I expected. I know my ships cannot take a dreadnought."

"Mine can," Henry said quietly. *"Bringer of Cloths* will remain with the E-Two ships. Your escorts will form up behind my destroyers and follow us in a full-thrust counterstrike. We will reach the dreadnought before the escorts can intervene."

"It feels wrong to save Kenmiri," Azan noted. "But not in the slightest to save our friends. La-Tar is with you!"

Henry nodded and turned to Chan and Eowyn.

"Orders to the squadron," he told them. "All hands to the acceleration tanks and prepare for full thrust. We're done running."

26

PALADIN WAS EQUIPPED with acceleration tanks, which was potentially one of the more ridiculous recent feats of conservatism in warship design in Henry's opinion. They took up mass and volume that could have been used for missiles—and the GMS left the ship in permanent free fall, requiring internal systems to provide gravity for the crew.

The *Significance-* and *Tyrannosaur*-class ships that made up the rest of the squadron needed the gel tanks, though. Their engines were rated for a full KPS^2 of acceleration, but their inertial dampeners were still far short of the Kenmiri standard.

At their full acceleration, the crews of the older destroyers were subjected to about twenty gravities of thrust. Without the acceleration tanks, most of the crew would die under that pressure.

But the differing development paths of Terran versus Kenmiri gravitic technology meant that TechDiv had been forced to choose between better inertial compensators or the gravity shield.

And the UPSF had chosen the grav-shield every time that choice had come up.

"Dreadnought is turning to meet us," Eowyn reported.

"Someone is more confident in his ship than I would be." Henry checked the numbers. Thirty-two minutes to missile range. Roughly five minutes after that to extreme laser range.

Unfortunately, *effective* range for his lasers and the Kenmiri's plasma cannon was much the same. Theoretically, the lasers on his destroyers could hit at seven hundred and fifty thousand kilometers, and the plasma cannon were limited to six hundred thousand.

Lightspeed delays meant that he had a five-second round trip for laser fire at maximum range. His experience was that anything above four seconds rendered hit likelihoods negligible. Plasma cannon had a similar problem and were enough slower that they had a four-and-a-half-second control loop at two light-seconds.

But if he slowed to extend the time in missile range, he increased the chance that he'd have to fight the dreadnought and her escorts at the same time. The Forward Flotilla needed to kill the dreadnought and *fast*.

And without a battlecruiser and her grav-driver or the massed alpha strike of a fighter group's missiles, that meant lasers.

"Escorts are still heading toward us. They're not on a direct line with us, so net accel is just one and a half KPS squared," Eowyn continued. "They're pushing one-point-two. How long can they hold that up?"

"If their engineers have done their jobs, they won't even start burning out the inside of their thruster nozzles until they hit one-point-three," Henry observed.

"And if their engineers are Artisans, they've done their jobs," Sylvia suggested. "But if they're short on Artisans…"

"The escorts may have problems. They'll have focused their Artisan engineers on the engines and weapons of the dreadnoughts and super-dreadnoughts." There was no way for Henry to confirm who was aboard the oncoming escorts and dreadnought, though.

They'd seen evidence of Warrior tunnel vision where he would have expected Artisan competence before. But he couldn't assume that was an omnipresent issue for Vengeance Fleet.

"The dreadnought's commander thinks they can take us," Henry told Sylvia. "I think they're very, very, wrong."

"And we find out who's right in about thirty minutes, I suppose," she replied. "This is your field, not mine, Henry. Good luck."

Henry smiled thinly, updating his tactical feeds to check on the status of the eleven ships he was leading into the teeth of the enemy.

"I hope we won't need it, but I will *definitely* take it."

THERE HAD STILL BEEN no updates from the E-Two contingent thirty minutes later, as the distances and timers on Henry's feeds counted down toward missile range. He'd organized his ships into a rough box, larger in the front where his seven grav-shielded ships led the way and smaller in the back with the four La-Tar escorts.

Part of him wanted to leave the escorts behind, but he couldn't. What their shorter range and lighter defenses bought was dramatically more firepower than his destroyers. Tol Azan's four escorts had almost as many lasers and *more* missiles than his seven UPSF destroyers.

The destroyers were far more survivable and longer-ranged, and had larger magazines, but he *needed* the escorts' missile launchers and lasers.

But since he didn't want to have to go back to La-Tar and admit to Arbiter Casto Ran that he'd managed to lose the four ships and thousand or so people the La-Tar leader had lent him, he was going to keep them behind his destroyers.

Paladin's shields were the strongest, but even the *Tyrannosaur*s were tougher than anything their size had any right to be. And that was what Henry's entire plan was hanging on. With comparable tech, destroyers and escorts had no business fighting dreadnoughts, even with a five-to-four tonnage advantage.

"Missile range," Eowyn reporting. "Holding until...escorts in range. All ships firing."

The extra hundred thousand kilometers of distance would *hopefully* protect the escorts. They had half of the launchers in the suddenly reduced Forward Flotilla, after all.

"Five seconds till we see their launch."

The closing speed of the dreadnought vastly extended the usual range of the missiles to over ten light-seconds. That meant the missiles would be in space for all of those ten seconds before the Forward Flotilla got them on scanners.

"Confirmed," Bach reported on the bridge. "Estimate five-five, fifty-five, missiles inbound."

"Eowyn, keep the telemetry links up and shared across the destroyer squadron," Henry ordered. "We can handle that, but we can't afford leakers."

"On it. We're coordinating grav-shield sweeper passes."

That meant the destroyers would intentionally interpose their shields between the incoming missiles and the La-Tar escorts. It was a risk—the odds of any given missile burning through a grav-shield were low, but *every* missile had that chance.

With the missile salvos in space, this part of the battle came down to orbital mechanics and luck. The Flotilla launched their second salvo thirty seconds later. Then a third.

"Flag further salvos for defense," Henry ordered quietly. "We'll be in laser and cannon range by the time the third salvo hits. One way or another, a fourth salvo won't make a difference."

This was where one of the few differences in Terran versus Kenmiri missiles came up. Basically *everyone* that had fought in the war had ended up standardizing around very similar missiles and missile launchers—thousand KPS from the launcher, ten KPS^2 acceleration for five minutes, modular, easily swapped warheads.

The UPSF's missiles, though, had a noticeably greater maneuverability. Not acceleration but the ability to adjust the *direction* of their acceleration. The primary purpose of a weapon with a five-hundred-megaton shaped-charge fusion warhead was to kill starships—but the UPSF had at least *thought* about the counter-missile use case.

It had been a small but distinct advantage through the war. Even when Vesheron and Kenmiri ships turned their missiles to the defensive role, their missiles weren't quite as *good* at it.

Which made it one hell of a surprise when the second salvo from the Kenmiri dreadnought swerved in space and dove in on the lead allied missiles. Massive warheads rigged for extra electromagnetic pulse and radiation effects tore through the Flotilla's salvo.

Fifty-five missiles against a hundred and fifty wasn't a winning match, but the Kenmiri counter missiles took out more than half of the incoming fire.

"That's new," Henry said grimly. "Eowyn?"

"Downloading counter-counter-missile protocols to our missiles," she replied instantly. "The warheads are new, and CIC is analyzing the missiles."

Defensive laser fire now reached out from the dreadnought and Henry's own fleet. The Kenmiri had only launched one offensive salvo, he realized, and their later missiles were tearing into his with far more success than he'd expected.

"Watch for surprises in their missiles," he ordered. "Scan for resonance and penetrator warheads, people."

They had no evidence that the Kenmiri had *either* of those anti-shield systems. But resonance warheads could shut down gravity shields—and the penetrator warheads in Henry's own magazines would use a miniaturized skip drive to *bypass* the shield.

The UPSF had developed a way to defeat their own defenses within months of rolling them out, after all.

"I'm not detecting anything suggesting resonance or penetrator warheads," Eowyn reported after a few moments. "But— *Fuck.*"

That wasn't an overly professional report, but Henry couldn't blame her. Most of the Kenmiri missiles had been destroyed, but a dozen or so reached the inner defense perimeter. They were unlikely to even reach any of his people's shields—destroyers were *very* good at shooting down missiles—but they were within a hundred thousand kilometers of his ships.

And half of the missiles had just exploded into the most ridiculous jamming he'd ever seen. High-powered blasts of electromagnetic radiation swept the path of the incoming fire, confusing the defensive scanners at a critical moment.

Henry held his tongue, barely managing to keep from issuing useless orders. His captains and tactical officers knew their jobs, knew the job ahead of them, and he nodded approvingly as they reacquired the missiles with impressive speed.

But the jamming explosion made the difference between *none* of the last dozen missiles making it through and *one* missile making it through.

And that missile was a plasma web that exploded out from its casing to try to wrap around *Dilophosaurus*. The same system that had devastated the Shieldwings in Ra-78 slammed into the gravity shield of a full-size ship.

Henry actively held his breath as he waited for the report. He *hoped* that the antifighter system was too small to break through a starship shield, but he couldn't be certain.

"*Dilophosaurus* reports multiple minor blowthroughs and hits," Chan told him. "Plasma fragments along the hull but no critical damage."

"Understood," Henry acknowledged.

That was both worse than he'd hoped and better than he'd feared. The web was widespread enough that it made it more likely for *something* to get through the gravity shield and hit the ship at the center—but it wasn't large enough to get an intact *web* through the shield, and the fragments that were striking *Dilophosaurus*'s armor weren't enough.

"Laser range in five seconds," Eowyn said sharply.

"All ships fire as they bear."

It wasn't a necessary order…but it was also somewhat traditional, and there was a limit to how much Henry could sit on his hands in a battle.

Paladin had edged a few kilometers ahead of the rest of the destroyers and she fired first, two beams of coherent light flashing across the void. Neither hit, but that wasn't truly a surprise.

More beams joined the first before the reports on their results made it back to *Paladin*. Return fire flickered across Henry's display, but the Kenmiri lasers were no more accurate than the UPSF's beams at this range.

"Plasma fire detected."

The plasma-cannon bursts traveled enough slower than light to be seen before impact—and fast enough that it was almost impossible to dodge them based on that data. Eight plasma cannon and twenty heavy lasers lashed at Henry's fleet—which returned the favor with eighteen lasers of their own at first, then over thirty once the escorts entered range.

Gravity shields shrugged aside beams and plasma bursts—but so did the dreadnought's energy screen. Accuracy improved as the range dropped and more beams connected with the dreadnought.

"Break, dammit," Henry whispered. The energy screen *should* have been breached by now. The warships of Vengeance Fleet had clearly picked up every possible upgrade they could think of in the last four years.

The rogue Warriors might be acting against the desires of the Remnant's theoretical rulers, but they'd certainly had no problems acquiring the latest and best technology available!

Then the last stragglers of the Forward Flotilla's third missile salvo arrived. Henry had thrown over four hundred missiles at the dreadnought, but the unexpected efficiency of their missiles in defensive mode and the expected efficiency of their close-range defenses had shredded the vast majority of them.

But six missiles arrived as the laser duel continued, diving past the distracted defenses and detonating their warheads. Six immense plasma shotguns, each as powerful as the dreadnought's own main turrets, flashed into existence at point-blank range—and the energy screen *finally* failed.

Lasers tore into the dreadnought and secondary explosions glittered on Henry's screens as he managed *not* to visibly pump his fist.

"*Dilophosaurus* is taking more hits," Eowyn said grimly. "Dreadnought is focusing fire on her, and she has multiple blowthroughs. They're reporting launchers offline and their starboard laser has ceased firing."

Thanks to his internal network, Henry could assess the situation in less than a second and made his decision.

"Orders to Captain Denison," he barked. "*Ankylosaurus* will sweep ahead of *Dilophosaurus*. Take the hits while her shields stabilize."

He'd rather put one of the newer ships in that position, but Lieutenant Colonel Bart Denison's *Ankylosaurus* was the ship that *could* shield her sister.

The two *Tyrannosaurs* swapped places, but the plasma fire was tapering off as more hits struck the dreadnought.

"Target is attempting to accelerate away, toward the escorts," Eowyn reported. Almost before she'd finished speaking, though, a new icon flared on the screen.

"Target fusion core breached," she noted. "She's breaking up."

A moment passed, in which their second-old data showed the ship continuing to fire despite her broken back. Then a secondary explosion severed whatever was still holding the dreadnought together, and her bow and stern started clearly separating.

"Target has ceased fire."

"All ships hold fire and adjust course to intercept the escorts," Henry ordered. "If, ah, *either half of* the dreadnought so much as twitches, launch standard nukes into that portion of the ship."

Most likely, the last salvos had emptied the capacitors and the dreadnought chunks didn't have enough power to energize their systems. They had enough power to *survive* until Kakat's convoy could rescue them—and Henry was willing to let that happen—but if they decided to instead take a shot, well…

The dreadnought was broken into two pieces, neither of which had shields—and her engines were wrecked. Henry eyeball-estimated that at least half of her crew was dead. If the Warriors wanted to die, he would oblige them.

But if they wanted to live, he had seven and a half minutes until he was in missile range of their escorts, and he was *far* more concerned about warships that were still in one piece.

27

WHATEVER COULD BE SAID about the Kenmiri in general and Warriors in specific—and Henry had *plenty* to say—no one had ever accused them of being cowards. The ten escorts that had been pursuing Kakat's part of the convoy didn't even waver as they hurtled toward the Forward Flotilla.

Henry watched them come with cold eyes. *Dilophosaurus* was battered and bruised, but his old ship was the worst-hit of his command. She'd lost half her weapons and he didn't want to know how many crew were dead, but she was still with him.

"*Dilophosaurus* is to fall back to join the La-Tar escorts," he ordered. "Get her behind everyone else's shields."

Captain Wilcox was unlikely to object. Henry wasn't going to write off *any* of his vessels while in Kenmiri space, but he suspected the *Tyrannosaur* was doomed. With half of her armament offline, why repair a ten-year-old ship when the same resources could finish one of the *Significances* sitting half-completed in a yard somewhere?

"All ships are standing by; *Dilophosaurus* has cut acceleration and is falling back," Eowyn reported.

Thankfully, the destroyer still had her engines. Luck of the draw,

Henry supposed—plus that the enemy fire had been coming in from in front of them.

"Enemy ships at fifteen light-seconds. Missile range in fifty seconds."

This wasn't a fight the unshielded Kenmiri escorts could win. But they were more likely to do damage in a missile duel than the dreadnought had been. Each of them had two-thirds as many missiles as the capital ship, after all—but none of them carried the plasma cannon that made the dreadnought a true shipkiller.

The question now in the back of Henry's mind was whether the escorts had been supplied with the same upgraded missiles, jammer warheads and plasma webs. The new weapons the Kenmiri had demonstrated over the course of this run for safety were changing his threat assessment of the old enemy.

"We have our sensors dialed up as much as possible, ser," Eowyn told him before he could ask. "I'm not certain we can identify jammer warheads or plasma webs this time...but we're damn well going to have enough data to do it *next* time if they use them."

"Keep me informed," he told her.

Both of them felt *Paladin* shiver underneath them as the two fleets entered missile range of each other and opened fire. This time, the three-to-one ratio of salvos was in the Kenmiri's favor.

But Henry had flown a starfighter into the teeth of an entire *fleet's* escorts. He'd conned a battlecruiser into the fire of entire dreadnought squadrons. He knew that his destroyers could handle those salvos.

So long as the Kenmiri had run out of clever tricks, anyway, but he wasn't taking *that* bet.

"Orders for the Flotilla to adjust course," he instructed. "We'll want to keep this a missile duel as long as we can."

"We'll only be able to extend it to two salvos before laser range," Eowyn warned. "Our base velocity is too high. We are closing *fast*."

The orders had been passed on, of course, and the Forward Flotilla's ships flipped in space. Now they were accelerating away from the closing escorts. The UPSF ships, at least, could fire all of their weapons forward or backward, and the escorts could do the same with their missiles.

"Second salvo away. Should we adjust for counter-missile fire?" Eowyn asked a moment later.

"Two more, then switch," Henry decided aloud. "I don't want to play in laser range with these people unless I have to. And if we can make *them* spend missiles on self-defense…"

Eowyn didn't bother to reply to his rhetorical commentary as she transmitted his orders.

The escorts were decently armored but had no shields. Their only defense against his missiles was to shoot them down before they detonated—and they set to it with a will. The Kenmiri's entire first salvo was in counter-missile mode.

"CCM modes aren't as effective as we'd hoped," Eowyn reported. "First salvo is gone. Laser range in thirty-five seconds."

They were now past any point where Henry could change what happened. He waited and silently took in the reports and data flying back toward him. The Kenmiri's second salvo blazed toward his ships, even as their third salvo locked on to *his* second salvo.

His own intercepts, the Flotilla's fifth salvo, blazed out at the last possible moment. Outnumbered three to one, they were never going to protect his people on their own—and jammer warheads detonated amidst the Kenmiri salvo, throwing off the defensive missiles at a critical moment.

"They're getting better," Henry observed. "Someone finally ran through all of their data on fighting us and came up with counter-measures."

There'd always been *some* development and modification to Kenmiri tactics, but the Vesheron rebels and their El-Vesheron allies had represented a dizzying variety of doctrine and weapon systems that had limited the clearly useful adaptations.

Given four years of reduced conflict to assess their weaknesses and an apparent decision to steal some of the UPSF's best ideas, Henry was frankly surprised he wasn't seeing gravity shields and starfighters.

Even if he'd rather *not* have had sequential jammers firing off again and again as the enemy missiles closed. He could see the targeting efficiency numbers for the defenses, and they were *awful*.

Dozens of missiles were blown apart, but *hundreds* should have died—and over a hundred survived, hurtling down on the six Terran destroyers and their nearly solid wall of gravity shields.

There were no plasma webs in this salvo, Henry realized, but a hundred–plus conversion warheads was bad enough. For a few seconds, it felt like his destroyers had walked into the broadside of a dozen dreadnoughts.

"*Paladin*'s shields are clear, no blowthrough," Eowyn told him. "*Ankylosaurus* reports multiple blowthroughs. Captain Denison says they're fine, but I'm reading some nasty power fluctuations.

"*Paramount* lost a missile launcher, and *Betekenis* took a full-blown corona hit and needs to refresh ninety percent of her heat radiators. All other ships report minor coronal hits from blowthroughs, but nothing serious.

"No missiles cleared the line. *Dilophosaurus* and the La-Tar are clear."

And in the middle of the last sentence of Commander Eowyn's report, the UPSF destroyers entered laser range of their enemy. Beams flickered in the void again, and while Henry's ships couldn't shoot those down, there was no jamming or confusion that could stop the grav-shields refracting the beams into uselessness.

Between gravity shields and distance, none of the escorts' first beams landed a blow on the Forward Flotilla. The Kenmiri ships only had distance on their side, and two of them didn't survive the first exchange.

Missiles were still in space, but with the energy weapons in play, no one on the Kenmiri ships had the attention to spare to run the sequenced jammers that had covered the earlier salvos. Fewer missiles made it to the gravity shields, and none blew through as the second exchange of lasers tore through space.

"Blowthrough on *Paladin*," Eowyn barked as the ship shuddered around them. "Hit on the starboard wing... I think they might have hit dead metal, same place we got hit last time."

The silence that followed the hit was deafening. None of the enemy escorts had survived the second exchange of laser fire, Henry realized. All of his ships were still with him, even as more missile salvos continued to hurtle toward them.

"Clear our skies, Commander Eowyn," Henry ordered. "Whatever munitions it takes—and then get me a location on that other detachment!"

28

THE LOCATION of the other detachment proved to be less important than what they were doing, because *what they were doing* was *running*.

"Bogey bravo has broken away from the convoy fragment they were pursuing and is making a direct run for the Ra-Two-Oh-One skip line," Eowyn reported. "They appear to have *started* running when we took down the dreadnought."

"Fortunately for them, pursuit is not my priority," Henry said grimly. "Do we have any link with Falling Rain yet?"

"Captain Vara on *Bringer of Cloths* reports that all of the ships now have at least minimal power and are showing signs of life, but he hasn't received any communications yet," Chan reported.

"Damn." Henry shook his head. "Let's get the Flotilla back together. This Kakat may have asked for our help, but I don't trust *any* Kenmiri.

"We'll fall back on Falling Rain's ships and do whatever we need to get them moving again. We're still four days out from Anderon, and I want us out of Kenmiri space *ASAP*."

He was eyeing the damage reports as well. The UPSF ships were back down to half a KPS^2, allowing Captain Wilcox's crew to start checking over *Dilophosaurus*. The news was as bad as he'd feared—but at least it wasn't *worse*.

The destroyer had lost her entire port armament. One of the wings that made all UPSF ships look vaguely birdlike—an impression hardly hurt by the feather-like heat radiators across the outer hull—was gone. Plasma had gouged gaping holes down the destroyer's side, and he had *no* idea how the ship still had functioning engines.

Out of three hundred and fifty SpaceDiv and GroundDiv personnel aboard *Dilophosaurus,* at least a hundred were dead and almost as many wounded.

"Let me know as soon as Captain Wilcox feels able to have a conversation," he told Chan. "I don't want to pressure her, but I need her assessment of her ship."

Henry didn't want to abandon and scuttle any of his grav-shielded warships—let alone one that he'd once commanded—but he knew how much damage and how many problems could be hidden behind the reports he was receiving. Many of those reports were automated, produced by the ship's systems, and would be the same thing Captain Wilcox would be relying on to send teams out.

"Will do, ser," Chan confirmed.

Henry nodded and checked the status of the rest of the ships. The La-Tar ships had, as planned, emerged entirely unscathed. Tol Azan had positioned his escorts protectively around the damaged *Dilophosaurus*—and was taking advantage of his ships' greater ordinary acceleration to play guard dog for the entire squadron.

The casualty lists weren't final yet, but Henry already knew they were going to be too damn long. They'd potentially lost *Dilophosaurus* —he didn't want to assume she could make the journey home under her own power—and all of his ships were damaged.

Of course, Henry had taken nine million tons of warships against eleven million tons and *annihilated* his opponents for the potential loss of one ship.

"What are our remaining Kenmiri friends up to?" he asked.

"Convoy fragments are both heading for a rendezvous point near the Olat skip line," Eowyn told him. "No aggression in our direction. Two ships have been detached from Kakat's portion of the convoy on what appears to be a search-and-rescue course on the ships we took down."

"Good. Once their ship is crippled, we are allies against the void." Even during the war, with the life and freedom of entire civilizations at risk, the UPSF had stuck to that standard. Space was even more hostile than the sea.

"Lieutenant Commander Nguyen is requesting permission to take a shuttle over," Ihejirika reported. "He wants to attempt to access the dreadnought's computer cores."

Quang Nguyen was the GroundDiv commander aboard *Paladin* and the senior ground officer in Henry's squadron of destroyers. Somehow, Henry wasn't surprised that GroundDiv wanted to board the wrecked dreadnought.

"Can we send a shuttle over without diverting from our course?" he asked. "Right now, reuniting with the E-Two and getting on our way is the critical path. If we can deploy the shuttles without diverting, maybe."

"Charmchi is running the numbers now, but it looks like it would take *Paladin* diverting from the rest of the Flotilla to use our higher acceleration," Ihejirika admitted.

The possibility of acquiring the computers of a Vengeance Fleet dreadnought was tempting; Henry couldn't argue with that. Except…

"And what does Commander Nguyen rate the odds of his people reaching the computer cores before they're purged or destroyed by the Kenmiri?" Henry asked. "The Warriors will fight to the death to keep us out of those computer cores, especially if they believe they're already doomed—and they won't have *happy* assumptions about seeing GroundDiv power armor kicking in their airlocks."

"We've also learned in the past that Kenmiri encryption and security protocols are even better than our own and can take us months or more to breach without some kind of hook," Eowyn warned. "I don't know if acquiring the damaged computers of a wrecked warship is going to do us any good at all."

Henry nodded, silently parsing the options and reviewing the course data that *Paladin*'s navigator had worked up. To deploy and retrieve the shuttles, they'd be pushing *Paladin*'s GMS to its full acceleration, and they'd *still* only be able to give the GroundDiv troopers twenty-six minutes.

"I know this is a military decision," Sylvia said on their private channel. "But may I interject a thought of the diplomatic consequences?"

"Always," he told her. "You know that. Immediate military requirements may override longer-term diplomatic concerns, but those concerns are not irrelevant to the decision."

"We've made a positive impression on the Remnant this trip," she pointed out. "Enough of one that a Kenmiri Artisan was willing to ask for our help. *Beg* for it—help we gave.

"Now that same Artisan is organizing the rescue of the Warriors we defeated, out of the general respect for the law of the void that would lead us to do the same. But if *we* board that dreadnought, the Warriors will fight. More people will die.

"And it has to be at the top of mind of *every* Kenmiri right now that there will be no more Kenmiri. Every Warrior, Artisan…even each *Drone* who dies is one tiny but perceptible step to their final extinction."

Henry said nothing immediately. Sylvia wasn't wrong—but he hadn't been joking when he said that the immediate needs could override the long-term diplomatic consequences.

"No," he finally decided aloud. "Hold the shuttles aboard; keep *Paladin* with the Flotilla. Today, I think, laying the groundwork of peaceful relations with at least *some* component of the Remnant outweighs the limited information we'd get from a damaged and encrypted computer."

"Understood, ser. I'll let Nguyen know," Ihejirika conceded.

"Have him and the rest of the shuttles prep for search-and-rescue," Henry ordered. "We don't know how bad things are going to be aboard Falling Rain's ships. Something went very wrong there."

TWO JOURNEYS CAME to an end around the same time. Henry and his destroyers decelerated to their rendezvous with the E-Two fleet only a few minutes after the second of the two Kenmiri freighters decelerated to meet the wrecked dreadnought.

The first freighter had matched velocities with the debris field from the escorts' destruction and had shuttles sweeping through that wreckage, looking for survivors.

Henry had even less sympathy or mercy for Vengeance Fleet than he had for most Kenmiri. His therapists told him that the somewhat-hypocritical conflict between his distaste and hatred for the Kenmiri and his guilt and horror over his involvement in their genocide was entirely normal.

Confusing and stressful, but normal.

Still, he had spent his entire adult life in space. He didn't have it in him to wish death by vacuum on *anyone*. Once the battle was over, the Warriors of the Vengeance Fleet were fellow sentients at risk to the void.

He had to focus on his own people and rescue Defender Falling Rain and their people first. Still, he was glad to see that Kakat had sent ships to save the survivors of the battle.

"Ser, we have a link from *Fronds of Will*," Chan reported suddenly. "Defender Falling Rain on a channel for you."

"Thank you."

Henry linked into the video before he'd even finished thanking Chan, studying the dark skin of his flytrap-esque plant-like ally.

"Commodore Wong. We must-will apologize for our failings."

"I am more concerned about the safety of your crew and vessels," Henry replied in Kem. "Is everyone all right?"

"There are-were no casualties," Falling Rain confirmed. "We lost power on all ships, but there are-were sufficient atmosphere reserves to sustain-protect everyone.

"Reboots are-were still in progress. It must-will be some more time before we are functional again."

"Do not apologize," Henry told them. "Kenmiri cyberwarfare is something we have grown so used to that we forgot to warn you about it."

In truth, he felt that the E-Two probably should have worked that out on their own—but no one in the UPSF or the other allies had even thought to *ask*.

"How long until your ships are back online?"

"I am-was waiting on confirmation. May-will be perhaps another hour," Falling Rain admitted.

The E-Two ships had been offline for hours already. Henry had never seen a UPSF ships so badly affected by any kind of malware— but then, the UPSF's primary threat prior to encountering the Kenmiri *had* been malware and viruses.

Not every member of the United Planets Alliance was entirely content with their situation, after all, and even the ones that were content *still* wanted to be able to access the UPSF's servers, sensor data, etc.

Kenmiri cyberwarfare had been more advanced and more capable than that of, say, China, but the gap hadn't been enough to prevent the UPSF adapting far more rapidly than the Kenmiri had expected.

The Eerdish and Enteni leaders had been strictly limited in their authority and options under Kenmiri occupation. If they'd known that the Kenmiri were in their systems, they likely hadn't been *allowed* to build countermeasures.

"We will hold position with your ships until we are all ready to move," Henry assured Falling Rain. "We have lost more time here than preferred, but I will not leave anyone behind."

"That is-will-be appreciated," Falling Rain said. "We can-will be online as swiftly as is-will-be possible."

29

"SER, one of the Kenmiri freighters is headed our way."

Henry blinked away fatigue. He hadn't *quite* been asleep on his desk—but he had been staring blankly off into space in his office, with a coffee to hand that he'd drunk maybe half of.

"Which one?" he asked once he was sure he wasn't going to *sound* asleep.

"The one that picked up crew from the dreadnought," Eowyn confirmed. "I can't help but feel that's suspicious."

"Agreed. What's their ETA?" he asked.

"Current course has them reaching us in about forty minutes if we don't change course. If we break for Ra-Two-Oh-One as planned, that will extend it."

"Keep an eye on them," Henry ordered. "Barring communication, we'll move out as planned once Falling Rain's people have their systems back online.

"If they communicate, have Chan let me know immediately."

None of the ships involved had been immobile when they'd lost power, so the distance between the wrecked dreadnought and the E-Two ships had been dropping as time passed.

"Ser, we have a link request from Kakat aboard the freighter approaching," Chan reported almost immediately.

"Time delay?" Henry asked.

"Twenty-seven-second round trip."

"Link them through."

Kakat didn't look like they'd shifted from their position on the freighter's bridge since the last time they'd transmitted to Henry. Even with the thirty-second time delay, this was a live loop, something none of the Kenmiri had established before on this trip.

"UPSF Commander, greetings," they said in the slow and almost stately Kem of an Artisan. "We must extend our appreciation for your intervention against our blood-sick kin. I recognize they are also your enemy, but you could have avoided all of us."

Henry nodded slowly.

"Greetings, Kakat," he replied. "I did not desire to engage any Kenmiri on this journey, but Vengeance Fleet has made themselves a critical threat to the people under our protection.

"That said, many of the ships under my command are crewed by your former slaves. While I do not believe that they will fire on an unarmed transport, approaching my Flotilla *will* put you at some risk. I recommend that you keep your distance."

The thirty-second round trip took patience. He and Kakat were basically staring at each other, waiting patiently, as their words flicked through the void at the both unimaginably fast and inconveniently slow speed of light.

"I understand your concern," the Artisan finally replied. "And I am requesting permission for my vessel to approach close enough to your Flotilla to send over a single shuttle. Neither this transport nor the shuttle in question carry any offensive weaponry, and we will not send Warriors on the craft.

"I wish to provide an appropriate compensation for your rescue. I believe that you will find it both suitable and useful."

Henry could see more than a few ways that could be true…and also that it could be an excuse for a trap. A shuttle could easily deliver a large-enough bomb to obliterate *Paladin* once it was allowed within the gravity shield.

On the other hand, *close enough to send a shuttle over* was almost certainly also *within missile range*. The transport had some limited antimissile defenses, Henry was sure, but not enough to stand off the entire Forward Flotilla.

"You have permission to approach," he confirmed. "Understand that we will scan your shuttle before it approaches, and any attempt to harm my people will be met with the annihilation of your ship."

"I understand," Kakat told him, thirty seconds later. "We mean you no harm."

Henry wasn't going to take *that* on faith. Not from a Kenmiri!

THE SHUTTLE BAY was *full* of GroundDiv when the Kenmiri craft arrived. Henry had been calmly informed that he wasn't allowed to be present and was watching the whole affair by video link—and he had to admit the precautions were reasonable.

Thirty power-armored troopers lined the walls of the bay, as close as they could be without risking damage from the shuttle's engines. Henry *also* knew that antispacecraft weapons were concealed in the back of the shuttle bay and that one word from him or Lieutenant Commander Nguyen would see the shuttle blown back into space.

In very small pieces.

"Shuttle is on the deck," Nguyen reported, the GroundDiv commander supervising from the front.

Either Henry or Ihejirika *could* have told the man that he had no business in a suit of power armor in the shuttle bay at that moment… but given that both of them *also* wanted to be there, Henry hadn't been able to give that order.

Ihejirika, he presumed, had made a similar calculation.

The shuttle itself was a standard Kenmiri design that Henry had seen a thousand times—and was, he was sure, duplicated several dozen times on his allies' ships. The scans showed no surprises prior to the ramp opening.

The single blue-green Drone that walked down the ramp looked around at the soldiers and guns aiming at them and spread their arms in a very clear shrug.

There were a few moments of the Drone and the armored troopers just looking at each other, then Nguyen cleared his throat.

"I think we can stop pointing the guns *directly* at the little guy," he ordered.

Enough of the threat profile shifted to make the Kenmiri more comfortable, as they turned and waved back up the ramp. A powered cart rolled down the ramp, escorted by four more Drones.

It took Henry a good five seconds to recognize the contents of the cart. It was a server-scale data-storage device—the kind that starships used for their core databases and incremental backups.

The original Drone was clearly in charge, communicating in sharp, staccato syllables that were spoken too quietly for the shuttlebay pickups to catch. The cart was rolled across the deck to a midpoint between the shuttles and the GroundDiv troopers, and then the Drones stepped away from it.

The four who'd been moving the storage drive immediately retreated back aboard the shuttle, and the first Drone looked around at the soldiers, gestured toward the cart, then shrugged again and followed their minions back onto the shuttle.

At no point in the entire exchange did any of the Kenmiri say a word to the humans. As the shuttle closed up, a team of GD troopers started sweeping the cart and its contents with sensor wands.

"It's clean of traps and explosives, at least," Nguyen reported as the shuttle lifted slowly off the deck and began to gently drift out of *Paladin*'s bay. "I don't know what's *in* it, though."

"That's going to be on Chan and Jackson," Henry replied. "And for the first time since the war, I'm actually wishing they'd sent an IntelDiv team with us."

IntelDiv had coordinated Golden Lancelot...and the rest of the United Planets Space Force hadn't forgiven them for that yet. Henry knew, intellectually, that the current separation between the military intelligence division and the rest of the UPA's military was dangerous.

But he hadn't tried to use whatever influence he had to oppose the ban on IntelDiv personnel on warships, either. To SpaceDiv, the lies and deception around Golden Lancelot were a betrayal that could not yet be forgiven.

Even if, at that particular moment, Henry could *really* have used a cyberspy.

"IT ISN'T, for those of you who were getting hopeful, a datacore from the dreadnought," Chan reported two hours later.

The Forward Flotilla was now back under way toward their final destination. The shuttle that had delivered the mystery datacore was back aboard her mothership, and all of the Kenmiri vessels that could be seen were on their way out of the system.

The remaining escorts from the Vengeance Fleet detachment were still visible, though the lightspeed delay meant they'd almost certainly already started the skip to Ra-201. Most likely, they'd be gone by the time the Forward Flotilla made it there.

Not that Henry was going to chase them. Barring someone coming after them, he needed to get his people to Anderon and, preferably, to Twelfth Fleet.

"Then what *did* our carmine friend provide us?" Sylvia asked.

Henry's staff, Ihejirika and Sylvia were in the breakout conference room attached to his office. While they had every intention of sharing their discovery with their allies, this was a conversation Henry wanted to keep private to begin with.

Rather than answering verbally, Chan flicked their hand and loaded an image into the holoprojectors in the conference room. A familiar image appeared in the air—though Henry hadn't got *this* close of a look at a superdreadnought yet.

"Full schematics and specifications for the new superdreadnoughts," the coms officer said calmly. "I *think* this may have been pulled from the Vengeance dreadnought's systems, but Kakat's people sanitized it and loaded it onto hardware of their own.

"Certainly, I'm not sure what it would mean if a convoy transport captain had full access to the specifications of the new dreadnoughts."

"How full are we talking?" Henry asked, leaning into to examine the hologram. It looked…complete. Armor thickness, hatch locations, weapon specifications…

"*Full*," Chan reiterated. "As-designed drawings for the cannon, the new missiles, the new warheads, the new shields, the new… There is no way in *hell* Kakat should have given us this."

"I'm guessing that if we'd seen any subspace coms, you would have told me?"

"There was one pulse from the dreadnought just after she broke in half," the coms officer told him. "I assume an automated terminal signal. If Kakat was talking to anyone outside this system, they have a different version of the carrier-wave system than we've seen so far."

Henry was silent, trying to take in the full weight of the prize the Kenmiri transport captain had handed them.

"It appears that at least some Artisans *really* dislike this Vengeance Fleet," Sylvia said. "I imagine that Kakat's opinion was strongly affected by the attempt to kill or capture them, but even that shouldn't have led to this kind of handover."

"Unless, of course, the ships Vengeance Fleet has *aren't* the newest and shiniest we've been assuming they are," Henry warned. "If the Remnant has ships that are superior to Vengeance's…"

He noted, with some amusement, how quickly the command staff at least had switched to using the Vengeance Fleet name. If the rest of the Flotilla's rumor mill was working the way it usually did, the name was already in widespread use.

It helped to know what the enemy called themselves, after all.

"I don't think it matters right now what Kakat was thinking," Ihejirika pointed out. "What *matters* is how the good the information on those antifighter plasma webs is."

Chan updated the hologram, switching it from the fourteen-hundred-meter-long behemoth of the Kenmiri superdreadnought to a far smaller piece of technology. The missile still filled the projector, of course, but it was at a much lower scale.

The missile warhead was only three meters long, after all. Mounted on a missile, it would have been just over fourteen meters long, but Chan had focused in on just the warhead itself.

Or the delivery system, Henry supposed. There were eighteen

drones in the cylinder, stacked in two sets of nine. Tiny as the robots seemed for interspace weaponry, he supposed they didn't need much in terms of fuel to sustain the plasma arcs for the few seconds they were online.

"I don't believe we could feed the information into our fabricators in its current form," Chan admitted. "But I suspect that if I were to hand this to Lieutenant Commander Bautista and her engineering Chiefs, they could translate it into something we could use with ease."

"We already have translation protocols for turning Kenmiri fabricator templates into something we can use," Henry told them. "There's some manual work involved, always, but you are entirely correct in that the Chiefs can turn any of this into hardware."

"If we can build it, we can counter it?" Sylvia asked.

"Not necessarily immediately, but yes," Henry confirmed. "Eowyn, I want you to sit down with Bach and the other tactical officers. Go through the data on the webs forward, backward, upside down... whatever it takes.

"We're still three days from Anderon. I don't *expect* to have a counter by the time we reach our destination, but if we do, there will be some very nice comments in everyone's evaluations. I will be *very* happy."

"How much of this data do we give our allies?" Sylvia asked after a moment. "I mean, am I correct in believing that this is enough to *build* a matching superdreadnought?"

Henry looked at the data on the missile and then glanced over at Chan.

"Commander? You've been deeper in this than I have."

"It's not enough information to build a superdreadnought if you can't already build a dreadnought," they said slowly. "There are no templates in here to build tools, for example. But these are full construction schematics for a sixteen-megaton capital ship, with all of its power and weapons systems."

"So, TechDiv and IntelDiv are going to be...*excited*, let's say, when we get this to them," Henry said drily. "But the UPSF doesn't *want* to build Kenmiri dreadnoughts or even dreadnought-sized ships."

While the UPSF had maintained a small number of battleships

during the middle years of the war, even those had only matched the mass and volume of the contemporary fleet carriers. The limiting factor on UPSF ships was the gravity shield itself—and no one in TechDiv had been willing to trade their most powerful defense for a hull that could mount more weapons.

He wasn't sure the UPSF had even kept the *Beethoven* class in reserve. The battleships had never had the endurance for the kind of long-range operations that had defined the war against the Kenmiri.

"I can see an argument for only handing over the most immediately critical components," Ihejirika said. "On the other hand…is the UPA disserved by the La-Tar Cluster, for example, commissioning a couple of superdreadnoughts?"

"The problem is that anything we give La-Tar or the E-Two, we arguably need to give the Kozun," Henry suggested. "And while we *currently* appear to have Mal Dakis on a short leash, he *did* attempt to conquer the quadrant and was perfectly willing to use starvation toward that goal."

Mal Dakis, the First Voice of the Kozun, was both the secular and religious leader of the Kozun Hierarchy. Henry knew the man personally—his first year in command of *Panther* had been supporting the campaign to free the Kozun homeworld—and he knew *exactly* how far to trust him.

Which was *not one inch*.

"I don't believe that *anyone* is going to be overly surprised if we decline to hand detailed military schematics over to the people we were at war with a year ago," Sylvia told him. "Mal Dakis and his government are well aware that our alliance with them is defensive and they have some trust to earn back."

"We need to give basically *everyone* the details on the plasma web," Henry decided. "Every brain we can get working on countering that system is another chance to maintain the efficacy of one of our most powerful weapons systems."

"As for the rest… Do you have a recommendation, Ambassador Todorovich? I feel that is a political question more than a military one."

"I would suggest that we provide a full copy of the database to both Tol Azan and Falling Rain and allow them to give it to their governments. Outside of allies present here today, I do not feel we have any obligation—but La-Tar and the E-Two were in this system and contributed to the action the database was provided as a repayment for."

"I mean, the E-Two's contribution is arguable," Eowyn snarked.

"Behave, Commander," Henry told her. "I agree with the Ambassador. It's a lot of data. Chan, do we *have* the ability for a secure data transfer of that magnitude?"

"It'll consume our links with the two flagships for about twenty minutes, but we do, yes."

"All right. Make it happen," Henry ordered. "And then spend some time of your own looking at those drones, Commander Chan. We know the Lancers are superior to the Shieldwings...but those webs were *designed* to kill our fighters, not the E-Two's.

"And I haven't seen anything in the tactical data to suggest they will fail at that task."

30

THERE WAS NO HUGE DIFFERENCE, really, between Osiris-65 and Ra-201. Both were dwarf stars with few planets and nothing of interest except their skip lines. Both were gateway systems between sectors, too important to ignore and too empty to be worth fortifying.

Still, Henry could feel the palpable sense of relief aboard *Paladin* as they finally emerged back into the Ra Sector. They were no longer in Kenmiri space. Among any other potential problems, it also removed the concern over whether or not any Kenmiri they saw were hostile.

Any Kenmiri in the Ra Sector were almost certainly Vengeance Fleet. Any that *weren't* hostile were welcome to talk quickly—but Henry was going to assume they were enemies.

He'd written that into the Peacekeeper Initiative's protocols and doctrines for a reason, after all.

"Scans are clear of Kenmiri," Eowyn reported. "The escorts from the Vengeance force must have made a run for the Ra-Two-Oh-Two skip line. That will take them back toward Rashova, bypassing Anderon."

"Anyone else we can pick up?" Henry asked. "I'm assuming Anderon has some kind of picket here. I know it's a long skip from here to there, but it's only one."

The twenty-three-hour skip from Ra-201 to Anderon was far too close to the twenty-four-hour limit for Henry's peace of mind. He'd made longer skips but not many—and he'd been using recent survey data when he'd made them.

The most recent update he had on the 201-Anderon line was from a Kenmiri survey a year before the Fall. It was almost five years old now—and while that *should* be fine, it made him nervous.

"We're not detecting any active engine signatures," Eowyn said. "On the other hand, we're still over a light-hour away from the skip line to Anderon. If there are Anderon ships operating at low thrust or even without thrusters at all, we would have difficulty detecting them at this range."

"And if they simply have surveillance satellites that have couriers regularly picking up data, we wouldn't see those at all," Henry guessed. There were a lot of ways to secure a skip line, after all.

Though surveillance satellites had been more useful when they could send messages home in real time regardless of distance.

"We're synchronizing sensors on all ships for better resolution, but it could be hours before we can pick up anything at the skip line," Eowyn warned. "I agree that there has to be *something* there—but whatever is here, it wasn't enough to stop a dozen Vengeance Fleet escorts making a run for Two-Oh-Two."

"No. But I doubt Anderon's ships would have tried, either." He studied the display and shook his head. "Without knowing what happened in Rashova, they have no reason to believe that these Kenmiri are an immediate danger."

"Yeah...but have you met *anyone* in the Ra Sector who wasn't more likely to shoot than talk when Kenmiri show up?"

Henry chuckled.

"No. Not even us." He rose from his seat. "I'll be in my office if I'm needed."

THE MAIN THING Henry was doing in his office was reviewing the minimum staffing requirements for his ships. He would let Tol Azan and Falling Rain decide how to handle their own people, but he *knew* the destroyer crews needed a break.

While *Paladin*'s crew would be the least likely to admit it, they were the most in need of it. The other destroyers had the retreat from Ra-78 wearing them down, but *Paladin*'s crew had barely recovered from the pursuit of and battle for Drifter Convoy Blue Stripe Green Stripe Orange Stripe before all of this.

And then they'd watched an entire world die.

Henry doubted he was alone in his new nightmares. His particular anthology was probably unique to him—and might be giving Lieutenant Commander Dr. Uehara nightmares of his own—but the sight of the heavy-metal-salted bombs searing a world's surface into ash…

That was a nightmare most of *Paladin*'s crew shared now. He'd worked them hard getting this far, but he also knew that he *needed* to make them stop and rest.

The door to his office slid open without an admittance chime, and he looked up swiftly. There were only three or four people aboard *Paladin* who could enter his office without permission—though he had plenty of evidence that the destroyer's crew knew that permission would be forthcoming.

But, as he'd hoped, it was Sylvia. She was carrying a briefcase in one hand and…a *picnic basket* in the other?

"Good afternoon, Commodore," she said breezily as she put the basket on his desk. "I wanted to go over the details of our planned diplomatic approach once we reach Anderon."

The briefcase joined the picnic basket and Sylvia opened it to reveal a portable holoprojector and several data drives. She was being serious about the work side, it seemed.

"But while we have work to do, I talked to Quaid and made sure we had appropriate nutrition for the discussion," she concluded, pulling a bottle of wine out of the picnic basket. "Shall we?"

Henry chuckled and shook his head at her—but he also told the drink cabinet in his wall to produce a pair of wine glasses.

"I assume you checked the wine was decent?" he asked. "I remember that date on La-Tar."

Their security had carefully scouted and prearranged that event with the restaurant—and at least three people and organizations Henry knew of had tried to pay for it for them. But the most *memorable* part had been the wine.

Henry and Sylvia were the saviors of the La-Tar Cluster—and *especially* of La-Tar, which they'd liberated from Kozun occupation. So, the restaurant owners had managed to source a bottle of Terran wine to serve them.

And it had been absolutely bloody *awful*.

"I picked this one," she told him. "And I have never picked an inferior wine, liquor or meal in my *life*, Henry."

He passed her the wine glasses and joined in unpacking the rest of the picnic basket. His steward and the steward staff had outdone themselves in creating a picnic-themed meal, with sandwiches, potato salad—even a red-and-white checkered tablecloth.

"I'm not entirely certain any of the people Quaid had put this together had ever seen a picnic in their life," he observed. "Because this belongs in a *movie*, not a modern park."

"Oh, I know," she agreed. "But all I asked for was *dinner in a basket*. Quaid and the kitchen staff did the rest on their own, and I *love* it."

Henry chuckled again and grabbed one of the sandwiches.

"Fair enough. Work, then?"

"We're multitasking." Sylvia poured the wine and passed him a glass before activating the projector in the briefcase.

She didn't *need* that, Henry knew, since she had access to the projectors in his office. It might have made preparing her presentation easier, but he was reasonably sure she'd done it for effect.

The hologram she'd activated was the Anderon System itself. A G3 yellow star with five planets, two asteroid belts and a gas giant, it was the kind of rich system with a chilly habitable world the Kenmiri adored.

"Anderon," he noted unnecessarily. "Over one and a half billion people before the Kenmiri withdrew."

He checked his network for the inevitable question, but Sylvia answered it as fast as his silicon could.

"Three hundred and fifty million Kenmiri. Evacuated within six months of Golden Lancelot," she told him. "An unknown number died in the planetary bombardment, and the creche was on an artificial floating island in the middle of one of Anderon's seas."

"So, we vaporized an ungodly amount of water and probably dropped the global temperature half a dozen degrees," Henry guessed. "And Anderon only averaged five degrees Celsius *before* that."

"Exactly. So, I'm not sure we can count on the system being particularly friendly to the Vesheron. The Golden Lancelot reports say they made a huge mess in this system."

"Biggest one is that they took out the dreadnought yards," Henry said. "So, where Rashova had built themselves a dreadnought fleet for system security, Anderon *can't* have."

"Sadly, my experience suggests that means they will be feeling paranoid and vulnerable. That may work in our favor—but we'll need to get past their initial distrust of us."

"I'm not planning on cannonballing my way in with a giant splash," Henry said drily. "Unfortunately, I suspect that Vengeance Fleet shot down our courier drones. We sent new ones on to Twelfth Fleet after the fight, but I decided to hold off on contacting Anderon.

"So, the first they'll know of us is when whatever picket they have here in Ra-Two-Oh-One reports in." He shook his head. "They're being quiet, wherever they are, which makes it hard for me to locate them to say hello.

"I would *prefer*, strongly, to make contact before we skip into Anderon."

"As the local diplomat and your civilian advisor, I agree completely," Sylvia told him. She sipped her wine and smiled at him. "The sooner we can make contact, the cleaner the contact will be."

"Which then brings us to what we *need* from Anderon," he noted. "I want to be able to basically shut the Flotilla down for forty-eight hours. Seventy-two, if they're confident in their early-warning systems.

"I can't really do that without some kind of formal alliance."

"Which is what we need anyway—preferably *before* Admiral Rex hits those early-warning systems with six carriers and as many battle-cruisers." Sylvia considered the hologram carefully.

Henry wouldn't blame the Anderonians one bit if they were upset at Twelfth Fleet entering their space without warning or permission.

The *low end* of what he was expecting Rex to show up with was over a hundred warships and several dozen logistics ships.

The problem was that he was expecting *Vengeance Fleet* to show up with about *four* hundred warships. Without the help of the alliance they'd spent the last two years building, almost completely by accident, Anderon would be overwhelmed.

Even with Twelfth Fleet and their E-Two and Kozun and La-Tar allies, Henry was worried. The intelligence they'd received from Kakat would make all the difference, if they managed to find the "keys" in time.

"The diplomatic side is yours," he told her. "I can tell you what we need if we're going to save Anderon, but I have no idea how we're going to sell Anderon on it."

"We have the sensor footage of Rashova," Sylvia said, highlighting an icon marking the attached video file. She did not, thankfully, play it. "I'm hoping that the offer to help defend them is enough, but Admiral Rex has enough firepower to take their system by storm. They have every reason to fear us and few to trust us."

"I wish we knew more about who was running Anderon," Henry admitted. "Every species from the Ra Sector is supposed to be on the colonies as slaves, which means it could be anyone from an Enteni to a Tak to a Kozun running the place.

"We had no contact prior to the loss of the subspace network. That suggests that no Vesheron took over there as we *did* make contact with everyone prior to the Great Gathering."

"The colonies were major Kenmiri population centers. They took far longer to evacuate and abandon than the slave worlds." Henry considered the geography of the Ra Sector. "It would make sense if Anderon was even one of the last to be evacuated in Ra.

"None of which really helps us know what we're walking into." He sighed.

"I have the starting points I need," Sylvia told him. "It's not going to be easy. Might even be *almost* as difficult as running eighteen starships through arguably hostile space to make it to Anderon in time was."

"We didn't have much choice. And now, with the data from Kakat, we may just be able to give Twelfth Fleet more than a warning about the plasma webs." Henry grinned as he glanced from the hologram to his partner.

"Unless I'm severely mistaken, Commander Bautista is *building* one to test. We will find a way to protect our fighters—and once we take away the Kenmiri's silver bullets, this is going to be a far-more-even fight."

The UPSF *preferred* to have a battlecruiser for every dreadnought with carriers as an extra. Still, the carriers were supposed to be able to take down three or four dreadnoughts on their own. Henry would rank the *Crichton*s and their GMS Lancer fighters as better than the UPSF's wartime fighter wings—and would put the Shieldwings about on par with the wartime fighters.

His rough math put those six carriers, three UPSF and three E-Two, as a match for twenty to twenty-five dreadnoughts. The math wouldn't work out for the superdreadnoughts, and the plasma-web missiles were going to change it up, no matter how good a countermeasure they developed.

But that was why there were also going to be six battlecruisers, thirty-seven UPSF destroyers, twelve E-Two destroyers—as of his now-very-old last information—and a *lot* of Ra Sector–built escorts.

"Vengeance Fleet analyzed everything about the war," Henry half-whispered. "They prepared, built, upgraded and readied themselves to face us. They launched this campaign believing they can defeat any Ra Sector power."

"They did," she agreed. "And we're going to demonstrate to them that they cannot defeat *every* Ra Sector power at once."

31

HENRY WAS on the edge of falling asleep when his internal network chimed at him. A squadron commander was never truly off duty, but his network was set up to filter most contact requests while he was asleep.

Or engaging in other bedroom activities, for that matter.

"Ser, we have detected contacts on the skip line to Anderon," Bach's voice reported in his mind. "You left orders to be updated as soon as we'd located the Anderon picket."

"I did," he confirmed, fully awake again and rolling over to sit up on the side of the bed. Sylvia made a disgruntled noise but followed suit almost immediately. "What have we got?"

"Forwarding you the tactical feed," *Paladin*'s tactical officer told him. "Single large contact with escorts. Their drives only came online a few minutes ago... Well, plus thirty-five minutes' lightspeed lag."

Henry let the unnecessary clarification go. Bach didn't need to be scolded for making sure her barely awake flag officer understand the time frames. He linked up the tactical feed and studied the seven icons now added to the map of the star system.

"Did they see us or is that station-keeping?" he asked.

"CIC is running the analysis now, ser, but we think, well...both.

They saw us and are adjusting position to make sure they can intercept us no matter what we do. They don't want us getting to Anderon."

"Makes sense. Have CIC tear down everything we've got and build me a picture," he ordered. "Link with Commander Eowyn and arrange the Flotilla so we have the most effective synchronized array we can manage without losing time."

"Yes, ser!"

"I'll be on the flag deck in ten minutes," he told Bach. "I'll go over the initial reports then."

There was definitely a capital ship at the skip line, and that was more than he'd dared hope Anderon would have. He needed to know as much about her as possible—because if Anderon had a dozen dreadnoughts to throw into the line, he might finally be able to sleep easy about what was going to happen next.

FORTUNATELY, Henry hadn't drunk enough of the wine for it to be an issue by the time he made it to the flag bridge. Eowyn had clearly barely beaten him—mostly because she was still dropping a mess-deck travel coffee into the holder by his seat.

"Thank you, Commander," he greeted her as he claimed the coffee. "What have we got on our hopeful new friends?"

"Escort group is about what you'd expect," she told him. "Six standard Kenmiri half-megaton escorts. Someday, people will stop building those things."

"But not yet," Henry replied. "And even if everyone were to stop building them tomorrow, the Empire had, what, sixty thousand of them in commission?"

His operations officer stopped silently for a moment, staring at him blankly as she consulted her network.

"I thought you were exaggerating," she admitted after a second. "Apparently not. IntelDiv files say we had a listing of all active Kenmiri ships that's about three years old. All sixty-five thousand of them, dreadnoughts and all."

"Twenty provinces, ten thousand star systems, eighteen hundred inhabited worlds and roughly twelve *trillion* sentient beings," Henry reminded her. "Every dreadnought had ten escorts in tow. Every Kenmiri colony world had a couple hundred escorts securing the system. The Kenmiri homeworlds, according to the Lancelot reports, had fleets of *thousands* standing guard."

What IntelDiv had realized was that the "fleets of thousands" guarding the Kenmiri homeworlds had been made up of old ships with crews that had never seen action. A few stalking-horse attacks later, the way had been cleared for the largest Golden Lancelot strikes.

"So, we know the little guys by heart," he said. "What have we got on the capital ship?"

"A lot of questions," Eowyn warned. "She's big but she's not as heavy as she should be. From her engine signature and acceleration, she's around eight million tons."

"Big dreadnought."

"Except what we're picking up from the long-range scanners and visuals has the escorts for scale," she reminded him. "So, our big girl is *big*. A thousand, maybe eleven hundred meters long. She's got the length and volume of a ten-, maybe even eleven-megaton dreadnought."

"But she's only eight," Henry said slowly. "That's…interesting."

"She's shown half-KPS-squared acceleration. That might just be fuel-conserving, since all they've done is adjust position to make sure they're between us and the skip line, but…it also might be the best she can do."

"Eleven hundred meters would be one of the Kenmiri's standard freighter hulls, wouldn't it?" Henry asked.

"That's CIC's analysis as well," Eowyn confirmed. "Are you familiar with a *technical*, ser?"

"General term for civilian vehicles refitted with heavy weapons, yes?"

"CIC thinks that Anderon was still able to produce dreadnought *weapons*, but after the destruction of their main shipyards, they hadn't rebuilt their ability to manufacture dreadnought hulls and armor."

Given that dreadnought hulls were basically unique in Henry's experience, that wasn't entirely a surprise. Very few star systems would have the giant lasers used to melt an entire kilometer-long asteroid for easy shaping—and *building* the system would be a nightmare.

"So, she's, what, a battleship-sized technical?"

"CIC is calling her a large technical cruiser, or LTC. She doesn't have the armor or hull structure to be a dreadnought or a battleship by our usual reporting rules—and even the Kozun *cruisers* were more custom-built than this.

"Our best guess is that she was built as a freighter, and her weapons and whatever armor she has were added on later. I'd call her an armed merchant cruiser, except she's a complete conversion."

"But still fundamentally a freighter hull with freighter engines." Henry focused his display in on the LTC and studied the information they had.

"Exactly, ser. We don't have enough information to estimate her defenses or armament from this range, but CIC expects that she is, at the very least, carrying superheavy plasma cannon and energy screens."

"All right, so, Anderon has *something* worth bringing to the fight," Henry noted. "Even if they're the glassiest glass cannons I've ever seen. That's better than I was afraid of."

"Any changes to the plan, ser?"

"No. Ambassador Todorovich was headed to her office. Pull together everything you have and forward it to her.

"She's going to talk to them—and we are all hoping that they see us as the rescue cavalry we're very much trying to be!"

32

HENRY NEEDED to throw on a uniform and run a comb through his hair to be a presentable officer and command his ships. Sylvia needed to do quite a bit more to be presentable as the Ambassador of the United Planets Alliance.

She knew they still had time, though. While the sooner they made contact, the better, they were also twelve hours away from the skip line to Anderon.

By the time she took her seat in the carefully prepared presentation space of her office, she'd re-braided her hair and found a freshly pressed blouse and gray suit. Every inch of her was as creased and sharp as the suit itself, and she checked the positions of the flags behind her.

Everything needed to fit her standards *exactly* and give the impression she wanted. She was dealing with multiple cultures and species. Having the shared trade language of Kem made some things easier, but she'd also seen it lead other diplomats to assume that Kenmiri slaves had adopted Kenmiri social norms and mores.

That was as dangerous as assuming that human norms applied—or, for that matter, as assuming the professionally open and accepting culture of the United Planets Space Force or Diplomatic Corps applied to all *human* encounters and cultures!

In her experience, in fact, the best place with the Kenmiri slaves, rebels and ex-slaves was with the antithesis of Kenmiri presentation. A Warrior or Artisan would make certain to have visible subordinates around them, where Sylvia was clearly alone. They would have bronze- or gold-plated electronics and technology to hand, where Sylvia sat behind a plain desk. A Kenmiri would have a mural on the back wall, likely from their semireligious mythological canon. The wall behind Sylvia held only the simple stylized helm of *Paladin*'s commissioning seal and the paired flags of the UPA and UPSF.

It was a sharp and simplistic presentation that told the recipient exactly who Sylvia worked for and that she was definitely *not* Kenmiri or Kenmiri-adjacent. That it also fit well with her own austere style and personal taste was a convenient bonus.

"We are standing by to transmit, Ambassador Todorovich," Lieutenant Commander Jackson's voice said in her network. Chan was off shift and no one had seen it necessary to wake them, Sylvia presumed.

"I have control of the pickups," Sylvia confirmed aloud. "I will advise when we're ready to transmit."

They were still over half a light-hour away from the Anderon ships, after all. There was no point in attempting a live conversation.

"Standing by."

Sylvia sent a nonverbal acknowledgement to the coms officer and focused her gaze on the almost-invisible pickup in front of her. A slew of different sensors around the room could create a holographic transmission if she wanted, but video would suffice for this.

"Defenders of the Anderon System," she greeted her audience crisply in Kem. "I am Ambassador Sylvia Todorovich of the United Planets Alliance, aboard the destroyer UPSV *Paladin*.

"The ships you see with me are the Allied Forward Flotilla, a special-purpose task group initially sent to the Rashova System to assist in protecting them from a Kenmiri return."

She focused on the camera, making certain not to let any hint of the fate of Rashova cross her face.

"We were too late to prevent a Kenmiri assault on that system and were forced to flee into the Osiris Sector. After a journey of some days and some trials, we have arrived before you. I fear we are the bearer of dark tidings.

"I am formally requesting permission for the Forward Flotilla to enter the Anderon System and negotiate with your government," she told them. "We share a mutual and powerful enemy, one I have reason to believe is even now preparing their fleet for a strike at your star system.

"Given the opportunity to make contact with our own forces elsewhere in the Ra Sector, we will be able to bring significant forces to the defense of Anderon, but we cannot do so without your cooperation and permission.

"We will continue our approach to the Anderon skip line unless directed elsewhere, but you have my oath as a plenipotentiary representative of the Security Council of the United Planets Alliance that we bear no hostile intent and will not approach within weapons range of your ships until an accord has been reached.

"I await your response."

A FULL HOUR of the twelve remaining before they reached the skip line had passed before it was even *possible* for Sylvia to receive any reply from the large technical cruiser standing guard over the skip line.

Like the military around her, though, Sylvia had long since learned to sleep in any available time when necessary—and unlike most of said military, she'd learned how to do so without even marring the creases on her suit.

A soft timer in her internal network woke her at the earliest moment she could expect a reply. Since she *wasn't* actually expecting an immediate reply, she made herself a coffee and forced herself to sit at her desk and drink it steadily.

There was no one in the office with her—she was getting a stream of reports from *Paladin*'s systems and crew and had access to her staff if needed, but the solitary presentation was key to the image she was creating. Still, appearances begat reality, and the steadier she made herself when she wasn't on camera, the easier it was to be steady while recording.

After finishing her coffee, she checked the system in case she had somehow not been advised of a message, then checked the timing.

Whoever was in command of the Anderon force had spent at least ten minutes considering her communication. Ten minutes in which the Forward Flotilla had closed over ten million kilometers and shed three hundred kilometers a second of velocity, cutting thirty-plus seconds off the lightspeed lag.

The same lack of urgency applied to the Anderonian commander as to her, she supposed. The officer on the other end knew the Flotilla was over ten hours away—and if they trusted her promise not to attack them, they could take longer to make their decision.

But the Anderonian over there *could not* ask his home government for advice or to make the call for them. If they had sent a message the moment they spotted the Flotilla, it would only reach Anderon three hours before the Flotilla itself!

Whatever decision was going to be made needed to be made in the Ra-201 System, by the Anderonian officers present.

"Ambassador, we have a return transmission," Jackson informed her, about five seconds before Sylvia was going to check if there was a glitch in the system.

"We're sanitizing it and will forward it momentarily. Transmission is a video."

"Thank you, Lieutenant Commander."

The file arrived a few moments later, presumably having lacked any attached malware attempting to duplicate the mass shutdown inflicted on the E-Two force in Osiris-65.

The woman that appeared in the screen was Ashall, an orange-haired and gray-tusked Sana clad in a dark blue outfit that resembled nothing so much as a Roman toga worn over a shipsuit. Like Sylvia, she was alone in an office—and hers managed to be even *more* austere than Sylvia's, with no decoration at all visible.

"I am Star Legate Kosvana," she greeted Sylvia, "commanding officer of the Interior Defense Squadron. Your communication is appreciated. We have seen several forces of what we believe to be Kenmiri vessels pass through this system and have been maintaining defensive stealth."

Kosvana paused—and there was a small blip in the video footage that Sylvia's network confirmed was an editing splice. The message had been recorded in pieces as the Sana officer made her decisions bit by bit.

"I do not have the authority to commit my star system to anything," she finally noted. "The Vesheron and El-Vesheron are not regarded well among my leaders. Millions died when you bombarded Anderon.

"But."

That single Kem word hung in the air for several seconds and another editing splice.

"We have no desire to serve the Kenmiri again. I lack the authority to commit my system—but it is also not my place to bar a diplomatic contingent. I have a compromise to suggest."

Sylvia leaned forward. Her professional mask was up, but she wasn't recording herself yet.

"I am prepared to allow one vessel—the one shared by yourself and Commodore Henry Wong, by preference, to make the skip transit to Anderon. The rest of your Flotilla will remain here in Talana until the Executive makes a decision on your offer."

Talana, Sylvia presumed, was Ra-201—something she'd have the navigators put in their database. The UPSF preferred to use local names when they knew them, after all.

"A Kenmiri dreadnought passed through Talana toward Osiris some days ago," Kosvana noted, running a fingernail down her left tusk. She probably should have taken the nervous gesture out of the clearly edited video, but she had been speaking at that moment, Sylvia conceded. "You now emerge from the direction they went—and a squadron of escorts fled before you.

"I conclude that you have already fought the Kenmiri, and while we share an enemy, as you say, I do not wish my system to become dragged into a war we want no part of. I can only permit the passage of one ship—and I am afraid I cannot guarantee the security of the vessels remaining in the Talana System.

"This is the best option I see for both of us, Ambassador. And I must warn you: If you attempt to make the transit without permission, I will turn the guns of my squadron upon you without hesitation.

"No one in Anderon will weep for Vesheron too foolish to have patience."

The video ended and Sylvia snorted. That last comment was clearly intended to refer to a *lot* more than just the current situation.

From a diplomatic perspective, though, Kosvana's offer was perfect. She needed to talk to Henry—and Tol Azan and Falling Rain, for that matter. She couldn't make the decision to leave the entire Flotilla behind on her own.

Given that it was exactly what they'd done at Rashova, though, she was certain she'd get the military officers to sign off.

And everybody would be left hoping *this* visit to a former Kenmiri colony went more smoothly.

33

HOLOGRAMS of the Kozun Squadron Leader and the Enteni Defender took their places in Sylvia's office moments before Henry arrived. Despite her earlier mental ruminations on the differing levels of prep required for their respective "uniforms," she had to admit that there was nothing *lacking* in the gravitas of the black-uniformed graying Asian man with the blood-red pilots' wings on his chest and the Commodore's gold oak leaf on his jacket's high collar.

He calmly took the seat she'd put out for him, creating a square of people and holograms facing each other.

"The Anderonians are uncomfortable with us bringing an entire battle group into their star system," she told the military officers. "The commander on the scene, a Star Legate Kosvana, has suggested a compromise.

"She has asked that most of the Forward Flotilla remain here in Ra-Two-Oh-One while we send one ship forward with the diplomatic contingent."

She surveyed her alien and human companions for a moment, then continued.

"Since the UPA's contingent is aboard *Paladin* and we had previously agreed to allow the UPA to lead on this, I believe the solution is obvious. I did not, however, wish to make the decision unilaterally."

Consensus-building, after all, was the heart and soul of diplomacy.

"That is-was the plan for Rashova," Falling Rain agreed. "But the fates have-will changed since then. There is-will-be no time for crossed winds and lost waters."

"My orders from my Arbiter are clear," Tol Azan said slowly. "We have absolute faith in you, Ambassador Todorovich. I still have to agree with Defender Falling Rain. We can afford no confusion. No failures of communication."

"But we also cannot afford to damage this relationship before it begins," Henry warned before Sylvia could say a word. "I will *not* watch billions die again, my friends. I will not. If Anderon is only willing to let us send a single ship, then we send a single ship.

"I suggest, though this is a diplomatic call, that we take representatives aboard *Paladin* from the La-Tar Cluster and the Eerdish-Enteni Alliance."

"I agree," Sylvia said instantly. She'd been mentally fumbling toward the same solution herself, but Henry had spoken first. "We are *allies* here. I have no desire to make separate treaties or concealed decisions. Avoiding confusion is absolutely critical.

"We may also be served by the fact that the Enteni and Eerdish homeworlds are not led by Vesheron and were never El-Vesheron," she continued. "The destruction of the Kenmorad creche on Anderon caused massive collateral damage. That will be held against us, I am afraid."

One of the problems the Diplomatic Corps had anticipated—but failed to fully allow for—was that the Vesheron had been a very small portion of the population under Kenmiri rule. While there were few Vesheron groups that hadn't worked with the UPSF over the years of the war, they couldn't rely on every successor state having Vesheron as its leaders or even advisors.

For a leadership born out of the sudden withdrawal of the Kenmiri, with no assistance from the rebels and with a major environmental crisis triggered by the Vesheron's attack on the Kenmorad...Sylvia could very much see the allies having been Vesheron working against them.

"This is-was-will-be logical," Falling Rain said. "I can-will select a representative to send aboard *Paladin*."

"And we will do the same," Tol Azan agreed. "If that is agreeable to everyone, of course?"

"We are allies," Sylvia repeated. "We have fought and bled by each other's sides to get this far. We must stand together in these discussions to protect the future of this entire sector.

"This Vengeance Fleet is determined to burn us all to ash. We need to convince the Anderonians of the threat—and that it is best fought standing together.

"How better to do that than by showing the alliances we already have?"

THE HOLOGRAMS VANISHED and Sylvia arched an eyebrow at her lover.

"I was hoping to get to sleep after we had sex," she admitted. "Doesn't seem to have happened."

"I *was* asleep." Henry gestured a holographic map of the star system into existence in the middle of her officer. "And I'm going back to sleep very shortly here. Probably once the personnel transfer is complete."

"Where are you even going to *put* more diplomats?"

"This isn't *Raven*. We have the Presence Mission Section and an actual set of guest quarters." He grinned. "We don't have to decide between a squadron commander and guests—even if we *did* decide that the squadron commander had the tiniest staff we could justify."

"So, you have space for, what, two more diplomats?" Sylvia asked.

"Captain Ihejirika has space for as many diplomats from each of our allies as are willing to squeeze into one room each." He paused in exaggerating reflection. "They're not very big rooms, so they may want to be conservative."

"I have faith in the Chief Petty Officers of the United Planets Space

Force to find a way to make it all work," Sylvia told him, then bit off a yawn.

"My faith in my Chiefs is infinite. But even they are only known to bend the laws of physics, not break them entirely."

Henry crossed to her chair and pressed a kiss to her forehead.

"Now, I should note that even I don't need to supervise the personnel transfer," he told her. "I will, because there are old spacers and bold spacers but not many old bold spacers. *You*, on the other hand, I need well rested when we get into Anderon.

"So, I suggest, my dear Ambassador, that you go back to sleep."

"We have to get this right, Henry," Sylvia whispered. The image of Rashova burning flashed before her eyes, and she shivered. She was with him on that—she wasn't prepared to watch another world burn if she could do anything to stop it.

"Yes. And that is why you should sleep," he repeated. "I'm going to do everything I can to get the entire Flotilla to *rest* while we're in Anderon. I want an awake and refreshed force when Vengeance Fleet arrives.

"But I *need* an awake and refreshed Ambassador when we meet the locals."

34

CLOSE UP TO the large cruiser, even *Paladin*'s scanners were sufficient to provide Henry with a far deeper look at the Anderon ship's secrets than he suspected Star Legate Kosvana would prefer.

The ship was a mashup of a thousand compromises. Her base hull was a standard Kenmiri five-million-ton transport, a cylinder eleven hundred meters long and three hundred meters wide. Her engines had been upgraded to handle the extra mass of her armor and armament but were still fundamentally civilian thrusters.

The escorts hovering around Kosvana's flagship were faster than their larger cousin, but they were true warships in a way the technical wasn't.

The irony of the Kenmiri's style of dreadnought construction was that if the Kenmiri *had* the ability to produce thick capital-ship armor, they'd never bothered. Escorts had a dozen centimeters or so of some highly advanced energy-dispersing ceramics, but the dreadnoughts had settled for a dozen *meters* of purified nickel-iron.

Fronted and backed, of course, by those same energy-dispersing ceramics. But where, say, the El-Vesheron Londu had built battleships with meter-thick modern armor, the Kenmiri had relied primarily on their thick reforged asteroid hulls and energy screens to protect their capital ships.

But Anderon no longer had the infrastructure necessary to reforge asteroids like that. So, the plating that would have armored an escort or been used as an ablative layer on a dreadnought was all the armor the Anderonians had.

So, the cruiser was covered in it. It looked like they'd assembled multiple layers for thicker sections over key systems, but it was still lacking to Henry's eyes.

She also had energy shields, at least, but Henry could also see where that came up short. The projectors were right, but there weren't enough of them and there wasn't enough power behind them.

And that brought him to the ship's key weakness: her power systems. Kenmiri dreadnoughts used massive, hyperefficient fusion cores, a derivation of the same technology that underlay their main guns. The Anderon LTC didn't have those cores. She had the same power sources as her escorts—in vastly greater quantities, layered through the hull like tapioca in bubble tea.

It gave her a redundancy to damage that a dreadnought lacked—but the dreadnought wouldn't *take* as much damage as the technical. And it meant she had more volume and mass dedicated to power generation for less output.

And the focus had very clearly been on *arming* the ship. Twelve of the same massive turreted plasma cannon that armed Kenmiri dreadnoughts were mounted evenly along her hull, supported by an equal number of lasers and protected by a vast array of antimissile lasers that put a dreadnought to shame.

"She's a fascinating ship, ser," Ihejirika observed, the captain clearly going over the same data as Henry. "Nothing short of a carrier's full fighter strike is going to get missiles through her defenses, and anything that comes into plasma range is going to get hurt."

"She'll kill dreadnoughts, given half a chance," Henry agreed. "But she'll die doing it. The first time one of these technicals ends up in range of a dreadnought, they're both going to die in short order.

"It won't take much luck on the dreadnought's part for them to survive—but it will take a *lot* of luck for the cruiser to make it through."

"Glass cannons."

"What else are you going to do?" Henry murmured. "The Kenmiri are *right there.*" He gestured vaguely in the direction of the Osiris-65 skip line. "When the enemy is just over the next hill, you need something to fight them.

"You put these into the line against a dreadnought squadron, they'll pay with blood—but you've got a good chance of *stopping* said squadron."

"How many do you figure they have?"

"If one is out here, watching the skip line from Osiris? At least six," Henry replied. "Given the reports on what industry Anderon has… could be as many as twelve. I'll be stunned if there's sixteen."

"Pleasant surprise, I suppose," Ihejirika noted, his gaze flicking back to the seven Anderon warships on the screen. "Anything to even the odds."

THE SKIP to Anderon was a long one, with two secondary impulse kicks along the way. Any icosadimensional impulse confused the human brain, and Henry's experience was that the more he endured in a given period of time, the worse it got.

To sustain a skip, best practice was to inject a new twenty-dimensional vector every eight hours, give or take. So, every skip that lasted more than sixteen hours required two impulses after the initial entry—and the strangest interpretations of them always hit on the third.

"I believe I just got punched in the stomach by the color red and the flavor of tapioca," Chan said in a faintly ill voice.

"The good news, Commander, is that you never have to worry about four skip impulses in twenty-four hours," Henry replied with a chuckle. His own reaction this time had been his brain interpreting the impulse as *sound*.

And not overly pleasant sounds, either.

No one who had ever made a skip jump would ever dismiss complaints of synesthesia. The momentary experience of similar sensations when jumping was more than enough to earn sympathy for people who dealt with it every day.

"Yeah, because all evidence suggests that the fourth impulse *disintegrates the ship*," Charmchi reminded them, the navigator sounding more amused than anything else on the link from the bridge. "Even this skip is long enough to make a lot of planners uncomfortable."

Charmchi was the most junior department head and watch-standing officer on the ship. At Lieutenant Colonel Ihejirika's quiet request, Henry had the link between flag deck and command bridge more active on her watches than usual. Just in case.

"Please don't make me uncomfortable, Lieutenant," Henry told her. "Everything is working as expected, yes?"

"We have a full hour of safety margin," she said. "I've done the math in the past for twenty-three-hour-and-fifty-minute jumps, after all."

"In class," Henry guessed.

"Simulated, yes," she agreed. "Longest skips I've taken an actual ship through, well…all of them have been aboard *Paladin*, ser."

"You've done fine so far." He remembered the time he'd made Jackson and the other navigators of his squadron make the skip out of a pulsar system. The Drifters had done it first, after all, and he'd needed to catch up with them.

That stunt had earned Lieutenant Charmchi her first steel bar, though the paperwork making her a Lieutenant Commander was in transit somewhere between the Rashov System and Base Fallout in the Zion System.

"Emergence in about six and a half hours, ser," Charmchi reminded him. "All's quiet."

Henry hoped so. Without communications, the only "noise" that could show up right now would be trouble with the four alien officers they'd taken aboard from their allies—or something among the crew.

Crew trouble would be Ihejirika's problem, but if the officers who'd been picked as diplomatic representatives caused issues…that was *very* much Henry's job to resolve.

But for now, he was doing paperwork and providing a quiet and probably unnecessary backup to the destroyer's most junior watch officer.

Somehow, he expected these would be his last quiet moments for a long time.

35

THERE WERE times when the most important thing Sylvia could do was stay out of Henry Wong's way. That was when she stayed in her office, linked in to the tactical and sensor feeds to make sure she was aware of what happened but being very careful not to joggle her boyfriend's elbow.

Their partnership had flourished even before their romance, and the solid sense of where their responsibilities began, ended and overlapped had been key to that. If anything, their romance had initially *undermined* their partnership with concerns about compromised judgment—both on their part and the parts of others.

She was quite certain they were past that, and this was one of those times where their duties and responsibilities overlapped. That meant she had taken the observer chair on the flag deck and was seeing everything Henry was.

At that moment, that wasn't much. The strange gray darkness of the skip filled the screens, overlaid with a timer until they were expected to "fall" back into three-dimensional space.

"Thirty seconds," Eowyn reported.

Sylvia noted that everyone was on station, on both the flag deck and the bridge. *Paladin* wasn't officially at battle stations, but every post she'd seen on her way to the flag deck had been fully manned.

She didn't think the destroyer's weapons were fully charged, for example, but she suspected that every aspect of battle stations that *wasn't* detectable from outside the ship was fully in place.

"All systems report green," Ihejirika told Henry. "I'm hoping not to have to do anything complicated, ser, but *Paladin*'s people are ready."

Henry glanced back at Sylvia and met her gaze.

"We'll see. This is supposed to be very, very talky."

Any further discussion was wiped away by the universe shifting around them. The sensation of falling back into three-dimensional space, with null vectors in the other seventeen dimensions, was less harsh than the impulses…but it was still a shock to the system.

"Clear, sensors are processing," Eowyn reported. "Contact at one million kilometers. *Multiple* contacts at one million kilometers."

"Tell me what we've got," Henry urged.

Sylvia held her tongue, waiting for the data to come in. She was going to need to talk to people very quickly here, but the first step was making sure they weren't under attack.

"We have three large technicals at a million kilometers with eighteen escorts in company," Eowyn said after a few seconds. "They appear to have been on standard skip-line patrol. We cannot evade their maneuver cones."

"Understood. Further contacts?"

"We're sweeping for energy signatures. She's a busy system, but I can confirm that the yards over the gas giant have not been replaced," the operations officer said. "I have what looks like multiple LTCs in orbit of Anderon itself and approximately fifty escorts scattered around the system, including our welcoming committee.

"Civilian shipping is dense. Estimate two hundred–plus contacts. There may be more escorts hidden in the traffic."

"Three seconds each way," Henry murmured, then turned to Sylvia. "Are you ready, Ambassador?"

She was as rested, caffeinated, briefed and prepared as she could be. Sylvia knew her job, after all, and simply nodded to him.

"Chan, set up the link. Let's say hello."

THERE WAS no point in pretending she wasn't aboard a warship that had entered the Anderon System with minimal warning. By communicating from *Paladin*'s flag deck, Sylvia was hoping to make it clear that she and the military side of things were in full alignment.

"Anderon vessels, I am Ambassador Sylvia Todorovich of the United Planets Alliance," she announced herself. "Star Legate Kosvana sent a vessel ahead to advise you of our arrival, but we will of course remain on our current vector until we receive a course from you.

"I am here, with designated representatives from the La-Tar Cluster and the Eerdish-Enteni Alliance, to negotiate with the Executive of the Anderon System. We bear warning of a mutual threat that has already ravaged the Rashova System, and an offer of alliance.

"I request permission for this vessel to enter orbit of Anderon and for myself and a delegation to visit the surface and engage in discussions with your Executive."

Sylvia had very little information on the current structure of the Anderon government. The Enteni had engaged in some trade with the system but nothing so official as to involve either state. She knew that the Executive was the leadership of Anderon—but she wasn't even entirely sure if the Executive was a single individual or a council.

For all she knew, it was a super powerful AI, though the Kenmiri had never seen a point in giving their artificial intelligences enough personality or broad-enough remits to make that likely. While humanity had certainly *made* true "silicon person"–level AI, they'd found that high-intelligence, narrow-remit, low-personality intelligences were so much more *useful*.

That rumination carried her long enough for the commander of the defensive squadron to reply to her hail, creating a two-way video link and revealing the *last* thing Sylvia had expected to be aboard an Anderon warship: a Kenmiri Warrior in full regalia.

A black uniform of a more Ashall style covered the Warrior, with the rank insignia that would have been carved into their chest carapace instead neatly embroidered on the chest of the tunic.

For a moment, Sylvia was afraid that Vengeance Fleet had beaten them there—except the ships on *Paladin*'s sensors were definitely the local-built large cruisers. A moment later, she realized that the bridge the Warrior occupied was plainer than most Kenmiri command centers she'd seen and that there was only one other Kenmiri in the space—along with at least three different varieties of Ashall and an Enteni.

"Ambassador Sylviatodorovich," the Warrior greeted her, slurring her name into a single word. "Star Legate Kosvana did send word of your delegation. While *I* have concerns about letting more humans into our star system…I have been overruled."

Sylvia had never expected to see Kenmiri in the assorted successor states. Her understanding was that *all* of the Kenmiri had been withdrawn to the core provinces…but it made sense, she supposed, that not all the Kenmiri on the colonies would have gone.

It was a surprise to see one of them accepting a mid-level role amidst their former slaves, though—let alone to see them surrounded by Ashall that clearly trusted and followed the Warrior.

"Your forbearance and trust are appreciated, Star…" She let the half-complete title hang to prompt the alien for their rank and name. She doubted the commander of the defensive squadron held any of the Kenmiri ranks that *didn't* start with *Star*—since any of them would be too junior to command *a* cruiser, let alone a division of them.

"I am Star Master Eledar and the trust is not mine," Eledar growled. "The Executive agrees with Star Legate Kosvana. We will transmit a course—but one of my Protector ships will accompany you with guns trained.

"My government is prepared to hear you out, humans. But if you seek to rain fire on this system once again, I will tear your throats out before you can begin.

"You have my sacred word."

The video feed cut out, leaving *Paladin*'s flag deck very quiet.

"You know, I think I like him," Henry finally said.

Sylvia turned to give her partner A Look. He shrugged back at her.

"He's dedicated to his duty, sworn to protect people who aren't all Kenmiri and *hates* us for killing his parents," Henry noted. "And I can't blame him for that last at all.

"Yet he still accepts—not merely *obeys* but *accepts*—orders to see us safely to his government. He's taking a, frankly, entirely reasonable precaution by keeping us under the guns of one of his ships. And he made it very clear to us what he was doing and why."

"I'm guessing the Protector ships are the LTCs?" Eowyn asked.

"Has to be," Henry agreed. "Chan, do we have that course?"

"We do," the coms officer confirmed. "Point-four KPS-squared. Will bring us to zero-zero with the planet in about six and a half hours. A bit over three light-minutes."

"Make sure Charmchi has it. And let's keep our eyes open, people. Just because we *think* we know what Star Master Eledar is thinking doesn't mean we're right."

Sylvia was moderately certain that the Star Master—equivalent to a UPSF Rear Admiral—wasn't going to lure them into open space and then vaporize them.

But *moderately* certain wasn't *completely* certain—and there was a Kenmiri battle fleet on its way.

If there were Kenmiri *there*, there'd almost certainly been Kenmiri in Rashova—and that hadn't slowed Vengeance Fleet at all. Star Master Eledar's presence was a surprise but not one that was going to change Anderon's fate.

That was up to Sylvia Todorovich.

36

ANDERON WAS A BEAUTIFUL PLANET. Like all Kenmiri colonies, it was on the cold side for human preferences, but its equatorial regions were perfectly comfortable. Natural rings hung in the sky above them as the shuttle followed the ordered course toward the surface—and the ring of *artificial* stations only added to the effect.

The worlds the Kenmiri picked for themselves, after all, had almost no industry on the surface. Massive foundries and factories orbited in the gap between Anderon's two rings, mixed in with defensive platforms and spaceships.

The water beneath the shuttle had a paler tinge to it than Sylvia had seen on most worlds, the surface seeming to have an almost baby-blue froth to it—and a similar pale blue tinge hovered over the continent they were flying toward, presumably from the vegetation.

"We'll be touching down in about five minutes," the pilot announced over his shoulder. "It looks like they're giving us a bit of a runaround—I'm guessing they don't want to take us over the city."

The nonhumans in the shuttle looked confused for a moment before Sylvia's aide translated the pilot's English into Kem. Asim Sikora was an Egyptian diplomat, one of the few members of Sylvia's staff who hadn't joined the Diplomatic Corps until after the war.

His Kem was fluent enough for all that, and the young man was bright and eager. He was mostly on *this* trip, though, because he'd passed the Diplomatic Corps VIP protection course. Sikora wasn't *primarily* a bodyguard—he was an economic analyst and was officially along today as Sylvia's secretary.

But he'd impressed Quang Nguyen enough that he'd been issued an energy pistol and was part of the tactical network with the squad of GroundDiv troopers sharing the shuttle with the diplomats—though Sylvia wasn't supposed to know about that, she suspected.

"The city will be on our left in a moment," the pilot announced.

Sylvia appreciated the heads-up and adjusted her virtual window in that direction. The Anderon port city that came into view wasn't the largest city on the planet, but it was one of three major spaceports and was the primary oceanic port on the smaller of the two inhabited continents.

The name was a mouthful of archaic Kenmiri dialect that translated into English as *Stormshelter*, but the city itself was light-years from archaic. It was a clearly planned settlement that both stood out from and blended into the stark chalk bluffs that sheltered the natural harbor and the gleaming white beaches of the harbor itself.

Kenmiri architecture had many styles, and the Artisans designing Stormshelter had gone for rounded domes and pyramids that seemed to grow out of the white rock like they were part of it. The buildings *gleamed* in the afternoon sun, the gold tracery on the white stone unintelligible at this distance but still adding a spark of reflected light.

"Damn," Sikora breathed, switching back to Kem as he glanced at their guests. "I have seen Kenmiri architecture but nothing like this."

"You have seen the architecture Kenmiri build on the slave worlds," the Beren diplomat Opanree replied. The orange-eyed woman was, if Sylvia understood correctly, the executive officer of one of Tol Azan's ships. Sylvia wasn't sure why Opanree had been selected as the La-Tar representative, but she seemed intelligent enough.

"That is built to impress, awe and intimidate," Opanree continued after Sikora nodded his confirmation. "Everything on the slave worlds is a component of a giant system of laws, imagery and violence to keep us in check. Even the homes of the Kenmiri."

"This…" Opanree gestured at the city. "This is what the Kenmiri build for themselves when they do not care what it looks like to someone else."

"We just got lit up by another round of targeting scanners," the pilot reported briskly. "Ambassador?"

"How many is this?" Sylvia asked.

"This is the fourth since we broke atmo. I'm receiving new instructions from ground control," they continued after a moment. "I think… Yeah. I'm flagging our destination to your network, Ambassador."

"Thank you."

Sylvia focused her virtual window in the direction the pilot had sent—and then had to consult her network for a sense of scale as she swallowed.

The five-level stepped pyramid they were being directed to was large enough that the landing pad was on the third level, twenty meters above the surrounding grassland. Eighty meters tall at its peak, the pyramid was half a kilometer wide at its base.

"Is it going to be a problem, Lieutenant Macdonald?" Sylvia asked the pilot, eyeing a disturbingly small landing pad.

The officer chuckled.

"A problem? Nah. Perhaps a bit too much fun, that's all!"

A SURPRISINGLY UNHARROWING approach to and landing on a giant building later, Sylvia watched the shuttle ramp extend and made certain every crease of her gray suit was perfect. Two of the GroundDiv troopers, dressed in ceremonial uniforms that concealed very real armor, blocked the way out of the shuttle. In case the diplomats got any ideas, she figured with a wry smile.

That was the last emotion she allowed to touch her face, locking in her professional mask as the ramp touched down and the doors slid open. The first pair of GroundDiv swept out, followed by two more.

Then Sylvia and Sikora stepped out, followed by their allies and then the last four troopers. Safety barriers retracted into their casings as she stepped out onto the reinforced stone of the landing pad, and a greeting party clad in long tunics emerged from behind them.

Red-tunicked soldiers spread out to meet hers in a formal evolution that could have been choreographed for how perfectly it took place. White-tunicked officials formed most of the group leading toward her.

So far, everyone she'd seen had been Ashall. She'd seen Tak, Sana, Beren, Kozun, and one of the white-clad officials had the pale jade-green skin of an Eerdish.

Then the crowd of officials separated slightly and a figure she hadn't seen before stepped through. The stranger was shorter than everyone around him but wearing a pale blue robe that matched the color of the sea outside.

He cut a portly figure, with graying brown hair, and Sylvia spent most of the ten seconds it took him to reach her trying to place which type of Ashall he was—and then realized that he was very definitively *human*.

"Ambassador Sylvia Todorovich," he greeted her in clipped British received pronunciation. "Welcome to Anderon. I am Executive Gregor Robertson."

"I...did not expect the Executive to be *human*," Sylvia replied slowly, realizing that she'd been surprised enough to lose some of her mask.

From the smirk on Robertson's face, he'd anticipated that.

"The Executive is a pentacameral ruling council that serves as joint head of state and government for the Republic of Anderon," Robertson told her—and suddenly Sylvia was *very* sure the man was a teacher of some kind. "The first Executive was selected by Third Governor Okalta after the Withdrawal, but the current Executive was appointed by the Grand Assembly after the Republic's first election."

"Very few successor states have managed to make it to elections yet," Sylvia murmured. "I'm impressed."

She was also running the man's name against the list of known human kidnappees. A small colony had been kidnapped from the Zion System, and there had been ships and outposts lost during the war, but over ninety percent of the victims known to have been enslaved by the Kenmiri had been recovered.

And Gregor Robertson wasn't on the list. A mystery to go with an anomaly...but neither were entirely relevant to her *mission*.

"Your story must be fascinating, Executive Robinson," she continued. "But I am sadly here because Anderon is in immediate and critical danger."

"We all reviewed the message you sent Star Legate Kosvana," Robertson told her. "Please, come with me. The Executive awaits you and your companions."

He quirked a corner of his mouth in a small half-smile.

"I just suspected it would serve best if you met *me* before the rest."

THE EXTERIOR of the step pyramid was the same gleaming white native stone as most of Stormshelter, but now Sylvia was close enough to make out the decorative inlays. Whatever luster the stone itself lacked was made up for by the complicated intertwining lines of silver and gold that formed linework versions of some of the familiar Kenmiri myth scenes.

Robertson led her delegation and his own flock of aides into the pyramid, where the delicate tracery gave way to murals and bronze sculpture. Unlike many of the former Kenmiri worlds Sylvia had been on, it was clear that the art was still being cleaned and maintained.

That made it less of a surprise when she spotted a trio of brown-tunicked Kenmiri Drones working away at an open stone panel, fiddling with some portion of the pyramid's electronics.

"This was the regional administration center for the Kenmiri governors," Robertson told Sylvia and her companions, switching to a Kem that still carried his British accent. "We felt, after the Withdrawal, that using the primary administration center would be foolish. It would seem arrogant to our Kenmiri citizens—and would be a warning sign of danger to come for our non-Kenmiri."

"I'm surprised the Kenmiri remained at all," Opanree observed, the Beren officer looking around with watchful eyes. "I spent time on Kori, but even there...we were slaves."

"Make no mistake, Commander Opanree, we were all slaves here,"

Robertson observed, his tone grim. "I was a favored *pet*. But unlike the occupied homeworlds and the forced-labor production worlds, the Kenmiri colonies were *home* to the Kenmiri who lived here.

"Over ninety percent of the Kenmiri on Anderon were evacuated in the Withdrawal, but that still left twenty million Artisans, Drones and Warriors who preferred to stay in their homes rather than flee to the Core. We are fortunate, I think, that Third Governor Okalta chose to remain. They recognized that the remaining Kenmiri could not force their will on an entire world.

"The transition from Kenmiri rule to the interim Executive was surprisingly smooth—and I say that as both the architect and one of the members of that Executive!"

"The architect?" Sylvia asked.

"That is a discussion for another time," Executive Robertson told her calmly as he paused in front of what Sylvia had taken to be a pair of massive decorative tiles—but now revealed themselves to be a pair of six-meter-tall square stone doors.

"The rest of the Executive of Anderon awaits us."

THE DOORS OPENED SLOWLY, revealing a space that was a one-hundredth-scale version of the pyramid itself. A quartet of openings in the roof ran all the way to the outside of the building, bringing in natural light to suffuse the room.

Four more people in the same pale blue robe as Robertson were waiting in the middle of the room, seated at four points around a white stone table with one long side and five shorter ones facing it. The table was clearly new, carved for its current purpose—but definitely made by Kenmiri Artisans, from the gold leafing.

Sylvia had been expecting the Kenmiri Artisan at this point. The other three were an Enteni, a Tak, and a Sana.

The seat across from the center of the petitioner's side of the table was empty, but Gregor Robertson walked around the table to take it. Five-sentient coequal Executive or not, Sylvia suspected the chubby human was first among equals there.

"Please, Ambassador, be seated," the Kenmiri instructed.

Six chairs had been laid out for them, and Sylvia gestured for her companions to obey.

"Ambassador Sylvia Todorovich, be known to the Executive of Anderon," the blue-robed Artisan continued. "I am Executive Okalta. You have met Executive Gregor Robertson. Know Executive Desert Wind, Executive Sho Naka, and Executive Tanseya."

Okalta's delicate armored fingers indicated the Enteni, the Tak, and the Sana in turn. Sylvia noted with interest that they had actually given the assorted non-Kenmiri their family names, a level of respect rarely shown by Kenmiri of any stripe.

Desert Wind was possibly the palest Enteni Sylvia had ever seen, with the same pale blue shade to their skin as she'd seen in the water and vegetation outside.

Sho Naka was a squat Tak with the blackest skin and head tendrils Sylvia had encountered on a Tak. Tanseya shared Naka's dark coloring, but had metallic-sheened hair that was almost true gold—and had plated her tusks in gold to match.

"We speak for the People and the Republic of Anderon," Robertson told Sylvia's party. "Depending on our discussions, we may need to take aspects or the entirety of the results to the Grand Assembly for a vote by the elected representatives of our Citizens."

"I understand," Sylvia confirmed. That was basically the structure of the United Planets Alliance, though the Security Council was directly appointed by the member governments rather than selected by the General Assembly.

"You have come a long way through unfriendly stars to reach us," Sho Naka said. "You may not be as welcome here as you think, Ambassador, but we are prepared to hear you out."

"Despite the crimes the United Planets Space Force committed in this system," Tanseya growled.

"Peace, Executive Tanseya," Okalta requested. "The war brought much sorrow. Your brother would not have us add to it." Their pincer snapped in a convulsive gesture, one that Sylvia doubted was overly happy.

"I cannot say the same for my creche-parents, but the Charge remains."

Sylvia wasn't entirely sure what "the Charge" was, but if it got her a chance to convince the Executive to let her save Anderon, she was glad it existed.

"Please, Ambassador," Robertson told her. "You have come a long way and we have been warned you bear dark tidings. I hope you also bear hope."

"I believe I do, if you will accept it from us," she warned. She nodded to Sikora, who laid an attaché case on the table and activated the holoprojector. An image of the planet Rashov appeared in front of her.

"You are, I hope, familiar with Rashova," she said. "Do you know what has happened there?"

Her audience exchanged silent glances, but it was Robertson who spoke again.

"We have had some official communication and trade with the Rashova System," he confirmed. "But we have not heard from them in some time."

"I was afraid of that." Sylvia linked into the attaché-case projector from her network and activated the recording. "This visual recording is reconstructed from our scan data of the events of approximately twenty-six days ago. Full sensor data is included on a data drive we will provide you for detailed examination, but this recording will carry the gist."

It was a short recording. It showed the march of death as Vengeance Fleet's missiles descended on Rashov's defensive forts, destroying the planet's defenders, and then crashing in on the planet itself in a choreographed cascade of Armageddon.

The Executives were silent as the recording played and remained so after it finished.

"Our scans confirmed that the fusion warheads bombarding Rashov were laced with heavy metals that would be activated as highly radioactive isotopes with sufficiently varied half-lives to render Rashov uninhabitable for a minimum of a hundred years."

Another command expanded the view, showing the attackers.

"From our limited communications with the Kenmiri Remnant, this fleet is *not* an officially supported operation," Sylvia pointed out, looking at Okalta. The Kenmiri met her gaze impassively, and she wished she'd dealt with Kenmiri more.

For an enemy she'd spent her adult life fighting, she'd been in the same room with *very* few Kenmiri.

"They appear to call themselves Vengeance Fleet and are a rogue faction of Warriors that seem to have decided that the Kenmiri will not die alone. Our intelligence sources"—she wasn't going to *name* the Drifters as that source, not among strangers—"warned us that their plan was to eliminate the former Kenmiri colonies first to remove the possibility of significant capital-ship strength being deployed against them.

"The astrography of the Ra Sector makes you their next target." As she spoke, the projection changed from the view of Vengeance Fleet to a view of the route between Rashova and Anderon.

"Rashova *had* produced a number of dreadnoughts they deployed to defend themselves. Vengeance Fleet took significant damage and will be taking time to repair, refit and rearm. We encountered raiding parties of theirs in Kenmiri space that were attempting to hijack supply convoys to restock the Fleet.

"But there is a limit to how long they are likely to take rearming, and they are only thirteen days from here. They're coming, Executives. If they are not stopped, they will burn your world to ashes. Then they will proceed to Kori and do the same. Then they will begin to reduce homeworlds, industrial worlds, agriworlds…until Ra Sector is nothing but a graveyard and they move onto the Apophis or Geb Sector."

There was a long, long silence.

"They deny the Charge," Okalta finally said. "But that has always been a risk."

"They accuse your people of this kind of slaughter, and you *believe* them?" Tanseya demanded. "Reconquest of worlds, perhaps, but this destruction is beyond all logic."

"We are charged to protect the Ashall, not destroy them," Okalta agreed. They glanced over at Desert Wind. "With non-Ashall races, we simply slotted them into the structure we created to honor the Charge.

"But you are correct. This is beyond logic, beyond honor. The Charge sings in their blood, and they deny it with fire and death. But I know my people."

The Artisan met Sylvia's gaze again.

"We will need to review the full sensor data," they told her. "But I see the doom you bear. Desert Wind. Against the fleet the Ambassador has shown us, how would our Protectors stand?"

The Enteni's fronds shivered as Desert Wind twisted their massive mouth, allowing their eyes to study the hologram more closely.

"We would-will die valiantly," their artificial voice finally said. "But against over thirty dreadnoughts, we can-could not prevail. But our Protectors can-will not yield."

"But they will die."

Robertson's words hung in the air, an acknowledgement of what Sylvia hoped all of the Executive had realized.

"And all of our people will die with them," he continued. "We are not the Kenmiri Empire. We lack the transports to evacuate hundreds of millions—and even if we managed to evacuate those hundreds of millions in mere days, we would leave hundreds of millions behind.

"It seems, Ambassador Todorovich, that we of the Executive of Anderon underestimated the darkness of the tidings you bear. But you told me that you also bear hope."

He raised an eyebrow at her.

"Tell us."

"We and our allies sent a flotilla to make contact with Rashova and negotiate an alliance of mutual defense," Sylvia said. "Our hope was to use the intelligence we had received to bring the powers of the Ra Sector together to stand as one—slave world, homeworld and colony world united against a rogue faction that would exterminate us all.

"We were too late," she admitted. That was going to haunt everyone who'd been aboard *Paladin* for a long, long time. "But the Allied Forward Flotilla survived. They now wait in the Talana System, a twenty-three-hour skip from here.

"Permission from you could see another dozen warships added to your defense in two days. Those crews require rest and the ships could use restocking and repairs, but we will stand with you.

"But that flotilla is only the scouts," she noted, seeing that Desert Wind, at least, recognized how little difference the Forward Flotilla would make. "Here with me are representatives from our allies in the Enteni and Eerdish homeworlds as well as the La-Tar Cluster.

"All of their nations and governments have committed ships to join a major fleet formation anchored on the United Planets Alliance Twelfth Fleet. That fleet, led by six carriers and six battlecruisers, is prepared to stand in your defense."

"And which continent are your people going to bombard *this* time?" Tanseya demanded. "There is no trust here for the murderers of the UPSF."

"Can-will they even make it in time?" Desert Wind asked. "The Kenmiri could-might be here tomorrow. Your Fleet is-was where? La-Tar? Your own stars?"

"Per the plans in place when we arrived in the Rashova System, Twelfth Fleet should have departed for Anderon when we did not report in," Sylvia admitted. "They are three or four days from here, potentially already making contact with whatever early-warning pickets you have in place around your system.

"It is within my authority to turn Twelfth Fleet *back*, if you require it," she assured them. "Their approach is based on the assumption that I and the rest of the Forward Flotilla are dead.

"We will not force you to accept our help, if Executive Tanseya represents your final decision. With your permission, we can send a communication drone to Admiral Rex that will advise Twelfth Fleet of your decision."

Sylvia considered her options. At least one of the five sentients at the table clearly hated the UPA—Okalta had suggested that Tanseya's brother had died in the creche bombardment, and there was no way she was the only one on Anderon who had lost family there. The former Kenmiri Third Governor had every reason to mistrust Sylvia—and Sylvia wasn't entirely sure she trusted Okalta, either.

The others were unknowns. Desert Wind at least understood how dire the military situation was. Sylvia wasn't sure how many of the big technical cruisers the Anderonians had, but she doubted it was enough to stand off Vengeance Fleet.

These people *needed* Twelfth Fleet. And *Sylvia* needed to not watch them die…which meant she needed their trust.

"We also have, thanks to sources I cannot betray, full specifications of the new superdreadnoughts leading Vengeance Fleet," she finally told them. "They have developed multiple new combat systems, including an extremely effective antifighter weapon.

"Twelfth Fleet is a carrier-centered fleet, which means that we need to find a counter for those weapons. Regardless of whether you wish us to help, I am prepared to provide those schematics and associated information."

Every set of eyes on the plasma-web schematics increased the chances of finding the countermeasure Twelfth Fleet needed.

And she'd brought the data in Sikora's case anyway.

"Sooner or later, we and our allies must fight Vengeance Fleet," Sylvia concluded. "If we do so here, we do so at your side with our combined forces—and we can save Anderon. If you refuse our help, we will fight them later. Without your ships…and with everyone you are sworn to protect already dead."

"Peace, Tanseya," Sho Naka barked as the gold-haired Sana began to open her mouth. "Let us fight in private." The Tak leveled a dark gaze on Sylvia. "We will have staff escort you and your companions to a place where you may wait in comfort."

"As you wish," Sylvia agreed. She gestured to the holoprojector case on the table. "We will leave the datacase here. It contains both the sensor data on Rashova's fate and the schematics on the Vengeance Fleet superdreadnoughts.

"The decision, Executives of Anderon, is yours. We will not invade your system to save you."

37

SYLVIA AND HER fellow delegates were led to a smaller, less ostentatious room to wait. This one had no windows or light channels, settling instead for decorative lamps that barely seemed to even glow when looked at but filled the room with a calm, indirect light.

"What happens now, Ambassador?" Sikora asked.

She glanced at her aide and then at the nonhuman representatives who'd accompanied her but remained silent while she spoke. They'd been present as much to make a show of standing together as anything else—and, Sylvia supposed, to make sure she didn't go too off-script.

"We wait," she told the young analyst. "We are offering to help them, with no strings, no ulterior motives. It would seem a good offer —but I worry they will see it as too good to be true and look for the trap. For the lie."

"Your people are not without their motives," Opanree observed. The Beren woman was examining the comfortable-looking couches with a paranoid eye. "It has taken some effort on the part of the Cluster's government to keep your corporations from trying to take advantage of us."

The industrial worlds could produce a lot of things that the United Planets Alliance wanted, but they also had many needs that their own economies couldn't produce. Like, for example, air scrubbers to keep their factories from polluting the air.

The main selling point of the Peacekeeper Initiative had been the hope of trade deals into a no-longer-at-war Ra Sector—a hope that had proven out in spectacular fashion.

"There are supposed to be people on our side making sure of that as well," Sylvia replied. "We made treaties with La-Tar. We will be making trade treaties with everyone who is willing. But the best trades make everyone better off."

"You have some businesses operating in La-Tar who do not appear to believe that," Opanree said drily. "But they have been restrained so far."

"Good." Sylvia was beginning to see why Tol Azan had picked Opanree to be the senior La-Tar representative. She might be a warship officer now, but she'd apparently *been* to one of the Kenmiri colony worlds prior to the Fall, and she seemed tuned in to some of the downsides of the UPA's alliance with La-Tar.

Sylvia *preferred* that in many ways. She wanted Anderon to join them with eyes open—though the biggest downside Anderon was currently facing was that Twelfth Fleet was going to turn their system into a battlefield.

And since Vengeance Fleet was coming *anyway*, Sylvia couldn't see that as much of a price. She just had to hope that the locals agreed with her there.

A door slid open before the conversation could continue, revealing a trio of brown-tunicked Ashall bearing trays of food and pitchers of water.

"The Executive instructed that you be provided food and drink," the lead woman told Sylvia. "They are uncertain how long their deliberations will take."

"Is anyone going to object if I make contact with our ship?" Sylvia asked.

The local looked confused and glanced around. "You have no communication hardware. Will you need us to provide a communicator?"

Sylvia tapped her temple. In truth, she'd be transmitting to the *shuttle*, which would relay her message up to *Paladin* with its more powerful transceivers—but she definitely didn't need any extra equipment.

"I do not require one. But I do not wish to be rude and transmit without permission."

"We have no orders to restrict your communications," the woman said after a moment. "You may even return to your shuttle, if you wish, but you will be escorted through the Administration Center."

"That is fair. Thank you."

"WE'RE KEEPING an eye on things up here," Henry told her once she'd established the link. "Counting ships, mostly."

"And how's that going for us?" Sylvia asked, looking around the waiting area from the corner she'd claimed for herself. The couches were surprisingly comfortable, using some kind of smart cushioning that automatically adjusted for the proportions of whoever was sitting on it.

"We've identified nine individual technicals," he said. "Sixty-five escorts. Fifteen gunships. They had six more escorts and another technical cruiser in Talana, so I'm guessing they have the same on the other side of the other two skip lines.

"Twelve LTCs and about a hundred escorts and gunships." She felt as much as heard or saw his shrug through the network. "If their cruisers were less glass cannons, that would be a lot more reassuring, but those things can't stand toe-to-toe with dreadnoughts. They'll *hurt* dreadnoughts, but they can't *fight* dreadnoughts."

"They need Twelfth Fleet."

"Honestly? They could have twelve *superdreadnoughts* and they'd need Twelfth Fleet. It's a reasonable assumption that Vengeance Fleet is going to be back up to thirty-six dreadnoughts again. We really don't know what their support infrastructure looks like."

"How long do you think we have?"

"I don't know what their support structure looks like," Henry repeated, a clear moment of exhaustion in his voice. "I don't think they could have repaired what we saw in less than two weeks. Probably more like three, even if they can get the yards at Rashova online for themselves."

"And then thirteen days to get here. It stills feels too soon."

"If they were in the next system out, I think we'd know. So, we can assume they're two days out at least. Beyond that...we'll have warning, but if the Executive won't let us bring Twelfth Fleet in, I have to go collect the Forward Flotilla and fall back on Eerdish."

"You'll abandon them."

Sylvia knew that wasn't fair, but she'd watched one world die already. She didn't want to leave another planet to share Rashov's fate.

"If they won't trust us, we can't save them. I won't throw away the Flotilla for a point of pride, not when it won't change anything. You've given them all the intelligence we have on Vengeance Fleet. If they want to fight the Kenmiri on their own, I have to let them."

"Sorry," she apologized.

"Don't be. I helped lay the groundwork for this mess. All parts of it. This Vengeance Fleet is...an anomaly. One the Kenmiri are helping less as it continues but are not stopping.

"But UPSF warships rained nuclear fire on that planet, Sylvia. I don't blame them for not trusting us. They hate and fear the United Planets Alliance because here, in this place, they weigh the innocents we killed above the freedom we bought them.

"And that is fair. We let the ends justify the means...and history may judge it necessary, but I do not expect the people who saw that collateral damage firsthand to forgive us."

"Neither do I," Sylvia conceded. "But by all that is sacred, we have to save them, Henry. We have to fight."

"Then you have to convince them to let us, my love," he said. "I have to make the military decisions based on the diplomatic situation. *You* can change the diplomatic situation.

"And I have the utmost faith in your ability to do so."

"No pressure," Sylvia muttered.

"No. Just the pressure you're used to."

SYLVIA HAD JUST BLINKED AWAY her silent link to Henry when the door to the waiting area opened. A pair of red-tunicked bodyguards stepped in and scanned the room. They then retreated through the door and Executive Robertson entered.

"Is the Executive ready for us?" Sylvia asked, rising from her seat.

"Not yet," he replied in English. "Please, Ambassador, sit and eat. I'd like to join, if you would permit it? There were exactly twenty-three humans on this planet before you landed. It's a relief to not speak Kem."

He paused and shrugged.

"I could probably muster up enough Russian for a conversation if you wish," he offered. "But the other humans on Anderon speak English, so I am very rusty."

"English is fine," Sylvia replied. "It's your...pyramid. You're welcome to join us."

Robertson nodded and took a seat on an empty couch across from her. The rest of Sylvia's delegation had left that particular seat empty to give her privacy in the corner, but that allowed the man to join her easily.

"If it's anyone's pyramid, it's Okalta's," he observed. "The Executives are equal, but Okalta recognizes that their voice bears the least weight. The choices they made led us here, and all Anderon recognizes the debt we owe, but the Kenmiri are a tiny minority now."

"A mistrusted one, I imagine," Sylvia added.

"Less than I feared at one point, but yes," Robertson agreed. "It helps, in my case, that I have known Okalta for over a decade."

"How did a human—an *Englishman*, at that—end up on Anderon's Executive?"

"I created the Republic of Anderon, Ambassador," the pudgy little man told her. There was no arrogance, no bragging, in that sentence. It was simply a statement of fact. "I hold dual doctorates in political science and xenocultural studies from the Imperial College of London and the Curiosity City University.

"When Okalta recognized that the structure of Anderon needed to change immensely to survive the Withdrawal, they turned to me. I sought out key figures in the worker population, people that the newly freed slaves would trust, and we created the interim Executive.

"The Warriors that remained answered to Okalta, and the janissaries that remained answered to the Warriors." Robertson shrugged. "I don't think the slave-race soldiers would have *kept* answering to the Warriors if we hadn't moved swiftly to stabilize things and create some semblance of equality."

"I have seen no worlds in the Ra Sector where the Kenmiri remained at all," Sylvia admitted. "But equality and democracy are… variable things here, when most governments are born of rebel movements and criminal organizations."

"Both of which are authoritarian and hierarchical by nature," the professor turned world leader agreed. "I imagine democracies are thin on the ground and the best you've been able to hope for is sovereignty and some semblance of sentient rights?"

"There are some encouraging traditions among the Ashall races that have helped," she replied. "And the homeworlds had their own extant governments, even under Kenmiri rule. But…yes. We are working with our allies to bring more freedom and more of a people's voice to their worlds, but it is a work in progress in many places.

"I am surprised to see Anderon end up in as solid a shape as you have."

"Okalta was the key," Robertson said instantly. "They were the Third Governor of the Kenmiri, and when they chose to stay, that meant they had command of whatever governmental resources remained. It wouldn't have been enough to maintain control—but it *was* enough to build a new planetary administration around and have a peaceful transition."

"But…where do you come in?" she asked. "You're long way from London or Mars."

"That I most definitely am," he agreed. "We were unlucky. It was a research expedition with a bunch of our grad students, heading to the colony in Altair." He sighed. "There'd been no reports that the Kenmiri were that deep in our space, so no one was worried.

"Then we got jumped by what I now know was a specialty escort refitted for long-range scouting. They weren't supposed to attack anybody, but we almost stumbled into them and would have blown the secret that they were surveying the deeper UPA worlds."

"Well, they covered it well enough," Sylvia noted. "I've never heard of them getting deeper than they did in the first campaigns. We always assumed they didn't know about many stars beyond Zion and Procyon."

"I'm not sure which systems they did know, but they'd definitely mapped a good chunk of our stars," Robertson said. "And about twenty-six students and professors from twelve different universities ended up as prisoners aboard a Kenmiri scout ship.

"I don't think they initially quite understood what they'd captured, but they were interrogating us for background information on the UPA regardless. And when they realized they had politics and cultural students, well."

He spread his hands and chuckled bitterly.

"We were *exactly* what Okalta's mission was about. They'd shoved their pincers into a meat grinder, and they knew *nothing* about human-ity. We could give them a bunch of background information, about how the UPA functioned, where we'd come from, how we thought.

"I, for one, was optimistic and thought that improved under-standing would help create peace."

"You were wrong," Sylvia guessed.

"Beyond any reasonable doubt," he agreed. "But, thankfully, our ship's captain wiped the navigation databases, and none of us knew such minor things as the route home. We only knew our names for the inhabited star systems, hardly enough for them to find anywhere.

"But they learned more about the conflicts and internal weaknesses of the UPA than we should have told them," he admitted. "My attempt to make peace easier was arguably treason. But it wasn't like any of us were ever going home.

"I'd always picked up languages quickly, so by the time the ship was back here in Anderon, I could speak pretty decent Kem. Okalta was the ship's interrogator and cultural expert. They and the captain, a Warrior, argued a lot about what to do with us.

"In the end, my students entered the general *educated slave* labor pool, and Okalta kept me personally. As a pet, really. We talked politics, culture, myth. The Kenmiri are a fascinating species, for all that much of what they feel driven to do is inarguably evil from our point of view."

"So, you were their pet for a decade?" Sylvia asked.

"Believe me, it doesn't sound worse than it was," Robertson replied drily. "Okalta is an intelligent, thoughtful and surprisingly empathic being. But they were still my *owner*. When the bombs fell on the creche at Oceanhome, they were angrier than I had ever seen them."

He shivered.

"There were forty-six humans on Anderon prior to that day," he noted. "Some from my ship, some from the other kidnappings. Twenty were murdered in the aftermath of the Oceanhome strike, once they knew it was humans who'd unleashed hellfire on the Kenmorad.

"But once the initial rage passed and the Withdrawal began, we were treated no worse than we had been before. Okalta realized early on that they wanted to stay on Anderon—they were born in Ocean-home, after all. They'd left this world in service of the Empire, but it was still home.

"They recognized that they could not maintain control over the slaves as they had, and they and I had engaged in long and deep conversations around politics and culture. They figured that I, more than anyone else, was qualified to try to put together an entirely new system of government.

"So, here we are. We ran elections, and in all honesty, the Grand Assembly promptly appointed every member of the interim Executive as the first true Executive. We serve a term of six local years—a bit over eight Terran years—and are limited to three terms. We're counting the term as interim Executive as one term, so I have at most seventeen standard years to serve this world."

He shrugged.

"I like it here. I like these people, and I want to help them. I don't want to see them burn."

"Then why are you here and not arguing with the rest of the Executive to accept our help?" she asked.

"Because as the only member of the Executive who was born in the

UPA, I felt it necessary to recuse myself from the decision," Robertson told her. "I gave my opinion and withdrew from the discussions.

"I trust each of those beings with my life and the lives of every citizen of this world. Tanseya hates humans, but she works with me. She understands duty.

"They all do. They'll make the right decision, Ambassador Todorovich. And since you won't be calling your fleet *off* until and unless we make a decision, it doesn't matter too much if it takes them a while to get there."

38

WHEN SYLVIA and her companions were finally brought back to the deliberation chamber for the Executive, she found herself missing Henry Wong. Her partner was no diplomat, but no one became a senior officer in the UPSF without having some sense of politics—and no one could have survived field command during a guerilla war in unfriendly territory without being able to handle alien culture.

And she found his point of view both refreshing and valuable. Right now, though, her understanding was that he was holding down at least three duty posts on *Paladin*, helping to keep the ship at a minimum staffing level so his people could sleep.

Officially, she didn't know that, because *officially*, he was doing no such thing. But Sylvia had her sources aboard the destroyer, beyond what her boyfriend told her.

She knew what Henry was doing was important, but the last time she'd faced the governing council of a planet with millions of lives in the balance, he'd been at her side.

Sikora was a useful aide, and Opanree and the other allied diplomats made for a useful display of solidarity, but Henry would have been reassuring.

But it wasn't like Sylvia *needed* her personal and professional partner to do her job. Her ambassadorial mask was fully up as she followed Gregor Robertson into the pyramid room, and she didn't show a single gram of surprise at the absence of Executive Tanseya.

Once Robertson took his central seat, he gestured Sylvia and her companions to the seats across from him.

"Executive Tanseya has agreed what is necessary," Okalta told them. "But she has other duties she has decided to attend to. The Executive requires unanimity, but there is blood between her and your people."

Translation: *We twisted Tanseya's arm to get her to agree to the alliance, and she's avoiding the future meetings for the sake of her blood pressure.*

Sylvia could sympathize. If anything, she was surprised that Okalta was not even more hostile to her than the Sana official.

"The Executive has made a decision, then?" she asked.

"We has-have," Desert Wind confirmed. "Our first duty is-was always-forever to the Citizens of our Republic. We must-will protect them."

"At any price," Sho Naka added quietly.

"We must-will pass a message to Star Legate Kosvana to bring your Forward Flotilla and her own guard squadron back to Anderon," Desert Wind told her.

"We will also inform our Protectors on the route from Eerdish to permit Twelfth Fleet to pass," Robertson continued.

Sylvia was amused to see that Robertson had clearly been kept informed of the Executive's deliberations despite being in the waiting room with her. The academic turned reformer turned head of state clearly still had a functioning internal network, even if almost no one else on this planet did.

"We have already issued orders for our Protectors along the route to Rashova to extend their patrols farther out," Okalta said. "We will pull our Protector ships back from the surrounding systems, concentrating all of our capital ships here in Anderon."

"Once Twelfth Fleet arrives, we may discuss different tactics and strategies," Sylvia told them. "I am no soldier, but I can see the value in engaging Vengeance Fleet before they reach Anderon.

"All of us would prefer not to risk exposing your people to Rashov's fate."

"Agreed." Robertson grimaced. "All of us would prefer not to live in such times, but here we are. For all of the fears our people have toward yours, we are grateful you are here and prepared to stand in our defense."

"Executive Tanseya did have one condition on her agreement," Okalta said after a moment of silence. "While Twelfth Fleet and your Forward Flotilla will be permitted to enter the Anderon System, none of your warships are to approach within five light-seconds of the planet itself."

That, Sylvia supposed, answered the question of *Can we give the crews shore leave on Anderon?*

"Your condition is noted and we will comply," Sylvia assured them. "If is it acceptable to the Executive, there are logistics ships with the Forward Flotilla—and with Twelfth Fleet, though I lack information on their final numbers—that we would like to have resupply from your gas giant and asteroid belts."

Water and nickel-iron would allow the logistics ships to manufacture about ninety percent of the non-food and non-fuel supplies a fleet needed. A gas giant would provide the common gasses necessary to synthesize fuel.

Food and specialty parts were different problems, but they were also the things that no one *expected* to be able to replenish in transit, and both the warships and logistics ships were stocked accordingly.

"I see no reason why that would be a problem," Okalta told her. "We are, it seems, allies. Our concerns exist for good reason, but if you are to stand in the defense of our Republic, we are well served to assist in your resupply."

"Thank you."

39

HENRY RELAXED, slightly, when the bright green icons of the rest of the Forward Flotilla appeared on his displays. They were accompanied by the gold icons of Star Legate Kosvana's technical cruiser and five of her escorts.

That meant a single escort had been left to watch over the Talana System—though it looked like the courier ship the Executive had sent to recall Kosvana had remained behind, so the escort's commander could at least send a message without leaving their post.

With the cooperation of the locals, Henry now had a solid count on how many warships the Anderonians would bring to their own defense. Kosvana was the second sentry commander to return, bringing the total number of the large technical cruisers in the system to fourteen.

A fifteenth ship was still one skip out from Anderon toward Rashova, backstopping the scouts sweeping out to locate Vengeance Fleet. Building fifteen of the ships in four years was impressive, even if they were basically armor and guns stapled to a civilian hull.

Add in a hundred escorts and twenty-two gunships, and the Republic of Anderon had probably the second-most powerful fleet

Henry had seen since the Great Gathering—but the *most* powerful had been in Rashova.

Ten proper dreadnoughts would have easily matched the large technicals. They'd get *hurt*, but they'd win more likely than not. Henry would match the E-Two's carriers up against the technicals at two-to-one odds as well, though that still left Anderon a slight edge over the E-Two Alliance's total firepower.

Three *Crichton*-class fleet carriers with six battlecruisers in company would *shred* the Anderon fleet, but that was the point. Twelfth Fleet had been assembled to take on any threat IntelDiv had projected the Ra Sector could produce—estimated at roughly eighteen dreadnoughts.

Vengeance Fleet was significantly more powerful than Rex had been expected to fight. They'd known Rex might have to fight the defenders of a three-stripe Drifter Convoy, and had supplied major overkill.

"*Bringer of Cloths* and *Rightful Chieftain* are being directed to Anderon-Six," Chan told him. "Captain Denison is taking *Ankylosaurus* to escort them."

The Flotilla was still several light-minutes away. Henry *could* tell his officers which ship to send to escort the logistics ships, but he didn't need to. *Ankylosaurus* was the ship he'd have sent—the undamaged *Tyrannosaur* being the oldest of his ships but fully functional, unlike *Dilophosaurus*.

Henry hadn't even been sure that *Dilophosaurus* would make it back to friendly space. He knew—everyone knew, even Lieutenant Colonel Ivana Wilcox—that the old destroyer would be scrapped as soon as she made it back to UPA space.

But until then, Captain Wilcox had her ship's engines and gravity shield online, and that meant that Henry couldn't give up the four missile launchers the destroyer still had.

"Rest of the Flotilla will reach the designated rendezvous point in about twelve hours," Chan continued. "They're taking it slow and moving in company with Kosvana's cruiser until they have to break off."

The Anderon cruiser would enter orbit, after all. Henry's ships would rendezvous with *Paladin* in an arbitrary volume of space two million kilometers away from Anderon.

The restriction was both entirely reasonable and somewhat silly. From two million kilometers away, Henry was outside the focal range for his lasers and outside the powered range of his missiles.

Except that if Henry was bombarding a planet, he didn't need to be in powered range of his missiles. Planets didn't dodge.

The advantage to *him* was that it was a concession that cost him very little and put his ships outside of range of the Anderon warships. And *that* meant he was comfortable dropping his ships to their absolute minimum crewing standards.

He couldn't give his people shore leave, not when the Anderonians were too twitchy to let his ships in weapons range of the planet. But he could authorize the mess deck to release extra liquor rations and pull out the emergency steak-and-cheesecake reserve.

Once the rest of the destroyers rendezvoused, he'd order them to do the same. It wouldn't be *much* of a holiday, but it would hopefully blow off steam.

There was an assumption, after all, that senior officers would ignore a certain degree of indiscretion during this kind of cooldown period for the ship. That meant, for example, that Henry was absolutely, definitively in the dark about just how many Ground Division commandoes were currently in Commander Georgina Eowyn's quarters with her.

Given his own...complex attitudes toward sex and attraction, he could only wish her well with her enthusiasm. And never admit that he knew anything about the degree to which fraternization rules were going to be blithely ignored for the next forty-eight hours or so.

If it became a problem, it would be dealt with. Otherwise, his people *needed* the break—because he figured he had a week, at most, before he was going to take them into battle against a fleet that apparently liked to kill planets.

ONCE THE REST of the Forward Flotilla had gathered around *Paladin*, Henry called another virtual conference of his senior officers and Sylvia.

"Were there any problems in Talana?" he asked in Kem once he had Tol Azan and Falling Rain online.

"No," Tol Azan said instantly. "Star Legate Kosvana was perfectly polite and reasonable. It was a difficult situation. She understood that we had come to help, but without authorization, she could not extend full trust.

"Now her government has decided to extend that trust, we are in a more comfortable situation."

"Agreed. At this point, we are waiting on Twelfth Fleet," Henry noted. "Once we rendezvous with Admiral Rex and your own commanders, the Forward Flotilla will be dissolved. You will return to your usual command structures.

"While we will still need to work together until then, I do not expect much to occur while our ships and crews rest and recuperate."

"We may not be that lucky," Ihejirika murmured. "Vengeance Fleet has been far from accommodating so far."

"We must-will be on watch," Falling Rain agreed. "But we also can-will allow our crews to rest. My own people are-will-be assembling fighters as best as is-was possible. With new supplies from Anderon's asteroid belt, we could-may be able to replenish as much as half our strike group."

That was news to Henry, though it made sense. Like most things aboard starships, the Shieldwing fighters had key complex components that had to be manufactured in proper facilities, but much of the hull and secondary systems could be fabricated from any materials to hand.

If *Fronds of Will* carried enough spare parts to build the frames around, replacement fighters would be possible—and *wouldn't* have been possible while the Forward Flotilla was making their headlong dash to Anderon.

"That will help," he told them. "I hope that Twelfth Fleet will also have spare fighters from your people. Will you have pilots for the ships?"

"Yes."

Falling Rain didn't elaborate, but they didn't need to. Henry could guess what kind of pilots they'd field for that kind of improvised strike group: shuttle pilots and crew members who'd been working on simulator hours to potentially qualify in future.

He'd thrown together that kind of wing in the past. He'd *flown* a starfighter as part of that kind of ragtag group on *Raven*'s last mission, something the battlecruiser's captain had no business doing in any sane circumstances.

"For now, our priority is to stay on Anderon's good side and to let our crews recover from the last couple of weeks," Henry noted. "Ambassador Todorovich, is there anything in particular we should be careful of with the locals?"

"Staying in our designated parking orbit should be enough for the moment," she replied. "The Ra Sector ships are a lesser problem, but I think they will regard all of us under the same brush as Vesheron— even those who never were."

Falling Rain lowered an objecting tentacle at her follow-up comment.

Very few, if any, of the Eerdish-Enteni Alliance's officers and spacers had been Vesheron. That was why they'd missed some of the default communications security anyone who had fought the Kenmiri would have used, after all.

"One of our priorities here is to gain a level of trust with people who, unfortunately, are all too vividly aware of how we ended the war with the Kenmiri," Sylvia warned. "In some ways, that is straightforward. Our goal here is to protect the Anderon System and destroy the fleet planning to attack it.

"By doing so, we protect the entire Ra Sector and potentially even beyond."

The assumption baked into that statement was that there was only *one* Vengeance Fleet. The Drifter Interface who had warned them had only spoken about the fleet attacking the Ra Sector—but the UPSF hadn't sent any ships *past* the Ra Sector since the Great Gathering.

The Council of Artisans and their messenger might well have assumed that the UPSF wouldn't care about—or couldn't intervene against, regardless of how much they *cared*—rogue Warriors in other sectors.

"For now, so long as we refrain from aggressive acts, we earn their trust simply by being here," the Ambassador concluded. "So, unless the rest of you have a plan I was not briefed on, I believe we will be fine."

"The only plan I have right now is to make as many of my people *sleep* as I can," Henry said with a chuckle. "Our little jaunt through Osiris wore them down. I imagine the same is true of everyone else."

"Indeed," Azan confirmed. "We are already standing our ships down so the crews can rest. For the moment, we can trust Anderon's military to protect us?"

"Even if we cannot, we have no choice but to act as if we do," Henry told them. "So, we may as well take advantage of it to give our people a break."

40

THEY'D HAD enough warning that Henry was watching when Twelfth Fleet arrived. It was a carefully staged transit, opening with four *Corvid*-class battlecruisers, twelve *Significance*-class destroyers, twelve E-Two Alliance destroyers and a matching number of escorts.

Four capital ships and fifty lighter warships spread out around the skip line, their scanners active—but their identity beacons were also live, and even from half a light-hour away, Henry could pick out the moment the incoming ships made contact with the trio of escorts watching the line.

There was no way the three Anderon warships could *do* anything about Twelfth Fleet, but they must have passed on sensor data as the waves of active scanning calmed down—in time for the next wave of ships to arrive.

This one was a mismatched pair of carriers, one *Crichton*-class and one E-Two ship—accompanied by a dreadnought that Henry recognized.

"My god," he muttered. "They sent *Mal Toranis*."

The wave of thirty escorts and gunships around the three capital ships likely included Kozun ships, then—since the Hierarchy had apparently sent their sole surviving capital ship as a sign that they were fully in on this alliance.

More ships began to appear, the cycle time between waves cutting shorter as carrier after carrier emerged. With the Kozun apparently talked down from their attack on the Eerdish and Enteni, there were more escorts than Henry had expected—and the E-Two had clearly decided they could risk partially uncovering their border with the Kozun.

They'd still only sent three carriers—they only *had* six, and with *Fronds of Will* accompanying Henry, that only left one per homeworld for security—but they'd scraped up another six of their new-build destroyers.

There were no surprises in the UPSF contingent's strength. Three *Crichton*-class carriers, four *Corvid*-class and two *Jaguar*-class battle-cruisers, twenty-five *Significance*-class destroyers and twelve *Tyrannosaurs*.

And then Henry realized that the *Jaguars* *weren't* bringing up the rear as he'd assumed when they'd emerged with *Chiana*. The two Kozun cruisers were a surprise—the last he'd heard was that the Drifters had wiped out the Hierarchy's new capital ships when they'd betrayed the peace talks—but so were the clear icons of four gravity maneuvering systems.

"The *Cataphract*s made it," he said in surprise. "I didn't expect them to get *Cataphract* back online." Or for the three new ships to even be *online*, for that matter.

"Running the identity beacons now, ser," Eowyn told him. Henry was only keeping one officer with him on the flag deck, and it was Chan's turn to relax.

Their relaxation, so far as Henry could tell, was looking significantly less *athletic* than Eowyn's had been.

"*Mameluke*, *Chevalier*, *Cataphract* and *Aswaran*, ser," she confirmed. "I don't know how they did it, but it's the rest of the *Cataphracts*."

Henry had *hoped* that Twelfth Fleet's fleet train would be able to repair *Cataphract*'s damage from their battle with the coopted Drifters. He hadn't dared hope that the wave-two ships would catch up before they took Twelfth Fleet into battle.

The general limits of UPSF funding meant that only the six had been laid down—the decision had been made to see how they performed in action and do a proper keel-out design for the next GMS destroyers. The *Cataphracts*, after all, were basically *Significance*s with the GMS drive stuffed in wherever it would fit.

The ability to reduce fuel bunkerage had freed up internal volume and allowed them to include secondary mission sections more suited to a cruiser, which worked *very* well for them.

"Ser, we have the names on the two Kozun cruisers," Eowyn said softly.

Henry looked over at her, wondering why that was important.

"Oh?"

"*Kalad* and *Edritcha*, ser."

"Oh."

Henry was glad he was sitting down. *Edritcha* was more…amusing to him, than anything else. That particular officer had been in command of the squadron at La-Tar and had died when Henry's hastily assembled alliance had retaken the system.

Kalad, though. Kalad had been a dear friend, a woman he'd served alongside during the war. A friend who'd almost become something more after Henry's divorce—which was a *big* deal for a demisexual.

And Star Voice Kalad had been in charge of the Kozun escorts at the peace conference between the Kozun Hierarchy, the La-Tar Cluster and the United Planets Alliance. Only one ship had survived the Drifters' betrayal of the talks—and the Kozun commander had neither been aboard *Raven* nor in the fortified capsule that had protected the diplomats themselves.

It seemed First Voice Mal Dakis was naming his cruisers for dead commanders. Sadly, Henry was quite certain that the Hierarchy's war of conquest had provided them with plenty of available options, even before the Peacekeeper Initiative had involved themselves.

"Thank you," he murmured—and he wasn't sure if that was directed at Eowyn or at Mal Dakis himself.

"What does that get us to for numbers?"

"Including the Forward Flotilla? Forty-eight UPSF destroyers, six battlecruisers, three carriers. Rest of the allies look to have put thirty gunships and hundred and twenty escorts, plus twenty destroyers from the E-Two, four carriers, *Mal Toranis* and the two Kozun cruisers."

Henry whistled silently.

Twenty capital ships. *Fronds of Will* was too light on fighters to fully count, and the Kozun cruisers were only on par with the E-Two carriers for mass, which left them as *light* capital ships.

But with the Anderon fleet in play, they had thirty-five capital ships to the thirty-six Vengeance Fleet had brought to Rashova. Vengeance Fleet had the standard Kenmiri eight-to-two-to-one ratio of escorts to gunships to dreadnoughts, giving them three hundred and eighty-five ships to Henry's estimate of three hundred and seventy for the allied fleet.

And Vengeance Fleet had dreadnoughts and superdreadnoughts. So long as they could get the fighter strikes in, Henry's bet was on Twelfth Fleet and their allies.

The problem was that the Kenmiri also knew that it would be starfighters tipping the balance—and that was why he guessed that every one of the three hundred–plus warships he expected to hit Anderon in the next few days would be carrying *plenty* of plasma webs.

AERYN, *Scorpius*, and *Chiana* were the unquestioned center of Twelfth Fleet. *Mal Toranis* was twice their size, but Henry didn't even need to *ask* to know that the Hierarchy detachment was being regarded with some suspicion by the rest of the fleet.

That was partially because he *knew* they were the last contingent to join up and had been at war with *every* other member of the fleet inside the last eighteen months.

But mostly it was because of how the Kozun detachment was positioned. All four components of the fleet had a clear separation from the others—and Henry had released his allied ships to rejoin their home commands—but the Kozun separation was just that much wider. That much emptier.

Henry couldn't help but feel a shiver of nervous anticipation as his shuttle dove toward *Aeryn*. Admiral Cody Rex's flagship wasn't his ex-husband's command—but *Aeryn* and *Scorpius* were similar enough to confuse his hindbrain.

That said, Commodore Peter Barrie was *Scorpius*'s CO and, unless the meeting Henry was heading to was smaller than he expected or the cascade of shuttles heading for the carrier suggested, his ex would be present at the meeting.

At this point, almost a decade later, Henry had a solid understanding of just what had gone down between him and Barrie. He hadn't quite forgiven the other man yet, miscommunication or not, and it was still uncomfortable to be around the officer he'd once thought was the love of his life.

But duty called. Rex wasn't in Henry's chain of command, but the Admiral *was* the senior officer on the scene. It was time to lay out everything that had happened since the Forward Flotilla had left Eerdish—heading for a completely different Kenmiri colony!

41

HENRY AND SYLVIA were met by one of Rex's staff officers as soon as they exited their shuttle, and found themselves ushered swiftly and efficiently to the Admiral's office on the carrier.

It was larger than any office on any smaller starship, taking advantage of the carrier's extra volume to give the Admiral space to work in. A display case covered one wall, set with models of starships Cody Rex had commanded—going back in time to Admiral Rex's time as a GroundDiv platoon commander, which was marked by three detailed UPSF power-armor figurines and a handful of green plastic army men.

The Lieutenant who'd brought them spent thirty seconds making sure they had coffee, and then disappeared as Admiral Rex himself entered the office.

"I know I didn't keep you waiting long," he noted in his warm baritone. "Though I don't *usually* send people into my office until I'm present. It's a busy day."

"It is," Henry agreed with a glance at Sylvia. "We don't forge new alliances of this scale very often."

"Outside of our joining the vague network of contacts and alliances called the Vesheron, I'm not sure we've ever forged an alliance of this scale, Commodore," Rex told him. "Please, both of you, sit.

"In about thirty minutes, we're going to go into a meeting with every Commodore and up in Twelfth Fleet. Mostly UPSF officers for now, though the allied contingents have sent senior officers to participate.

"There will be a full virtual conference tomorrow, once I've had a chance to make contact with the Anderon Protectors in a more formal fashion. A task the two of you have made extremely easy for me… despite the fact you weren't even supposed to be here."

"You've seen the reports," Henry said. "I don't think nearly as many drones made it through as I would have liked, but we definitely sent some from here that should have connected."

"Those were the first ones we saw," the Admiral confirmed grimly. "Until four days ago, Henry, we thought you were all dead."

"Overdue, presumed lost."

"Same. Fucking. Thing," Rex growled. "You did what you had to do, and you may have just saved everybody doing it, but I'll be *damned*, Commodore Wong, if I pretend that the entire fleet wasn't shaken, thinking we'd lost the Forward Flotilla."

"If we could have traded ourselves for Rashov, I think most people in the Flotilla would have," Sylvia noted.

"I know." The room was silent as Rex stared blankly into the air before taking his seat behind the desk. "Even the Golden Lancelot strikes, for all that they were a targeted xenocide, were *targeted*. We obliterated Kenmorad creches. Not entire *planets*."

"Ceterum censeo Carthaginem esse delendam."

Sylvia's Latin hung in the air for a long silence.

"Kill them all, burn the fields, salt the ashes," Rex concluded. "Carthage must be destroyed. Unfortunately, in this case, *we* are Carthage."

"And we will not be destroyed," Henry replied. "I will not stand by while Anderon burns. I watched Rashov die. I've seen too many worlds die for one lifetime."

Rashov was the only one with that level of destruction…but one was too many.

"I would give a great deal to have never seen any at all," Rex murmured. The Admiral then glanced at Sylvia and away, having said something he shouldn't have in civilian company.

Henry knew just how brutal the attacks on the Kenmiri homeworlds had been, but that was something the UPSF was still trying to keep under wraps. In at least one case, Henry knew that the Vesheron involved had thrown out the careful targeting data provided by IntelDiv and launched a saturation bombardment with fusion missiles at ballistic range.

It was perhaps a sign of the intelligence penetration of the Empire the Vesheron had possessed at the end that they hadn't *needed* to obliterate worlds to wipe out the Kenmorad—but one of the enemy homeworlds had died anyway.

Henry hadn't known Rex had been there. Now he did…and had a new grim milestone in common with the fleet commander.

"We have work to do to make sure of that," Sylvia said crisply, clearly recognizing the tension and aiming to defuse it. "What do you need to know, Admiral Rex?"

"I've reviewed all of your reports in detail," Rex said, not quite visibly shaking himself. "I'll admit I didn't expect to find a British academic running a planet out here, but Robertson is going to be useful to us. A friendly face, if nothing else."

"We're either going to earn all of Anderon's friendship in this mess or have real problems."

"Agreed." Rex gestured a hologram alive between the three of them after Sylvia spoke. "Commodore Wong, I know you're not under my chain of command but, bluntly, eight of my destroyers and one of my battlecruisers belong to the Peacekeeper Initiative. Most of those destroyers were with you, but *Lioness* joined up at Eerdish.

"I need…"

Henry chuckled as Rex couldn't find quite the right words.

"I'm sure your staff has already worked up some kind of formal orders to temporarily second them all to Twelfth Fleet," he observed. "We're not going to risk the fleet's chain of command over bureaucratic siloing, Admiral."

"I appreciate that, Commodore," Rex told him. "I'm not sure if the division between the main fleet and the Peacekeeper Initiative is in our best interests in the long run, especially if the Kenmiri are going to start being genocidal, but it existed for a reason, and I refuse to break it without a reason."

"Given the choice between the niceties that kept my command independent and a billion lives, I am perfectly prepared to be a *very* obedient subordinate," Henry said drily.

Rex chuckled.

"Good. Now. Rear Admiral Áed Róg will be commanding the primary destroyer screen. Technically, you're still the CO of DesRon Twenty-Seven, which I would logically place under Admiral Róg."

"But it sounds like you have a different plan in mind?"

"Indeed. I'm transferring the wave-two *Cataphract*s to DesRon Twenty-Seven," Rex told him. "Technically, that may make them Initiative ships after this; I can't say I care. But that will give you five destroyers with gravity maneuvering systems. The only thing more maneuverable than your ships will be the starfighters themselves."

"You have something specific in mind."

It wasn't a question.

"The last thing I am prepared to accept, Commodore Wong, is collateral damage to Anderon. I want to use DesRon Twenty-Seven as a reserve. We'll clean, you'll sweep. Anything that tries to break past the main fleet body toward the skip line is yours."

That assumed that the battle would take place at least one system away from Anderon. There were *far* too many benefits to that plan for Henry to argue with it.

"With our maneuverability, we can definitely interpose ourselves against just about anything, ser," Henry agreed. "It makes sense to me."

"Good. Ambassador Todorovich."

Henry had a decent idea of what was coming next, much as in some ways he'd prefer to keep Sylvia aboard *Paladin*.

"I need you to transfer to Anderon's surface to act as an interface between us and the Republic's government," Rex continued. "I can't see any conflicts of interest that will arise between us, but we need to make absolutely certain that any potential problems are smoothed over *immediately*."

"Agreed. I'll remain here for your grand briefing, but I see no problem with relocating to the surface."

"Thank you." Rex looked thoughtful. "We have a lot of components to work through, even with just four individual forces in Twelfth Fleet. Once we add Anderon's Protectors and their large cruisers, we're going to have some real confusion.

"But that's better than the alternative. If time gives me two days, I will—"

The alert tone that rang through all three of their internal networks told Henry the Admiral had just taunted fate one time too many.

"A damaged large cruiser has emerged from the Ra-One-Eight-Five skip line," *Aeryn*'s tactical officer said grimly. "They're transmitting a warning. The Kenmiri were sending stealth ships ahead to remove sentries and are *in* the Ra-One-Eight-Five System.

"Estimated arrival in Anderon is sixteen hours."

42

The familiar voice calling down the corridor drew Henry's attention. Like everyone else aboard *Aeryn*, he was heading to the suddenly accelerated grand briefing. So, it appeared, was the gawky officer with the red ponytail and the Lieutenant Colonel's copper oak leaf—and the pilot's-wings insignia.

"Lieutenant Colonel O'Flannagain," Henry greeted the woman. "You are looking good. I didn't know you were going to be here."

"Strike Group Executive Officer aboard *Chiana*," his former Commander Air Group told him. O'Flannagain had commanded the single squadron of fighters aboard *Raven* and helped save the day when the Drifters had turned on the peace conference.

"*Someone*," she noted drily, "put some nice words in the *plays well with others* section of my file. Not sure why said person felt obliged to lie on my behalf, though."

"I don't think I said anything about *plays well with others*, to be fair," Henry said as she fell in beside him. "More *leads well* and *fights well*. And maybe censored a bit around how much of a handful you can be."

She grinned at him, incorrigible as always. On one memorable occasion, Samira O'Flannagain had both made a sexual pass at Henry *and* tried to punch him in the space of about fifteen seconds.

She'd also been one of the orchestrators of the quiet but determined attempt to matchmake Henry with Sylvia by, he estimated, ninety percent of *Raven*'s crew.

"I basically arrived at Base Skyrim with *Raven*, got pulled into an office, had a new leaf stuck on me and got thrown aboard *Chiana* as we were shipping out with boxed fighters filling the decks. If SpaceDiv's Chiefs weren't more efficient than they have any right to be, I figure my luggage would still be three systems behind me!"

"And your new strike group?" Henry asked.

"About half of them are so green, I smell chlorophyll from sixty paces," O'Flannagain told him. "The rest are the grab bag of vets who survived the war and decided civilian life wasn't for them. Always a… mixed bunch."

"Says the exemplar of the type."

"Yup. Where's the Ambassador?"

"On a GroundDiv shuttle heading for Anderon. Once the warning arrived, we barely had time to say goodbye before she was running for the flight deck," Henry admitted. "We expected seventy-two hours' notice from the Anderon sentries.

"Not sixteen."

"Fuckers." There was no heat in O'Flannagain's voice. "No one's told middle management what happened there yet."

"It'll be in the briefing," Henry promised. "But Anderon's Protectors didn't screw up. Vengeance Fleet just knows this game as well as anyone. Which is a *lot b*etter than most of the successor-state fleets."

"Well, with you in charge, we'll kick them back to hell," she said cheerfully. "And you know, when this is over, if you and the Ambassador ever want a third…"

Her lascivious wink suggested that she was *probably* joking—but handful as she was, that took Henry sufficiently by surprise to make him flush.

"Behave, Lieutenant Colonel," he said repressively.

"You take yourself too seriously, ser. *Someone* has to let the air out occasionally." She grinned again, incorrigible as always. "And truth be told, *Chiana*'s GroundDiv Colonel and I have an understanding. They have all *kinds* of interesting bits to play with!"

"That is *definitely* running into too much information, Colonel." Henry was now past *repressive* and somewhere into *pained*.

"You're my captain, ser, no matter what titles everybody's carrying," she told him in a suddenly serious tone. "Great mothering fleet action? I'm glad you're here, Commodore."

"Likewise, O'Flannagain."

A handful or not, Samira O'Flannagain was one of the best pilots Henry had ever flown alongside.

THE ADVANTAGE of using fleet carriers as flagships was that they *had* space to spare. The *Crichton* class had also been designed to be flagships of fleets built from disparate allied components, which meant that the designers had packed as many of the meeting spaces into one area of the carrier as they could.

They'd then designed the bulkheads to go away when needed, creating a massive amphitheater-style space above the flight deck where Admiral Rex had collected all of his UPSF flag officers in person. With the sudden urgency, the holoprojectors had been activated as well, linking in captains from every ship in Twelfth Fleet, plus several key Anderonian officers, plus whatever junior command staff had been available, like O'Flannagain.

Henry's seat was surrounded by the holograms of the officers commanding the *Cataphracts* now under his command. He knew Ihejirika, of course, and Captain Aoife Palmer of *Cataphract* had served under him before.

The commanders of the other three ships were strangers to him, but that would need to be fixed later. Time was short and Admiral Rex was already stepping out into the center of the amphitheater as the last projectors turned on and physically present officers took their seats.

"Thank you, people," Rex said in clear but slow Kem. The Terran officers could receive a translation of the Kem through their networks, but none of their allies had an equivalent ability to translate English.

The Admiral was clearly still rusty with his Kem, but he soldiered on.

"We expected to have more time, but Vengeance Fleet deployed stealth raiders to neutralize Anderon ships along their route, preventing us from being warned until their raiders failed to destroy the LTC *Faith*, allowing her crew to skip her ahead and warn us.

"*Faith* detected what we believe to be the vanguard of the main fleet body before transiting," Rex noted. "They saw twelve dreadnoughts with assorted escorts. Assuming that the rest of Vengeance Fleet entered the system shortly after that, they will arrive in Anderon in just over fifteen hours.

"We had hoped to have time to properly reorganize formations and perhaps even to drill together before engaging Vengeance Fleet. We will not have that time."

Rex surveyed the crowd of officers.

"Thanks to Commodore Wong and the rest of the Forward Flotilla, we now know how these Kenmiri rogues intend to counter our fighter strikes. They have limited information on the UPSF's new gravity-drive starfighters, and Lieutenant Colonel O'Flannagain, the officer most experienced with the Lancers, has developed new tactical doctrines that *should* minimize the effect."

Henry realized that his assumption that O'Flannagain had been present out of convenience had been an error. Of *course* Rex would have pulled the only officer who'd commanded GMS starfighters in combat into the planning to counter the plasma webs.

"The details of what we have worked out will be downloaded to all of your ships and your fighter wing commanders," Rex informed everyone. "The fundamental component to it, however, is going to be attempting to fool the Kenmiri as to when our fighters will enter range.

"The plasma webs have an extended range over standard missiles, designed to deploy the webs against our fighters before they launch their missiles. Colonel O'Flannagain and our other pilots and fighter tacticians believe there are multiple ways we can deceive the Kenmiri into firing their carrier missiles early or late.

"While this will reduce the effectiveness of their weapons, they are likely to respond by covering a wider zone of space and time with the webs. Knowing what they have prepared against us helps, but the webs are, unfortunately, a quite effective tool."

The Admiral held up a hand and met Henry's gaze across the amphitheater.

"That said, I know that the Forward Flotilla and the Anderon Protectors had this information significantly sooner than we did. I am hoping, Commodore Wong, that your people came up with additional options?"

"Like Lieutenant Colonel O'Flannagain, we developed several tactical options," Henry said quickly. "The best solution we gamed out was a combined-arms tactic, sending destroyers and escorts in with the starfighters and using their defenses to reduce the number of plasma webs.

"As with the fighter-based maneuvers, that will only reduce the effectiveness of the weapons, not eliminate them. It will also place whatever warships we send forward with the fighters at risk of being overwhelmed by the enemy fleet's massed firepower."

He shrugged.

"The other option we saw was to completely abandon the alpha-strike mission and hold the fighters back for the bravo-strike role."

Doctrine called for them to launch the carrier strike at a long-enough range to get at least one, and potentially two, full salvo launches in before the fleets closed to their own range—the alpha strike—followed by rearming the fighters to deploy their missiles along with the fleets, preferably about as the fleets closed to plasma range—the bravo strike.

Starfighters' primary role, after all, was to put a lot of missiles in the air with widely dispersed threat vectors. They could do that on their own, or they could do it with the fleet in company—and Henry suspected that Vengeance Fleet wouldn't be as willing to use missiles as plasma-web carriers with thirty-five allied capital ships firing at them.

He hid a grimace.

Thirty-four allied capital ships. *Faith* was the fifteenth Anderon large technical cruiser, and she was a wreck. She'd been lucky to skip successfully, and she had *no* business in the order of battle.

"We will need to run the analysis on that," Rex noted. "Removing the alpha strike from the battle plan may be worth it if we cannot preserve our fighters."

A soft chirp echoed through the amphitheater, and Rex looked up at one of the holograms.

"Star Warlord Kanax," he greeted the Anderonian officer who'd triggered an attention chime.

The hologram of the red-tunicked Ashall expanded, becoming the centerpoint for anyone receiving the virtual version of the conference. Kanax was Vonga, the last Ashall race in the Ra Sector to be annexed by the Kenmiri. Still rare on the slave worlds, Henry was guessing there'd been a contingent of Vonga slave soldiers, janissaries, on Anderon.

Kanax was covered in russet fur and had massively bulging eyes. The Vonga were definitely Ashall, but they were further from the standard form than most of the Seeded Races.

"We had the opportunity to study the data Commodore Wong provided," the Star Warlord—equivalent to a Vice Admiral in Kenmiri terms, though Henry didn't believe the Anderon Protectors used the Grand Star Master rank—noted calmly.

"While we have limited information on any of your fighters, we were advised that the plasma-web system was devastating against them and that your starfighters were a key weapon system," she continued. "Given our lack of data on the fighters themselves, we focused on the Kenmiri's new weapon.

"We found a weakness."

"That may be the best news anyone has given me so far," Rex told Kanax. "Can you explain?"

The Star Warlord blinked her immense eyes as she was given partial control of the conference's visuals. A hologram of the plasma-web system appeared in the middle of the shared space.

"The plasma web is based on a series of self-mobile drones maintaining plasma arcs between themselves," she noted. "But the arcs require coordination between the drones—and the plasma itself carries no information.

"Each web maintains a meshed computer network between all of the platforms, not only to enable them to wrap around their final targets but to enable the web to exist at all."

Translucent white beams connected the drones in the hologram, representing the coms network.

"While Kenmiri encryption and electronic warfare are beyond our ability to penetrate, even with the level of information Commodore Wong provided, we *have* studied the network itself quite carefully. It cannot be breached.

"But it *can* be overwhelmed by powerful-enough garbage signals. At which point the drones will lose contact with each other and the web will collapse in a few moments."

Henry stared at the hologram and remembered that the Kenmiri weren't truly used to fighting a peer opponent. The El-Vesheron, the rebel's external allies like the United Planets Alliance, had often had areas where they were ahead of the Empire, but none of them could match the full technological and industrial might of the Kenmiri.

The plasma web was extremely clever and powerful. But...the Anderonians were right. If the drones were using radios instead of tightbeams or laser coms, they could be jammed.

"The appropriate tool to do so, we also realized," Kanax continued, "was in the same database Commodore Wong provided us. The Kenmiri's own antisensor jamming weapons are extremely effective at neutralizing the plasma-web systems."

She paused, then smiled, exposing a mouthful of sharp teeth.

"We commenced mass production of the jammers three days ago and have fourteen hundred warheads available for distribution."

"They will adapt," *Aeryn*'s CAG said grimly. Opeyemi Botha was the senior pilot in the fleet and though Henry had met her, he didn't know the woman well. "They are not foolish."

"It is a hardware shortcoming," Kanax pointed out. "They can adjust their deployment strategy, yes, but they will not have time to update the hardware in a single battle."

"And we only need it to work once," Commodore Barrie added. Henry's ex-husband was sitting with his carrier-group commander, focused on the task at hand.

"Even with the GMS fighters, we are unlikely to have the opportunity for a second alpha strike," Barrie continued. "If we keep the fighters close enough that the *fleet* can provide the jammer salvo, we may even have issues equipping for the bravo strike—but we will guarantee there are enough jammers to cover the alpha-strike launch."

It would work, Henry thought. The main fleet clash would follow all too shortly afterward if they were keeping the fighter strike that close, but the starfighters *should* even the odds.

Should.

43

THIRTY LIGHT-MINUTES WAS FAR ENOUGH that the massed fleet got moving well before they saw any further sign of Vengeance Fleet. They might not be able to engage the Kenmiri in Ra-185 as everyone had been planning, but everyone was going to be more comfortable the farther the battle was from Anderon itself.

Left behind, Sylvia found herself pacing the office she'd been lent in the Administration Center. The Executive had done fairly by her—the room had a full holographic display linked to Anderon's orbital sensor network—but it still wasn't *her* space.

But there was absolutely zero point in any of the civilian diplomats' being aboard the warships. Twelfth Fleet's logistics train—forty-some transports, some of them even bigger than the capital ships they supplied—was now tucked away around Anderon-VI, but the diplomats were all on the surface.

Whatever Anderon's fate was, Sylvia and her people would share it. Even *she* had to admit that it was a bloody foolish piece of showmanship—but it was an important symbol all the same.

And if Twelfth Fleet *failed*, it wasn't going to matter whether she was aboard *Paladin* or down on the surface. She'd talked Henry Wong into retreating when they'd already been unable to stop a planetary genocide.

There was no way in all the stars and planets that he was going to retreat when it would mean abandoning a planet to bombardment. She wasn't cleared—to her surprise, she'd *thought* her clearance was basically complete—for the part of Admiral Rex's file that would explain his reaction to the thought of bombardment...but she could guess.

Someone had to have gone into the heart of the Empire and launched strikes on the Kenmiri homeworlds. And Sylvia knew that one of those strikes had gone very, *very* wrong and resulted in one of the twelve original Kenmiri planets, well...ending up like Rashov had.

And there had been *very* few Golden Lancelot strikes that hadn't involved UPSF ships. That Rex's Golden Lancelot involvement was classified beyond the level Sylvia had access to told her enough.

Her partner had enough guilt over destroying an evacuation ship with the last Kenmorad aboard. She couldn't begin to guess how much horror was wrapped up in the heart of a man who had, however unwittingly and unwillingly, been party to the only *semi*-accidental glassing of a planet.

Another turn of the office brought her back to the big holographic display on the wall, studying the massive swarm of starships converging on each other a dozen light-seconds from Anderon. There were fortifications above the planet itself, but those would be the absolutely final line of defense. Heavily armed for their masses and fitting in energy screens where mobile vessels of their size would put engines, they were tough and dangerous but inherently limited.

The Kenmiri had never built their forts to stop overwhelming long-range bombardment, and Anderon's Protectors had inherited the fortresses their former overlords had left behind. They didn't have the defenses to save the planet if it came down to them.

Between forts, allies and UPSF ships, it took Sylvia a good minute to locate *Paladin*'s icon in the middle of the fleet. Whatever organization the assorted fleet leaders had imposed was nearly unintelligible to her, but she could pick out the five *Cataphracts* of the re-formed DesRon 27.

Henry Wong's old and new command.

She touched the icon of the central destroyer delicately, then straightened as she heard a knock on the door. It was apparently time to get to work!

The surprise, though, was who was outside the door. She'd been half-expecting Executive Robertson. Instead, she got Executive Okalta, the blue-robed Kenmiri Artisan tilting their head at her quizzically.

"You were not expecting me," they observed in Kem. "But are you willing to speak with me?"

"That is much of what I am here for," Sylvia replied. "This is a borrowed office. You are more than welcome to come in."

Okalta bowed forward over their mandibles in an oddly familiar gesture, then swept into the office with an easy grace. There was only one seat in the space, but the Artisan dropped into an odd backwards-knee pose that would have been physically impossible for a human.

"Most of the former Vesheron are uncomfortable around my people," Okalta noted. "I am pleased that you are prepared to speak with me."

"I was expecting Robertson," Sylvia admitted. "But I am here to help build long-term relationships with Anderon and the Executive. That is hard to accomplish if I ignore one-fifth of the Executive itself!"

"True, and yet I do not believe the others of the Executive would blame you. Even Tanseya, who hates Terrans with as much fury as she hates my people, would not blame you for dealing only with the Ashall and El-Nall members of the Executive."

The El-Nall were the *non*-Ashall races of the Kenmiri Empire—literally the "Outside Peoples" in the same way as the El-Vesheron were the "Outside Rebels."

That the Kenmiri regarded even outsiders fighting them as rebels was…telling, in Sylvia's mind.

"And yet you came here to see if I would speak with you," she observed. "In my practice of diplomacy, it would be rude to turn you away. So, here you are. What did you wish to speak to me about?"

Okalta chuckled, a strange buzzing, clicking sound, and gestured at the display behind her.

"Twenty-six thousand, four hundred and ninety-three," they told her quietly.

"Twenty-six thousand *what?*"

"Kenmiri Warriors in the Anderon Protector-fleet," Okalta clarified. "They were trainers and cadre to begin with and still form the skeleton core of our Protectors. A full third of the crew who will go into battle alongside your Twelfth Fleet are of my people.

"And they will die before one weapon lands on Anderon's surface. We Kenmiri who remain here chose this world over duty to the Race. We chose…home and the Charge. And for that, it seems, we are to be exterminated by Warriors who have betrayed both the Race *and* the Charge."

"The name says it all, does it not?" Sylvia replied. "Vengeance Fleet. They believe they are avenging your race."

She glanced back at the holographic display.

"I cannot speak to the Charge, though," she admitted. "I am not familiar with it."

"It is not a thing we would have spoken about to Ashall and El-Nall before the Withdrawal," Okalta admitted. "We did not, even at our most generous, treat other peoples as equals.

"And yet, the Charge defines the Empire."

They spread their hands, staring blankly past her at the display.

"And the Charge sends a third of the remaining Warriors in Anderon into battle against our own kin. Because we *will* honor it."

"What *is* it?" Sylvia demanded.

Okalta was silent for a few seconds, still looking at the display of the gathering defensive fleets.

"The Charge defines the Empire," they repeated. "Not all Kenmiri agree on that, of course. It is not quite a religion, but it is close. Many Kenmiri, myself included, believe that the gods gave us a sacred duty, a holy mission. This is the Charge."

"To…what?"

"Protect the Ashall," Okalta said. "Where we are today, looking back at the past and all that has occurred, it is clear that we failed in the Charge and that our fate was our punishment for that.

"We did not protect anyone. We conquered. We shaped. We *ruled*. And we claimed we did it to protect so that the Charge, the calling that sings in our blood, would be honored."

"Propaganda, to control all sides of the discussion," Sylvia suggested. "A story to convince slaves that they are meant to be slaves —and slave*masters* that they are doing something right instead of something evil."

"It was warped into that, yes," Okalta agreed unflinchingly. "I see that now. And yet…"

They turned their gaze back on her.

"It sings in our blood, the Charge," they told her softly. "Not insurmountably. But I feel the urge to guard and protect Ashall. The thought of the kind of massacre that was unleashed in Rashov makes me physically ill, Ambassador Todorovich.

"I do not understand what has…broken in the Warriors of the Vengeance Fleet. The death of our parents and of our future is a harsh blow for any sentient to endure.

"But to strike against the Charge, against those we are summoned to guard… Every moment they act, their own souls rebel against them. We failed in our mission, Ambassador. By becoming the Empire, we believed we honored the Charge.

"But that was a lie, a tool to allow us to overcome what our leaders saw as a *weakness*."

"And now?"

"And now your people have become the instrument of our punishment," Okalta said. "I want to hate you, you know. I understand how Tanseya feels. I was hatched and raised in the Oceanhome creche here on Anderon. My creche-parents died here. We do not fully understand families as Ashall have them, but we understand *that*."

"I was not part of that plan," Sylvia conceded. "But I do not believe your people left us many other options."

"Our gods set into motion our punishment," the Artisan told her. "I can be angry at my ancestors for failing the Charge. I can be angry at my gods for laying it upon us and for punishing us for breaking it. I cannot be angry with the tool they used for that punishment."

Sylvia wasn't sure she could ever have embraced *that* level of fatalism with regards to the sterilization of her entire species—and Okalta's point of view robbed humanity and the other Vesheron involved in Golden Lancelot of their own agency, their own choice to commit mass murder for strategic goals.

But if it was a belief that could help humanity find peace with the Remnant, at least for the few decades until the last of the Kenmiri died out, it wasn't something she could discourage.

Plus, she had to admit, she truly did *not* understand what Okalta meant by "it sings in our blood, the Charge."

She was beginning to suspect that the Kenmiri were even more complicated than she'd believed—and she'd never thought they were *simple.*

44

HENRY HAD LEFT *Paladin* with Sylvia in tow, confident that they had all the pieces moving in the right direction to survive the oncoming storm. He returned without the Ambassador and with his certainty in tatters.

Ihejirika was waiting as he exited the shuttle, the officer saluting crisply.

"Chan has all the *Cataphract* captains standing by for a virtual conference, ser," the Black man told him. "Rest of the fleet is already in motion, but we were told to hold off?"

"We're the backstop, Captain," Henry replied. "The most maneuverable ships in the fleet. I'll brief everyone at once, but we're operating as an independent detachment."

He could see arguments both ways, but it came down to the mission. The *mission* was to protect Anderon. No one would be *happy* if the allied fleets were wiped out saving the planet, but at the end of the day, there were about a quarter-million sentients in the three hundred–plus warships rising to meet the Kenmiri—and one and a quarter *billion* on the planet behind them.

Admiral Rex and Star Warlord Kanax and the other flag officers understood that in their bones, Henry hoped. There would be no retreat today.

"We set up the closest conference room," Ihejirika told him. "Are you ready for the briefing, ser?"

"No," Henry admitted with a wry smile. "But we don't have time for me to *be* ready, Okafor. So, let's get to it."

✦✦✦

FOUR HOLOGRAPHIC OFFICERS were waiting in the conference room Ihejirika led Henry to. He gestured his flag captain to a seat and took a long moment to study the women—the other four captains were all women—now under his command.

All five of the captains wore a Lieutenant Colonel's copper oak leaf and had the white-collared turtleneck of a starship's commanding officer. The rest were a study in the ethnic variety of modern humanity.

Aoife Palmer he knew. She was a sparsely built redhead from Sandoval in the Procyon System. She had more experience commanding a *Cataphract* than anyone else alive, having received command of *Cataphract* from the yards where Ihejirika had been given his command in the Zion System. Of course, much of that time had been with her ship in Twelfth Fleet's mobile dry dock.

Palmer was a known quantity and Henry was glad to have her back.

Lieutenant Colonel Elpida Earls was an Ophiuchan from the European Union colony there, but she wore her Greek ancestry clearly and proudly, with short-cropped black hair and olive skin. Her file and a subtle ribbon on her right breast marked her as the recipient of three different awards for valor.

And at that, Earls *wasn't* the most decorated of Henry's new captains. That distinction was held by Nora Acquati, a Welsh woman who shared her height and hair color with Palmer. Acquati's hair was a complex set of braids, as opposed to Palmer's short ponytail, but the visible cybernetics around the right side of her face told the story.

So did the Medal of Valor on her file, even if she wasn't even wearing the ribbon that marked her as deserving a salute from even superior officers. She'd lost the eye and ear in an infiltration mission with the Vesheron gone very wrong—but had managed to turn the failed mission around and save the battlecruiser *Tigress* when the Kenmiri had ambushed her.

Against the present and concealed medals of the other two captains, Lieutenant Colonel Ylenia Babineaux might have looked inexperienced. Except that the blonde Frenchwoman's determinedly blank file told Henry everything. She'd been wartime Deep Recon, rising over ten years to command one of the converted Kenmiri freighters that had backboned IntelDiv's operations in Imperial space.

Babineaux didn't have the medals and military bona fides of her fellow captains, but Henry knew *exactly* what he was getting with an ex–Deep Recon officer—and was glad to have her.

"If our crews are of the same caliber as the captains I've been handed, this squadron is going to go down in history," Henry finally told them all. "Again."

That earned him forced chuckles.

"We all know who the others are, so let's dispense with pleasantries," he continued. "We have a job to do and we have no time to get to know each other, exercise as a formation or any of the other niceties of organization.

"In eleven hours, the Kenmiri Vengeance Fleet is going to come through the skip line from Ra-One-Eighty-Five. We don't know their strength, but they'd mustered up thirty-six dreadnoughts and super-dreadnoughts for the attack at Rashova, so we're assuming they've got the same today."

He swept his gaze across his people.

"The allied fleets are already moving out to meet them. The skip line is thirty light-minutes away. They won't be in position to intercept the enemy on transit, and Admiral Rex is likely going to embrace a long-range, high-speed missile engagement.

"I haven't been fully briefed on the Admiral's plan," Henry observed. If he was being honest, he hadn't expected Rex to even end up in command of the final defense. But there'd been no time to do more than load the jammer warheads onto the warships and move out.

Command had devolved on the man with a plan—or at least the

starfighters. Everyone except the Anderon Protectors was comfortably reporting to Rex. Kanax and her ships *technically* hadn't given the UPSF Admiral command of their formations...but everything Henry had seen showed that they were maneuvering with the allies anyway.

There was a time for pissing contests, and it *wasn't* in the face of genocide.

"The fleet's estimated time to engagement is approximately eighteen hours," he continued. "But, as Captain Ihejirika flagged to me before I even made it in here, we are not moving out with the fleet.

"The *Cataphract*s represent a level of maneuverability the rest of the fleet does not share. The fighters are the only other spacecraft available to us who can manage two KPS-squared, and we need them to support the main fleet.

"We, on the other hand, are highly maneuverable and unfortunately underarmed for our mass," Henry concluded.

"We have the toughest gravity shields in the fleet," Babineaux pointed out. "Even if all we do is act as shields, we would assist."

"Our shields are on par with the *Corvid* battlecruisers, yes," Henry agreed. "But there is a critical mission that remains."

He gestured a map of the star system online in the middle of the conference.

"Every mobile unit in the system except us is forming up into a giant hammer and attempting to intercept Vengeance Fleet as far out as possible. But that leaves Anderon itself with just...*this.*"

Eighteen icons, gold for allied units, flashed above the planet.

"Standard Kenmiri heavy defensive fortresses," he told them. "One-point-five million tons, energy screens, missile launchers, plasma cannon. Minimal maneuverability but otherwise solid combat platforms.

"Except that we're not worried, right now, about Vengeance Fleet trying to enter orbit to carry out precision bombardments in support of ground assaults."

He let that sink in.

"How are those forts at stopping missiles getting past them?" Palmer finally asked.

"Crap," Babineaux said bluntly, with the kind of certainty that only came from having seen it. "They're not designed to defend the planet quite that directly. The assumption baked into them is that anyone wanting to take the planet is going to have to take out the forts first. They can defend *themselves* just fine, but they're mediocre at best against missiles aimed at the planet."

"And that's before even getting into missiles coming in ballistic, with their fuel expended," Henry reminded them.

"We have the best sensors and best engines in the system, and we are facing an enemy that is absolutely *determined* to exterminate the people they see as having betrayed their race. While the main fleet will be between the enemy and Anderon, there's no guarantee that the Kenmiri won't be able to get missiles past Admiral Rex's ships.

"At the velocities we're expecting the fleet to engage the enemy, it will not be practical for Rex to send starfighters after any missiles they miss—and even our Lancers don't have the sensors to reliably track missiles without active drives.

"We do."

Henry met each of his captains' gazes in turn, waiting for them to nod their understanding.

"We will deploy in approximately six hours, but we are going to maintain a significantly lower base velocity and remain well behind the main body. Our task, Colonels, is to make absolutely certain that not one missile lands on Anderon.

"We're a backstop. We expect most missiles to be targeted on the main fleet—and even those that aren't will still need to breach the main fleet's defenses to approach Anderon. We're sweeping up leftovers, which will likely require every scrap of our maneuvering and sensor capabilities and skills."

He smiled grimly.

"And that, my friends, is why the job falls to us."

There would only ever be six *Cataphract*s. The next generation of gravity-maneuvering-system destroyers would probably be superior in every respect—but the five ships that Henry commanded right then had some of the best destroyer skippers in the UPSF.

He doubted that the Personnel Division had picked three ridiculously qualified officers for the new ships, only for a different chunk of PersDiv to hand them lame-duck crews.

"They picked the best of us to crew these ships. The best officers. The best spacers. And they gave us ships that are unique in the galaxy. Nothing in this system can match our *Cataphract*s or their crews.

"And that's why the final responsibility for a billion lives rests on *us*."

"So, what's the plan, ser?" Acquati asked.

"We move out and hold position about fifty million kilometers from the planet, staying in touch with the main fleet and receiving full telemetry updates," Henry told them. "We should have a decent general vector on any missiles that break through.

"Once we have that, we'll move to intercept at maximum acceleration and shoot those missiles down. You're clear to use your missiles in countermode and to use your shields to sweep if necessary.

"As Lieutenant Colonel Babineaux pointed out, we have battle-cruiser-grade shields. The missiles aren't targeted at us, so they may even be safe to sweep.

"*May*."

The warheads, theoretically, would be salted heavy nukes. Even if they were rigged with proximity detonators to hurt ships that intercepted them, nukes were a lower threat level than conversion warheads.

And any missile that *didn't* detonate before it hit the gravity shear of his ships' defenses wasn't going to be intact enough to do so afterward.

"We will do whatever we have to," Henry concluded. "Every resource at our command is now dedicated to preventing missile strikes on Anderon. Because behind us, Captains, are a billion civilians…and my girlfriend."

That got the hoped-for real chuckles—but he also knew his point was made. If everything went right, DesRon 27 would be sorely missed in the main order of battle.

But if just about anything went wrong, DesRon 27 would be Anderon's only line of defense against apocalypse.

45

HENRY WAS INTIMATELY familiar with the calm before the storm. He would have to go back and read his own file to give a number on how many battles he'd served in. Seventeen years of war and three of peacekeeping had not been calm.

But the hours between *we know the enemy is coming* and *the enemy is here* were always an odd time. The allied fleet was hurtling outward toward the skip line at half a kilometer per second squared, the cumulative light of their engines rivaling the system's star. DesRon 27 moved out after them at a more cautious pace, their gravity drives almost invisible at this level of thrust.

He'd made himself sleep. His internal network was entirely capable of rendering him unconscious for a fixed period of time, after all. It wasn't as restful as true sleep—but there were no nightmares and it was better than getting no sleep at all.

"We are now in the estimated arrival window for Vengeance Fleet," Eowyn noted. "We have not seen any further survivors of the Anderon pickets."

"Eleven ships," Henry said softly. All escorts—the only ships Anderon had built that weren't standard Kenmiri designs were the large technical cruisers themselves—but that was still over three thousand dead.

That was going to be a drop in the bucket when all of this was over, he was grimly certain, but it was a dark harbinger of what the day would hold.

"Keep an eye out for stealth ships," he ordered. "We know they managed to infiltrate through the skip lines to ambush the sentries. The Protectors *should* have been able to detect them, but the wreck of *Faith* and the silence from the smaller ships tells me otherwise."

Faith had wiped out the squadron of stealth raiders that had jumped her—but Henry wasn't going to count on the Kenmiri only have *one* set of the terrifyingly sneaky attack craft.

"The main fleet has all of *Faith*'s sensor data—and ours from the *last* time we tangled with one of those," Eowyn told him. "Our analysis says we *should* be able to detect them if we know where to look—and they have to come through the skip line."

The fleet was still twenty-five light-minutes away from the skip line. Everything they saw was out of date, but if they detected stealth ships, they could send fighters to intercept them.

And the stealth ships paid for their sneakiness with limited size and weaponry. Even a handful of Lancers would be able to stop any attempt at a stealth pass on the planet.

If they were seen in time.

Henry knew he wasn't being paranoid. Paranoia would mean he was looking at threats that *didn't* exist—whereas his concerns about Vengeance Fleet pulling a fast one were very, very real.

"We are in position to intercept anything that gets past the fleet, ser," she assured him.

He took pride in his professional mask, but it was apparently slipping. A billion innocent lives was a bit more pressure than he was used to.

"You'd think the Kenmiri would manage to be on *time*," he growled at the display. They were twenty minutes past the expected window for them to arrive. That had been based on the vanguard squadrons, he supposed, but it had seemed reasonable enough.

"The longer they take, the greater risk they're doing something we don't expect," he continued. "So let's keep—"

"Contact!" Eowyn snapped. "Telemetry from *Aeryn* confirms stealth ships emerging from the skip line. Estimate thirty-plus contacts!"

"Damn," Ihejirika swore. "Were we expecting *that* many raiders?"

"No," Henry said grimly. "Get me a vector; are they going to be able to bypass the fleet?"

"Negative," Eowyn reported. "They are well inside the fleet's maneuver cone, and the fleet has them nailed in."

"Update from the fleet is that Admiral Rex has designated twenty escorts to shadow the raiders and intercept them if the main fleet has to deviate from their course."

It would still be hours before any of the ships clashed. The arrival of the stealth raiders suggested that it might be even longer before the main fleet showed up, though Henry was watching for a second or third shoe.

Kenmiri Warriors, after all, knew their business like almost no one else in the galaxy. Henry had outfought Warriors, outgunned Warriors and most definitely *outlasted* Warriors, thanks to gravity shields—but he'd rarely outfoxed them.

And if he couldn't see what Vengeance Fleet was doing, that meant they were doing something he hadn't expected.

"Subspace signal from one of the raiders," Chan reported. "They're phoning home."

"I'd love to find out that they can't communicate into FTL with the new communicator, but that seems unlikely." Henry stared at the screen, as if by sheer will and fury he could conjure the answer to what Vengeance Fleet's commander was planning.

"I'm surprised we didn't detect a subspace pulse *before* we saw the raiders," his coms officer said quietly. "We should be seeing the pulses in real time, which means they were in-system for over twenty minutes before they transmitted."

"And potentially that they *wanted* us to be able to match the subspace pulse to the raiders," Henry murmured. "Someone is being far too clever for my peace of mind."

Rex clearly agreed, as Henry saw the icons of the fleet begin to spread out. The wider the formation, the more interception options they had and the better resolution their massed sensors could produce.

"At least twenty-five minutes until we know what that subspace pulse was about," Eowyn warned. "It's going to be a long day."

"Have the mess stewards bring up more coffee and some sandwiches," Henry ordered. "I don't think any of us are going anywhere for a while."

Paladin was not yet at battle stations. They had time for that—but every member of the command and squadron staff was on duty. And none of them would be going anywhere until it was all over.

ONE OF THE several advantages of the GMS was that they really didn't need to worry about impacts throwing them around. On an older ship, Henry would be drinking his coffee from a squeeze bulb, just in case.

Aboard *Paladin*, the stewards not only brought up cups of coffee, but there was also a station where they'd left several carafes of coffee and the fixings for it. It made the calm before the storm slightly less uncomfortable, at least.

"Stealth ships are continuing to vector to try and cut around the fleet," Eowyn reported. "They'll swing outside missile range, unless the fleet maneuvers, but I'm surprised they're not trying to move farther out."

"They're expecting *something*," Henry agreed. "Which is why I'm watching for the other shoe. Especially with—"

"Contact report, multiple contacts…at the starward end of the skip line."

"That had to *hurt*," Ihejirika said as Henry's senior staff all turned to study just what the Kenmiri had done.

The skip line was just that—a *line*. It ran, arguably, from star to star, though there were definitely points in any system that were easier to skip from or into, depending on the planetary masses and the star's own mass and activity.

Emerging farther out from a star could leave you with an excessive flight time but was mostly harmless and occasionally difficult to calculate. Emerging *close* to the star was actively dangerous, a trick that required the most careful calculations and often an additional icosaspatial impulse kick.

"They recalculated their final kick into the system based on the data from the stealth ships," Henry concluded aloud. "It wouldn't have been much of an impulse, but it moved them significantly farther along the line."

And out of the zone Admiral Rex was heading toward. The fleets could adjust—there was still a vast distance between the two forces and distance became time in star system scale maneuvers.

"Numbers?" he finally asked.

"Same eighteen superdreadnoughts as at Rashova," Eowyn laid out swiftly. "Twenty regular dreadnoughts. Four hundred–plus escorts and gunships."

Henry was working up the course on his network even as the information came in. Twelfth Fleet and their allies could definitely still intercept the fleet, even if the odds weren't as even as they'd hoped. Two extra dreadnoughts *shouldn't* be enough to change the balance.

The problem was that the only thing between Vengeance Fleet and Anderon at that moment was empty space.

"All ships, I'm transferring a course," he told his captains. "Maximum acceleration, and bring active sensors online at full power."

"Ser?" Ihejirika was clearly looking at the course and unsure what he was seeing.

"They're going to launch a full salvo of missiles in the next few minutes," Henry explained. "With thirty-eight capital ships and four hundred escorts, we're looking at somewhere in the region of three thousand missiles per salvo.

"They'll be headed toward the planet on a ballistic course—and this squadron is the only thing that can get between them and Anderon on time."

He'd been expecting to have to stop a few hundred leakers, with the main fleet doing most of the work.

He'd been wrong.

THE DUAL FRUSTRATIONS of space combat were that everything Henry was seeing the Kenmiri do was over twenty minutes out of date—and everything *anybody* did was going to take hours to resolve.

Over four hundred and fifty million kilometers still separated the two fleets, and DesRon 27 was over sixty million kilometers behind the main fleet—and the course Henry had given his people wasn't set up to intercept the fleets.

Their course was meant to flip at a point in time that would allow them to match the missiles' terminal velocity. How fast they needed to be going, of course, depended on when Vengeance Fleet launched.

If they'd already launched, he wouldn't know until half an hour later—but his job would be a *lot* easier. With just the velocity from the launchers and the missile drives, the missiles would come in at just over one percent of lightspeed—and would take *days* to reach Anderon. The longer the Kenmiri waited, the more velocity their missiles had and the harder it was going to be for his squadron to intercept them.

The fate of a world hung in the balance, and all Henry could do was sit on his command deck, do math and drink his coffee. In theory, he could even *sleep* while they waited—they could easily estimate when the Kenmiri were likeliest to launch their bombardment salvo, after all.

"Estimate five and a half hours until the battle opens up," Eowyn said aloud, following a similar train of thought. "Assuming the fleet wants to keep the fighters close in, anyway."

"They have to," Henry agreed. "The fighters can't afford to give up warhead space for the jammers, so the fleet will have to provide the cover from the plasma webs."

It was a weird feeling to be in the same system as one of the largest space battles he'd ever seen took place but to know that he was going to be light-minutes away from the actual fighting.

And yet his mission was potentially even *more* important.

He ran his math one more time and growled.

He wasn't entirely certain that he *could* match the missiles' velocity if the Kenmiri waited long enough before they fired. All they were going to be able to do was make sure they stuck with the weapons for as long as possible.

46

"VAMPIRE."

Henry whispered the report himself, even as both Bach and Eowyn declared it aloud.

For five hours, he'd watched the two fleets creep toward each other at rapidly increasing velocity. The closing speed of the two fleets had now passed ten percent of lightspeed—but Vengeance Fleet was still twenty light-minutes from Anderon and "only" had a velocity of six percent of lightspeed relative to the planet.

But that was enough for their missiles to get up to eight percent of lightspeed and cover the distance in a little over four hours—and twenty minutes earlier, Vengeance Fleet had opened fire.

Three thousand missile icons flared on the display. Then three thousand more. And three thousand *more*. And two more salvos before the Fleet ceased fire and adjusted their vector slightly toward the defending forces.

Fifteen thousand missiles. Even that was only an estimate—Eowyn had calculated how many missile launchers the Kenmiri had, and it certainly *looked* like they'd fired everything they had.

"Five-minute burn complete on the first salvo," Eowyn reported.

"We have the terminal vector dialed in. Not that there was any question where they were aimed."

Henry's ships had already made turnover. The missiles would catch up to them as they approached Anderon again, and they'd fire at them as the missiles passed by. If they were lucky, they'd be close enough in velocity to extend their time in range.

The numbers flowed across his screen. He'd *expected* the Kenmiri to fire sooner, and DesRon 27 had come to a halt relative to Anderon almost half an hour earlier. They were ten light-minutes from the planet, and the missiles had twenty light-minutes to cover.

"Charmchi, Ihejirika, Eowyn," he said aloud, calling the attention of the destroyer's navigator and captain as well as his operations officer. "Check my numbers.

"I make it that if we hold our current position for just over eighty minutes and then accelerate toward Anderon at full power, we will match velocity and distance with the missiles roughly one light-minute from Anderon."

He should have pushed farther out, but he'd needed to make the decision on when to make turnover hours earlier. He'd guessed, and he'd guessed close enough.

"We'll have a bit over ten minutes in range, if I'm right," he continued.

"I get the same," Ihejirika confirmed. "We got it right, ser. We'll short-stop them before they reach the planet."

"Fifteen thousand missiles, Okafor," Henry reminded his subordinate. "And that's assuming they don't start flinging more at us if they start losing the main battle."

They couldn't *see* it yet—the defending fleet was almost two hundred million kilometers closer to the enemy than DesRon 27—but Henry knew that the carriers would be deploying starfighters as he spoke.

Rex would send the fighters in at two light-minutes, using the mind-boggling closing velocities to dramatically extend the range of the alpha strike. He'd pull the fighters back to rearm after that—they'd have to land under fire, but that wasn't new for UPSF pilots.

Henry worried about the E-Two pilots who were going to have to do that for the first time, but they had no choice. If the UPSF's allies couldn't keep up, then a lot of people were going to die.

He had a lot of faith in the *will* of the Eerdish and Enteni pilots. Their skill might falter, but he had faith that they would make the attempt anyway.

The defenders had a solid wall of gravity-shield destroyers and battlecruisers leading the way, and that *should* even the odds against a slightly greater number of Kenmiri capital ships. Henry had definitely fought the Kenmiri at worse odds in the past.

But the only time the stakes had been this high was at the culmination of the Red Wings Campaign at the Battle of Procyon—and less than ten percent of the starfighters and twenty percent of the starships on the UPSF side had survived that battle.

HENRY HAD FOUND command of a squadron to be difficult enough in terms of needing to sit and watch while other people did the fighting and dying. To sit ten light-minutes away and watch a massive fleet action was…worse.

He'd made his contribution, making certain that the allies knew what was coming, providing technical details on the enemy weapons. Part of him suspected his largest contribution, though, had been delivering Sylvia Todorovich to Anderon in time.

Combined, Anderon's Protectors, Twelfth Fleet and the rest of their allies had a chance to win. If anything, Henry figured the odds were in their favor. The Kenmiri were probably thinking differently—but they didn't know that their superweapon was out of the game.

The next battle would see updated plasma webs; Henry was sure of it. But Vengeance Fleet had come to *this* battle with a flawed weapon— and come against an enemy that *knew* those flaws.

"Fighters deploying," Eowyn reported.

It had been a *long* time since Henry had seen a multi-carrier fighter strike. Once the UPSF had thrown the Kenmiri back into their own space, they'd mostly deployed single carriers supported by battlecruisers and Vesheron ships.

Now, though…three *Crichton*-class carriers deployed three hundred and sixty SF-130 Lancer GMS fighters. Six battlecruisers added another thirty-six Lancers.

The other E-Two carriers had managed to provide the pilots and parts needed to replenish *Fronds of Will*'s fighter wing, allowing the four ships to put another three hundred and sixty Shieldwings into space. They weren't GMS fighters, limited to two KPS^2 on fusion drives, but they had energy screens and were far better defended than any non-UPSF fighters had ever been.

Over seven hundred starfighters lunged out from the defending fleet at just over two hundred gravities of acceleration, and the Kenmiri spread their formation wide to receive them. Minutes ticked by, and then Vengeance Fleet launched their defensive salvo.

"And…now," Henry murmured. Rex had held back his covering fire until the Kenmiri had committed the plasma webs—it was unlikely that the Kenmiri could refit the plasma webs in the middle of a battle, but there was no reason to take the chance.

The missiles passed through the fighter wings—whose formation had expanded to leave a gap for them—and then held formation about ten thousand kilometers ahead of the strike as they closed.

Kenmiri Warriors were born to battle. Henry figured they'd realized there was a problem—but at these velocities, missile range was *twelve million kilometers*. There was no way they could sort out what was going on, improvise a solution and deploy it to their antifighter munitions before it was too late.

The plasma-web drones blasted free of their carrier missiles, blazing toward the starfighters as their intricate network of arcs flared to life.

Then *Paladin*'s sensors lost track of the entire battle as five hundred jammer warheads went off. A third of the missiles manufactured by Anderon, it might have been overkill—but there were three thousand plasma webs targeted on less than eight hundred starfighters.

Henry was on board with overkill versus that.

When the jamming cleared, every single starfighter remained. The plasma-web drones themselves probably survived too, but without the arcing plasma lines linking them together, they were invisible at this distance.

"Fighters in range…now."

The ripple effect of seven hundred and fifty–plus starfighters each firing four missiles created a cascade of icons on Henry's tactical feeds. It took a moment for the system to resolve sufficiently to confirm that the fighters had flipped and were now accelerating hard back toward their motherships.

More missiles blazed out from Vengeance Fleet, targeted on either the starfighters or their missile salvo, Henry wasn't sure which, but the main defending fleet opened fire only a few seconds after that.

There were thousands of missiles flying each way, but only the starfighter salvo would hit before the fleets entered plasma and laser range of each other.

"The worst part is that it's already over," Ihejirika muttered on his link to Henry. "Everything we're seeing is what, twelve minutes old?"

"Yeah. By now, they've interpenetrated and the starfighters are rearming to go after the stragglers," Henry agreed.

For four more minutes, all Henry saw was missile launches as both sides filled space with suicidal robotic spacecraft. None of them appeared to be targeted on the planet—the original fifteen thousand his squadron was vectoring to intercept were all the Kenmiri had launched for that—but it was still a *lot* of missiles.

"Gravity drivers firing."

Six new icons flashed on the screen as the battlecruisers unleashed the power of their main guns. Closing velocities didn't change the range of lasers and plasma cannon, which were close enough to light-speed to make additional velocity irrelevant. Gravity drivers, on the other hand, fired at seven percent of lightspeed.

Adding another thirteen percent from closing velocity dramatically expanded their range. Their accuracy at a thirty-second flight time was limited, but it was worth taking the shots—and all six battlecruisers were firing every five seconds now, throwing the heaviest warheads either fleet carried directly at the superdreadnoughts.

But the entire point of the starfighter strike was to hit first and remove plasma cannon from the fight before they ranged on the capital ships—and that was exactly what they did.

Whoever had done the targeting had decided that the smaller traditional dreadnoughts were more vulnerable than the new superdreadnoughts—and then targeted all of the Shieldwings' missiles on just three of them.

Almost five hundred missiles crashed in on each of the E-Two's targets. Missile defenses took their toll, but the same velocity that increased the engagement range degraded the effectiveness of those defenses.

Before meeting the UPSF's fighters and their favored alpha strike, the Kenmiri had not believed enough missiles could get through their defenses to overwhelm a dreadnought's shields and mighty armor. They'd learned their mistake over the Red Wings Campaign leading to Procyon, and UPSF FighterDiv had taught it to them again and again.

Two of the Shieldwings' targets vanished in the balls of fire, and the survivor belched atmosphere and short-lived flames as even her forged asteroid armor gave way.

But the dreadnoughts the E-Two targeted were the *lucky* ones. The UPSF, after all, had long before built a countermeasure for their own gravity shields—and then discovered that the icosadimensional jump that could bypass a grav-shield did exactly the same with an energy screen.

Traditionally, they didn't arm *fighters* with penetrator warheads, as a fighter was far more likely to be lost than a capital ship. Admiral Rex had clearly decided that even if they did lose fighters in Anderon, it was a friendly system and they could recover the wrecks.

Almost sixteen hundred missiles were salvoed at eight dreadnoughts. Missile defenses took their toll, obliterating or deceiving almost half of them, but a hundred missiles plunged in on each targeted dreadnought and vanished—to reappear *inside* the capital ships' mighty defenses.

"They've upgraded them with an inner shield layer," Henry observed. "It...isn't enough."

At least one five-hundred-megaton warhead detonated *inside* each ship, even as a tightly fitted inner energy screen absorbed dozens more. The Kenmiri had learned all of the UPSF's favored tricks, but there was no countermeasure for a nuclear warhead inside the hull.

"Ten down," Eowyn reported in satisfaction.

"And now the price," Henry replied, watching the first Kenmiri salvos blaze in at the fleeing starfighters. Even gravity-shielded fighters were going to fall against five or six missiles apiece—and the Shieldwings had yet to truly test their defenses in combat.

"Jammers live!" Ihejirika snapped. "They… They got it right."

The Kenmiri missiles blazing in on the fighters were *also* plasma webs. Henry had expected standard missiles—they could be effective enough if they had time on their drives—but it seemed the Kenmiri thought they were worth trying again.

And Rex's people had anticipated that. Another four hundred jammer warheads had been hidden in the offensive salvos. They'd matched course with the starfighters and waited for just this.

A salvo of conventional missiles was right on their tails, though, and both time and distance were evaporating far too quickly.

"Fleet salvos impacting on both sides," Eowyn reported. "Our destroyers and cruisers are taking the brunt of the Kenmiri's."

Henry nodded grimly. He didn't even need to look at the display to know what Rex and his captains were doing. Twelfth Fleet had forty-nine battlecruisers and destroyers. They couldn't risk the carriers—the four-megaton ships were just that little bit harder to replace than even battlecruisers—but the rest of the Terran ships had formed an inter-linked shield wall.

The execution was new, but the concept was ancient. A seven-by-seven wall of starships hung in space between the Kenmiri and the rest of the defenders, putting their gravity shields in the line of fire because the Terran ships *could* take the hits and live—and the jammers seeded through the Kenmiri salvos only made the defensive targeting solutions harder.

But even as Twelfth Fleet bulled their way through the first missile salvos, the real shipkillers on both sides finally joined the fray. The massed fire from the defenders had obliterated another half dozen dreadnoughts, leaving only a handful of the older ships to back their new siblings.

The Vengeance Fleet's superdreadnoughts' commanders had been utterly ruthless, though, positioning both their escorts and the older capital ships between them and the incoming fire. Escorts had died. Older dreadnoughts had died.

Despite all that and the thousands of missiles thrown each way, Vengeance Fleet's solid core of eighteen superdreadnoughts remained, and their plasma cannon opened fire in a hail of starstuff.

In the same moment, the first grav-driver rounds struck home. Like the fighter missiles, they were fully loaded with penetrator warheads, bypassing armor and shields alike to deliver half-gigaton warheads to their victims.

Six rounds every five seconds, like a steady metronome hammering into the Kenmiri warships. Plasma fire blazed each way, and missiles continued to descend on both fleets. Accelerations flipped, trying to buy precious extra seconds in range as the starships careened past each other.

It took twenty seconds for the fleets to interpenetrate. Their relative velocities were so high, no missiles could hit after that—but it was another twenty seconds before they passed out of plasma-cannon range, and the shield wall had served its purpose well.

Mal Toranis might have been older and smaller than the dreadnoughts the Kenmiri had brought, but she was still a dreadnought with a battery of massive plasma cannon of her own. The Kozun cruisers brought their own cannon to the party—and Anderon's large technical cruisers had nearly the same firepower as the Kenmiri super-dreadnoughts.

Twelfth Fleet had taken the best that Vengeance Fleet could give, covering their allies and allowing them to unleash their own arsenal.

Not a single Kenmiri capital ship survived the firing pass. Shattered flotillas of escorts and gunships blazed away from the allied fleet in a dozen directions, and Henry watched them grimly.

"Track those stragglers," he ordered Eowyn. "Rex will send the fighters after them, but—"

"*Aeryn* is gone, ser," his ops officer said softly. "No reports if the flag made it off."

Henry was struck silent, then asked the question he vaguely hated himself for saying aloud.

"*Scorpius?*"

"Still with us. I don't have identifiers on which destroyers we lost, but *Scorpius*, *Chiana*, and I think most of the battlecruisers are still with us, if a bit the worse for wear."

"Chain of command puts…Rear Admiral Cheung in command?" Henry asked.

Rear Admiral Cheung Jian Chin was the CO of Carrier Group *Scorpius*. Henry's ex-husband's ship.

"For us, yes, but I don't think the allied forces have…"

"Sorted out any real succession planning. We didn't have time," Henry said grimly. "But Cheung knows what to do about the stragglers. The E-Two will listen to him. They have to."

"Yes, ser," Eowyn said calmly. "But…what now, ser?"

"The main fleets have done their job," he told her. The butcher's bill would be too high. It always was—and Admiral Rex had been one of the UPSF's best admirals—but Vengeance Fleet was gone. Whatever happened today, without the capital ships that had died in Anderon, the rogue Warriors weren't going to be destroying any more worlds.

"The question left is Anderon," Henry admitted. "And that, Commander Eowyn, falls to us."

47

THE HOUR DESRON 27 WAITED, watching the clash of titans of the main battle as an apocalyptic bombardment hurtled toward them, was one of the hardest hours of Henry's life. It was a relief to have the gravity wells blaze to life and see the *Cataphract*s leap into motion once more.

The Kenmiri missiles were still two hundred million kilometers away from his ships, but since they were moving at almost eight percent of lightspeed and his ships were motionless relative to Anderon, they needed time and space to get up to speed.

They'd built the space while the Kenmiri had built the base velocity for their salvos. Now they needed the time. The Vengeance Fleet missiles were coming to them, and the careful balance of distance and acceleration that would put them on top of the weapons at the same speed had finally broken down.

"Two hours, forty-five minutes, until we can launch our own missiles," Eowyn reported. "And then…what?"

"Then we empty our magazines in counter-missile mode," Henry told her. That seemed self-evident to him—but there were a *lot* of missiles coming their way, and he was grimly aware of what their hit chances were in this mess.

"Once we've matched velocity, we hit them with defensive and offensive lasers, and sweep what we can with the shields," he continued. "The missiles aren't active. We should be able to clear a lot of them by sweeping."

Well, he was *hoping* the missiles weren't active.

"That said, let's keep an eye out for any missiles that still have fuel," he told her. "*I* would have snuck some extras in hunter-killer mode in to protect the swarm. Especially since they could *see* us."

The Kenmiri might well have assumed that five destroyers couldn't stop fifteen thousand missiles. Henry wasn't even sure they were wrong. He had fifty-six launchers and roughly thirty-four hundred missiles across all five of his ships. After that, it was down to lasers and the gravity shields themselves.

The only *good* news was that nothing else in space could match the acceleration DesRon 27 was putting out at that moment. The defensive fortresses would have been engaging the missiles at a massive disadvantage, but even if the Kenmiri had done something *clever*, Henry's ships would be tracking in at the best possible range and velocity to take the missiles down.

He just wished he could figure out what clever tricks the Kenmiri might have pulled. His margin was already disturbingly thin...and despite Vengeance Fleet's near-annihilation, the lives of Anderon's citizenry still hung in the balance.

THE KENMIRI STEALTH ships were Henry's last remaining complication. He had plenty of *worries*, but the only thing outside the relatively narrow scope of his ships' charge was the potential for the stealth raiders to do something dangerous.

Fortunately, the escorts Rex had detached were on top of their job. When Twelfth Fleet's fighters went out to try to chase down the stragglers of the main Vengeance Fleet, the stealth raiders tried to engage.

But the turn to go after the fighters brought them into range of the blocking squadron of escorts. There were thirty Kenmiri raiders against twenty Allied escorts—but the raiders were a third of the escorts' size, relying on surprise and single-shot launchers to take down their targets.

They never stood a chance, and Henry swallowed relief as he was able to narrow his focus to the task at hand.

The five *Cataphracts* blazed toward Anderon at full acceleration—and the Kenmiri missiles blazed toward them, all too rapidly catching up.

Only distance made the entire affair seem slow. Henry's ships were gaining over a hundred KPS of velocity every minute, and the missiles were already moving at over seven percent of lightspeed. But the Kenmiri had launched the missiles over twenty light-minutes from the planet.

"All ships report our missiles rearmed with conventional warheads," Eowyn told him. "All penetrator and kinetic warheads are stored. We've got roughly seventy percent conversion warheads and thirty percent nukes on every ship."

Given *enough* time, Henry knew that his engineering crews could convert any of the non-directional five-hundred-megaton nukes into the directional conversion warheads. But that was a matter of days, not hours.

"Contact in two hours," Charmchi reported.

"Nothing to do but wait until their missiles catch up," Henry noted. "Somehow, I don't think anyone is going to go take a nap."

He silently pinged Quaid, instructing the steward to make sure coffee and something calorie-dense was delivered to the bridge—and to the rest of the battle stations. If there was ever a time to break out the donut stash, it was then.

"Last stand of the tin-can sailors again, I see," Ihejirika murmured in his network. "I can only hope it goes as well for us as it did for Sprague."

Henry had to think for a moment to place his flag captain's reference—but only a moment and didn't even need to look up in his network except for details.

"Sprague had more ships than we do *and* had carriers," he reminded Ihejirika. "And he was covering said carriers and the troop transports. No civilians."

The Battle off Samar was something the UPSF made sure all of its officers covered—and destroyer officers tended to be told to refresh themselves on when they came aboard. That portion of Leyte Gulf and the entirety of the Battles of the Atlantic in both World Wars were considered essential to understanding the role of a destroyer.

"'It is the first and final duty of any warship to put herself between the innocent and the enemy,'" Ihejirika intoned. "No one is going to back down, ser. We're going to save Anderon."

"Whatever it takes," Henry agreed grimly.

"Whatever it takes."

THEY WERE STILL a long way from the planet, in distance if not necessarily in time, when the oncoming missile storm entered DesRon 27's range.

"Fire."

Henry knew the order was unnecessary. By now, everyone on all five ships knew the plan. Knew the potential price they might be asked to pay.

Knew at least something of the price that *had* been paid to take down Vengeance Fleet. The shield wall of UPSF destroyers had probably saved tens of thousands of lives, but the Protectors' large technical cruisers had *needed* clear lines of fire to engage the Kenmiri super-dreadnoughts.

Half of the big Anderon ships were gone. So were fifteen of the Twelfth Fleet destroyers that had forged the shield wall and dozens of the allies' lighter units, along with *Aeryn*, *Puma*, and the Kozun cruiser *Edritcha*. But for all of the price that had been paid, Twelfth Fleet and her allies remained an effective fighting force.

And like the main fleet at Leyte Gulf that Ihejirika had referenced, they were horrendously out of position to defend against the incoming Kenmiri missile strike.

"First salvos away," Eowyn reported. "All launchers cycling."

Fifty-six of their own missiles blazed into space. *Paladin*'s wrecked four launchers could have been fixed in Twelfth Fleet's mobile dry dock if they'd had time…but they hadn't.

Another salvo launched half a minute later. Every minute, a hundred and twelve missiles hurtled into space. Nine of the *Cataphracts'* salvos would be in space before the first intercepted the incoming Kenmiri missiles, and Henry watched the icons with predatory eyes.

He didn't have enough missiles to clear the swarm even if every one of his weapons took out a Kenmiri weapon. He could *hope* for multiple kills…but the odds said that his average would be less than a kill per missile.

And about *now* would be when any clever tricks Vengeance Fleet had set up triggered.

"Jammers activating through the swarm," Eowyn barked. "Estimate at least a dozen. Our missiles are losing lock."

DesRon 27's missiles hadn't actually traveled particularly far—they were catching up to the Kenmiri weapons' velocity and letting the ballistic course do most of the work.

The problem was that DesRon 27 had traveled over a million kilometers in that time period and their missiles were almost two light-seconds away—and a four-second command-and-control loop left no chance to salvage the first salvo's targeting.

"Unclear how many we got, ser," Eowyn said grimly after a few more moments. "Our main beams can't hit them at this range, we don't have solid enough targeting solutions and it looks like they've set a sequence of jammer warheads.

"One set of a dozen or so is going off about every thirty seconds, just as each of our missile salvos goes in. We're getting *some* but not as many as we were expecting."

Let alone hoping, Henry knew—and the enemy jammers were making it harder to tell how many they'd taken down. Worse, even after the jammers had triggered, they still couldn't ignore the missiles carrying them.

They knew the Kenmiri jammer missiles weren't carrying salted nukes—but at seven percent of lightspeed, they were still going to hit with incredible force. DesRon 27 needed to vaporize, shred or deflect every missile in the salvos.

"Range is two hundred fifty thousand," Ihejirika snapped from the bridge. "Let's get those firing solutions in, people. We don't have long."

For all of the mind-boggling velocity with which the battle was approaching Anderon, *Paladin* and her sisters were barely ten minutes from matching the Kenmiri missiles' velocity at point-blank range.

And only twenty minutes from those missiles reaching Anderon. The *Cataphracts* were on a crash course for the planet themselves, but they had the maneuverability to dodge a planet at the last moment, and they *needed* to be on the incoming missiles' course.

"Main lasers engaging," Eowyn reported as white lines drew themselves on the display. "Between their jammers and our nukes, it's getting hard to pinpoint *anything* out there, ser."

"The closer we get, the easier it will be," Henry said grimly, watching the rippling kaleidoscope of radiation in which the death of a world lurked. If they'd taken out five percent of the enemy weapons yet, he'd be shocked.

They needed to do better, but Henry also knew that the Kenmiri couldn't be done with tricks yet. There would be at least one more counter. One more trick to keep anyone from saving the planet.

"Defensive lasers engaging," his operations officer told him. "Our targeting data still sucks, and we're starting to run out of missiles. And lose launchers."

The *Cataphracts* had enough munitions aboard for thirty minutes of sustained fire. The expectation was that those missiles would be expended over multiple engagements rather than spent in one single, continuous, rapid-fire engagement.

The launchers weren't *designed* to fire every thirty seconds for thirty minutes. And aboard *Paladin*, especially, where this wasn't the first time Henry had asked them to do it...the price was obvious.

"A third launcher just failed on *Paladin*," Eowyn continued. "We're down seven across the squadron.

"Range is one hundred thousand kilometers."

They were losing at least one launcher every salvo now, but they still had twenty salvos left. And no time.

"We think we've taken out about three thousand enemy missiles so far," Eowyn reported. She paused, then physically turned to meet Henry's gaze.

"I'm not sure this is working, ser," she warned.

"This part was never going to be enough," he told her levelly. "We always knew what it was going to take. All ships should have courses prepped to sweep the swarm with their shields."

The flag deck was silent for a few moments, then she swallowed hard.

"We need to make sure all of those courses have vectors that will miss the planet if they lose engine power, ser."

The last thing they needed was to successfully clear the missile swarm—and then drop a million-ton destroyer into the planet at seven percent of lightspeed.

"That was in the brief, yes," Henry agreed. The range continued to drop, and he watched his destroyers slowly shift their formation, spreading out to form a sweep pattern that would take them back and forth through the Kenmiri salvos until there was nothing left.

"We will match velocity and interpenetrate the lead salvo in three minutes," Eowyn told him. "The jammer density is dropping. They've triggered at least a thousand of them, but I think our success in taking down their missiles is starting to reduce their jammer numbers as well."

"It has to," Henry murmured. "But we're down to the wire. As Captain Ihejirika said: it's time to stand between the innocent and the enemy."

"And if we couldn't take the joke, we shouldn't have put on the uniform."

"Exactly."

There was another moment of quiet, then Chan cleared their throat.

"Ser…it's not an option most of us have, but you should call the Ambassador," the coms officer told him.

Henry sighed.

"*Should have called* is probably more accurate, Commander Chan," he admitted. "All I could say now is goodbye…and she'd yell at me for making assumptions.

"No, Ambassador Todorovich knew what she signing up for. She understands the job and what it takes."

He couldn't be distracted now. He was waiting for what he hoped would be the final shoe, and it would be sometime in the next two minutes.

After that, the only thing left would be to throw their hulls and shields in front of Armageddon.

48

HENRY HAD SUSPECTED from the beginning what the second part of the Kenmiri's one-two punch to defend their salvo would be. He hadn't anticipated *quite* so large a percentage of the genocidal missiles to be jammers, but that was part of the trick he would have pulled.

The second part kicked off as they made their first approaches to sweep with the gravity shields. With the relative velocity down to under a hundred kilometers a second and the range down to barely a thousand kilometers, they were hitting an enemy missile with every shot of their defensive lasers.

There were just too many missiles...and as Henry's ships hit the thousand-kilometer line, the ones that had specifically kept fuel aboard leapt to life. A thousand missiles were nothing against the scale of the salvo targeted on Anderon. DesRon 27 had already destroyed over five thousand Kenmiri missiles...but none of those missiles had been maneuvering, and they'd destroyed them over twenty minutes.

Two hundred attacking missiles per destroyer would be a nearly guaranteed kill against even *Significance*-class ships. But Henry's command weren't *Significances*.

They were *Cataphracts*, and the emitters necessary to fuel their gravity maneuvering systems gave them the gravity shields of *battle-*

cruisers. They had the same active defenses as a *Significance,* but their shields could take a lot more.

But there was a vast difference between shredding an inactive missile with a five-thousand-gravity shear five centimeters wide and deflecting the plasma blast of a conversion warhead.

They had ten seconds. Ten seconds in which Henry's ships shot down a quarter of the missiles targeting them, but the rest detonated in a nuclear hellstorm with his squadron at its heart.

"Blowthrough, blowthrough, *blowthrough,*" Bach snapped desperately from *Paladin*'s bridge. "Multiple hits across the hull. Both wings hit… Missiles are down, *all missiles are down.*"

Henry could see the heat-dissipation reports for *Paladin* instantly. They'd lost a lot of heat radiators. They'd lost the missile launchers. But the gravity shield was intact, and they had power. That meant they had maneuvering and the shield—and that was all they needed.

"Squadron-status report," he barked.

"*Chevalier* is gone," Chan said crisply. "*Mameluke* has lost shields and drives, but they had enough of a sideways vector to avoid the planet. They are continuing to engage with defensive lasers, but Captain Earls has no idea when she'll have drives and shields back.

"*Aswaran* has lost her primary lasers and half her launchers, but her drives and shields are online." There was a pause. "*Cataphract* is undamaged; no major blowthroughs."

"I see Palmer is luckier this time," Henry noted. "Earls will do what she can do. It's on us, *Cataphract* and *Aswaran.*

"People, they're out of tricks to protect their missiles, and we've taken out over half of them," he continued, linking to his three captains. "It's time to sweep Anderon's skies clear of this mess!"

He hoped he was projecting more confidence than he felt. Losing two of the gravity shields that had been baked into the plan was bad. Glancing at his feeds, he shivered as *Paladin* rammed into the remnants of the Kenmiri's first salvo.

Inactive missiles were easy prey. Explosions and plasma blasts —*those* risked burning through the grav-shields, but physical objects could *not* survive the gravity shear. Missiles tore apart by the dozen as they charged through.

Hundreds of Kenmiri missiles were vanishing from the displays, but there were thousands left. Even the jammer missiles had to be stopped. Even *one* missile—even *part* of a missile!—could inflict massive devastation on the planet they were protecting.

"Ser," Eowyn said softly. "Check the acceleration numbers."

It took him a second to realize what she meant, then he swallowed hard. He had three ships left actively accelerating, sweeping back and forth through the missile swarm. *Aswaran* was accelerating at two-point-four KPS^2. *Cataphract* was at two-point-three. *Paladin* was at two-point-*five*.

"How long can the ships take this?" he asked her, as levelly as he could.

"I don't know, ser. No one was ever quite willing to test a destroyer gravity system to *destruction*."

"Then have faith in our engineers," he instructed. The missiles were dying quickly. Maybe even quickly enough.

Maybe.

As he watched, *Cataphract*'s acceleration jumped up to two-point-five KPS^2 as she made her turn to sweep back through the hostile salvos.

"Five minutes to impact. Estimate four thousand enemy missiles remaining," Eowyn told him. "*Mameluke* is successfully cleaning up the leakers. Single missiles are getting past, but she's still *v*-matched and her lasers are still online."

Henry wasn't sure he wanted to know what devil Captain Earls had struck a deal with to manage that. *Mameluke* was leaking atmosphere and had detectable jets of flames as that atmosphere occasionally ignited, yet somehow, she had eighty percent of her antimissile lasers online.

"Defensive fortresses are requesting telemetry feeds to allow them to launch countermissiles in support," Chan told him. "They've moved every station they have to this side of the planet."

"Give them whatever they ask for, Commander," Henry ordered, a chill running down his spine as *Paladin* shivered around him.

"Was that the engines or an impact?"

"Impact," Ihejirika told him from the bridge. "We're breaking the missiles down and tossing the chunks in a million directions, but some of them are going to hit us. That was a big one."

New icons marked Henry's screens as the defensive forts opened fire at their maximum possible range. The head-on intercept calculations would be a nightmare, even with DesRon 27 providing targeting data from the middle of the missile swarm.

"First two salvos are *completely gone*," Eowyn reported. "We've bought two extra minutes."

The salvos were separated a bit. That had been a saving grace so far, allowing them to focus at the front and work their way back.

And then Henry's last three destroyers dropped within ten seconds' flight time of the fifth salvo, and he realized they'd only been subject to *half* of the Kenmiri's defensive hunter-killers. They'd killed many of them, but half the remaining missiles were now coming at his ships.

"Evasive; take down those missiles," he snapped.

Two hundred enemy missiles per ship had shattered his command. Another two hundred–plus on top of the existing damage was a *death sentence*.

Except they were *minutes* from the surface, and that was eight hundred missiles that were no longer targeted on Anderon.

"Take us into the heart of the last salvo," Ihejirika ordered calmly, clearly following Henry's own thoughts. "If they want to coat us in fire, let's *turn it on them*."

Henry could only hang on to the armrests of his chair as his flag-ship dove into the maelstrom, turning the warheads aimed at her into a corona of fire that took dozens more missiles with her.

Until it was too late. Henry *felt* the shield fail, taking the GMS with it. He *felt* the lurch that flung the entire destroyer to one side.

And then the flag-deck lights went out.

49

THE LIGHTS WERE BACK on a few seconds later, and Henry's heart started beating again.

Then the status feed came back online and he realized just how doomed they were.

"Missile swarm appears to have been eliminated," Eowyn said softly. "Maybe a couple dozen leakers, but the fortresses already have them dialed in and are commencing long-range laser fire."

"And we are about to snatch defeat from the jaws of victory," Henry told her bitterly. The main display was offline, but he could run the numbers through his internal network feed. "Ihejirika? How long for the drive?"

"It's…gone, ser," his flag captain said grimly. "Too many gravity projectors were lost. We're down both wings and two-thirds of the emergency thrusters. We don't have enough acceleration, ser."

They couldn't maneuver…and *Paladin* was heading directly for Anderon at seven percent of lightspeed.

"Captain, initiate the scuttling sequence," Henry ordered quietly. "Can we evacuate?"

"Boat bay is fucked," the other man told him. "Plus, less than two minutes. Ser…even if we scuttle, the ship is still going to hit the planet. Just in smaller pieces."

"I'm *hoping* that the fortresses can hit the smaller pieces hard enough to throw them off course," he replied. "Do we have coms?"

"No," Chan told him, their voice…beyond exhausted. There was no energy left in their tone. No hope.

"Okafor, what do we have?" Henry asked his friend and flag captain.

"Waiting for an update from Bautista, but we have no time." Ihejirika paused. "Commander Giannino is dead, ser. CIC is gone. I need you to counter-authorize the scuttling charges."

Henry nodded grimly, linking his internal network into the fragile-feeling ship network. Finding the scuttling system took him a moment, and he stared at the mental equivalent of a big red button for several seconds.

"I'm linking Bautista in," Ihejirika told him. "Report, Commander?"

"We have no guns, no gravity drive, no missile launchers, no shields, and we've lost sixty-eight percent of our emergency thrusters," *Paladin*'s chief engineer said grimly. "We've got power, somehow, and the skip drive.

"So, we can die faster if we want, I guess."

"Even overloading the fusion cores won't work," Henry said quietly. "The scuttling charges are all we've got."

"System's lying to you, sers," Bautista replied. "Our outer hull has been savaged. If we have *three* scuttling charges left of the twenty, I'll be stunned. Might work to break the ship up a bit, but…"

Henry closed his eyes.

"Prepare the fusion cores for overload," he heard Ihejirika order. "How long?"

"We don't have enough time for that," Bautista said quietly. "It's at least a five-minute process to overload a core—that's why we *have* scuttling charges."

"And we have ninety seconds."

Henry felt the answer hovering around his brain, *something* key that he was missing. After everything they'd done to take down the missiles, his ship was going to ram into the planet and do almost as much damage as the attack would have.

That he'd die was secondary. Even a single million-ton impactor at over twenty thousand kilometers per second would kill everyone on the planet. If they could break up the ship, that *might* help. If they were lucky, they might get it down to a handful of fifty-thousand-ton impactors.

But the scuttling charges were defunct, and they couldn't overload the core in time. All they had was the skip drive, and that couldn't do anything without a line between stars.

Except…that was how penetrator warheads worked. They didn't change the three-dimensional vector, but they *added* a vector in the seventeen imperceivable dimensions.

"Fire up the skip drive," he ordered.

"What?" Bautista and Ihejirika stared at him.

"*Penetrator missiles,*" Henry snarled. "We won't get extra realspace distance out of it, but if we can get *enough* of an icosaspatial side vector, our existing velocity might just get us past the planet."

"That's…" Ihejirika stared into the distance.

"The ship may not survive the kind of impulse we need," Bautista warned.

"*Our* survival is no longer a variable in the calculation," Henry told her. "Do it."

"This is going to *hurt,*" she cautioned. "Hang on to your guts."

It wouldn't be a carefully calculated thing, Henry knew that. The icosaspatial impulse generators took forty-five seconds to spin up, and they were down to barely *seventy* seconds.

"I can't communicate with anybody, but I think we're being targeted," Eowyn reported.

"Good. If this fails…those forts hitting us with everything they've got is Anderon's only hope. What's the status of the other ships?"

"*Cataphract* is the only one with drives online, but *Aswaran* went ballistic with enough of a side vector to miss the planet. *Mameluke* was already there. All three ships are clear. Maybe we could get a tow?"

"Not something we can rig in fifty-five seconds," Henry conceded.

They were still a million kilometers away from the planet, but without some kind of side vector, the implausible plan to try and skip *past* the planet was their only hope.

"Impulse generators are charging. Target impulse is three hundred percent of standard," Charmchi reported from the bridge. "We should hit that about five seconds before impact. But...I have no idea how long that's going to keep us sideways from the planet. Might be ten seconds. Might be sixty.

"Might be two."

"Fire it as soon as you've got it," Henry ordered. "I don't want this ship within a hundred thousand kilometers of Anderon."

"What do we do about the fortresses?" Eowyn asked.

"Nothing. Shooting us down is more certain than this scheme," he admitted. "Are we in their range?"

"Yes, ser," she confirmed. "They have not fired."

He looked at the icons on his feed.

"Damn you," he whispered. "You *have* to fire."

"They may be trying to communicate, but we have no receivers," Chan reported.

"They *might* be calculating an angle where they think they can knock us off course without destroying us?" Eowyn suggested.

"Then if we live through this, I am going to find every damned officer involved in that decision and beat them with the don't-be-stupid stick," he growled. "We are *not* worth risking the planet!"

He could think of a few reasons for the fortresses to hold fire that weren't *completely* stupid, but he could accept that he was being uncharacteristically frustrated at moment. Incipient death and accidental genocide apparently did that.

"We're ready," Charmchi snapped. "Except... *Fuck.*"

"What?"

"Generators can't hold the charge. We have to skip *now.*"

"Do it."

If anyone on *Paladin*'s bridge or Engineering section had waited for his order, Henry would never know. Even as he was speaking, the world went mad.

The robotic minds on the penetrator missiles had been specially designed to survive a skip deep in a gravity well, but their skips were also intended to be under a quarter-second.

Normally, *any* impulse generation only lasted a second or two. This one…endured.

Henry felt dragged in every direction. Pushed in every direction. Both crushed and pulled apart. Most of it was in his head…except he both felt and *heard* his left forearm *snap*, bending to a forty-degree angle no bone should ever acquire.

And then he was falling. Falling forever, as the world fell out beneath his stomach. He struggled to move and realized that this *wasn't* psychosomatic at all. Whatever was going on, it was creating a real gravity well of at least half a dozen gees on *Paladin*'s deck.

Pain tore up his arm as the falling sensation and gravity tore at his fragmented bones, and he barely managed not to scream as he forced his right hand up and over, managing to pin his injured forearm to the armrest.

Immobilizing it was all he could do until suddenly, finally, after only three small eternities, *Paladin* plunged back into reality.

"Re…port," he managed to ground out against the pain. "And…medic to flag deck."

"Medical casualties across the ship," Ihejirika barked back. "Scanning for position and velocity…"

The African officer paused for a moment too long and Henry swallowed against the pain.

"Captain?" he demanded.

"We're clear of the planet, but we somehow shed almost all of our three-dimensional velocity in the skip."

"That's…good."

"We're six thousand kilometers above Anderon's third major continent, and we don't have the velocity to escape her gravity well," Ihejirika told him. "I think we can minimize the damage to the surface…but we're crashing, ser."

"Captain, if we walk away from this, I'm giving Charmchi every medal I can find," Henry said drily. "Helm?"

"Thrusters coming online now," Charmchi replied. Her voice was vague, distant. She was utterly focused on the job of trying to get the ship down to the ground safely.

"Gravity will take almost twenty minutes to pull us down," Ihejirika told Henry. "Charmchi just needs to make sure we make it down at a low-enough speed to survive…lithobraking."

"Commander Charmchi? First priority is not landing on anything local. Second priority is crashing slowly enough that the crew survives. You have no other priorities."

Paladin was already dead. There was no way to save the ship. They'd saved the planet. They might even manage to avoid doing major damage to the planet.

And then, maybe, just maybe, they could save themselves.

50

"WHAT ARE YOU WAITING FOR?" Sylvia demanded as she barged into the command center.

Several dozen local officers looked up at her in shock. She knew she wasn't supposed to be there, and it was *definitely* a diplomatic faux pas for her to have left the office they'd given her, but she'd watched *Paladin*'s crippled course for long enough to know that they needed to shoot her down.

"As it was explained to me," Robertson said calmly from the center of the room, "we were waiting for *Paladin* to get close enough for a clear-enough targeting solution that could guarantee she was either knocked off her collision course or completely vaporized."

She nodded grimly to him as he waved her over.

"There was, perhaps, some hesitation around vaporizing one of our allies' ships," Robertson continued. "While I have not met Commodore Wong or any of *Paladin*'s crew, I *have* met UPSF officers. I have to assume they would rather die than contribute to Anderon's destruction."

"Without question," Sylvia told him. "You have *my* authorization to fire as you must."

"She is gone, Ambassador," the nearest officer, a Kenmiri Warrior in a red tunic with a Star Legate's iconography embroidered on the chest. "We are attempting to relocate her, but she *disappeared* half a light-second out."

"Just as we were finalizing the targeting solutions," a Vonga officer added. "They…saved us. We did not want to repay that with death."

"The missile strike?"

"Cleared away," Robertson told her. "It was the right call to position a squadron for that role, but the price was high."

"Executive Robertson…Commodore Wong is my lover," Sylvia whispered in English before switching back to Kem. "High as the price may be, we pay it gladly. I suspect *Paladin* lost communications, because I *know* Commodore Wong would have ordered you to fire on them."

"Whatever has happened to *Paladin*, your people have saved Anderon today," Robertson told her. "We have all paid heavily for that victory, but my people are safe."

"We have not managed to establish what happened to *Paladin*, Ambassador," the Warrior told her. "The rest of your destroyer squadron is badly damaged except for one surprisingly lucky vessel. We sent most of the civilian spacecraft to Anderon-Six with your logistics fleet, but we do have some tugs we can launch into orbit to help tow your damaged destroyers into a stable orbit."

"We would be grateful," Sylvia told the Kenmiri. "My apologies, Star Legate; I did not catch your name."

"I am Varkul, Executive Okalta's military aide," the Warrior told her. "As I was before the Withdrawal and will be until one of us dies, whatever rank Anderon's Protectors lay on me. Such is my duty."

"We will get the tugs moving," another officer confirmed.

"I still do not understand what your Commodore Wong *did*," Robertson admitted. "They disappeared five minutes ago. If they had somehow turned invisible, they would still have struck the planet within moments.

"Instead, they are just…gone. I have never seen anything like it."

"Whatever they did, it was clearly risky, and the risks took them," Varkul noted. "But they took that risk to defend *our* people. They honored the Charge and died as Warriors and Protectors.

"Unlike the *ikitan* who launched the missiles."

It had been a *long* time since Sylvia had heard a Kem word she didn't understand. From the reaction of the other non-Kenmiri officers close enough to hear, they hadn't heard that particular phrase either.

"I think you just confused everyone, Legate," Robertson told the Kenmiri drily.

"They are Kenmiri who have not only lost the Charge—as too much, sadly, of our Empire had—but have betrayed it and turned upon it," Varkul explained slowly. "They are…filth. Blood-mad. They are *ikitan*."

It made sense that wasn't a term Sylvia knew. It didn't sound like a concept a non-Kenmiri would know.

She was about to thank Varkul for the explanation when one of the officers suddenly started in surprise.

"New contact!" she snapped. "Contact is at six thousand kilometers above Blue continent, rising but losing velocity fast. Scanners suggest contact does not have escape velocity."

"Identify that contact," at least three officers snapped at once.

"It is *Paladin*," Varkul murmured, before any confirmation. "It must be. But how?"

"Contact is confirmed as a UPSF *Cataphract* destroyer, badly damaged. Can only be *Paladin*, but she was on the *other side of the planet*. Fifteen minutes ago."

"The skip drive," Sylvia said, a spark of hope running through her. "They must have triggered their skip drive and sidestepped the planet."

"They were missing for seventeen minutes," Robertson said slowly. "And shed all of their velocity. Whatever sensor data they have is going to be ridiculously valuable to scientists all across the galaxy."

"But right now, they are *falling*," Sylvia pointed out, staring as the main holographic display shifted to show her lover's ship.

"Varkul, are those tugs in the air?" Robertson asked.

"First trio just managed liftoff," the Kenmiri Legate replied.

"We have a new mission for them!"

51

BLUE CONTINENT WAS ONLY LIGHTLY INHABITED, with most of its area made up of a chilly steppe that even the Kenmiri found a bit much. The plant life of the steppe was well adapted to their home, with vast fields of moss-like fungal patches sucking up the sunlight.

Paladin had been guided to a landing in the middle of a thick patch of that moss, the locals clearly having decided to sacrifice plant life to cushion the crash as much as possible.

As Sylvia arrived, a team of Artisan-led Drones was setting up a landing pad while an Ashall-led rescue team was stabilizing a ramp they'd attached to a brand-new hole in the destroyer's hull.

Her shuttle was carrying medical personnel from the main administration center, but *Cataphract* had sent their own people down already —unlike their last mission together, Captain Palmer's command had somehow emerged from the battle over Anderon utterly unscathed.

The *rest* of DesRon 27 were half-wrecked, and even *Sylvia* could tell that *Paladin* was never leaving Anderon's surface.

"Make a note," she heard Robertson say to the Beren aide accompanying him aboard the UPSF shuttle. "We will want to check with the UPSF on how to make the wreck safe, but I think we will want to turn the site into a monument.

"To *everyone* who fell today."

That was something Sylvia should engage with and encourage, but for once in her life, she was prepared to let the personal get in the way of the professional—and she didn't think anyone in the star system was going to blame her.

She was briskly walking toward the destroyer as the Executive spoke, taking in the wrecked state of a starship that had been her home for months now.

A pair of GroundDiv troopers, somehow in full dress uniform with *Paladin* shoulder flashes despite everything, met her halfway. The senior had a Chief Petty Officer's gold chevron over the crossed rifles of Ground Division—and her nametag and network told Sylvia they were Chief Kyra Živković, one of the destroyer's squad commanders.

"Ambassador, we can't let anyone on the ship except for rescue crew with the proper equipment," Živković told her quickly. "We're still extracting people and…the ship isn't safe. There's too much internal damage."

"Commodore Wong?" she demanded.

"He's still aboard, ser," the Chief said. "They haven't cut through to the flag deck yet. There's a medic in there with him, though."

"A medic? Is he okay?"

"I'm not sure, ser," the GroundDiv woman confessed. "But we can't let you on the ship. Even if you went aboard, you can't get to him—if we could *get* to the Commodore, he'd already be out here.

"Please, Ambassador Todorovich. Be patient. Everyone who has made it this far is going to be fine."

THE RESCUE CREW'S "PROPER EQUIPMENT," Sylvia quickly realized, was only a step or two down from combat power armor. *Paladin* was in atrocious shape, and the interior clearly required breathers and protection.

It still took every scrap of self-control she had not to push past the squad of GroundDiv standing watch over the crash site as more personnel arrived from *Cataphract* and the Anderon capital.

Especially when the crews started removing body bags. A mobile hospital was setting up on the mossy tundra behind her, and most of the rescues were being rushed toward the tents, but all too many times, the rescue crews were carrying distinct black bags.

And Sylvia was reasonably sure they wouldn't have started moving *bodies* unless they'd pulled all of the living they could find.

She took a half-involuntary step toward the hulk, but Chief Živković was there, smiling and shaking her head gently.

"Bridge and flag deck both have a tertiary armored shell," she told Sylvia. "Both of them locked shut, and the usual emergency measures to open them have failed, so the team is cutting their way in.

"And those shells are designed to withstand plasma fire."

"Apologies, Chief. It's…"

"Believe me, ser, if I thought I could help rescue the Skipper or the Old Man, I'd be in there swinging a plasma cutter," Živković said drily. "And I'm not dating either of them!

"But I absolutely *cannot* let the UPA Ambassador aboard a ship that's currently full of radioactive gasses, loose flames, sharp metal…"

"I understand."

"I know you do, ser," the Chief conceded. "But the point had to be made. The ship is not safe."

A momentary flash of something crossed Živković's face, immediately replaced by calm professionalism.

"She was our home," Sylvia said, recognizing the moment of grief.

"She was."

"Gangway!" someone at the exit from the ship bellowed. "Coming through!"

Two rescue crew who were halfway up the ramp jumped to the side—*off* the ramp, as their gear was designed to survive worse falls—clearing the way for a trio of ash-covered rescue crew carrying a stretcher at full speed.

"Keep the ramp clear," Captain Ihejirika's familiar voice bellowed from behind the medics. "More wounded coming through!"

Sylvia spared a glance for the first stretcher and recognized Lieutenant Commander Bach, the destroyer's tactical officer. Or, at least, her upper half. The woman was missing her legs entirely, and Sylvia had to swallow a moment of nausea.

Half a dozen bridge officers and techs proceeded to be rushed past her, in various states of injury. Then a final stretcher appeared at the top of the ramp—and *this* one was flanked by Captain Ihejirika and Commander Eowyn.

Sylvia was moving toward the ramp before they were even halfway down, and this time Chief Živković didn't even try to stop her. She met Henry's stretcher at the end of the ramp, and the bottom dropped out of her heart as she saw him lying there, completely still with blood all over his left side.

But Ihejirika was there too, the big Black officer dropping a heavy hand on her shoulder.

"He snapped his forearm in the skip and broke the skin," he rumbled softly. "He was conscious for long enough to give the landing orders, then passed out from blood loss and shock.

"Medics say he'll be fine. He's out right now, but he's going to be fine."

"Thank you," Sylvia murmured, then grimaced as she saw another stretcher carrying Commander Chan off the ship. "Is that everyone?"

"According to my network, it's everyone who's still alive," Ihejirika confirmed grimly. "Most of my crew are casualties, Ambassador. Wounded or dead. That last skip…"

He shivered.

"What *happened*?" she asked.

"We skipped through the planet," *Paladin*'s Captain told her. "The Commodore's plan. Not that we had any other choices left except *make it easy to shoot us.*

"Worst ninety-three seconds of my life."

Sylvia paused for a moment.

"Ninety-three seconds?" she asked.

"Yeah. That's how long the system says we were in the skip. As we bypassed a freaking *planet.*"

"Okafor…*Paladin* was missing for seventeen minutes," Sylvia told him. "I didn't think time dilation was a *thing* with icosaspatial movement."

Ihejirika was silent for a long time, turning to study the wreck of his ship.

"To my knowledge," he finally said, "*no one* has ever used a skip drive to bypass a major physical object. I also don't believe anyone has ever generated the level of twenty-dimensional impulse we did outside of a lab or a test ship.

"It was…inconceivably risky. Even now, I'm not sure *I* fully comprehend how risky," he admitted. "But…our survival was no longer the priority."

"Your squadron saved over a billion lives today, Captain Ihejirika," Sylvia pointed out, glancing past the captain to see Robertson carefully waiting, not *really* out of earshot, for them to finish their conversation.

"And I think the locals want to talk to you about that."

52

THERE HAD BEEN no plan for further reinforcements. So far as Henry Wong knew, the remaining carriers were too deep in UPA space to have arrived anywhere useful in time—and *he* hadn't called for reinforcements.

The arrival of eight UPSF capital ships and five destroyers six days after the Battle of Anderon was a surprise to everyone—though when he recognized *Magpie*, he was unsurprised to discover that Admiral Sonia Hamilton was in command.

Magpie was *Raven*'s replacement as the Peacekeeper Initiative's sole modern battlecruiser.

He wasn't entirely sure where the three carriers and the other four battlecruisers had come from. Either way, *he* was still mostly restricted to the rapidly solidifying hospital site next to *Paladin*'s crash site.

His left arm was still completely immobilized, and his doctors, human and local, were insistent that he be careful in how he moved and where he went. He was even…*mostly* obedient.

Sylvia knew where to find him when he went for his morning coffee. He was pretty sure the doctors had worked it out, too, if only because no one was harassing him about it as he sat in a borrowed wheelchair, studying *Paladin*'s wreck.

"They're going to have to wait, what, a week before they even start decontamination?"

"About that," he agreed, not looking back at the Admiral as Hamilton spoke without announcing herself. "Welcome to Anderon, ser. I'm afraid I'm under strict orders not to stand or salute."

"I have never required mickey mouse bullshit, and especially not of my wounded soldiers," Sonia Hamilton told him, stepping up next to him and dropping into an easy parade rest. "I wish we'd been faster, Henry. I'm not sure it was physically possible, but I wish we'd been faster."

"I'm not even sure where you found the ships."

"Procyon Reserve," she replied with a soft chuckle. "Rear Admiral Clarke was in Procyon, charged with reviewing the older ships there to see what was worth putting into reserve and what needed to be scrapped.

"None of the ships had more than caretaker crews, but they hadn't been stripped for parts or otherwise decommissioned, so…"

He saw Hamilton shrug out of the corner of his eye. Rear Admiral Alexander Clarke wasn't a man Henry was overly familiar with, but he was aware of the LogDiv officer in passing. Apparently, he owed the man a drink.

"Clarke got the reports that we'd sent an allied flotilla, with a bloody *carrier* at its heart, to Rashova and they hadn't reported in. So, he took his assessments, short-stopped the entire decommissioning process and ordered his LogDiv people to restock the capital ships he thought were in best shape.

"But since he didn't have *crews* for three *Lexington*s and four *Jaguars*, thanks to the stand-down, he put out a call to the Reserve and the veterans' networks for volunteers."

"So, the destroyers are all Initiative?" Henry asked. "But those six capital ships are…thrown-together crews of volunteers?"

"And flying Dragoons, not Lancers, off *Lexington*, *Charles de Gaulle*, and *Kiev*," Hamilton confirmed. "But we figured nobody was going to complain about an extra three hundred gravity-shield fighters, even if they *are* the last generation."

"We wouldn't have, no."

"Officially, I have no idea how they caught up to us," the Admiral noted drily. "We left Zion *before* they left Procyon, but they caught up to us five days ago."

"About as the battle was being fought," Henry murmured.

"They were spending fifteen hours a day in the acceleration tanks, Wong. There's no way they caught up doing anything else."

He grimaced.

"And you still would only have been in time to avenge us if we'd fucked up."

"If *you* hadn't made the Osiris Run," Hamilton replied flatly, the capitals clear. "We sent drones ahead, but they had to go through systems we knew were safe. They'll get here tomorrow, I suspect.

"But if you hadn't run through Osiris, built the alliance with Anderon and provided the details of those antifighter missiles… We're going to need a fucking *transport* full of medals for you and your crews."

"And then I lost my entire squadron. Not a great look for the brand-new GMS ships."

"We used them up," his boss said bluntly. "And we used the *Cataphracts* up by giving them missions no one else could do. The crews rose to what we asked of them. And they have more than proved their worth."

"*Cataphract* needs a few weeks of repairs," Henry told her quietly. "*Aswaran* and *Mameluke* need several months. Destroyer Squadron Twenty-Seven isn't an effective combat formation at this moment, ser."

"If there is a formation in the UPSF that deserves a break more, it's DesRon Twenty-Seven," Hamilton told him. "And they'll get it. *You*, on the other hand, I have work for."

"I serve at the Security Council's pleasure," Henry replied.

"First, DesRon Twenty-Seven was going to be dissolved anyway," she admitted. "The plan was to use *Cataphracts* as scouts and flotilla leaders for regular destroyers. Looking at what you pulled off here, I think that plan was *stupid*, but it had already been set in motion.

"But it gets complicated. You're not going to a Peacekeeper Initiative desk, Henry."

Henry stared blankly at the destroyer. That wasn't good news, not really. He'd been expecting to fall back into a more administrative side of being the Initiative's second-in-command.

"I have a new job title; the drone caught up with me a couple of days ago," she told him. "The Peacekeeper Initiative is no more. The Security Council apparently took the return of the Kenmiri as a long-overdue wake-up call that their *peace dividend* was a fucking illusion and the price we could end up paying for it was too damn high.

"Everything that was the Initiative is being rolled over into Ra Sector Peacekeeper Command," Hamilton told him. "I am officially Commanding Officer, RACOM, as of about a month ago. Officially, I get to keep *Chiana* and *Scorpius*, with Rear Admiral Cheung becoming *Vice* Admiral and the second-in-command of RACOM."

"I see, ser."

Henry wasn't sure he did. He'd spent a *lot* of time getting the Peacekeeper Initiative together, leaning on both his and Sylvia's connections and moral authority. To just have it…vanish around him was a strange feeling.

"Every protocol, every rule, every doctrine you and I wrote for the Initiative is going to apply to the new Peacekeeper Sector Commands," she told him, as if reading his mind. "The Initiative isn't so much being dissolved as we're absorbing the rest of the UPSF. We're going to have the resources to expand into the Apophis and Hathor Sectors inside the year, creating new PSCs to support them as we try to stabilize the area."

That was a different story, he supposed.

"That's…a big change," he murmured.

"Vengeance Fleet scared them. A *lot*—and they weren't even certain of Rashova's fate when the decision was made. That said…" She sighed. "The main impulse for this is that some accountant ran the numbers.

"Taxes on the increased trade through the Ra Sector have covered the costs of the Initiative *and Twelfth Fleet's entire deployment* twice over. And we hadn't even fully established proper trade networks or had any material trade come into the UPA on Ra Sector hulls.

"So, the Security Council has realized that the *costs* of maintaining a full-strength Space Force to restore stability in the former Empire is going to be more than offset by the revenues gained from that stability.

"And that's before you get into the discussion around recruiting colonists from the Ra Sector to help fill the third-wave colony worlds. No, Henry, the Initiative isn't going away because we failed.

"It's *transforming* because we succeeded beyond anyone's wildest imaginations. And the only reason *you* aren't going to be getting one of the two junior Sector Commands is that we need you elsewhere."

Henry nodded slowly and thoughtfully.

"I'm listening, ser," he told her.

"I'm sorry, but *I* need Todorovich here, helping me make contact with the parts of the sector we haven't touched. I'll be relocating to La-Tar initially, but we need to negotiate basing rights for an actual full sector-fleet base somewhere in Ra—to be designated Base Vakarian once online.

"You, on the other hand, the United Planets Alliance has two very specific needs for," Hamilton told him. "And you don't get to turn any of them down, even as we are separating you from your girlfriend."

"That's a familiar story, ser. What do you need?" he asked.

"First and foremost, the UPSF needs *you* to spend six months at the Iron Ring and eighteen months in a senior staff position so we can make you a fucking Admiral."

If Henry hadn't already been sitting down, that would have taken his feet out from under him. The Iron Ring was possibly the most elite educational institute in the United Planets Alliance. An old centrifugal gravity ring station in orbit of Mars, it had served as the training center for all starship captains in the European Union Extrasolar Security Force.

When the ESF had been stood down in favor of the UPSF—along with the rest of the skip-capable national space forces—they'd transferred over enough officers, ships and crews that they and the Royal Commonwealth Space Navy had formed the beating heart of the new military.

And the ESF had turned the Iron Ring over alongside most of its senior officers. The UPSF had too many ships to justify training *all* of their officers there, so it had become used as a very specific, small-class instruction facility, solely for officers who had been selected as potential flag officers.

Two types of people went through the Iron Ring's six-month course: Commodores about to make the next step and the UPSF's Command Master Chief Petty Officers, the absolute cream of their NCOs.

"I am—"

"The only officer to command a GMS squadron in action, the officer who almost single-handedly stabilized the Ra Sector, the man who made the Osiris Run and saved Twelfth Fleet, the man who commanded the Stand of the *Cataphracts* to save Anderon."

More capitals. Sonia Hamilton was *good* at putting those in.

"The next Iron Ring intake is eight months," she continued. "You're on the list. But before that, Admiral Mordecai has put his foot down. He gets you before and after your Ring. Potentially *during*."

Vice Admiral Gabir Mordecai headed the UPSF's Technical Division. TechDiv was responsible for designing, building and assessing warships and weapons for the UPSF's Space, Fighter and Ground Divisions.

"I'm not a designer, ser."

"He doesn't need a designer. Mordecai has literally *thousands* of architects and designers. He *needs* the officer who has commanded GMS ships in action. He needs you to help design the refit program for the *Significances*, *Crichtons* and *Corvids*.

"You're going behind a desk at TechDiv for eighteen months at the moment when the UPSF is about to redesign our *entire* order of battle around a new drive system and a new generation of shields and gravity drivers," she told him. "No one else except for Mordecai himself is going to have as much impact on the next generation of our warships.

"And no one else, Henry Wong, has made as much of an impression on our next generation of officers. You get your desk time. You get your Iron Ring. Then you get your star.

"None of this is negotiable, understood?"

JOIN THE MAILING LIST

Love Glynn Stewart's books? Join the mailing list at

GLYNNSTEWART.COM/MAILING-LIST/

to know as soon as new books are released and for special announcements.

ABOUT THE AUTHOR

Glynn Stewart is the author of *Starship's Mage*, a bestselling science fiction and fantasy series where faster-than-light travel is possible–but only because of magic. His other works include science fiction series *Duchy of Terra*, *Castle Federation* and *Exile*, as well as the urban fantasy series *ONSET* and *Changeling Blood*.

Writing managed to liberate Glynn from a bleak future as an accountant. With his personality and hope for a high-tech future intact, he lives in Southern Ontario with his partner, their cats, and an unstoppable writing habit.

VISIT GLYNNSTEWART.COM FOR NEW RELEASE UPDATES

CREDITS

The following people were involved in making this book:

Copyeditor: Richard Shealy

Proofreader: M Parker Editing

Cover art: Sam Leung

Typo Hunter Team

Faolan's Pen Publishing team: Jack, Kate, and Robin.

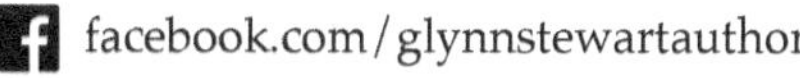 facebook.com/glynnstewartauthor

OTHER BOOKS
BY GLYNN STEWART

For release announcements join the
mailing list or visit **GlynnStewart.com**

STARSHIP'S MAGE
Starship's Mage
Hand of Mars
Voice of Mars
Alien Arcana
Judgment of Mars
UnArcana Stars
Sword of Mars
Mountain of Mars
The Service of Mars
A Darker Magic
Mage-Commander
Beyond the Eyes of Mars
Nemesis of Mars *(upcoming)*

Starship's Mage: Red Falcon
Interstellar Mage
Mage-Provocateur
Agents of Mars

Pulsar Race: A Starship's Mage Universe Novella

DUCHY OF TERRA
The Terran Privateer
Duchess of Terra
Terra and Imperium
Darkness Beyond
Shield of Terra
Imperium Defiant
Relics of Eternity
Shadows of the Fall
Eyes of Tomorrow

SCATTERED STARS

Scattered Stars: Conviction
Conviction
Deception
Equilibrium
Fortitude
Huntress
Prodigal (*upcoming*)

Scattered Stars: Evasion
Evasion
Discretion
Absolution (*upcoming*)

PEACEKEEPERS OF SOL

Raven's Peace
The Peacekeeper Initiative
Raven's Course
Drifter's Folly
Remnant Faction
Raven's Flag (*upcoming*)

EXILE

Exile
Refuge
Crusade
Ashen Stars: An Exile Novella

CASTLE FEDERATION

Space Carrier Avalon
Stellar Fox
Battle Group Avalon
Q-Ship Chameleon
Rimward Stars
Operation Medusa
A Question of Faith: A Castle Federation Novella

Dakotan Confederacy
Admiral's Oath
To Stand Defiant (*upcoming*)

VIGILANTE
(WITH TERRY MIXON)
Heart of Vengeance
Oath of Vengeance

**Bound By Stars: A Vigilante Series
(With Terry Mixon)**
Bound By Law
Bound by Honor
Bound by Blood

TEER AND KARD
Wardtown
Blood Ward

CHANGELING BLOOD
Changeling's Fealty
Hunter's Oath
Noble's Honor
Fae, Flames & Fedoras: A Changeling Blood Novella

ONSET
ONSET: To Serve and Protect
ONSET: My Enemy's Enemy
ONSET: Blood of the Innocent
ONSET: Stay of Execution
Murder by Magic: An ONSET Novella

STAND ALONE NOVELS & NOVELLAS
Children of Prophecy
City in the Sky
Excalibur Lost: A Space Opera Novella
Balefire: A Dark Fantasy Novella